NIGHT LIGHTS

NIGHT LIGHTS

OR

GOLF, THE BLUES, AND THE BROWN MOUNTAIN LIGHT

RAHN & TIMBERLEY ADAMS

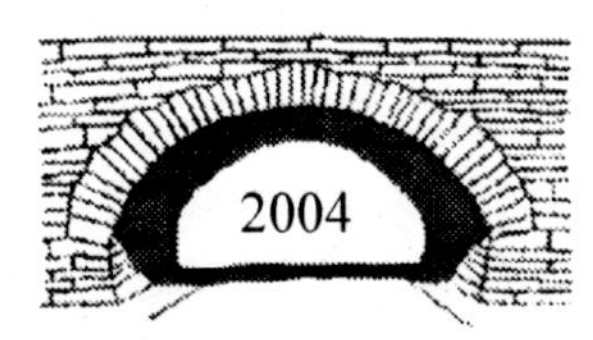

Parkway Publishers, Inc.
Boone, North Carolina

In memory of our brothers, Ken Adams and Tony Gilliam, and our fathers, John O. Adams and Edward "Nat" Gilliam; and in appreciation of our friends, Tim Adams, Jo Ann Canipe, Stan Carman, Arthur Daniels, Sandy Deal and Sander Gibson, who read and commented on all or part of this work in its various stages of completion.

The authors' profits from this edition benefit the
Edward N. Gilliam Scholarship fund.

For more information on the authors, please visit
www.gaillardiapress.com

Available from:
Parkway Publishers, Inc.
P.O. Box 3678
Boone, North Carolina 28607
www.parkwaypublishers.com

Cover design by Beth Jacquot
Cover art by Timberley Gilliam Adams
Photograph by Steve Adams

Library of Congress Cataloging-in-Publication Data

Adams, Rahn.
Night lights, or, Golf, the blues and the Brown Mountain light / by Rahn & Timberley Adams.
p. cm.
ISBN 1-887905-40-5
I. Title: Night lights. II. Title: Golf, the blues, and the Brown Mountain light. III. Adams, Timberley. IV. Title.

PS3601.D394N54 2004
813'.6--dc22

2004019580

* * *

Then they bare the first course with the blast of trumpets and waving of banners, with the sound of drums and pipes, of song and lute, that many a heart was uplifted at the melody.

– *Sir Gawain and the Green Knight*
(Jessie L. Weston translation)

And the three companies blew the trumpets, and brake the pitchers, and held the lamps in their left hands, and the trumpets in their right hands to blow withal: and they cried, The sword of the Lord, and of Gideon.

– *Judges* 7:20
(King James version)

Life is something like this trumpet. If you don't put anything in it you don't get anything out. And that's the truth.

– W.C. Handy
(*The New York Times* obituary)

* * *

ONE

Back when I was growing up—or when I was almost grown, I should say—there were three things I was really afraid of. Three things. I almost hate to think back to those days, because sometimes I catch myself feeling the same way now. But I've learned to live with my fears, I guess, through years and years of practice, and looking back isn't quite as painful as it used to be. You know, sometimes I think that's what life is all about—learning to live with fear and to endure the pain that goes along with it. But I sure did take my own sweet time learning that lesson.

Ever since that September morning when my high school civics class sat in stunned silence watching over and over the Twin Towers explode in balls of fire, then burn like horrible candles beneath coiling clouds of evil smoke, then crumble into dust, I've been afraid to fly. My teacher that day—a substitute—was a little old man everybody called Brother Josh who had retired a few years earlier as preacher at the Freewill church in my town. I remember that all he kept saying—muttering to himself, really—after we had seen the footage for the umpteenth time was, "God…my God…why?"

Back then, I thought that was an odd thing for a preacher to say, Freewill or otherwise, but now I kind of understand his confusion as well as his horror. But that's neither here nor there. I looked up "fear of flying" on the Internet recently and saw that its official name is *aviophobia* and that it became one of the most common fears in America back then—after 9/11, I mean. So I wasn't alone.

My second phobia and the one that has been hardest to hide is my fear of the dark (*nyctophobia*). A person can always take a car or bus or train or boat to avoid taking an airplane anywhere—unless time is an issue, that is. But everyone eventually has to click off the bedside lamp and try to go to sleep. Believe me, the average person can take only so many sleepless nights staring at a lightbulb. Sooner or later she's going to crash and burn. I know that from experience. You see, I've had professional help understanding why I'm afraid of the dark. They say it's because of what happened to my family.

When I was little, my mother and father got killed in a car wreck. So I had to go live with my elderly grandparents, and I wasn't even out of high school before both of them died, too—of natural causes. One of my counselors said my fear of darkness was really a fear of abandonment (*monophobia*), of my uncertainty about the future. He said it was a subconscious manifestation of the anxiety we all feel when we realize that we're going to die and that we're ultimately alone in the world. I didn't agree with him then and still don't, because I could sleep just fine as long as a night light was plugged in near me. And I didn't always like being around people, especially when they got on my nerves.

My name is Valerie Kirsten Galloway, but everyone who knew me then called me "Val," even though I liked "Kirsten" better, and even though old men, especially, were always calling me "My Gal Val," which annoyed the crap out of me after a while. My grandfather, Bronson Galloway, never annoyed me. He was my hero and always will be. Grandpa was a shrimpboat captain, just like Forrest Gump, except my grandfather was the farthest thing from being an imbecile. In fact, he didn't suffer fools well at all, although he was one of the most kind-hearted men I've ever known, once you got past his gruff exterior. Old Bron Galloway could have used some of Forrest's luck, though. After a long hard life of shrimping and doing whatever else a fisherman had to do to support his family, Grandpa's heart finally gave out. He died the spring of my eighth-grade year. That was when I met my best friend Bo—while he and his mother were on Easter break at the beach.

Grandma and I got along OK for the next three years, despite rambling around by ourselves in that old house on the mainland side of the Intracoastal Waterway near Shallotte Inlet. We didn't have any money to blow, but we got by well enough on our monthly Social Security checks and with some help from Aunt Elaine, Grandma's only surviving child. We had already sold Grandpa's beloved shrimpboat, *The Lady of Shallotte*, to pay his medical bills and funeral expenses. But then, during the fall of my senior year at Lockwoods Folly High School, Grandma got cancer and in three months passed away. They were both buried at Village Point Christian Church, in the same plot with my folks. That's why I didn't want to leave the Point. But I had no choice. I was running out of family. Or so I thought.

My story begins around noon on a partly sunny mid-June Saturday at the airport in Wilmington, N.C., which was about forty miles as the crow flies from my home at Village Point, a tiny fishing community near the only slightly larger coastal town of Shallotte. I was eighteen years old, having only a week earlier walked across the stage at Lockwoods Folly High to shake the principal's hand. Despite my fear of flying, I was seated on a small commuter jet parked at the terminal, waiting for my traveling companion to arrive, in hopes that he could help me take my mind off the takeoff and the turbulence and whatever else was in store before our scheduled 1:49 p.m. landing at the Hickory airport in the North Carolina foothills.

Unlike me, my friend, Bo Gaines, loved to fly. He also wasn't carrying the added baggage of knowing he was leaving the coast for good, as I was. You see, I was going to live with my aunt and her nineteen-year-old son near the mountain resort town of Blowing Rock, while Bo—a student musician whose real name was Lionel Hampton Gaines, after the jazz musician—was heading off for a four-week music camp at the college in Boone, only a few miles from where I'd be staying with my relatives.

I was beginning to think Bo was going to miss our flight when at last I saw him stroll through the door at the front of the cabin. He slowly approached with a slightly annoyed look on his dark handsome face. He was a year younger than me, but he handled himself more confidently than I ever did. I noticed that he had nothing with him—no carry-on bag, no cap, no jacket, no nothing that I could see. Well, nothing but a thin paperback book sticking out of one pants pocket. Of not quite average height and build, he was wearing light-brown Dockers slacks, a royal-blue short-sleeve Polo shirt and brown Topsiders loafers. His hair was natural but short and neat. He called it his "baby 'fro."

You could have described Bo as dapper, but you wouldn't have wanted him to hear you say it, because he lately had acquired a certain moodiness, possibly from a devotion to his musical hero, jazzman Miles Davis. Come to think of it, Bo even looked kind of like a younger, lighter-skinned Miles, at least when he had a trumpet stuck in his face. I was surprised that Bo hadn't carried-on his trumpet, because his horn meant so much to him. "Lips off the Connstellation!" he'd say if I tried to play the instrument, which had been his father's. Bo was the same way with his Martin guitar, but it was definitely too big for the overhead compartment.

Bo didn't spot me on the plane right away, probably because I was blending into the cabin's interior really well, as I was wearing my favorite style of clothes—plain. My favorite colors were earth tones. I always tried to blend in wherever I was. That should tell you something about me. I had taken up the ancient sport of golf and had begun to see myself in that light—as a golfer, a person whose passion is to chase a little white ball (in my case, an optic-yellow one) all over creation from sunup to sundown, beating that ball with a stick. Even so, I hated what the old-timers on the links called "go-to-hell" pants and the other garish golfing attire on sale in most pro shops. I wore whatever was comfortable and whatever could be worn more than once, maybe even several days in a row, without being noticed.

That day, on the airplane, I had on a pair of baggy slate-gray cargo shorts and nondescript running shoes, both items from the Wal-Mart back home, and a navy-blue T-shirt with "Cross Creek Country Club" and its logo of crossed golf clubs stitched in red and white on the pocket. All my shirts were seconds or over-runs from a knitware outlet store in nearby North Myrtle Beach, S.C. Since the shop did custom embroidering for local golf courses, I could buy customized tops—knit sportshirts as well as T-shirts—from places that I could never have afforded to play.

I found the outlet one time when Bo and his mom took me to North Myrtle for a concert at the House of Blues, Bo's favorite place on earth, he claimed. I don't remember the name of the guy we went to see—some old folk/rock musician from the Sixties or Seventies who came onstage with just his acoustic guitar. The only other thing I remember about the concert was that I got kinda tired of listening to the guy by himself, and I was ready to go home by the end of the man's first set. Bo, on the other hand, couldn't understand why I wasn't as thrilled as he was to hear this "living legend." But I could be that way back then—kind of impatient, or "hyper," as some people call it. My years of playing golf, however, have taught me patience, I hope.

While I'm trying to draw a picture of myself for you, I should probably go ahead and describe my looks in terms other than my clothes. I was of average height and weight for a girl—about five-feet-six and 110 pounds—and I kept my coarse reddish-brown hair cut short enough not to be too much trouble but long enough to be pulled back into a short ponytail and held in place with a golf cap and scrunchie. Although I was a golfer, I didn't have what could be called an "athletic" build, but I *was* in fairly good shape for a girl my age. At the same time, I didn't have the kind of figure that guys were always going on about. My face had too many freckles to be anything other than "cute," my boobs were a little too small, my waistline was a little too thick, and my hips, butt and legs weren't anything to write home about, if you were a guy who was looking for those kinds of things in a girl.

And if you *were* that kind of guy, I wouldn't have been interested in you, at all; in fact, I probably would have avoided you like the plague. Which probably explains why I had so little experience dating boys in high school—just some friendly outings with Bo or with one or two of the guys from the golf team. Lockwoods Folly didn't have separate teams for guys and girls then, so the boys were forced to get to know me, at least on the course. I never went to the prom. No one—no boy, I mean—ever took me out to the movies or out for pizza or out for anything else. I never went parking with a boy, unless you count the time me and three of the guys spent the night in a parking lot near Pinehurst No. 2 to get onto the grounds of the U.S. Open first. Nothing happened, though, except stupid guy stuff that was totally annoying.

Anyway, back on that airplane, Bo eventually reached our seats about halfway down the aisle and broke into a smile when he finally noticed me sitting there next to the window. "Hey, Val," he said, a bit louder than necessary. It was then that I noticed he was wearing earbuds attached to a tiny MP3 player clipped to his pants pocket. He pulled out the left bud and let it dangle over his shoulder down the front of his shirt. I could hear the tinny rasp of digital music.

"Sorry I'm running late," he added, taking the seat next to me. "Had trouble getting my stuff checked after Mom dropped me off. They went through both cases—even looked *inside* my guitar. You believe it? And then my MuVo and cell phone *and* my harmonica set off the metal detector." He patted his pants pocket.

I shrugged it off. "That's OK. What you listening to? Not Miles, is it?"

He grinned again. "Nope. Doc Watson. Here." He offered me the dangling earbud, which I took in my fingertips and held to my right ear. Through the tiny speaker I could hear a deep country voice that Grandpa, who had his own way with words, would have said was "smooth as molasses," accompanied by some nimble guitar-picking. "Cool, huh?" asked Bo, his dark eyebrows arching as if he were waiting for me to laugh at his taste in music.

The prospect of taking off within the next few minutes had my insides already tied in knots. It was all I could do to stay seated, as my heartbeat and breathing suddenly were trying to keep pace with Doc Watson's breakneck guitar. I listened to the song a few seconds longer, then handed back the earbud with trembling fingers. "Yeah, guess it's OK," I replied, taking hold of the armrest between us to steady my hand. "What about Miles? Thought *he* was your hero."

Bo touched a button on the player to turn it off and took the bud out of his other ear. "Oh, he *is*. Miles's the man, and I got him loaded, too," he said, patting the device on his belt. "But you gotta like Doc—best flat-picking guitar player in the world. And you know, he lives near Boone, where we're headed."

I chuckled nervously through my rising anxiety over our imminent takeoff. "Flat-picking? You mean like flats and sharps?"

Grimacing, Bo slapped me lightly on the arm and just shook his head, then carefully wound the earpiece wires into a plastic case he had taken from his pants pocket. "No, take my word for it," he said. "Doc plays *all* the notes great. And we gonna get to see him next month. DocFest—that's his music festival—it's the weekend before camp ends, and me and you are going, period." He patted my arm gently this time, apparently having noticed how I had latched onto the armrest.

"Val?" he asked, eyeing me more closely. "You gonna be solid with this? I mean, you cool with this?" I knew he was referring to the flight ahead and not to his assumption that we would go to the music festival together.

I nodded. "Have to be, I guess. I'm here. Not going anywhere." Our eyes met and held each other's gaze for a moment as, just then, the captain's monotoned greeting and preflight instructions came over the cabin loudspeaker along with the order to buckle up.

The stewardess—I'm sorry, female flight attendant—walked down the aisle and helped passengers with their seatbelts. It was a small commuter flight not even close to capacity, and the young woman reached us before I could get hooked in. As she started to lean past Bo to help me, he waved her off. "That's OK, ma'am," he said. "I got her." She smiled and nodded as she moved on.

"You're cool," Bo said, reaching to help me with the belt. It wasn't a question this time; it was a statement. Once I was buckled in, he leaned back in his seat to fish the earbud case from his pocket, then unclipped the player and handed both to me. "Here. Put these in your ears, close your eyes, and just sit back and listen. Don't even think about nothing else. You got Doc and Miles and some other guys *and* me to keep you company the next couple hours. Me and the boys'll take care of you, sister. All *you* gotta do is keep the faith."

He patted my arm again and gave it a couple of reassuring squeezes before leaning back to buckle himself in. Though I fumbled with it a bit, I managed to get the player hooked up and turned on before I noticed the plane begin to move. I took Bo's advice and closed my eyes, with no intentions of opening them, at least not for the next ninety minutes or so. Peeking only to find the volume button, I tried not to focus on the bittersweet feelings and memories evoked by the very first song on Bo's playlist, a friendly and familiar tune that could have been the soundtrack for our earliest adventures together at Village Point a few years earlier when Bo and I had first met. It was Lionel Hampton's "Flyin' Home," performed by someone named Charlie Parker, according to the scrolling LED readout on the player. Still, I couldn't help but notice the irony that, yes, I *was* flying, but to an unfamiliar home I had never seen before. And away from a home I might never, ever see again.

TWO

I guess the flight went well—for me, anyway. Once we got into the air and had leveled out, I *did* open my eyes from time to time. When I did, I kept my head turned away from the window and toward Bo, who spent the whole flight reading his paperback about Miles Davis's album *Kind of Blue*. That's why I had picked the window seat—not so I could look *out* the window and view the wild blue yonder, but so I wouldn't have to face the window while talking to Bo and look out accidentally. Every once in a while, I felt a jolt of turbulence; however, it wasn't enough to send me running and screaming down the aisle to lock myself in the john.

I just kept listening to Bo's music, and that was enough to keep me fairly calm. After the Charlie Parker record, Bo had loaded a bunch of songs by Miles and Doc Watson, and a single selection by a guy named Mike Cross. I recognized most of the tunes, but I hadn't heard many, if any, of the versions Bo had loaded on the player. I was most familiar with Doc's songs, mainly because they were traditional everyday kinds of tunes you might hear someone humming as they worked or played. I found out later that Doc called his music "traditional plus"—traditional music, plus anything else he wanted to play. In fact, a couple of the songs were ones I remember my mama and daddy singing or humming or whistling to me when I was little, back before the wreck that took them away from me.

Maybe it was the same with Bo, because he had lost a parent, too—his father, from cancer. Bo and his mom got along pretty well, though, since Mr. Gaines' death. She was a history professor in Raleigh and made more than enough money to support them. Like my Aunt Elaine, Dr. Marilyn Gaines was the kind of woman I wanted to become—smart and self-sufficient but caring and kind—even though I didn't realize that for some time yet. When she heard that we might have to sell our Village Point house after Grandma died, Dr. Gaines agreed to lease it from Elaine as a vacation home until we decided what we wanted to do with it. After dropping Bo off at the airport, Dr. Gaines was on her way down to Village Point for what would be longer than a summer's stay. She was taking the next year off from teaching to work on a book, and she said she wanted to write it at Village Point, near where she had grown up.

Her people had been slaves on one of the plantations near Shallotte. They had stayed in that area after the Civil War to work the cotton and tobacco fields but after the Depression had eventually moved off to urban areas where jobs were easier to come by, places like Detroit, Chicago and New York. That's how Dr. Gaines' family got up enough money to help her go off to college and make something of herself. She had gone to school in Philadelphia—a natural choice for a history buff, I imagine—and there she had met Bo's father, Lionel Hampton Gaines, Sr. I'm not exactly sure what Bo's dad did for a living. Bo didn't remember much about him, because he had died when Bo was just a baby. But I know Mr. Gaines really liked music, which apparently was why Bo had decided to make music his life. It was in his blood, I guess.

Back then I wished I knew what was in *my* blood—other than adrenalin, right at that moment—because there I was, eighteen years old and just out of high school, headed toward a new home and a new family, with not a clue as to what I was going to do with myself for the rest of my life. Becoming a professional golfer was by no means a reasonable career goal, mainly because it was a rare day when I broke ninety on any regulation course. That may sound impressive by most duffers' standards; however, a twenty-handicap wasn't going to get me on the ladies' tour, much less the men's, like Annika Sorenstam or, long before her, Babe Didrikson Zaharias.

By the way, I had three female sports heroes back then, like my three great fears. First came the Babe, who was one of the most versatile athletes of all time, male or female. She was a Texas girl whose father, like my grandpa, had worked on ships and sailed the world. Though she excelled in all sorts of serious and leisurely pursuits, she is best known as an Olympian and women's golf champion.

I also idolized the great Althea Gibson, who, like me, had lived in southeastern North Carolina. Althea was a champion at both tennis and golf back in her day. Actually, tennis was the first sport I had tried my hand at in school, but I gave it up when I popped a set of strings right away on the racket I had borrowed from another player and then found out how much it cost to have the racket restrung. That other girl said I probably wasn't "well-off enough" to play tennis. But I still liked Althea, partly because she hadn't always been "well-off" either. Bo found out for me that she also was a singer and had recorded an album in the 1950s, though I've never heard it and I don't think he had either. For that matter, the Babe entertained at parties by playing "hillbilly" songs on harmonica, according to what Bo learned on that computer of his. He was always on the Internet, looking up something, whenever I was at his house.

And my third female hero? Once again, like my third fear, I'll have to hold off on telling you, at the risk of wearing out your patience. Besides, I didn't know I wanted to be like this other woman until I moved to the mountains that summer.

I'm not sure if Bo used the Internet to find all the songs on the playlist I listened to during the flight that day. He must have, though, because it was an unusual assortment of recordings. As it ran, I peeked at each title that composed Bo's soundtrack, which included "Flyin' Home," "Night and Day," "Time After Time," "Basin Street Blues," "Stardust," "Autumn Leaves," "Sweet Georgia Brown," "Summertime," "Remember Me," "More Pretty Girls Than One," "Stormy Weather," "Sitting on Top of the World," "Will the Circle Be Unbroken," and, finally, "Farewell Toast/Boatman." That last one made me laugh out loud.

At the time, I thought it was an odd mix, but Bo explained to me later that his main interest in those songs had to do with how the different artists chose to interpret—or *cover*—tunes written by other composers. Also, Bo said he *did* idolize Miles and Doc but that he actually liked any artist who dared to take a risk and do something different, because risk and change were what life was all about, he said. Even then, I was amazed at how wise my best friend was, though I didn't necessarily agree with him about taking risks as we sat together on the airplane that day.

Back then my tastes in music were much simpler than Bo's; I generally just listened to singers and groups whose music I liked. Since I didn't own a computer and MP3 player like Bo and since I couldn't even afford a Walkman CD player and CDs, I was pretty much relegated to the land of scratchy AM/FM radio and almost obsolete cassette tapes. My machine's brand name was Realistic, and it must have been one of the first boom boxes ever produced right after the Eight-Track Era of the Information Age. About the size of a regular rural mailbox, the player/recorder had only one cassette deck, which could play either prerecorded tapes or record audio from whatever radio station I was listening to. I had inherited the boom box from my dad, who had bought the machine back when he was a teen-ager. According to Grandma, Daddy had saved up his money from digging clams and selling them to a supermarket in Shallotte one year. She told me that when she brought the boom box down from the attic and gave it to me a couple of years after the wreck.

Actually, I think she gave it to me not long after Grandpa got sick, because I remember listening to it the day after Grandpa died. I had been listening to some of Daddy's old tapes—the Beatles and Chicago and James Taylor—when I just happened to flip over to the radio right when the "Daily Obituaries" came on the local radio station. It was the most popular program on our town's little AM station, at least as far as Grandma and her friends were concerned. But as soon as I heard the somber-voiced announcer read, "Captain Bronson Benedict Galloway, 77, of…," I flipped the switch back to the cassette deck and fast-forwarded Daddy's copy of James Taylor's *Greatest Hits* to "Fire and Rain." Even now I tear up when I hear the verse about Jesus looking down and flying machines on the ground. I'm glad Bo didn't put *that* song on his playlist, even though it's one of my favorites.

You're probably wondering how—if I grew up so poor and couldn't afford to play tennis—how I could afford to play golf, truly a rich man's game. Well, it wasn't always easy, especially after I left Lockwoods Folly and couldn't play on the golf team anymore. That had been great, getting to play every day for free, even in the off-season, as long as I played at the no-frills locals course where our coach was the pro. Occasionally, a teammate or two would call me up to complete a foursome at their country club or resort course, and then I'd get to play on the lush fairways and perfectly-manicured greens that the rich folks were used to treading every time out. The other guys got a kick out of having me play with them, particularly when they were betting on the round and wanted to kind of sandbag whoever they were playing. As I've said before, I wasn't a great player, even for a teen-ager in the South Brunswick Islands, but I could more than hold my own with the high-handicappers who deigned to let me, a mere girl, join their foursome.

I had taken up the game during the summer before my freshman year at Lockwoods Folly. This was something else that happened as a result of Grandpa's death, believe it or not. Grandma and I were having trouble paying bills and making ends meet, so she asked around and found out that Billy Joe Pearlman, one of Grandpa's old fishing buddies, needed a hand at the mom-'n'-pop driving range and par-three course he had built all by himself with little more than a rented Bobcat earthmover. A good ole boy who had recently retired from a long and lucrative career as a cement contractor, Billy Joe had known next to nothing about golf course design before starting his little retirement project. All he knew was that he loved golf, owned forty acres of prime swampland near a booming tourist area and that he wouldn't mind spending his golden years as a golf pro—even though he wasn't an especially great golfer himself.

He was always claiming that he had played a lot better back before the war and that another North Carolinian named Billy

Joe—Billy Joe Patton, the amateur hero of the 1954 Masters golf tournament—had been named after him, but nobody with any sense believed him. I knew it wasn't true, because nobody outside our little corner of the world had ever heard of Billy Joe Pearlman and, besides, he was always saying something silly for a laugh.

Anyway, good ole Billy Joe paid me almost a minimum wage to keep the driving range and short fairways mowed two or three times a week depending on how much rain we got, and to pick up range balls and then wash and re-bucket them before sunset each day. For some reason, though, he wouldn't let me touch the special rotary-blade mower he had bought to cut the nine small but perfectly-round mounded greens sculpted into "Buccaneer Bill's Crossbones Country Club & Driving Range—9 Holes, Par 3, No Lights," as the sign out front read. Usually, folks just called the place "Billy Joe's" and left it at that.

The course *did* have a certain flair to it, though. Each green sported a kerchief-sized black pirate flag at the end of a seven-foot-tall pin. We *did* have one gas-powered cart to rent out, as well as one Billy Joe had modified to pick up range balls and another one for himself to ride around in. That one he had painted black to go with his pirate theme. The course, however, was so short that the tourists who were silly enough or lazy enough to pay an extra ten bucks to use the one available cart looked even more ridiculous herking and jerking from spot to spot to spot, chasing their $25-a-dozen balls from Astroturf tee to Bermuda-grass green. I kind of liked driving the ball-retriever, except that it didn't have headlights. That's why I had to get all of my work done before sunset, because the unlighted "B.J.," as the guys on my team laughingly called it, was situated deep enough in the pine swamp that I had trouble after dark finding my way back to the single-wide trailer that served as clubhouse.

One time when I got caught out on the course after dark, Billy Joe had to come and get me in *The Jolly Roger*, which was the name he had stenciled on his black cart. Additionally, he had painted a white number three with red trim on each side, as he was a really big Dale Earnhardt fan. The day Dale died at Daytona was probably the second worst day of Billy Joe's life, and I know because I was with him both days. "I like stockcars 'cause it's life or death out there on that track, kinda like bullfighting or boxing," Billy Joe told me once. "I like playin' golf 'cause it's just about life—the frustratin' part of it." He was always saying stuff like that, and sometimes it even made sense.

My teammates—the guys—were also always making fun of my mismatched clubs, even though I'm sure they understood why I didn't have an expensive, matched set like theirs, and I don't think they meant to be mean, necessarily. That's just how most high school boys are—kind of stupid and thoughtless sometimes. Or, at least, most of the boys *I* knew, except for Bo. They can't help it. It's in their genes. Anyway, since I didn't dare waste my wages buying golf clubs, I had to cobble together a set from the stray irons and woods that were always being left by careless tourists on the course and even at the driving range. It took me at least six or seven months, I guess, but I finally managed to adopt almost a full set of clubs, with all of my orphans coming from Billy Joe's place.

A full set is fourteen clubs; mine, however, consisted of only the twelve that I absolutely needed on the course, as I had no use for all the different wedges (attack, gap, lob wedges and those with various degrees of loft) that most golfers clutter their bags with. Just give me a good pitching wedge, and I'd be happy—even though Billy Joe said that if a golfer was going to carry only one wedge, it should be a sand wedge. And I never used a driver, instead choosing to hit off the tee with a more dependable three-wood. Even then, I often carried only six or maybe nine clubs onto the course, depending upon its length and difficulty. It made sense to me back then, anyway.

Three of my clubs—my first six- and nine-irons and the first few pitching wedges that I found—were subpar sticks, all off-brand knock-offs that I was always complaining about to Billy Joe when we would sit around in his golf cart and talk shop. "Just be patient, little Missy, just be patient," he would always say. "They's always another wayward club just waitin' to find a new home, you wait 'n' see." And he was right about all three clubs—six-iron, wedge *and* putter, three of the four clubs that will always be nearest and dearest to my heart. I just had to be patient.

For some reason, the duffers who played the B.J. or used the range must have identified more closely with their putters than with any other club in their bags, because in the three years I worked there, only one putter was ever left at the course. I found at least two $350 titanium drivers, several of those oddly-shaped fairway "metals" that were a cross between an iron and a wood, a bunch of custom-made irons from expensive sets, and fancy wedges of all brand names, shapes and lofts. I probably found more wedges than anything else, usually left on the fringe near the sand trap at the back of the fifth green.

Billy Joe's stated policy was to keep recovered clubs in the clubhouse under lock and key for six full weeks before putting them up for sale, just in case the owners returned looking for them. And despite the fun he took in playing Buccaneer Bill the Putting Pirate Captain, he stuck to his word, even when I had my eye on some really choice booty, like the Calloway Big Bertha II driver I found or that Nike CPR 56-degree wedge (which would have completed my fourteen-club set). And then, more often than not, Billy Joe would sell the club while I was at school on the very day the six-week waiting period ran out. Of course, I'd get mad when I got to work and found the club gone, but he'd just laugh and say, "Arrrrr, it's a mighty cruel world out thar, matey! It's every buccaneer for hisself!" Words to live by.

Like I said, Billy Joe was always saying goofy things like that. I think he and Grandpa used to sit around thinking up that crazy stuff when they went shark fishing or floundering together and would stay gone all night. Those were about the only times Grandma would get really mad and fuss at Grandpa, when he would come dragging in at sunup too tired to talk much to anybody. All talked out, I guess—knowing Billy Joe and my grandpa.

The only pieces of equipment that cost real money were my shoes, my glove, my cap, my golf bag and those four clubs, my four favorites. For my sixteenth birthday, Aunt Elaine and her son, Alan, had come to visit us and had taken us out for pizza in Calabash and then down to those big golf stores in North Myrtle Beach.

Aunt Elaine—her full name then, by the way, was Elaine Katherine Galloway Delacruz—always made a pretty good salary in her jobs as a newspaper reporter and later as an editor. But she never had money to burn when I was growing up, at least not since she and Alan's father, Lance Delacruz, divorced some years earlier. Before the divorce, the three of them—Elaine, Lance and Alan—had been fairly well off, you could say, because Uncle Lance was a big lawyer in the Wilmington area. He specialized in divorce cases, oddly enough. They had a big house at the beach near Wilmington and a big vacation home in the North Carolina mountains, the house I was moving to that summer. For a few years after the divorce, though, Lance was a real jerk about things and wouldn't even pay child support. He didn't start paying until about a year before I moved in with them, after Elaine finally took him back to court over it.

So it really *was* a special occasion when she took us all out on the town for my birthday that time, maybe because it was my *sixteenth* birthday and you know how everybody is always making a big deal about being "sweet sixteen" and all. Anyway, after dinner we were at the golf store when Elaine steered me away from the golf clubs and toward the shoe department and told me to pick out a pair of golf shoes. I tell you what, I looked long and hard at the newest and most expensive pairs of shoes—especially the Nikes, since that was what Tiger Woods wore—but I settled on a heavily-discounted pair of brown-and-white saddle oxfords that came with a free set of soft spikes and individual velour storage bags. I guess Aunt Elaine could tell that the cheaper pair wasn't my first choice, because when we got back to the car, she presented me with a white Nike golf cap and a Nike golf glove to make up for my not picking those more expensive Nike shoes after all. Actually, she said Grandma was the one giving me the cap and that Alan was giving me the glove, but I'm sure Elaine paid for everything. That's how Elaine was.

How I got my first golf bag and my four favorite clubs is another story, one that I'm not too proud of but will tell you anyhow, just for the sake of balance; I don't want you to think I'm a Miss Goody-Two-Shoes, as Billy Joe sometimes called me. Other times, by the way, he would call me things like Miss Too-Big-Fer-Yer-Own-Britches or Miss Got-Rocks or, my personal favorite, little Miss Vanasterbutt, whenever I was getting too full of myself, hanging around with my rich teammates on their fancy golf courses. Billy Joe knew how to keep me humble.

Anyway, I carried my hodgepodge of clubs in what golfers call a "Sunday bag," a thin little black nylon sheath with room for no more than five or six clubs. But it had a red Wilson logo on it, and it hadn't cost me anything—to begin with, anyway—because I'd found it at the B.J. and had waited the six weeks without anyone claiming it and had talked Billy Joe into letting me have it. What I'm getting around to telling you, though, and what I didn't tell Billy Joe right off then, either, was that I had also found three older but expensive clubs in the Sunday bag—a Ben Hogen forged six-iron, a Yonex pitching wedge and, the real treasure, a Ping putter, all three scratched and dinged from overuse and maybe even misuse but still in good playing condition. The two clubs other than the putter had been regripped, indicating that their former owner at least had known enough about the game of golf to realize he needed to keep a firm grip on his clubs at all times. I'm surprised he let them slip away.

As a matter of fact, I can usually size up most players pretty quickly just by checking out their grips—the actual grips themselves, not the position of the golfers' hands on their clubs, as so many teaching pros make such a big deal about. Proper grips and perfect swings and all that technical crap don't mean all that much when you get right down to it; it's where the ball lands after you hit it that counts. Or, as Billy Joe used to say, "they's more than one way to pluck a duck." Which brings me back to the story about how I paid for my four favorite clubs, including the three I had found in the Sunday bag but didn't tell Billy Joe about.

When I finally got up enough nerve to take the clubs out of hiding and use them on the course one weekend—I practiced at the B.J. all the time because it was free—Billy Joe spotted the expensive Ping putter right away and asked me where I got it. To make a long story short, I eventually told him the truth—that I had turned in the bag but had held onto the clubs. "I don't know why I didn't just keep the bag, too," I explained sheepishly. "I don't guess I thought it was fancy enough for me."

"Now wudn't that kinda stupid?" Billy Joe asked. "Ya know, the ole man that lost them clubs come in a week or so after I give the bag to you, and when he asked me about them, I said we hadn't found no clubs, just the bag. I told him some rascal must've picked them up right after he left them, 'cause you hadn't turned in nothin' but that bag, and you're an honest kid. At least your granddaddy told me you were. Anyways, I didn't figure you'd turn in the bag and not the clubs, too. That don't make good sense."

I really didn't know what to say at that point. I was so ashamed of myself for having violated Billy Joe's—and Grandpa's—trust that I just put my head down and, for one of the few times in my young life, started to cry like a girl. Of course, my show of emotion, as honest as it was, embarrassed Billy Joe to no end. "Now you can just stop that boo-hooin' right now, little Miss Fancy-Pants," he said. "You're actin' like I done went and told you you's fired or something."

"Well, aren't you gonna?" I sobbed.

"Hel—, I mean, heck, no." We were sitting side by side under *The Jolly Roger*'s plastic canopy to get out of the hot midday sun that late fall Sunday, and, as I kept crying, Billy Joe put his heavy arm around my neck and laid his rough cement-contractor hand on my far shoulder and shook me a little bit. "No, no, no," he said as gently as he could manage with his gruff voice. "I ain't about to let you go, big girl. You're about the only thing that gets me outta bed ever' mornin'."

He and I both realized how his last remark sounded, because I glanced over at him and he withdrew his arm as he struggled to explain. "No, now, I don't mean it *that* way, Val, so don't you go givin' me one 'o those looks of yers. You know me, Val. It's just that ever since I retired, I ain't had much to look forward to, not 'til I got this place up and running'. I always liked fishin' with your granddaddy, 'cause me and him always had a good time. But Bron couldn't go fishin' with me ever' single night, so I had to look for somethin' else, and this is what I settled on. Don't really know why; it just worked out this way."

"But you're not firing me?" I asked again.

He grinned. "*Heck*, no. Are you jokin'? I got just enough meanness in me to keep you 'round here the rest of yer life and make you work off what you done." Though I could tell he was starting to tease me, I also knew he was just getting wound up. "Ain't you the very Ike who's always goin' on about givin' folks second chances and not jumpin' to conclusions about folks just because of the way they look and such? Well, little Miss Vanasterbutt, you ain't gettin' off that easy. Nosiree. I felt so sorry for that ole boy whose clubs you took—even though I didn't know you took 'em—that I give him better clubs and a better bag than what he lost. Don't know why I was such a soft touch that day. Just was. Guess I felt bad 'cause I'd give away his bag. Anyways, big girl, I figure you owe me, oh, I don't know, somewhere in the general neighborhood of, oh, 'bout, hmm, 'bout let's say four days' pay—one fer each club you took and one fer good measure. I'd make you give them clubs back to that ole boy, but he looked like a tourist, and I didn't get his name and address. And, you're right, the bag ain't really worth nothin'."

Then Billy Joe said something else that still wounds me all these years later. "I may not know what it feels like to play like them great golfers you see on TV, but I know how to act like 'em, far as bein' honest and bein' a good sport and bein' a *golfer* goes. That's one thing I like about this game—it shows you for who you are and what you are. They's a lot of ways to tell a lie, but they's only one way to tell the truth. I don't know who said that first, but he was a smart man, and that's the honest-to-God truth. And you, Val, you *are* an honest girl, like your granddaddy said. It ain't like you to be dishonest and make a liar outta me—or him. Our word, our honor, is about all some of us golfers got. Val, you're a golfer, too. You ain't no sneakin' kid I can't trust, and I know you'll do the right thing here, and you won't never let me down again. Now will you."

It really wasn't a question. The definite way he said "will you" and his sober look left no room for me to say anything but, "I won't let you down again." And I never did pull another stunt like that in the next two-and-a-half years that I worked for Billy Joe.

I had to quit my job at the B.J. when Grandma got sick during my senior year, and I didn't see Billy Joe again until the funeral and then, for the next to last time, exactly one week before my flight with Bo. I ran into Billy Joe at the big golf store, one of his favorite places, too. He said my job was waiting for me if I wanted it; he even promised me a raise and more hours than I knew he could afford. I thanked him but said I was going to have to move to the mountains to live with Aunt Elaine and Alan. I was leaving the next week, I said. He nodded that he understood and told me to come see him at the course the next morning, because he wanted to talk to me before I left for the mountains, he said.

When I got there the next day—it was around ten o'clock, I guess—a hand-lettered "TEMP CLOSED FOR REPAIRS" sign was tacked to the locked clubhouse door, along with a smaller, folded note to me from Billy Joe. Neither he himself nor any golfers were anywhere to be seen, even though a strange vehicle—a muddy, battered old black Scout, a jeep-like vehicle that looked like it had just been driven out of the swamp—was parked next to Billy Joe's immaculate pickup truck in the lot outside the clubhouse. The note directed me to the farthest point from where I stood—the sand trap behind the fifth green at the very back of the course, where I assumed that Billy Joe was working with whoever owned the Scout, maybe some guy that Billy Joe had finally hired to replace me after our talk the previous night.

Anyway, what I found was a complete surprise. Lying there on the fringe was what turned out to be Billy Joe's going-away present to me, a new Wilson sand wedge, its steel shaft and silver forged head gleaming in the morning sun. My fourth favorite club. Taped to the shaft just below the grip was a yellow Post-It note that read: "V.—You earned this 1000000 times over—think of the beach and me when ever your in the sand—I miss you—I will always luv you. Come see me. By-by. B."

I rode my bike back to the course that night around closing time to thank Billy Joe, knowing that he would give me a ride back home, but, well, things didn't work out the way anyone would have planned, and I'd rather not talk about it just yet, even now. It was too much of a shock. I don't even want to think about it, to tell you the truth.

As Bo and I sat in the terminal at the Hickory Airport with all our baggage and waited for someone—either Aunt Elaine or Alan, we weren't sure who it'd be—to pick us up, I told Bo about Billy Joe's farewell gift and what my "old pro" meant to me. Bo said I was lucky to have so many people who cared so much about me. I knew he was telling the truth.

THREE

Bo and I waited in the terminal's outer lobby for about thirty minutes before he asked if I knew Elaine and Alan's phone number. That was his way of saying he was tired of waiting. Actually, I didn't mind the down time and I definitely was in no hurry to start a car ride up a winding mountain road; I was still shaky from the flight and from the landing, in particular. Taking out his cell phone and flipping it open with a flourish, Bo punched in the numbers I recited, then handed me the phone so I could talk to my aunt. I listened to at least seven or eight rings before I heard a click, then a glitch in the static, then a different sort of ring. "Yo," a deep male voice answered. "Hold on. I'm turning."

"Alan?"

"Hold on," he repeated. I heard road noise and what sounded like another, higher-pitched voice in the background. "OK. Val? That you?"

"Yeah. Where are you? I called your home number."

"Yeah, ain't technology wonderful?" Alan laughed. "Mom had to go in to work today, and she asked me to pick you up. I guess she figured I'd be late, so she must've set the call-forwarding to ring me instead of her. That's Mom for you—a step ahead of everybody."

I wondered what was going on with Alan that Elaine could guess he would be late, but I didn't bother inquiring right then. "Where are you?" I asked again. "We landed about an hour ago, I guess."

"Well, we're almost there," he said. "Hey, sorry you had to wait so long, cuz."

"It hasn't been *that* long," I corrected, letting his reference to "we" slide for the moment. "It took us a while to get our stuff. They were kinda slow taking it off the plane. We've only been waiting about a half hour, I guess. I was wondering—you gonna have room for all our stuff? What you driving?"

"My new truck," he replied. "Can't wait for you to see it. But, yeah, we oughta have room. What all you got?"

I explained that in addition to our suitcases we had Bo's guitar, trumpet and laptop computer, and my golf clubs. Alan whistled in surprise, as though he hadn't expected to be hauling so much cargo on this expedition up the mountain. "OK, well, we're turning into the airport now," he said, "so one of you come meet us out front, and we'll get this show back on the road. See you in a minute. I'm glad you're here, cuz." The connection went dead, and I handed back Bo's phone as I brought him up to speed on Alan's arrival.

Hickory, in the foothills, is ordinarily about an hour's drive from the Boone-Blowing Rock area where Aunt Elaine and Alan lived. "Ordinarily," I say, because that day Alan had several surprises for us, including a little side trip of which Aunt Elaine probably would not have approved. But that was Alan's way, as he was something of a daredevil.

My favorite cousin was nineteen years old, having just completed his freshman year at Appalachian State University in Boone. He was tall and handsome, and he knew it. Not that he was conceited, exactly. Extremely confident. Maybe that's a better way to describe him. Except for his uneven early-summer tan with its faint blotches of red and white here and there on his face and neck, Alan's looks hadn't changed much since I had seen him last at Grandma's funeral. His wavy light brown hair with blond highlights was still perfectly cut and groomed, as if he were in one of those "boy bands" that were so popular back then.

That day the clothes he wore made him look as though he had just stepped out of an L.L. Bean catalog, as if he really *were* taking us on safari—a crisp white longsleeved, multi-pocketed fishing shirt with rolled sleeves, scuffed dark-leather hiking books with gray socks, and a light khaki-colored pair of those convertible travel pants whose legs can be zipped off just above the knees. Alan drove the girls wild, as he was about six-feet-two and two hundred pounds, with handsome chiseled features and an athletic but not-too-muscular build, thanks in large part to all the outdoor sports he pursued. In warm-weather months when he wasn't in school, he spent most free hours backpacking, rockclimbing, whitewater kayaking or mountain biking. In the winter, he especially enjoyed cross-country skiing, snowboarding and ice-climbing.

Despite his extreme self-confidence, my favorite cousin, my exceptionally good-looking cousin, was one of the most gentle and most kind-hearted fellows you could ever meet. Still, as his choices in leisure pursuits attested, he was anything but a team player, as he was always going his own way. He used to play on the basketball team in high school but had given it up for tennis and then had given up the tennis team for all those outdoor sports, because he was such an independent soul. He didn't like having to depend on anyone else when it came to a sporting activity of any sort. In all of those respects, he was very much like our grandfather had been, though Grandpa's individualistic exploits were on the Carolina coast instead of in the mountains.

Alan's first surprise that day at the airport came when he pulled up out front in a brand-spanking-new, canary yellow Chevy Blazer ZR2, the expensive, off-road model loaded with all the extras. At Grandma's funeral Alan had been talking about wanting a new vehicle and had even asked his dad, Uncle Lance, to help him buy one. But I don't think Alan ever dreamed of owning anything like that Blazer, at least not until he got out of school and was making money on his own. I found out later that Lance had run out and bought the $30,000-plus Blazer for his son right after the funeral, partly to score Brownie points with Alan but mainly to show up Aunt Elaine, who, Lance knew, couldn't afford anything like that. He also knew that Elaine was still paying Alan's car insurance while he was still in school and that the new Blazer's collision coverage alone would increase her premium considerably. Uncle Lance was sneaky that way.

That quality—Lance's sneakiness—was also why he had given Elaine and Alan the mountain house in the divorce settlement, I later learned. The house, built into the side of a mountain basically, was located in a wooded, upscale subdivision near the Blue Ridge Parkway between Blowing Rock and Boone. On four levels from attic to basement, the river-rock and wood-frame mansion—and you *could* call it that without exaggerating—contained probably five to six thousand square feet of living space, not counting the huge decks, screened-in porches and flagstone patios attached to it on three sides. The fourth side sported an attached, three-car garage that itself was at least as large as the old cottage that Elaine and Alan had rented at the beach, back when they lived near us.

Lance had owned the mountain house for only a couple of years prior to the divorce; so when Elaine got the house in the settlement she still had to make mortgage payments on it, payments that took everything she made and more in her job at *The Linville Ledger*. As far as vehicles went, Elaine couldn't even afford a four-wheel-drive SUV for herself, even though having one would have made life much easier for her, especially in the snowy mountain winters. She still drove her old baby-blue Volkswagen Beetle whose torn cloth sunroof leaked like the dickens when it rained. I always loved that old car, though, and she did, too. I had hoped that someday it would be mine.

Alan's second surprise that day at the airport was sitting in the passenger-side front seat next to him. The girl wasn't a complete surprise, but Bo and I might have liked to have had Alan to ourselves for a little while before we had to share him with his new mountain friends. From the looks of them together, though, this girl was more than just a friend.

A natural beauty with long dark hair, Alan's companion smiled and waved to me without rolling down her window, as he hopped out of the Blazer and came around to meet me. "Hey there, cuz," he said, giving me a big hug. "Lacey'll stay with the truck while we go get Boo-Boo and your bags. Come on." (He was always calling himself "Yogi" and Bo "Boo-Boo," like in the cartoon, mainly because of the differences in their heights.) Even though I was the one who knew where Bo and our stuff were waiting, Alan led the way, as was his style. He really was smarter than the average bear, as his major in applied physics with a concentration in astronomy implied.

"What do you think of her?" Alan asked as we walked.

"She's pretty," I replied. "How long have you been dating?"

He laughed. "No. The truck. What do you think of the truck?"

I popped him on the shoulder. "What's the matter with you, Alan? You didn't even introduce me to her. But the truck, yeah, the truck is nice, I guess. It's really, uh, *yellow*, though, isn't it?"

"That's so everybody can see me coming, cuz," he said, playing along. "That's why Dad said he picked it out, anyway. But, hey, Lacey *is* pretty, isn't she? She's really nice, too. But she's kinda shy—until she gets to know you. You'll like her." Just then he spotted Bo. "Hey, hey, Boo-Boo!" Alan greeted, as Bo just shook his head and stood to gather his things. Alan slapped him on the back just a bit too sharply.

"Ain't changed a bit," Bo said with a weak smile, wincing slightly from the sting of the friendly slap. "Hey, man, you give me a hand with the guitar?"

"Sure thing," Alan said. "I'm glad you brought it, dog. I told my girlfriend how good you are. She likes folk music, too."

"Girlfriend?" Bo asked. I wondered what Bo thought about being called "dog," but he apparently chose to let it pass. "You got a girlfriend?"

"Yeah," I said, butting in. "She's really pretty and looks nice—nothing like any of Alan's old girlfriends."

Alan bumped me with his hip as the three of us walked along side by side, almost making me drop my golf bag. "Hey, what'd'ya mean by that?" he said. "I've never gone out with an ugly girl in my life."

"What about that groupie you had sophomore year?" I asked, referring to a girl Alan had escorted to the annual homecoming football game when he was a tenth grader at Lockwoods Folly. I called her a groupie once around Billy Joe, and he thought I'd said Alan was dating a "grouper," a kind of fish.

"She wasn't my groupie," Alan said, "and she wasn't ugly, either. She had a nice, well, uh, nice—" I thought he was going to say "gills."

"Not *even* a nice personality, Alan," I interjected. "She was mean as a snake and just went out with you because you were a jock. She didn't want to have anything to do with you after you quit playing basketball and tennis. And you *still* had a big crush on her."

"Yeah, I know," he admitted. "But you're right—Lacey isn't anything like that girl or anybody else I've ever dated. She's—well, you'll just have to see for yourself."

By then we had reached the Blazer. Lacey got out to help us load our gear into the back, and it was then that Alan made his introductions as we piled into the vehicle and started toward the mountains on the western horizon. Lacey Green *did* seem genuinely nice; still there was something different about her that I couldn't quite put my finger on. For example, when Alan stopped for snacks at a convenience store on the outskirts of a small town near the foot of the mountains, Lacey refused to let him buy her anything, even though she had no money and, like the rest of us, had missed lunch. Without losing her temper, she was adamant that he would *not* spend any of his money on her. She said she'd eat something when she got home. I figured she was as independent as Alan was and that she didn't want any guy to think she owed him anything, not even a nice guy like Alan. That's how I always was, anyway.

And there was something else that I picked up on as we left the main highway at the true foot of the mountains and turned onto a dusty, graveled road that wound for miles through a rocky river gorge and dark mountain coves toward a place that Alan called Kawana, near where Lacey and her elderly grandfather lived. Though Lacey was the local, the one who should have known the most about this isolated place where she lived, Alan did all of the talking, as if he were a Pisgah National Forest ranger.

It was obvious that Alan had spent a lot of time there in what he called the Wilson Creek Gorge, as well as in the Harper Creek and Lost Cove Wilderness Study Areas. It also became apparent that pretty Lacey wasn't going to volunteer any information about herself, her home or anything else, for that matter. She just sat and listened with a knowing look as Alan played tour guide. He had pointed out the brand spanking new Wilson Creek Welcome Center, and we even stopped there to use the clean restrooms. He showed us the ruins of an old cotton mill near Mortimer, a mill town that had flourished in the early 1900s until a flood washed out the railroad line that connected the mountain community with the outside world. With only a few summer homes and national forest campground there now, Mortimer was more like a ghost town than anything.

Alan also drove us through a community called Edgemont, which, like Mortimer, had seen more prosperous days. Back when the railroad was still running, flatlanders would come to the Edgemont Inn to get away from civilization and to enjoy the cool mountain breezes, Alan explained. However, the flood had also ended Edgemont's future as a mountain resort when the train could run there no more. In fact, floods nearly washed both villages off the map.

"Yeah, we've been getting so much rain the past couple months, I'm beginning to think it's 1917 or 1940 all over again," Alan said, referring to the two worst floods in history there. "The road was so muddy back in March, we almost got stuck in Lacey's truck on that rough stretch that runs right along Wilson Creek back before you get to Mortimer. The creek didn't get out, though. And Lost Cove Creek into Edgemont didn't flood this spring, either, far as I know. It usually takes a hurricane coming through to do the damage these areas got back in the day. But we got rain just about every day this spring. I sure didn't like the drought we *were* having, but I think I liked all the rain even less. I sure am glad we're getting some nice weather for a change now that summer is finally here. In my line of work, a man's gotta be able to see the sky."

"What line's that?" Bo asked.

"Astronomy," Alan replied earnestly. "I've always been fascinated by the stars, ever since I was a little kid when Dad and Mom and me still lived together. We used to go out at night and lay on our dock to watch the Perseids every August, and we'd see who could count the most shooting stars. I remember when you could see Hyakutake, the comet, so clear that one spring when Mom and I lived at the beach. We'd go out on the deck every evening and look at it together. Remember, Val? Bo? That was around the time Grandpa was sick, and the three of us were running around all over the place trying to find the Fountain of Youth. Remember?" He glanced up at our reflections in the rear-view mirror.

"Did you find it?" Lacey asked, breaking her silence. "The Fountain of Youth?" It was as if she actually believed we might have succeeded in our quest.

Alan looked at me again in the mirror. "Val?" he said. "You wanna answer that one?" Then turning to his girlfriend, he added, "Val and I kinda see that little adventure in a different light. And Bo won't take sides. Right, Bo?"

Bo only nodded, giving me an opportunity to answer Alan. I really didn't know how much I wanted to say right then, because that particular issue—whether or not we had found the Fountain of Youth—was a touchy subject between Alan and me. Being an aspiring scientist, my cousin had always taken the more analytic view of our search, as if our results had needed to jive with his narrow interpretation of The Scientific Method. I had always taken the more idealistic approach, as I don't always need to see something to believe in it—just as I believed with all my heart that I could help heal my grandfather by finding the legendary healing waters of Shallotte Inlet near our home at Village Point. But that's another story altogether.

"Well, I think we found it—what Ponce de Leon, the Spanish explorer, called the Fountain of Youth," I told Lacey. "My grandpa—Alan's and my grandfather—called it the Healing Hole, and *he* believed in it. He *used* it to heal all sorts of sick people. It's a little cove where these really rare reeds grow and produce something like penicillin when the tide gets high enough to flood the cove."

Alan snorted. "Now, Val, you don't know that for a fact. That's just what the old folks around there say. Now, tell the truth; have you ever met anybody who was healed by the water there?"

"No," I replied, "but Grandpa always said tha—"

"Grandpa didn't really believe in it himself," Alan interrupted. "He just took all those people there because *they* thought it would work. It was just that those folks were ready to try anything. It was their last resort, and Grandpa didn't want to put out their last little glimmer of hope. They were desperate."

"Are you saying *we* were desperate that Easter when Grandpa got sick?" I asked. "Or that it was just me? That *I* was the desperate one?" I was growing angry with Alan, as I always did whenever we discussed Grandpa's illness.

"Yeah, I think you were desperate," Alan said. "I think we *all* were, because we all loved Grandpa, and we all felt so helpless over what was happening to him, and we didn't want to lose him. It just hurt you a lot more than the rest of us, except for Grandma, I mean. You'd already lost your folks, and then here Grandpa was sick, and you didn't want to lose him, too."

Lacey turned in her seat to look at me. "You lost your parents?" she asked.

"Yeah," I said. "They died when I was little. Car wreck."

At first I thought she was going to say something else, but she merely nodded sympathetically and turned back to look at the road ahead. "I agree with you about Grandpa, Alan," I said, "but are you saying that all those stories about the healing waters are lies? That none of them are true?"

Alan nodded. "Well, not that they're *all* lies. I'm sure there's a grain of truth *somewhere* in the stories. That's the way it is with myths and legends and folk tales and stuff like that. Right, Bo? You're the expert on folk songs and all. Right, dog?"

"Yeah, I guess so," Bo replied. "It's kinda like this song I'm studying up on now; it's called 'Brown Mountain Light.' You heard it, man?"

"Yeah," Alan replied, "everybody around here has heard *that* song. Matter of fact, we're really close to Brown Mountain right now. That area we went through along Wilson Creek right after we turned off the paved road is called Brown Mountain Beach. The mountain itself is back in that direction." He pointed back over his left shoulder out the window, even though the trees along the road were too high and too thick to allow a view of the nearby peaks.

"I know," Bo said. "That's why I got interested in the song to begin with, 'cause it's one of the biggest hits anybody from up here ever wrote—it and 'Have I Told You Lately (That I Love You).' A dude named Scotty Wiseman wrote both those songs back in the Fifties, and they've been covered by a bunch of people. Back in the Sixties, a country 'n' western singer named Tommy Faile had a hit with 'Brown Mountain Light,' probably bigger than anybody else that ever did it. He played guitar for a man named Arthur Smith, the guy that wrote the *Deliverance* song, you know, 'Dueling Banjos' and another big hit called 'Guitar Boogie.'

"But, anyway, that band—Arthur Smith and the Crackerjacks—they were popular back when everybody only had AM radios to listen to. All the big stations had live country music shows like the *Grand Ole Opry* and *Barn Dance* and stuff like that. WBT—that was the big AM radio station out of Charlotte back then—had a live music show called *Carolina Hayride* that everybody around here listened to. The head of the company that owned the station—this guy named Julian

Price—even owned property up here in the mountains and donated it for a big park. That's what I read."

"Yeah, that's gotta be Julian Price Park up on the Blue Ridge Parkway between Blowing Rock and Grandfather Mountain," Alan said, clearly impressed by our friend's knowledge. "How do you *know* all that stuff, Boo-Boo? You know now, *I'm* supposed to be the *smart* one." I could see that Alan was grinning, not taking himself as seriously as his words suggested.

"The *humble* one, you mean," I laughed. Alan glanced at me in the rear-view mirror and winked. I added, "Bo *knows*, Alan. Haven't you ever heard that before?"

"Oh, shut up, Val," Bo scolded, then addressed Alan again. "I just like looking up stuff—doing research. It's a lot of fun to learn all the old stories about songs and about the people who write them and sing them. It tells you a lot about people—the songs they like to sing and how they make music. When I knew I was coming up here to camp, I did a little research on the music in these mountains. I just got started, though, and I still got a lot to learn. But, yeah, man, I agree with you that most folk songs have a little truth to them but that they get changed as they're being passed on from one person to the next. It's like that game where you whisper something in one person's ear, and they whisper to the next person what you said, and you go on down the line like that until the last person hears something that's totally different from what the first person said to begin with. The trick is figuring out how and why the story changed along the way—what reasons a person might have for changing a story. That's what I'm after—the truth.

"But, seriously, man," Bo went on, "I don't believe that the Brown Mountain Light is the ghost of some poor old slave who's wandering around the top of that mountain looking for his lost master, waving a lantern back and forth, like the song says. And I don't believe any of those other stories connected with the Brown Mountain Light legend—you know, the one about the Indian maidens looking for their fallen braves or the one about the old mountain guy who killed his wife and baby and buried their bodies up there. People just make up stories to explain all the stuff they don't understand. They just see what they want to see."

"Well, as far as the Brown Mountain Light goes," Alan said, "I've never seen it, and I've been around here a lot lately—hiking and camping. And on my bike. I just think there's some other explanation for it, for what people *think* they see or what they *want* to see. It's got to be *something*. There's got to be some kind of scientific explanation, and eventually somebody will figure it out." Alan nodded toward Lacey. "She hasn't seen them, either, and she's lived around here all her life. Right, Lace?"

The young woman nodded but said nothing. Even though I loved both my favorite cousin and my best friend, I couldn't agree with either of them on this topic. "No, you guys are just plain wrong," I said. "There *could* be a Light. There are some things we just don't understand and *can't* understand. I don't really know why I'm scared of the dark, but I am. That fear is real, even if it *is* all in my head. Or if it isn't real, then it may as well be, because it sure does feel real, to me, anyway. Like I said before, there are just some things you gotta believe in. I wish I could prove that to you, Alan. And to you, too, Bo."

FOUR

The four of us were mostly silent for the next few dusty miles, as we continued to wind through the forested hills. Alan did point out a trailhead along the way; he said it eventually led to the Greentown Trail, a steep footpath which led more or less straight up the mountain to a place on the main highway called the Barkhouse Lodge & Family Campground, where Lacey worked part-time. Several miles farther on, he pulled off at what was little more than a wide spot in the road next to a brown wooden Forest Service sign that read "Darkside Cliffs Trail."

"Anyone up for a short hike?" he asked, already unbuckling his seat belt. "This is the easiest one around here. Only about a half mile. Great view of the Brown Mountain Light, no waiting."

Lacey rolled her eyes but didn't seem too put out with him. "I'm gonna be late for work if we stay too long, Alan," she said. "I guess I oughta call Sonny and see if he can cover for me 'til I get there. He will, just 'cause I'm with you." Then she looked back at us. "It really ain't a bad hike, but you know you ain't gonna see the Light in the daytime. It's gotta be dark." It was the most she had said since our introduction a couple of hours earlier at the airport.

"But you said you haven't seen it," I said. "Have you?"

She lifted her dark eyebrows. "Not *me*. But my granddaddy has. He's seen it a hundred times, I guess. But he says you ain't gonna see it if you look for it. It's just one of them things. But I believe in it 'cause Granddaddy says it's so."

We were quiet as she took Alan's cell phone and checked to see if it had service before dialing the Barkhouse Lodge's number. She shook her head. "You gotta get another phone, Alan," she said. "We never can get any bars on it when we need to make a call from down here. Sonny's phone's better than this one."

"I know, I know," Alan said, "but Dad got a good rate, and he's the one paying the bill. He says this service is the best, and he won't pay for anything else. Maybe it'll work when we get out to the cliffs, but I doubt it. My phone is about worthless down here in these coves and valleys, and it isn't much good anywhere but right in the middle of town. If we can't get a signal out on the cliffs, you can use the OnStar when we get back to the truck, OK? We can hit a satellite, even from out here."

"OnStar doesn't use satellites for its phone service, does it?" Bo asked. "I think it uses cell towers, just like regular cell phones."

"Really?" Alan said. "But the GPS part is satellite, right? Gotta be. Guess that's where they got their name." Bo shrugged.

As Alan suggested, Lacey was able to get a cell phone signal, though only a faint one, once we had emerged from the woods to stand on the high cliffs, with their 180-degree view of what Alan identified as the Wilson Creek basin, Grandfather Mountain range and Blowing Rock. According to Alan, the Blowing Rock—the actual rock formation—was where a Cherokee brave who had been scorned by his lover tried to kill himself but was rescued by the swirling winds that blew him back to the precipice from whence he had jumped.

"That's another one of those old stories you hear all the time around here," Alan said, "but I sure don't know anybody who's thrown anything heavier than a leaf or piece of paper off the rock and had it come back to them. It's a good story, though."

The easy hike to the cliffs was a nice way to stretch our legs, especially after Bo and I had been sitting for so long that day, what with the plane ride and the long drive into the mountains. The trail itself had been simple to follow, with only one fork about halfway to the cliffs. It was no problem, though, because Alan had been there before and knew the way. He even took the time to point out his favorite wildflowers like the Jack-in-the-pulpit and plants like the skunky-smelling galax or mountain laurel, and even the different good and bad mushrooms that grew all over the place.

"Why do they call that the Darkside Cliffs?" Bo asked Alan as we walked back to the Blazer. "Darth Vader live back there?"

"Maybe so," Alan said, with a chuckle. "I don't know, I guess 'cause the trail runs through these laurel thickets the whole way to the cliffs. Look." He pointed up into the canopy of tall shrubs and trees that shrouded the pathway. "The sun's shining, but it's still dark on this trail. Imagine how dark it'd be at night."

I shook my head. "I don't *even* want to think about it," I said. Alan gave me a funny look but said nothing. I guess he was tired of hearing me whine about my problems—my fear of the dark and the other stuff.

We walked back to the Blazer, then continued on toward Lacey's home. At a dark crossroads deeper in the forest, Alan rounded a curve, then abruptly veered off the road and into a small parking area next to a battered green Chevy LUV pickup truck, throwing us forward in our seats as the Blazer came to a halt. Bo made a face, because the sudden stop had also jolted his instrument cases in the cargo area, but he said nothing. I was impressed with his restraint, especially since he lately had become so moody.

"Watch it, Alan," Lacey fussed. "You came within a hair of hittin' Granddaddy's pickup. He'd skin you alive if you smashed up his truck."

"Sorry," he said sheepishly. "That curve always takes me by surprise. Sorry." I could tell that Alan wasn't entirely sure of Lacey's affections from the way he looked at her as he apologized.

"That's OK," Lacey said. "No harm done." She calmed down as she unbuckled her seatbelt and started gathering herself to get out of the Blazer.

"Is this Kawana?" I asked Lacey, though she went on to act as if she hadn't heard my question.

"No," replied Alan, as Lacey opened her door. "Kawana's down that road there about three or four miles. This is Lost Cove. Lacey, I'll call you later. All right?" Without saying anything, she nodded and smiled as she closed the door and then turned to her grandfather's truck. Alan waited until she had cranked the motor and backed out before he threw the Blazer into reverse, left the parking area and headed on up the road. "She's had it rough," he said in explanation of Lacey's behavior. "She lives out here in the middle of nowhere with her old granddad, and he's a real character—you know, kinda *quarr*."

"You mean, like those hillbillies in *Deliverance*?" Bo asked half-seriously. "The ones that make the fat dude squeal like a pig?"

"No," Alan retorted. "I mean he's one of the orneriest old coots who ever lived in these mountains. The word on him is he used to be a moonshiner way back when and that he maybe even killed some folks who ran across his still way back in the hills behind his shack—

sheriff's deputies or federal agents or backpackers or somebody. Folks say he'd slit your throat as soon as look at you. His name's Oren Green, but everybody calls him Buck, I think because he carries around this big Buck knife on his belt all the time. He's real tall and skinny as a rail and real scary-looking, with wild hair and a big beard and no teeth. And he never talks. Like I said, he's *quarr*. That means he's so strange nobody wants to have anything to do with him. You guys better hope you never meet him."

"Have you ever met him?" I asked.

Alan broke into a grin. "Yeah, I've met him, and he isn't all that bad. I'm kinda pulling your leg. Folks just talk about him like that 'cause he keeps to himself and doesn't socialize much. They live in a little cabin way off in the woods by itself. Well, actually it was Lacey's parents' cabin, but they aren't there anymore."

I remembered that Lacey seemed to be interested in my parents' deaths, and I wondered if she, too, were an orphan. "Where are they?"

"Prison, I think." Alan looked in the mirror at us again. "Don't get the wrong idea, but Lacey comes from a long line of, well, I guess you could call them bootleggers. That part's true—about Buck, I mean. He did do a little moonshining in the old days and even served jail time for it. And then Lacey's mom and dad got in trouble for growing pot back in the Seventies and Eighties. I'm guessing they're in prison, 'cause I've never seen them and all Lacey ever says is they 'went away.' And it was about a year ago—maybe longer—that Lacey's older brother got busted somewhere else for running a meth lab with some friends of his. Lacey says he 'went away,' too.

"She has a pretty good attitude about it, though," he continued, "because she says it isn't gonna happen to her. She says she's gonna make something of herself, and she's going to college—well, technical college, anyway—and she works at the Barkhouse when she isn't at school. That's why I like her. She's tough—*and* pretty. A survivor."

I asked how the two of them met, and Alan explained that his astronomy class had gone on an outing once and that they had stopped for sodas and snacks at the Barkhouse Lodge where Lacey was running the front desk and lodge store. It was love at first sight, Alan claimed, and he then started stopping at the Lodge to talk to her every chance he got until the dark-haired girl agreed to go out with him.

"I wore her down," he laughed. "She wouldn't go out with me for the longest time, but finally she said she'd go with me up to Wiseman's View. That's a place up the road that overlooks the Linville Gorge. Matter of fact, Bo, Wiseman's View is supposed to be one of the best places you can go to see the Brown Mountain Light. That's kinda why I went up there with her. I took a chance, thinking maybe we'd see the Light and she'd get scared and want to snuggle up, but I think I was more nervous than she was. I'm used to being in the dark, what with being into astronomy and all, and I definitely like being in the dark with pretty young ladies every chance I get, but I'm telling you it was dark with a capital D-A-R-K up there on that mountain all by ourselves."

By then we had come to the end of the graveled road and were pulling out onto the main highway near a small community that Alan called Jonas Ridge. Its business district was basically a big general store, a fairly modern-looking but small post office, a couple of pretty little churches and a quaint old school building constructed mainly of fieldstone. Alan said some residential subdivisions, another church and then the Barkhouse Lodge stretched over the next several miles to the south on the same road.

We turned north toward Linville, the resort town where Aunt Elaine worked as editor of *The Linville Ledger*, a weekly newspaper that served the surrounding mountain communities including Jonas Ridge and the towns of Newland and Crossnore. A mile or so beyond Jonas Ridge in a small community called Pineola, we took the Blue Ridge Parkway—Alan's favorite road in the whole wide world, he said—toward Grandfather Mountain, so named because its ridgeline, when viewed from certain angles, resembles an old man's bearded profile. Grandfather also is one of the oldest mountains in the world, Bo added, having read up on things other than mountain music.

Along the way we stopped at the Lost Cove Cliffs Overlook—in the shadow of, believe it or not, Grand*mother* Mountain (named that because it lies beside Grandfather, I guess)—where Alan showed us a U.S. Park Service display about the legend of the Brown Mountain Light. The sign read:

> The phenomenon of the Brown Mountain Lights has puzzled observers for centuries. The earliest known accounts are based in Indian lore from the early 1700s.
>
> In 1913, the U.S. Geological Survey studied the lights and concluded that they were the headlights of locomotives. A few years later a flood inundated the valley and stopped movement over the railways. When the lights continued to appear, the skeptics had a field day at the expense of science.
>
> Another study in 1922 by the Geological Survey concluded that the lights came from a variety of

> sources—automobiles, nearby towns, and brush fires. Scientists explained that at sundown the peaks and valleys produce unstable air currents that refract or bend light rays. A light from the valley beyond Brown Mountain might be bent skyward away from its source.
>
> Questions continue to be raised. Are the lights caused by phosphorous, UFOs, radium ore deposits, or marsh gas, sometimes called the elusive "will-o'-the-wisp?"

The information sign also included a newspaper article about the Lights and a drawing of tourists viewing them. The article was from the Aug. 13, 1962 edition of *The Asheville Citizen.* It claimed that a Jonas Ridge man had led a twelve-man expedition onto the crest of Brown Mountain and that they had "watched the fabled lights flash out of nearby crevices" from atop a sixty-foot wooden tower that they had constructed. The man told the Associated Press reporter that the lights "came out in circles of about three feet in diameter…in colors of red, orange and the color of the moon." He added that one of the lights "came to rest on the men on the tower. It gave them a static-like feeling of dizziness. When they climbed to the ground, they were unable to stand up."

I laughed to Alan and Bo that the newspaper article reminded me of the Bible story about the Tower of Babel that Grandpa had read to me a couple of times. Alan noted that there was a place called Babel Tower below Wiseman's View in the Linville Gorge, which had all sorts of strangely-shaped rock formations, with names like Sitting Bear, Hawksbill, Table Rock, the Chimneys, the Mummy, the Camel and Shortoff. "I like hiking in the Linville Gorge," Alan said, "but you can't bike there 'cause the trails are just too steep, and, besides, I don't think it's allowed. That's why I like it down there in Lost Cove and Harper Creek, 'cause there are more good places to bike."

"I got an idea," Alan added, as he wheeled the Blazer away from the information sign. "How 'bout if we solve the mystery this summer?"

"What mystery?" I asked.

"The Brown Mountain Light?" Bo ventured. "Really?"

Alan nodded. "Sure, why not?" he said. "It'd be fun. And I bet I could write a research paper or something on it for the class I'm taking this summer. You guys could help me. It'd be fun proving there isn't anything to it—that folks are just seeing fireflies or automobile headlights or swamp gas or something and not ghosts or space aliens or the boogie man. We'd be famous."

"I don't know," I said, realizing that I'd have trouble wandering around in the dark with my friends. "I don't know if I can."

But Alan and Bo were already sold on the project, which would occupy our time and attention for the next three weeks. Alan said it would give me something to do other than sit around and pick my nose. He was always saying things like that, but I don't think he meant it in a mean way, necessarily.

Up the road in Boone, we dropped Bo and his stuff off at the big university where his music camp was being held beginning the next day. He gave me his cell phone number and made me promise to call him before we went looking for the Brown Mountain Light. Then we drove on toward Blowing Rock, turning off the main highway before reaching Tweetsie Railroad, which, like Grandfather Mountain, had long been one of the so-called High Country's most popular tourist attractions. It turned out that we could hear Tweetsie's whistle from Aunt Elaine's house in an area called Aho (pronounced "Ay-hoe," with a long A). Her house sat not far from Aho Gap, where through the distant trees I could just barely see a large building that resembled a medieval castle complete with round stone turrets. Or at least that's what I thought I saw. Maybe not.

All things considered, I could already tell that I had arrived at an unusual place—for me, anyway—a part of the world that was ever aware of, if not haunted by, the past. The sun was setting behind Grandfather Mountain as Alan and I pulled into the driveway of his house. Elaine was waiting for us, sitting by the phone in the kitchen as if she had been parked there for quite some time, judging from the look on her face. She wasn't a happy camper. And I could tell right away that we weren't going to be, either. As my old pro, Billy Joe, would have said about our situation right then, we were "up the crick and about to get paddled."

FIVE

Aunt Elaine had good reason to be upset with us—or with Alan, anyway, since she had given him specific instructions to drive Bo and me straight to ASU and then home from the airport, she said. She pointed out that *anything* could have happened to us down there in that "no man's land," she called it. We could have had a flat tire, we could have run off the road into a ditch, we could have driven off a cliff, we could have been attacked by a pack of man-eating bears, we could have been totally obliterated by part of the Russian space station falling out of orbit. And no one would have been around to call for help. All three of us were laughing by the time Elaine finished her litany of our possible fates on the side trip that Alan had taken us on that afternoon.

My aunt had a hard time staying angry with her son, though, mainly because he hardly ever did anything worth staying mad about. Nothing *had* happened to us that afternoon, had it? But Alan didn't say anything like that to his mom; a remark like that would have been considered disrespectful. However, Elaine was smart enough to figure it out for herself. She knew she was lucky to have such a good son, even though his father was a royal jerk most of the time. Also, Alan said he would have called her from Lost Cove if he had remembered to do so from the Darkside Cliffs—or if the phone his dad had bought him had been worth anything. I wondered if Alan knew that blaming Uncle Lance for Alan's own thoughtlessness would deflect Elaine's disapproval.

As I've already said, my favorite aunt was also one of my favorite people. She had been a loving daughter to Grandpa and Grandma, and she had been a loving wife to Lance until he went off the deep end when he turned forty and started fooling around on her. She was a great mom to Alan and a super aunt to me. She was a hard worker who always did things the right way even when she didn't have to, if that makes any sense. She could bait a hook with the biggest, juiciest worm you've ever seen and would fish with you all day, if you wanted her to. And then she would clean and fry up all the fish you caught, and they tasted as good as if you were sitting in some big fancy seafood restaurant in Calabash.

And she was beautiful. My gosh, she was beautiful, so strikingly pretty that it was hard for me to believe she and I were kin. I guess that's where Alan got his good looks, even though Uncle Lance, the dirty bum, was a good-looking guy, too. Elaine's long hair that she liked to have me French braid for her was actually auburn, not plain old reddish-brown like mine. Her electric-blue eyes pulled you to her like a magnet. She was taller than me but short enough that she had to stretch to give Alan a peck on the forehead when she forgave him that evening for being thoughtless on the way back home that day.

And she didn't take crap off anybody—except maybe the people she loved, I guess. Like Alan. And Lance, back when she was trying to make their marriage work and before she finally got fed up with the way he was doing her and finally told him to hit the road, Lance, and don't you come back no more, no more. That hurt her really bad, she told me once, but you can put up with only so much crap from a guy, she said. After a while, you've got to cut your losses and get on with it, she said—"it" being your life, I guess.

Anyway, after fixing us a late supper that first night at her house, Elaine showed me to my bedroom and told me that I could do anything I wanted with it. The room, on a front corner of the house's second story above ground, was larger than our whole living room back home—I mean, back at Village Point. On one side of the room was a window looking to the west where I would be able to watch the sunset over Grandfather Mountain every evening, she said, and on the south wall were French doors leading to my own private sundeck. The wallpaper was a sunny yellow print with tiny golden *fleurs-de-lis* within a light pattern of crossed golden lines. The bedroom suite—a large dresser, tall chest of drawers, sturdy upholstered chair and king-sized bed covered by a puffy golden comforter that matched the wallpaper—was French provincial, Elaine noted. My room had its very own bathroom. And low on the wall next to the bed, on my favorite side of the bed, there was an electrical outlet. Already plugged into it was a night light made of crystal-like clear plastic in the shape of a lighthouse.

"You'll be OK here," Elaine said, echoing Bo's remarks to me earlier in the day. She had noticed my interest in the night light. "It'll come on when the lights go out. I thought you'd like the lighthouse. We can't ever forget where we're from. Can we, Val?"

"No, ma'am," I replied. I knew that she really meant we could never forget Grandpa and Grandma. She just didn't want to upset me.

Billy Joe would have just come right out and said whatever was on his mind, even if he *did* stick his foot in his mouth. In that respect, he and Elaine were like night and day—or, as Billy Joe would have said, like "earl and water." It took me the longest time to figure out just who "earl" was, but I finally understood when Billy Joe told me to go check the "earl" on the course's tractor before I started mowing the fairways.

For some other reason, though, Elaine didn't really like Billy Joe. But don't opposites usually attract? Well, not in their case. Maybe it was because Elaine played tennis and didn't especially like golfers, but I doubt it was that. She just didn't want to be around Billy Joe, even for just a few minutes, like if he dropped me off at Grandma's house when Elaine and Alan were visiting and then would come in to say "howdy doody" to Grandma and maybe end up staying for a piece of her famous cornbread. Though she never said so, I honestly think that Elaine assumed Billy Joe was interested in Grandma romantically, and Elaine didn't want him presuming he could even attempt to take Grandpa's place.

Maybe he *was* trying to date Grandma, but I still don't think that would have been all that bad—not necessarily. For as much as I dearly loved my grandfather, I also soon realized that Grandma was desperately lonely and needed someone or something other than just her memories of Grandpa. She had me for company, but, as I myself have learned over the years, a woman needs a man friend, from time to time, anyway. I'm sure that if Elaine didn't know that fact before Grandma died, she was seeing it for herself that summer by the time I moved in with her and Alan.

Aunt Elaine's new friend that she had met through work was a man named Sonny Rose. Actually, G. Wayne Rose, Jr., was the name he used in the community news column he wrote for each week's *Ledger*, but everyone called him Sonny, probably from back when his father, the Rev. George W. Rose, Sr., was still alive. As I later learned from Sonny himself, authorship of "Jonas Ridge News" had been in his family for three generations, beginning with his maternal grandmother, Ila (pronounced "I-ler") Mae Loven Morgan, and continuing with his mother, Ola (pronounced "O-ler") Faye Morgan Rose, a schoolteacher and devoted wife to Preacher Rose there in the Jonas Ridge community for years. Miss Faye, as she preferred to be called, handed down the column to Sonny when she retired from Jonas Ridge School and then dedicated the next few years to caring for her elderly mother and then her cancer-stricken husband.

Rather than send either or both of them to an area nursing facility, Miss Faye had kept both Granny Iler and the preacher at home in her little house on Gingercake Mountain where she still lived when I met her. After both died within a month of each other, Miss Faye mourned for a long while and then finally went to work as a volunteer at the Jonas Ridge Public Library, which was housed in what had been the old school building before the school board started busing Jonas Ridge students to the new school over in Newland, Sonny said. She didn't take back the newspaper column, though, because Sonny had done such an "outstanding job" with it and had increased the *Ledger*'s readership due to his column's popularity, he claimed.

Elaine explained to me that people *did* read the "Jonas Ridge News" but not because of Sonny's writing or reporting abilities. She said simply that, unlike his mother and grandmother's ladylike approaches to the column, little Sonny was always "stirring up trouble." He didn't just report the tidbits of news and gossip generally found in articles of that type; he also used his allotted space to make editorial comments on whatever the local controversy of the week was, like how the new preacher at Cold Springs Bible Church was getting along with whichever faction of church members, or which graveled roads the Department of Transportation planned to blacktop next—an ongoing controversy where paved roads were still the exception.

Elaine said Sonny was a nice man and had been a good friend to her but that he was quite contrary—just like Mary of nursery rhyme fame—and proud of it. Billy Joe would have just called him a "big ole butthole" and left it at that. For several reasons that I'll try to explain later, I didn't really know how to take Sonny until I eventually saw what a fine, caring man he really was. He certainly didn't make a good first impression on me.

I met Sonny for the first time on the very next morning after I went to live with Elaine and Alan. It was a Sunday, and Alan and I were still in the doghouse over having scooter-pooted all over creation between the airport and their house the day before. So Elaine decreed that we *would* go with her to something called the Singing on the Mountain, an annual event that had been held for at least the previous seventy-five years in a meadow at the foot of Grandfather Mountain, one of those mountains that Alan had shown us on Saturday.

Grandfather, I later learned, is the highest peak in the Blue Ridge chain. Also, it was the largest privately-owned "biosphere," or nature preserve, in the world, with hiking trails and animal habitats and a nature museum. It was once home to the beloved Mildred the Bear and her cubs, North Carolina's real-life answer to Yogi Bear and Boo-Boo.

Speaking of my friend Bo, he went along with us to the Singing on the Mountain. I had called him at music camp on Saturday night after Elaine had given us our orders for Sunday. Bo, though, was thrilled about getting to attend the Singing. He said that he had read all about it and was interested in hearing several of the gospel groups that would be appearing from 8:30 a.m. to 12:30 p.m. and then again for three or four hours in the afternoon. The "preaching" was held around 1 p.m., so that all the folks who'd gone to their regular churches that morning could still hear the Singing's sermon, often by a famous preacher like Billy Graham.

Actually, Elaine had two reasons for going to the Singing—one, to cover it for the *Ledger*, as it was a genuine news event not just for locals but also for gospel music fans throughout the Southeastern United States, and, two, to support her friend Sonny, who dreamed of being good enough to perform at the Singing. This year he was "on standby," in case a replacement act was needed. At first I was a little worried that I didn't have "Sunday clothes" to wear there, but Aunt Elaine said the Singing was fairly informal and that we could wear school-type clothes.

Ordinarily, music campers like Bo were not allowed to come and go on the university campus as they pleased; they could leave only on the weekends. Also, the camp rules plainly stated that the young musicians were not allowed to ride in motor vehicles, even the AppalCart bus line, except on Saturdays, when they could ride the bus just about anywhere in and around Boone and Blowing Rock. On Sundays they had to have written permission in advance from their parents to travel anywhere off campus with anyone, including relatives and friends of their families. Anticipating that Bo would want to visit me in his free time while in Boone, Dr. Gaines had already sent the proper paperwork to camp officials, clearing the way for her son to enjoy his stay and to explore the mountains with Alan and me.

It was just after seven o'clock that bright Sunday morning when we picked up Bo in front of his dormitory on the hill near the football stadium and then headed toward Grandfather Mountain, about a thirty-minute drive southwest of Boone on good, well-traveled roads including one known locally as the Yonahlossee Road (Cherokee for "Trail of the Bear"). If we hadn't picked up Bo, we might have avoided Boone altogether and driven to Grandfather via the Blue Ridge Parkway and over the famous Linn Cove Viaduct, a huge concrete bridge built in a breathtaking S-shape around part of Grandfather's waist, as it were. It's the big white bridge used in a lot of those car commercials on TV.

Aunt Elaine, who for some reason had insisted on driving us in her VW, said she usually drove to and from Linville every day on the Parkway because it was much less traveled than the main highways, even in the cool summer months when tourists were on the roads with their mini-vans and travel trailers. Also, she liked to look at the trees as she slowly cruised the two-lane road that generally followed the crest of the Blue Ridge range, and she often stopped at overlooks along the way to look "off the mountain," as locals put it. Her favorite stops were the Thunder Hill Overlook near Aho and the Wilson Creek Valley Overlook near the Viaduct.

When Elaine guided the straining Beetle into a grassy parking place in a lower section of what is called MacRae Meadows there below Grandfather Mountain, I remember noticing that the two cars next to us were both convertibles—a jet-black Ford Mustang and a lime-green Dodge Challenger with a black racing stripe down both sides. It seemed odd to me that I was seeing more ragtops in the mountains than I had seen at the beach, where the weather is more conducive to driving with the top down. Of course, I soon learned that Elaine was at least partly the reason the two convertibles were parked there beside us, because both convertibles belonged to Sonny, and Elaine had made a sort of deal with him that involved her Beetle and the Challenger.

Besides playing tennis, Elaine and Sonny had started doing a lot of things together, stuff like cruising the Parkway on sunny days, or strolling around Bass Lake, Trout Lake or Price Lake, or maybe even hiking the trails in the area, like the Tanawha Trail (Cherokee for "eagle") near Grandfather Mountain or, once, the steep Greentown Trail from the Barkhouse Lodge, where Sonny lived, down to Kawana, near where Lacey and Buck stayed. To Sonny's credit, he always tried to include Alan in the couple's outings; however, the Greentown hike was the only invitation that Alan accepted, and he did so mainly because he wanted to try out a new mountain bike his dad had given him for his birthday—an expensive Iron Horse Maverick Sport.

All of this sounds as if Sonny and Elaine were dating, and maybe in some respects they were. But Sonny was the first to point out that he was just an old bachelor who happened to like the company of intelligent women and that he had no interest whatsoever in marrying anyone, period. He was too set in his ways, and, besides, he was too busy to get married, he would always say. And Elaine, for her part, claimed that she wasn't ready yet to be tied down again by *any* man, after what she had just been through with Lance Delacruz, and I knew she meant it. Still, if Sonny wasn't dropping in on Elaine and Alan at the Aho house, then the two of them were always driving over to the Barkhouse to see Sonny—or, in Alan's case, to see Lacey.

"Well, what do you know," Elaine mused, motioning toward Sonny's Mustang. "I never thought Sonny would get up early enough to beat us here this morning—or that he could get his mother over here at this hour. He must really be nervous about maybe singing in front of so many people. They say they're expecting at least ten thousand people today. You believe that, Val?"

"Yeah, I guess," I replied. "But where they gonna put everybody?"

She motioned toward a boulder-strewn grassy knoll just beyond the parking area for a half dozen motorcoach buses, apparently the transportation and touring quarters for the more successful gospel groups scheduled to appear later in the morning. "This year they're setting up the stage over there so it faces Grandfather instead of having him—the mountain, I mean—as a backdrop," she explained. "Come on, guys. Let's find Sonny and Miss Faye. They're probably eating breakfast—if Sonny can hold anything down."

With each of us carrying a blue folded-up sports chair, we strolled past the buses and through the seating area where people already were claiming spots in front of the stage, with its simple, black-painted, wooden pulpit in the middle and pole-mounted Peavey loudspeakers on either side. Sure enough, sitting together at a picnic table in the roped-off section where vendors' booths stood between the stage and woods were a short, stout, blond-haired guy in a black Western suit and a sweet-looking, gray-haired lady in a flower-print dress and cardigan sweater. Both had white Syrofoam cups of coffee in front of them; the woman also nibbled at a country ham biscuit wrapped in white wax paper. From what Aunt Elaine had already told me about them, I knew they had to be Sonny and Miss Faye.

Right then, Sonny didn't have much going for him, as far as I was concerned, mainly because he was a teacher—well, actually, a history instructor at Skyland Technical College in Foscoe, a community up the road not far from Boone. If I have his list of vocations and avocations straight, Sonny taught history classes during the school year; ran the lodge, where he lived, all year and the campground during the late spring-to-fall tourist seasons; and traveled throughout the area, sometimes as far away as the neighboring county seats of Lenoir and Morganton, performing as a gospel singer on weekends year-round, mainly at church services and small singings. In addition, he played tennis with Elaine every chance he got and even distributed, at this own expense, free Bibles, New Testaments and gospel tracts throughout the area. Another of his hobbies, believe it or not, was restoring classic cars—well, *kind of* classic cars, which I'll explain later.

Sonny was a real busy beaver to be sure, which was why he had come to rely more and more on Lacey's help at the lodge and, to an ever-increasing extent, at Miss Faye's house, too. He often paid Lacey and sometimes even her grandfather, old Buck Green, to go there and assist Miss Faye with whatever needed doing whenever Sonny had too much going on at the college or in his various other pursuits. According to Alan, Lacey might help Miss Faye around the house with the cleaning, while Buck might mow the grass and do other outside chores on occasion. Alan told me that even he himself had been recruited a time or two to do various things for either Sonny or Miss Faye. But they were nice people, my cousin assured me, and Sonny paid well for a person's services when he was forced to ask for them. And Sonny wouldn't ask you to do anything that he himself wouldn't do if only he'd had the time, Alan added. My cousin apparently liked Sonny a whole lot more than I did at first.

I guess I should describe Sonny's physical appearance and the way he usually acted, and maybe that will explain why he made such a bad first impression on me. Also, I should admit that the circumstances under which we first met probably had much to do with my initial, faulty notions about him. It wasn't just that he was one of those busybody teachers who were always feeling so sorry for me and always trying to "help" me somehow. There was more to it than that. For starters, I just didn't trust Sonny's looks, what with his scissor-cut, blown-dry and feathered-back blond hair and his thick, reddish-blond mustache. He was about my height and about twice my width, and he always wore clothes that he apparently thought made him look younger than the middle-aged man he was. I'm guessing he was around forty-five then, maybe just a year or two older than Elaine. She said he tried to jog a few miles every day to keep his weight under control but just couldn't seem to shed any pounds.

Whenever he turned into "The Gospel Singer," whether he was leading the singing on Sunday morning at Cold Springs Bible Church or performing in front of other Christian groups, Sonny donned a dark Western-cut suit with a crisp white shirt, a black bolo tie with a silver-and-turquoise clasp, and shiny black cowboy boots, but no hat because he didn't want to mess up his hair. He never explained to me why he dressed up like a cowboy in church, but it made about as much sense as some of the other things he did. Sonny *did* explain, though, that he always wore the bolo because neckties cut into his neck, constricted the flow of blood to his brain, and kept him from singing his best. I guess he was being serious. Also, the necktie was an authoritarian symbol, he said, while a bolo stood for the pioneer spirit of the Old West and the inherent freedom of Americans, in general, to make whatever fashion statements they pleased.

Billy Joe would have simply stated that Sonny's whole getup looked like "horse crap," plain and simple. Billy Joe always said he wouldn't be caught dead with *anything* around his neck, except maybe a noose, and that would only be if any of his ex-wives ever caught up with him. I think he was just kidding—about the wives, I mean.

I also didn't like that Sonny appeared to be a Ford man when it came to his favorite cars. I found out later that he drove two vehicles most of the time—when the weather was nice, the black Mustang convertible or, with rain in the forecast, an older-model but immaculate white Ford Bronco like the famous one in the O.J. Simpson case. As if Sonny were a Western hero and the two vehicles were his trusty steeds, he had named the black Mustang "Champion" after Gene Autry's mount and the white Bronco "Trigger" after Roy Rogers' famous horse. I guess that made him, in *his* mind, anyway, a singing cowboy of one sort or another, whatever the weather. Also, on his right hand he wore a large silver-and-turquoise signet ring with a star shape engraved into the stone, and on his left wrist he sported a matching ID bracelet bearing only his initials. He wore no wristwatch because it made his forearm look too fat, he said.

Vain about his appearance, Sonny was always fussing over his fingernails with clippers or an emery board. He had quit smoking cigarettes years before I met him, because the habit adversely affected his singing voice, he claimed; however, he *did* like to puff on a big fat dark cigar whenever he cut the grass around the lodge on his green-and-yellow John Deere lawn tractor. He wouldn't smoke when mowing his mother's lawn, though, because she and Preacher Rose had opposed all "worldly" pleasures, sins such as smoking, drinking, cussing, gambling and especially fornicating, because it, of course, led to dancing. I once heard Sonny tell that joke to Aunt Elaine over dinner with Alan and me at the pizza place near Pineola. He hee-hawed and snorted so hard that iced tea squirted out his nose. Even I laughed then.

But, as I've said, that Sunday morning at MacRae Meadows I was in no frame of mind to like Mr. G. Wayne "Sonny" Rose, Jr., and he did very little that day to change my attitude toward him. After exchanging quick hugs and pleasantries with Sonny and then his mother, Aunt Elaine glanced back at us and said, "Miss Faye, you know Alan. And this is my niece Valerie Galloway from Village Point and her friend—*our* friend—Lionel Gaines from Raleigh. He's here for the music camp in Boone. And I'm sure Sonny's told you, Miss Faye, that Valerie—I mean, Val, that's what we all call her—she's staying with us now…." Elaine's voice dropped off, as though she had something else to say but didn't know exactly how to say it. It wasn't like her to become "plum flummoxed," as Billy Joe would say whenever he was at a loss for words, which wasn't very often.

It took Sonny a couple of awkward moments to come to his lady friend's rescue. "Have you folks had breakfast yet?" he asked, holding up his half-empty coffee cup. "I could use a refill, and I'd be more'n happy to get you something. Valerie? Lionel?"

"No, that's OK," Aunt Elaine said. "I'll get it, but you can help me carry it. Let's see—coffees and ham biscuits all around? Everyone *does* drink coffee, right?" We nodded. She and Sonny walked together toward the booth run by the volunteer fire department, leaving us at the table with Miss Faye.

"Sonny and I really think a lot of Elaine," the lady said between tentative sips of coffee, though it couldn't have still been hot enough to burn her faded pink lips. Even without makeup to highlight them, her blue eyes twinkled as she turned her head slightly to watch Sonny and Elaine standing together at the food booth. "I just wish Sonny would realize I'm not going to live forever and that he needs somebody to grow old with. You know what I mean?" For some reason, she looked at me instead of at Alan, as if she were actually waiting for me to answer.

"Uh, yes, ma'am," I said. "I guess so."

She must have read my confusion, because she continued, "Usually it's the woman who has to deal with it, isn't that right, Valerie? These old men we take up with just go about their business like they're going to be around forever, and then when they go—and they always do—we're the ones left behind to carry on. That's usually the way it is, anyway. Isn't that right, honey?"

I shrugged, not knowing exactly what to say. I was plum flummoxed. Alan, however, wasn't bashful, as he apparently knew the elderly woman fairly well. He said firmly but politely, "Mom's OK, Miss Faye. She likes Sonny a lot—and I do, too—but the business with Dad is still too fresh for her to get married again just yet. And, besides, Dad would probably go ballistic and do something stupid."

Alan chuckled, then continued, "Dad was out on the golf course when Mom had the support papers served on him, and they say he got so steamed that he ran off the cart path on the way back to the clubhouse and drove into a pond. All his buddies still give him a hard time about it and call him 'Cart Man,' even though he doesn't think it's funny. It didn't just make him look silly; he had to pay to get the cart dried out. He said that'd be the last dam—, uh, the last time he'd play golf there or anywhere else."

Just as well, I thought. The only thing I envied about Uncle Lance was that he had once played Cape Fear Country Club, which was one of the oldest golf courses in the whole state, dating back to 1896. It was even a couple of years older than the oldest Pinehurst course. I don't think any of that mattered to Lance, though.

"Do you see your daddy very often, Alan?" Miss Faye asked, choosing to ignore that he had almost cussed on a Sunday morning.

"Every once in a while," Alan replied, "usually around Thanksgiving and Christmas, and then once or twice in the summer when I'm not in school."

"Oh, I'm so sorry," Miss Faye said. "I know that must be difficult."

"No, no," Alan said. "We stay in touch good enough, and, besides, I'd rather be with Mom. We've been through a lot together."

"'*Well* enough,'" Miss Faye corrected.

Alan smiled. "That's right. You were a schoolteacher. Sorry."

"That's quite all right, Alan." She turned again and looked up as Sonny and Aunt Elaine returned with the coffee and biscuits. "Well, it's about time you two got back. What in the world have you been talking about? Anything *important*?"

"Oh, Mama," Sonny scolded. "Don't start that again." We sat in silence for a couple of minutes as we ate. Then Sonny reached across the table and patted my hand. "Well, aren't you just a pretty little girl," he said to me. "You must have all sorts of boyfriends back at the beach."

"No, not really," I said. He hadn't picked my favorite topic.

"Oh, come on now," he insisted. "I bet you were one of the popular girls at your school—Lockwoods Folly, wasn't it?"

I could feel my eyes narrowing as I glared at him. "Why do you say that?" He still wasn't scoring any points with me. It irritated me that Sonny apparently didn't see Bo sitting right there beside me. We weren't a couple, as such, but we *were* best friends.

"Because you're just about the prettiest girl I've ever seen," Sonny continued, letting me know for sure that he was blowing smoke. "And I bet the boys around here will just go bananas when they get a look at you. Isn't that right, Mama?" She nodded.

I don't know if the "bananas" remark offended Bo or not—I don't guess so—but he politely excused himself and walked off. If he *had* cared, I'm sure he would have said something. It also made me wonder how much Aunt Elaine had already told Sonny about me, and why he didn't assume that Bo and I were together—even though we weren't. Sonny seemed to be making an awful lot of assumptions about me, not to know me any better than he did. I hated having anyone take one look at me and try to size me up based just on how I looked.

"What are you gonna do after this summer, Valerie?" Sonny asked. "You going to school? Or are you gonna go to work?"

"I don't know," I replied. I really *didn't* know, but apparently he didn't believe me.

"Now, you've got to have some idea," he persisted. "Like, when I graduated from high school, I knew exactly what I wanted to do. Have you been accepted anywhere yet? To any colleges, I mean?"

I frowned. "I haven't applied anywhere."

"Well, why not?" He waited for my reply. When I didn't answer, he gave me this impish sort of grin and said, "You could go to one of my old schools—Bob Jones University. I lasted all of six weeks before I got homesick and went home. But Mama and Daddy both liked it there. That's when they started courting, as a matter of fact. Course, all they did was sit and talk in this big old room with about a hundred sofas called the Dating Parlor. Lord, I don't know why I couldn't hack it there, but I just couldn't. Guess I was just a big baby."

"Bob Jones?" I said. "You mean *Bobby* Jones, the golf champion?" I wasn't going to say it out loud, but if the great Bobby Jones had started a college, I *might* consider going there.

Sonny laughed. "Not hardly. No, Valerie, the one *I'm* talking about was a great preacher, and the college he started is one of the strictest ones in the whole country. But it'd be a great place for a girl like you who doesn't want to worry about drinking or drugs or, well, anything bad. They don't allow any of that. They don't even let you listen to rock 'n' roll there, still yet. That sound like your kind of place?"

I could feel my face starting to flush, and I was ready to snap at him when Aunt Elaine spoke up. "Sonny, don't push her," she chided. "She had her hands full this past year. We all did. And I've told her, she can take as long as she wants to, to make up her mind. There's no hurry, as far as I'm concerned." She gave me a hug to calm me down. "Maybe you and Alan better go see where Bo got off to, Val. The Singing is supposed to start before long."

As we were walking away, I heard Sonny say to Elaine, "Well, it isn't good that she hasn't applied *anywhere*. She'll have a hard time getting into a good school this late." I couldn't hear Elaine's reply because her back was to us.

Alan put his arm around my shoulders as we walked back toward Aunt Elaine's car, where Bo was waiting. "Don't worry about it, cuz," Alan said. "Sonny means well. He's just trying to be helpful, being a teacher and all."

"I know," I said, "but I'm tired of everyone trying to help me with all my problems. I wish everyone would just leave me alone. You know?"

"Yeah." He withdrew his arm, intentionally mussing my hair in passing. "But, you know, all us poor ole folks wouldn't be trying so hard to hep ya if ya wudn't sech a perty little thang!" He laughed at his own Sonny impersonation.

"Oh, stop it," I said, elbowing him in the ribs as we reached the Beetle. Bo, leaning against a front fender, appeared lost in thought. Our friend stared off into the sky toward Grandfather's distant summit some three thousand feet higher in elevation than where we stood in the meadow. I almost hated to interrupt him. "You OK?" I asked. "Bo?"

"Yeah, you all right, Boo-Boo?" Alan echoed.

"I'm OK," Bo said. "I was just thinking...."

"Uh-oh, he's been thinking again, Val," Alan said. "What about, dog?"

"About the Light."

Alan looked up at the sun. "What about it?"

"No," Bo said, "the Brown Mountain Light. You know, sometimes you're about the dumbest guy I've ever met."

I waited for Alan to punch him, but my cousin just laughed out loud. "But I'm smarrrrr-ter than the average bear! Right, Boo-Boo? Lighten up, dog. I'm just kidding."

Bo grinned. "Oh, shut up—and quit calling me 'dog.' You're white. White. Not black, Alan. I don't care how good you were at basketball. You're still white. But that's OK. Some of my best—wait a second—*all* of my best friends are white, come to think of it. I gotta get me some friends with some soul."

Alan and I both knew he was kidding. "You mean I'm not a…*brutha*," Alan said in mock horror, checking the backs of his hands as if their color had suddenly changed.

"Naw," Bo said. "We'll always be brothers—all three of us. Even Val."

"Hey! Watch it, buddy," I said with a smile. "I may act like one of the guys, and I may even look like one, but you don't have to rub it in."

"Aw, Val," Bo retorted. "Ain't nobody gonna mistake you for a guy." He paused. "Especially not up here in these *hollers* where girls are scarce." He didn't even wait to see what I would say; instead, he took off up the hill and motioned for us to follow him.

As we walked, Alan could have pointed out that Sonny's earlier remarks to me had been more or less along the same lines as Bo's were right then, and that I wasn't mad at Bo as I had been at Sonny. But Alan didn't mention it.

About then, the Singing started, but it wasn't Sonny or one of the groups that Bo wanted to hear, so we kept walking until we reached a stadium, of all things, in the meadow—a green unmarked athletic field surrounded by a gray, quarter-mile, cinder track, with no seats or benches but with a grassy incline on one side for spectators.

"This is where they're gonna hold the Highland Games in a couple weeks," Alan explained. "Me and Mom came last year right after *we* moved here. If you think there's a lot of people here for this thing today, just wait until you see the crowd of people that come for the Highland Games. Rain or shine, the whole place'll be packed."

"Why?" I asked. "Are we coming back here for that?"

Alan nodded. "Yeah, I guess so. Mom'll want to cover it for the paper, I guess, 'cause it's a big deal. She'll get us all passes—you, too, Bo. And it *is* a lot of fun. There's all sorts of music—you know, bagpipes and drums and fiddle-playing and all—and all sorts of Scottish stuff, like herding sheep and tossing telephone poles."

"It's called a cabar," Bo offered. "That's Gaelic for 'pole.'"

"Yeah, cabar-tossing," Alan said. "That's it—like tossing telephone poles end over end and using pitchforks to toss bales of hay over goalposts and all sorts of neat Scotch stuff."

"The word is *Scottish*," Bo corrected. "*Scotch* is a whiskey. That means 'water of life.'"

"Whatever," Alan said. "Anyway, Val, you'll get a kick out of the athletic events, and you'll like all the music, Bo."

"When is it again?" Bo asked.

"It's in about three weeks, I'm pretty sure." Alan scrunched up his face, thinking hard. "Yeah, it's in three weeks, 'cause the Fourth of July is weekend after next—a week from this Friday—and the Highland Games are always the week after July Fourth. The games start on a Thursday night with a race up the mountain, and then—"

"Up the mountain!?" I exclaimed. "What kind of race? Cars?"

"Nope," Alan replied. "It's a six-mile footrace that starts down at the foot of the mountain in front of the newspaper office there in Linville. Sonny says he's entering the race, but I'll believe it when I see it. I don't think we'll have time to drive up the mountain today, but we probably will sometime during the Games, and you'll see how tough it is. Just *driving* up the mountain—and back down—gives some folks the willies. It's a real bear. Matter of fact, that's the name of the race—the Bear."

"You're kidding," Bo said.

Alan shook his head. "No. The Bear. Just like Mildred the Bear and her two cubs, Mini and Maxi." He chuckled.

"Mini and Maxi?" Bo asked. "Oh, come on. You're making that up."

"Nope," Alan said. "Mini and Maxi. You aren't the only one who knows how to use the Internet, Boo-Boo. Look it up."

"I will," Bo replied. He added that he would like to attend the Highland Games but that he didn't want us to miss seeing his guitar hero Doc Watson, whose music festival near Boone was scheduled for the same weekend.

We had been following the circular route of the cinder track, enjoying the softness of its finely graveled surface, and had almost completed our third circuit when Bo happened to notice a brown fieldstone obelisk standing on the plateau above the stadium's seating area. We walked up the hill to the cairn-like monument to read a relatively small bronze plaque mounted beneath a large Celtic cross on the side facing the stadium. It read:

In Memorium
AGNES MACRAE MORTON
October 7, 1897 - April 22, 1982
Co-founder of the
Grandfather Mountain Highland Games
1956
May the blessing of Light be on you–
May the blessing of Rain be on you–
And may the blessing of the Earth be on you–
May the Lord bless you and bless you kindly.

"Who was she?" I asked Alan. "I mean, other than co-founder of the Games." For some reason that I couldn't explain then, I was strangely drawn to that monument and those words.

Alan shrugged. "I'm not sure, Val. I think a man named Hugh Morton owns the mountain—that whole mountain, believe it or not, and the meadows here. He's a famous photographer and has taken pictures of all sorts of famous people and important stuff. I guess the MacRaes had something to do with the mountain to begin with. You know, I wonder if they lived in Wilmington, too. There's a MacRae Park there that Mom and Dad used to take me to. But I'm not exactly sure who Agnes here was—other than what it says."

That was Bo's cue to step in. "Don't worry, Val," Bo said, pretending to loop his thumbs under make-believe suspenders. "*I* can use the Internet, and *I* can read, so *I'll* look it up for you when I get back to the dorm tonight. OK?"

Alan jumped Bo and started wrestling playfully with him. I just shook my head at my two idiotic companions. The amplified music from the Singing was loud enough that we probably would have kept circling the track if Elaine hadn't come for us. She said there was an outside chance that Sonny might get to sing in a few minutes, and she wanted us to sit with her and Miss Faye. As it turned out, Sonny's services weren't needed after all, but he made the most of the situation by passing out some CDs and cassette tapes of gospel songs that he himself had written, recorded and produced, hoping to drum up some invitations to church singings in the future.

Sonny even gave Bo a copy of what he apparently thought was his best CD, one called *The Bold Rebel Flag (Is My Old Rugged Cross)*. The cover art showed Sonny, dressed in a gray Confederate cavalry officer's uniform, standing in front of a blood-red Rebel flag with its white stars and navy cross. With a clenched jaw, Bo looked over the front and back of the jewel case, then got up and left. I saw him toss the CD in a trash can as he headed for the parking area. I figured I'd better leave him alone for a while, because I could tell that he was steaming. I thought he might eventually return, but he didn't. And we couldn't find him when Alan and I went looking for him a couple of times during the afternoon. I even missed the preaching as I searched for Bo in the meadows and surrounding woods.

Bo was missing the gospel music that he had looked forward to hearing, while I was missing the gospel itself—the "good news" that I had been needing so badly for so long. The last sermon I'd heard back home was one entitled "What Would Jesus Drive?" and I'd thought it was kind of a ridiculous thing to consider in the first place. Jesus didn't drive. Jesus didn't even ride, unless you count the donkey that one time. Jesus walked. And if Billy Joe had ever been asked the same question, he would have answered, "Why, the green, o' course."

Whether as a sermon topic or not, vehicles were a main concern of the day, at least as far as my group was concerned. The car deal that Aunt Elaine had made with Sonny involved exchanging her Volkswagen—the little Beetle with its cloth sunroof, the car I thought of as my own—for the racy Dodge Challenger convertible Miss Faye had driven to the meadows that morning. Elaine said Sonny wanted to fix up the VW and put it on display at his campground. He would pay her for the Beetle and loan her the Dodge until she could find a new car for herself, she explained. That, in itself, would have been enough to rub me the wrong way, because, as I've said, I had always dearly loved that VW and had hoped that Elaine would eventually give it to me, not to some idiot like Sonny.

But Bo's problems with my aunt's friend had top priority on our way back home. Bo reappeared after the Singing, meeting us at the edge of the parking area. As we rode back toward Boone in the convertible, Elaine looked up into the rearview mirror at Bo next to me in the back seat, then over at Alan in the front passenger seat. I figured Alan had told her about Bo's reaction to Sonny's CD. "Don't be upset with Sonny, Lionel," she said. "He doesn't mean for that album of his to be offensive."

"But it *is*," Bo replied.

"I know," Elaine said, "and I'll talk to him about it. But up here in the mountains, the Rebel flag is still a big deal. They say it represents Southern heritage to them, not racism, the way we look at it down on the coast. There really aren't that many black people up here, you know. I'm sure you've already noticed that."

"Yeah," he said. "But Southern heritage? How do they figure that? I'm as Southern as they are—I come from Southern slaves—and that flag represents nothing but hate—to me, anyway. Besides, the men who lived up here in these mountains weren't always loyal to the Southern cause. They didn't always keep the faith. Mom told me that several hundred men, white men, from western North Carolina fought in Union regiments. She said a lot of Rebel soldiers, hundreds of them, deserted whenever it suited them, especially for spring planting and to harvest their crops. Some things were more important to them than that piece of cloth that rednecks are always waving around."

"I know, and I don't necessarily agree with the Southern heritage argument, but that's what they say," Elaine repeated. "From what I've seen and heard, things up here have changed *a lot*, especially over the last twenty or thirty years. And—you're right—it used to be really bad for black folks all across this state. But we've got to trust that people can change. And that they're sincere about the feelings they try to express—like the feelings in that song on Sonny's album. Like I said, he really doesn't mean for it to be offensive. But that's the way he is—not just with that Rebel flag song, with a lot of things.

He's always sticking his foot in his mouth, and that makes editing his column a real challenge, if you know what I mean." She managed a nervous laugh.

The talk with Aunt Elaine—just getting it out in the open—did seem to ease Bo's mind a bit, and I knew him well enough to know that he and I were OK, even if he wasn't going to become a Sonny Rose fan anytime soon. And for my part, I certainly had no intentions that day of becoming a Sonny Rose "grouper" either.

Later that night before I went to sleep, I called Bo in his dorm room and talked to him for a few minutes. He couldn't talk long and couldn't tell me if he had found out anything new about Agnes Morton, because it was after "lights out," and if he got caught on the phone after curfew he'd be in hot water. He also didn't tell me his thoughts about the Brown Mountain Light, from when Alan and I had interrupted his musings that morning at Elaine's car.

"Well," I said. "I just wanted to make sure everything's OK."

"It is," he replied. "We're solid. Look, Val. Don't worry. You know I'll keep the faith."

As I hung up the phone and thought about the events of the day, holding them up against all I knew about Bo, I was sure he would never compromise his belief in himself or in his friends. Several years earlier when the three of us—Alan, Bo and I—were seeking and, I believe, finding the healing waters of Shallotte Inlet, we had started calling ourselves the Kindred Spirits, and our motto was "We Are One," kind of like the Three Musketeers.

That night as I lay in bed and endured that anxious moment between turning the bedside lamp off and seeing my little crystal lighthouse come on, I wondered for the first time if Alan and Aunt Elaine might have changed since their move to the mountains and if they might have become as blind to some things as many of the people that I had just met seemed to be—Sonny Rose, for instance. And I wondered if maybe it was me, maybe I was the one who couldn't "see the dang ocean for all them dad-blasted waves," as Billy Joe would sometimes say when he came back from surf fishing. Maybe I *couldn't* see the forest for the trees. Maybe we *were* all alone.

SIX

The next day was Monday, the middle of Aunt Elaine's work week since *The Linville Ledger* went to press in the early afternoon every Wednesday so it could be mailed out before the post office closed that day. Because most *Ledger* subscribers—a good many of them Floridians with resort property in the Linville area—received their papers through the mail, each week's edition was dated Thursday, and no papers were placed in distribution racks around the area until the day after it was actually printed. The deadlines each week for contributed material, such as Sonny's "Jonas Ridge News" column, were 5 p.m. Monday for regular columnists and noon Tuesday for the general public, so that Elaine would have time to edit the articles and get them laid out and typeset by presstime Wednesday.

My aunt's title was editor, which certainly sounded impressive; however, the *Ledger*'s editorial staff was basically one person, Elaine, whose full-time job was to coordinate a group of community correspondents, like Sonny, and other part-time columnists. There were the men's golf columnist, Duffy MacGregor, and his ladies' golf counterpart, Kitty Forrest. Several area ministers wrote columns with religious bents, probably to offset the several ladies whose lengthy articles reported on partying and dancing at the Linville area country clubs and resorts. Each town and, for that matter, each wide spot in the road within the paper's coverage area had a correspondent to share whatever had gone on with their neighbors, friends and families the previous week. As a result, the *Ledger*'s editorial standards were dubious at best. There was no telling what might get into the paper, depending on what axe an individual columnist had to grind at any given time. And Sonny, as I've mentioned, always seemed to have bigger axes to grind than the Jolly Green Giant. That was just how he was, Elaine always explained apologetically to disgruntled subscribers.

Also, Aunt Elaine and many of her writers doubled as photographers, so the paper wasn't going to win many press awards for photography. My aunt, though, had won several awards over the years, mainly for her own writing but also for picture taking. One photo that didn't win anything other than a spot on my "Wall of Fame" was of Jack Nicklaus, the Golden Bear, visiting a new course he had designed in the area. Elaine sent me a copy of it because she knew I was a golfer.

I always wished I could write—or do *anything*—as well as my aunt did. But the only talent of mine that Elaine thought she might put to use at the paper was my ability to snap a decent picture now and then. For my twelfth birthday back at Village Point, Grandpa and Grandma had given me a little black plastic Kodak 35mm camera that couldn't have cost much but was priceless in terms of the fun I had with it then and the memories that it preserved for me now. More than any other subject, I liked to take pictures of Grandpa working on *The Lady of Shallotte*, and a couple of times before he had his first heart attack he took me out with him so I could get photos for him of different places along the coastline from offshore. Even then, I couldn't afford either to waste film or get it processed as soon as I finished a roll; I had to be selective about pressing the shutter release.

It was always like Christmas morning on the appointed days when I could finally go pick up my packet of negatives and prints at Wal-Mart. I always wanted to use the store's one-hour photo service but had to have my film sent off for the five-day processing because it was cheaper that way. And I never got double prints, except for the couple of times I took the pictures when I went out with Grandpa. I guess he knew even then that his days on *The Lady* were numbered.

That first Monday morning I lived in the mountains, everybody but little old me had a place to be—Aunt Elaine at work, Alan in his summer school class and Bo at music camp. I heard Elaine leave home first that morning, around 7:30 so that she could get to her office in Linville by eight o'clock. She had told me that she would be at work until at least six or seven o'clock that evening and that she might not be home for dinner until as late as eight or 8:30, depending on how work went. Sometimes she had to go visit her writers at home or work to goose them up if their articles hadn't shown up at the *Ledger* by deadline.

Then I heard Alan banging around down in the kitchen around eight o'clock that morning. His class ran from nine o'clock to noon Monday through Friday throughout the short summer term. Not that first week I was there, but the second week he—as well as Elaine and Bo—would have Friday off for the Fourth of July holiday. I was already looking forward to the day off, even though every day was shaping up to be a day off for me.

I had slept OK the night before, I guess, but I didn't want to get out of bed just yet. My cousin had another idea, though. "Hey! Sleeping Beauty!" Alan shouted up the stairwell toward my room. "Get your lazy butt down here!" He waited to see if I stirred. "Hey! No kidding! You gotta get up now! You're gonna make me late!"

Make *him* late? That was news to me. "What?!" I yelled back as I threw off my covers and rolled out of bed. I slept in gym shorts and a T-shirt, so I didn't have to dress before going downstairs to join him at the kitchen table.

He pushed a pink Tupperware cereal bowl already filled with Wheaties across the table to me and nodded at the half-empty quart container of milk at his elbow. As usual, he was wearing clothes that appeared to have been bought at a wilderness outfitters—a gray Royal Robbins V-neck T-shirt, tan Columbia hiking shorts, and gray and yellow Nike trail-running shoes. Resting on the table was a light green cap with "Life is good!" embroidered in white on a black oval-shaped patch with white trim. I had seen that logo before on outdoor apparel, and I could never figure out if that was a manufacturer's name or just some company's idea of an upbeat motto that kids would like.

"Hope you don't mind powdered milk, cuz," he said, not looking up from the back of the cereal box, which had a photo of Tiger Woods and his picture-perfect follow-through on the front. "Mom's on another one of her diet kicks. Said she gained a couple pounds over the weekend—probably from the ham biscuits yesterday—so now *we* gotta pay for it. First thing she does is pour out all the two-percent and mix up a quart of this chalky crap that's supposed to be milk. I figure we'll be using it for at least a week, until she loses five pounds. Just hope she isn't shooting for ten."

"That's OK," I said. "Back home we drank it all the time, anyway."

Rising to clean up his mess, he filled me in on the day's schedule. "OK, here's the plan. Mom said you're supposed to go to school with me, and then I'm supposed to haul your butt over to the *Ledger*, and I think she's got something there for you to do this afternoon. Matter of fact, I think she's got something for *me* to do, too, but she said she has to check on some stuff first and she'll let us know when we get there. Got it? Got it. Now, eat your Wheaties, get your butt dressed—casual attire will be fine—and meet me at the Blazer in, oh, let's say, fifteen minutes. I gotta see a man about a dog. A big dog." And with that, he was up and gone, down the hall to the downstairs bathroom, slamming the door behind him.

I finished eating, then washed both of our bowls and spoons and left them in the dish drainer. Before going back upstairs to dress,

I wiped off the table and looked over Tiger's perfect follow-through one more time, wondering if I would ever get to meet him, as Aunt Elaine had seen Jack Nicklaus up close for that newspaper picture of hers. *Probably not*, I thought. *He's too important, and I'm too…too… nothing.* When Alan's toilet flush awakened me from my daydream, I bolted upstairs, pulled on my gray cargo shorts, a clean black T-shirt (one with Billy Joe's crossbones emblem on the pocket), white footie socks and my Wal-Mart special running shoes, then scrambled to catch up with Alan in the garage. I almost forgot my white Nike cap but remembered to grab it from the hatrack as I hurried out the door. "I didn't lock it," I said, as I got into the Blazer.

"Don't worry about it," he replied, starting the vehicle. "I got it." He reached up to a black panel above the windshield and tapped two black buttons, one that opened the garage door behind us and another that made the lock on the door into the house click loudly. "Dad thinks of everything," Alan added. "I can run just about everything in the house from this panel—lights, air conditioner, burglar alarm, even turn the TV and stereo on and off. Only thing it can't do is put something in the microwave and have it ready to eat when we get home."

"You're kidding," I said.

"Nope. It's kinda scary, how everything's run by computers now. Course, it takes money to pay for all this stuff, and I don't know how long Mom can keep coming up with the house payments. After I turn twenty-one, Dad won't have to keep sending us checks every month, and then me and Mom'll be on our own. She'll probably have to sell the house and find something smaller, probably closer to Linville, too. Probably around Foscoe, near the college where Sonny teaches."

By now we were on Aho Road heading toward the main highway to Boone. I had been awake since around six a.m., and the thought of that unpleasant character Sonny Rose hadn't entered my mind until Alan had to go and mention him right then. "Why do you like that guy?" I asked. "Doesn't it bother you how he acts around Aunt Elaine? And the Beetle. He took the Beetle!"

"No, he didn't," Alan corrected. "Mom sold it to him. He's helping us out. He's not charging Mom anything to borrow the convertible, and he'll loan her that car or one of his other cars for as long as she needs it, until she can buy herself a new one."

I said nothing for a few seconds as we stopped at the intersection with the main highway and as Alan looked both directions to pull out. He muttered and shook his head at the heavy traffic, most of which appeared to be tourists on summer vacation. "I know how you feel," Alan said, as he finally found an opening in the stream of vans and SUVs. "Sonny kinda comes on strong at first, but he *isn't* a bad guy. You'll see. You just have to spend a little time with him and get to know him. He's probably Mom's best friend right now."

Keeping in mind that Aunt Elaine had never liked Billy Joe Pearlman, a sometimes off-putting character who was one of *my* favorite persons, I didn't know if I even wanted to give Sonny Rose a chance, as Alan was suggesting I do. "You guys don't need his help," I suggested. "You could get a part-time job, Alan, and then it wouldn't be so hard on Aunt Elaine to pay bills and stuff."

He shot me an annoyed look. "I *did* try to get a job," he said. "Last winter I wanted to work at a ski slope, but Mom wouldn't let me. She said it's more important for me to do good in school than work a part-time job. She says she wants me to enjoy my college years, because once I get out and get a job, I'll be working for the rest of my life."

I nodded. "That makes sense, I guess. But I still think that guy Sonny wants something, or else he wouldn't be pushing himself on you guys so much. Nobody acts the way *he* does without wanting something in return."

"I'm telling you, Val, you've got him all wrong," Alan insisted, shaking his head. He paused to point out the window as we passed Tweetsie Railroad on the hill to our left. I could see the stack of the famous steam engine puffing clouds of gray-white smoke as it sat on the tracks behind the replica of a Wild West town. Just then, the train's distinctive whistle cut the morning air. "Old folks around here claim that no other train whistle sounds like Tweetsie's," Alan said. "Back in the early 1900s, it ran from Johnson City, Tennessee, to Boone by way of Foscoe and Linville and some of those mining towns over near Mount Mitchell. Sonny's always telling how Gene Autry—you know, the singing cowboy that did 'Rudolph the Red-Nosed Reindeer'—he bought that engine, old No. 12, the last one, after the railroad line stopped running, and then he sold it back to the people who built the tourist attraction. That's what Sonny says. He used to work summers at Tweetsie, back before he opened the Barkhouse. I think he played one of the bad guys who rob the train."

"You see?" I said, glad that Alan was back on track. "What's *that* all about? The singing cowboy stuff." I was referring to Sonny's apparent obsession with the Old West and with matinee idols like Autry and Roy Rogers.

"That's just his thing, Val," Alan insisted. "Or *one* of his things. He's into a lot of stuff, and he's done more stuff than anyone I know. He even worked up at that old theme park on Beech Mountain back in the Seventies, the Land of Oz. I think he was the Scarecrow or Tin Woodman or Cowardly Lion or something one summer. Maybe he was a Munchkin, I don't know. But give him a break. You know how it is to really be into something and kinda play at whatever it is, like you're a cowboy or a pro basketball player or a rock star or something." He gave me a quick glance. "Or even a famous golfer, maybe."

"I never said I wanted to be a famous golfer."

"Well, then what *do* you want to be?" my cousin asked pointedly. "You got mad yesterday when Sonny pushed you a little bit on the subject. But you really do need to be thinking about it."

"I know. But he was pushing a *lot*. And it's none of his business."

"Well," Alan said, "he was just thinking about Mom, I guess, and just wondering how...."

He chose not to finish the thought, but I was pretty sure I was reading him loud and clear and could finish the sentence for him. "Wondering how you and Aunt Elaine are going to make it with *me* around," I blurted. That was about all I could take right then, and—like that time a couple of years earlier when Billy Joe had made me feel bad about myself—I burst into tears.

Alan looked over at me. "Stop crying, Val," he said, and touched my knee. "I didn't mean it the way you make it sound. You're taking everything the wrong way. Don't be so sensitive."

"I can't help it," I offered weakly.

He glanced at me again and shook his head. "You and Lacey," he muttered, then began braking the Blazer as we rounded a wide curve that wound down and around a hill past the "Welcome to Boone" and Boone Golf Club signs and then leveled out at the first traffic signal on the outskirts of town.

From the traffic light where we sat, to the university at least three miles away, there stretched a burgeoning commercial strip which included shopping centers and franchise restaurants and hotel chains and even the occasional mom 'n' pop business that had so far managed to survive the development boom. The Town of Boone was named for, of course, Daniel Boone, who had kept a hunting cabin at the foot of nearby Howard's Knob, Alan explained.

"Sonny went to Chapel Hill in the late Seventies," Alan noted, as we turned onto campus and headed for a parking lot near the stadium. "He went to that other college first but came back here and went to a community college before transferring to Carolina. I think he and Mom were there around the same time, but they didn't know each other. She was in the journalism school; Sonny was a business major, I think."

"He hasn't always wanted to teach?" I asked, wiping my eyes with my fingers. "You mean, he did something else for a living? Full-time?"

"Yeah," Alan said. "He told Mom he was in business for about ten years, out in California and up in New York and even in Japan, I think, and that's how he made enough money to come back here and buy the Barkhouse and campground and fix them up. He said he'd had enough of big cities and big business. And I think that was about the time his dad got sick, too, so I guess he really came back to help take care of his dad. I think he's been teaching at Skyland Tech for about ten years. After he moved back here, he went to ASU and got the history degrees he needed to teach at Skyland. He says he likes working there, even though he doesn't get to teach kids like the ones at the university."

"What do you mean by that?"

We pulled into a parking space fairly close to Bo's dorm. "Oh, you know," Alan said, stepping on the parking brake pedal and jiggling the shifter to make sure the Blazer was in gear. "Technical college is kind of like two more years of high school," he said. "You get all kinds there, even old people who go back to school just for the heck of it. And most of the students here at ASU are regular college-age kids—you know, like you and me."

"Well, is everybody expecting me to come here, too, like you?" I asked, as we got out of the vehicle. "Would you guys think bad of me if I decided to, say, go to Skyland for a couple years? Like Lacey's doing."

Alan pushed a button on his key chain to click the door locks and tweek the horn to set the vehicle's security system. "Naw, that wouldn't be bad," he replied, "if that's what you want to do. And if you've got a plan, like *she* does. Come on. Walk with me." We hurried down the hill past the bronzed statue of a seated Daniel Boone, crossed the street and headed toward the four-story red-brick science building with its telescope dome on the roof. Alan held up at a crosswalk near the corner of the building. "The library is that way," he pointed. "I'll be in class until noon on the dot. Take a walk around campus and see what you think, then meet me back at the truck by, say, 12:15. OK? That'll give me time to talk to my professor after class, and you won't have to wait at the truck too long. I love ya, cuz." He gave me a peck on the cheek and smiled before turning away and heading to class.

I spent the next three hours walking around the hilly campus of brown fieldstone, rough red brick, gray-white concrete, and green grass and trees, not only to take a quick peek at the big university but also to take a good long look at myself and try, try again to start coming to grips with what I wanted to do with my life. Until then, I really hadn't slowed down long enough—not in months, anyway, not since those long-distant days before Grandma's illness—to actually get my bearings and map out some kind of route to take through life. I had been running from one place to the next, not really knowing where I had been or where I was headed.

After only an hour, I had seen enough of the university to know that I liked the buildings and grounds well enough, but I had no clue as to what in the world I would study even if I *could* get myself accepted for the upcoming fall semester. That was pretty much out of the question, anyway. But even at Skyland Tech, where I could get in just by filling out a form and paying my money, what could I do, other than just mark time for two years? Certainly not major in golf. I wasn't good enough, and I never would be. I didn't need to go to school to be a waitress or to learn how to flip hamburgers or to clerk in some store, even in the nice big ones on the strip coming into town.

Turf management, maybe? No, seriously. Greenskeeping. That was an important part of the sport I loved. And at least I would be working in the golf industry, I figured, even if I wasn't playing golf for a living. I had considerable experience, about three years of it, mowing fairways, even if it was only at the B.J. back home. That brilliant idea came to me after two hours of walking and watching the university maintenance guys mow the grass between and around the buildings, also around the time I started getting tired and decided to chill in the library until noon. Maybe I could find a copy of *The Idiot's Guide to Golf Course Design* or *Turf Management for Dummies* or maybe this month's edition of *Weed Wackers' World* there. But who was I fooling?

SEVEN

As I was leaving the university library, I happened to notice a rustic wooden sign by the door to one large room on the top floor. The sign indicated that the room housed the university's Appalachian Collection—books and other materials pertaining to the Appalachian Mountains region, I gathered from stepping inside for a quick look. Though I wasn't crazy about Alan and Bo's idea to investigate the Brown Mountain Light, I thought it might help for them to know about that special section of the library. Of course, Alan probably already knew about the Appalachian Collection from having used the library for his previous classes, and Bo, as curious as *he* was, might already have found the collection online.

Still, I knew I needed to mention the collection to Bo when I talked to him that evening on the phone. Based on what he had told me about the music camp's tight schedule, there was only a slim chance that I would run into him on campus during the day, even though Alan's Blazer was parked so close to Bo's dormitory. Also, I didn't dare try to call Bo on his cell phone, because it would get him in trouble, he said, if the phone happened to go off in the middle of a practice or, heaven help him, a performance. For that reason, he wasn't going to carry the phone with him, at least not for the time being.

So you can imagine my surprise when I arrived at the Blazer before Alan did, and I found that Bo had already been there, that he had spotted the bright yellow vehicle and had left a note for us under a wiper blade. It was written on blank staff paper, like the kind that composers write songs on. The note read: "Alan, Tell Val I found info on A Morton. Also on BM Lites. Call me tonite (Mon.) at 9 SHARP. Gotta go. Bo"

I knew I could count on Bo not to forget anything. And I was glad that his mother, Dr. Gaines, was living in our house near Village Point. Two neighbor families there got upset when Aunt Elaine told them Bo and his mom would be leasing the house, but they had no reason to be angry. Marilyn Gaines was a fine lady with a long family history around Village Point, a stronger connection with the place than those two families had, what with their big houses and expensive cars and big sportfishing boats. Those people were just mad because Marilyn and Bo were black.

It didn't take long, though, for Elaine to set them both straight—the two fathers of the two families, that is. She told them that if they were the fine Christians they were always claiming to be—especially during election campaigns when they weren't shy about pushing their "kinder, gentler" politics on everyone—then they should be happy to have two new neighbors that they could love as they obviously loved themselves. That last time I talked to Billy Joe, at the golf store the week before I left the coast, my old pro laughed when I told him how Elaine had stood up to those two men. "Good," he said. "Let 'em stick *that* in their craws and chew on it."

He might have looked and acted like a redneck and he might not have gone to church much in his life, but Billy Joe Pearlman—like my grandfather Bron Galloway—was a good man. And if there really is a heaven, I'm sure that's where he went, even though he despised the men who wore the little "WWJD" bracelets to the course but would tell racist or sexist jokes in the clubhouse and cuss louder than anybody when they sliced their balls into the pond off the first tee. When he'd hear the splash, Billy Joe would say, "Proof they *is* a gawd."

One of Grandpa's favorite sayings at a time like that was, "Watch who you make light of, 'cause what goes 'round comes 'round." Billy Joe and my grandpa both hated phonies worst than just about anything, and I learned to be that way, too—one who hated phony people, I mean, not to be a phony myself.

At least I hope I wasn't a phony, even if I *was* warming up to the idea of becoming a greenskeeper but was afraid to tell anyone, even Alan, right then. Alan, the boy genius, wanted to become a great astronomer like Carl Sagan or a great scientist like Albert Einstein or maybe some great mathematician like Stephen Hawking or whatever the heck a person does with a degree in applied physics. And then here I was, Alan's stupid little girl cousin from the coast, seriously considering mowing grass for a living. Billions and billions of blades of grass.

That's kind of what I was thinking about when Alan finally got back to the Blazer from his class. He was only about five minutes late, so I wasn't upset with him, just anxious to get to Linville to see what Aunt Elaine had for us to do. I showed him Bo's note as we left Boone, then listened as Alan filled me in on the conversation with his professor after class. "He said I could write my research paper on the Brown Mountain Light," Alan said, "if I come up with a new angle on it."

"What do you mean?" I asked. A green and white billboard on the right side of the road caught my attention as we sailed down what Alan called Rockcrusher Hill and into a sharp curve to the left. The sign was for a par-three course called Willow Creek.

Alan replied, "Well, most scientists think it's just refractions from light sources in Lenoir. That's a town that's about, oh, I guess fifteen or twenty miles beyond Brown Mountain on a straight line from most of the places the Light's usually seen. They're almost positive it isn't swamp gas or foxfire or St. Elmo's fire or anything like that, 'cause investigators have been all over Brown Mountain and they can't find anything to support those other theories."

"Do they know what they're talking about?" I asked, trying not to forget to ask about Willow Creek but not wanting to change the subject so abruptly.

"Of course," Alan said. "They're scientists, aren't they? But lately they've been studying other stuff around here besides the Brown Mountain Light, like light pollution."

"Light pollution?" I pictured vanloads of tourists littering the roadside with dead disposable flashlights.

"Yeah. You know, when shopping centers and places like that have such bright lights that they light up the night."

I shrugged. "Isn't that the point—to light up the night?"

"No, not the night *sky*, which is what happens," he explained. "And then people can't even look up at the stars, because the sky is too bright and the stars get drowned out by the city lights down here. It's getting to be a problem everywhere, but it's more of a problem around here than at Village Point."

"You mean, like when we'd go out on the beach at night and could see Myrtle Beach glowing to the south?" I asked.

"Exactly," Alan replied.

"Or when we saw the space shuttle take off from Cape Canaveral that one night?"

"Well," he said, "that's a little different. You wouldn't say the space shuttle causes light pollution."

"Why not? Because *you* want to be an astronaut?"

"I didn't say I wanted to be an astronaut."

By then, that golf course billboard was the last thing on my mind. "I was thinking about that a while ago, Alan," I said. "All you guys keep giving me a hard time about deciding what to do with my life. Well, what are you going to do with a college degree in applied physics?"

Alan didn't answer right away. As we drove through the Foscoe community, he pointed out the campus of Skyland Technical College on the hill to our right. "Sonny's office is in the building on the back side of the campus," Alan noted. "Oh, yeah, and you'll be interested in this. There's a nice golf course up the road behind the college—up on the mountain."

"Willow Creek?" I was thankfully thinking of golf again.

He gave me a funny look. "No, Willow Creek is the par three back toward Valle Crucis. The course up there is Hawksnest. It's a ski resort in the winter and a golf course the rest of the year. I've played it a couple times. It'll give you a good workout. Here's something else that's interesting. The name of the little town up there on top of the mountain is called Seven Devils. They say it got that name from being 'cold as seven devils' up there in the winter, and that's about the truth."

"Seven devils are cold?"

Alan grinned. "No, Seven Devils *is* cold. Now, shut up and listen to me a second, and this'll be the end of it, as far as I'm concerned." He paused to check his watch. "I thought we were running late, but Mom probably isn't even back from lunch yet. Sometimes she goes walking at MacRae Meadows—you know, where we were yesterday at the Singing.

"Anyway, you wanna know why I'm studying astronomy?" he continued. "I'll tell you. It's because if there's any answers to the big questions we have, they're out there." Extending an index finger on the steering wheel, he pointed into the sky through the windshield. "I know, that sounds like *The X-Files* or something, but it's true. The answer to every single question is somewhere up there in the stars, if you just know where to look and can figure out what you're looking at."

"As long as there isn't any light pollution around you, right?" I quipped.

"You got that right, cuz," said Alan. "Yeah, I know, environmentalists can be a real pain in the butt sometimes. We call 'em 'tree-huggers' up here. But if you stop and think about it, what else do we really have but the earth? And take that golf course I was talking about—or *any* golf course, for that matter. Did you know environmentalists hate golf courses, 'cause they create runoff and pollute the groundwater with pesticides and herbicides and stuff? You know, when you look at it that way, it makes you feel kinda guilty just to play a round of golf."

"Not me," I said, realizing that maybe I *was* a phony after all. "Golf's about the only thing that got me through all the stuff with Grandpa. And with Grandma."

"What stuff?" He glanced over at me.

"You know."

I could tell he didn't want to push me, as Sonny had the day before, but that he wanted to know what was really going on in his cousin's head. "You mean, all that stuff you got the, uh, help with?" he asked. "Like being afraid of the dark and all?"

"Yeah." That was about as much as I was willing to give him right then. "Have you ever played Willow Creek?"

"Oh, yeah," he said. "It's nice, for a par three. Nine holes. Kinda hilly. Doesn't cost much—nine bucks, I think. A buck a hole. Can't beat that, can you?"

"Nope," I replied, glad I had successfully changed the subject, something I had become an expert at in recent months. "Not with a stick."

Alan laughed. "Is that something that old guy at the beach used to say? That guy you worked for? The one Mom didn't like—Billy Bob or whatever?"

"Billy Joe," I corrected. "Alan, you knew Billy Joe."

"Not like you guys did. Village Point wasn't exactly the most happening place to hang out. The guys at school would have laughed me off the court—basketball *or* tennis court—if I'd spent as much time at that little golf course as you did. And wasn't Billy Joe the old guy who was always hitting on Grams after Granddad died?"

"No, he wasn't hitting on Grandma," I said. "He was just trying to be nice, because he and Grandpa were good friends. You know that. What's the matter with you?" I wasn't especially mad at Alan, just a bit perturbed that his memory could be so selective. After all, wasn't he supposed to be the genius in the family?

"Whatever you say, cuz," he said, then pointed out a couple of other golf courses on the road to Linville—up the mountain on the right, Linville Ridge Golf Club, the highest course east of the Mississippi, and in the river valley on the left, Grandfather Golf & Country Club, Alan noted. "I think Grandfather's the second toughest course in the state," he added, "next to Pinehurst."

"Number two?"

"Yeah—I think," he replied, though I wasn't sure if he knew I was referring to the Pinehurst No. 2 course and not to what he had just given as Grandfather's toughness rating among other state courses. "There are four *big* courses up here that everybody wants to play. They even call them the 'Big Four'—Grandfather, Linville Ridge, Linville and Elk River, over near Banner Elk. Knowing Sonny, I bet he's played all four of them. Maybe he'll take you with him sometime."

"Yeah, maybe," I said. Maybe I had misjudged Sonny. Maybe he wasn't such a bad guy after all. Maybe I was full of crap just like those phony tourist golfers at the B.J. Maybe I'd just better shut up and see what Aunt Elaine had waiting for us at the *Ledger*.

When we got there just after one o'clock, Elaine, who apparently hadn't been back from lunch very long, was on the phone, taking notes at her desk. She hadn't even had time to take off her navy blue Prince windbreaker, the type of jacket she usually wore as part of her warmup suit for tennis on cool mountain mornings. Putting her hand over the phone's mouthpiece, she whispered for us to wait in the outer lobby.

There we found copies of the previous week's paper, as well as the *Ledger*'s quarterly tourist-oriented supplement called *Linville Living*, which contained information on the little town and its surrounding area. I learned that Linville—the town, the river, the gorge and the falls—all had been named for a man and his sons who were hunting in the area back in the 1760s when they were attacked and scalped by a Cherokee war party.

Alan was about as fidgety that afternoon as those poor Linville boys must have been almost 250 years earlier; however, my cousin had no choice but to wait for his mom to get off the phone, since we still didn't know what she wanted us to do for her.

"Do you have to keep doing that?" I asked, referring to the way Alan insisted upon chewing his fingernails and spitting out nail fragments on the carpet.

Alan scowled. "I'm about to starve."

"Well, you're not eating *that*, are you?" I said. "Then why didn't you stop at that McDonald's we passed on the way here? We could've got something there. I'm kinda hungry, too."

"You kidding?" he replied. "Mom would kill us if we walked in here with burgers and fries when she's on a diet. Maybe I didn't explain it clearly this morning, but the rule around *our* house is, if Mom's on a diet, then *everybody's* on a diet. I can't wait to find out what this one is. We've done 'em all—Weight Watchers, Special K, Atkins, Duke Rice Diet, Sugar-Busters, Eat to Win, Eat to Lose, Eat This, Eat That—"

"OK, I get the idea," I groused, turning back to the paper I was reading. "Go ahead and chew your nails. I don't care."

The newspaper office occupied a small rock building on a corner of the main intersection in Linville. The two roads that crossed there led travelers to Linville from the four corners of the earth—well, actually, from Boone, Blowing Rock, Jonas Ridge and Newland, the seat of Avery County, of which Linville was a part. Linville, as a tourist retreat, was settled—or incorporated, rather—just before the turn of the 20th century and within a decade had built a reputation as a favorite summer playground of some of the Southeast's richest and most influential families. Linville, situated in the green Linville River valley between the slopes of Grandfather Mountain on the east and Pixie Mountain, little more than a tall hill, on the west, competed through the next century with Blowing Rock as a destination for rich lowlanders seeking relief from the summer heat, as the region's average summertime high temperature hovered in the mid-seventies.

Back then, Linville and Blowing Rock were connected by what was called the Yonahlossee Trail, a winding road running part-way up and then around the southern and eastern sides of Grandfather Mountain. The road once had been the stagecoach route between Linville and Blowing Rock, both before and after the original Tweetsie train ran through Linville to Boone. Since then, much of the route had been claimed by construction of the modern highway, which passed right outside the office door. However, one short, seldomly-used, unpaved section of the old roadway remained, winding uphill the three dusty miles from Linville to MacRae Meadows near the gated entrance to Grandfather Mountain's famous peaks, its hiking trails and its terrific Mile-High Swinging Bridge, so named because its elevation was right at 5,280 feet above sea level (but only about eighty feet above the actual ground it crossed).

Looking at the photos in the supplement, I swore to myself right then and there that no one, not even Alan and a team of wild horses, would ever drag me across that Mile-High Swinging Bridge, even if it *was* only eighty feet off the ground. That was high enough for me. As Billy Joe used to say after a fishing trip in rough seas, "They's nothing' like keepin' yer feet planted in good ole Mama Dirt."

"She done yet?" Alan asked, nodding toward his mother's office down the hallway.

I leaned forward to listen for Aunt Elaine's voice. "Nope," I said presently. "She just asked something about a meeting tonight."

"Great," Alan said, shaking his head. He began untying and retying his Nikes, as if he intended to go on a long hike.

From the *Ledger*'s lobby, I could look out the front window across the intersection at another rock building, this one a Texaco service station with its famous star-shaped sign. Then cattycorner from us was the big yellow wedge-shaped Grandfather Mountain sign with the mountain's name and "Carolina's Favorite Scenic Attraction" motto in rust-colored wooden letters. Behind the twenty-foot-tall sign were a number of wood-sided buildings which constituted Linville's main business district. On the outskirts of town but within walking distance was MacGregor's Grill, where Elaine often took her meals—when she wasn't on a diet, that is. Near the corner directly opposite the newspaper sat the tiny Linville Post Office, whose proximity conveniently allowed the *Ledger* pressmen to haul outgoing mail bags full of newspapers there in nothing more than a golf cart-like four-wheeler each Wednesday afternoon.

According to the newspaper article I was reading about Linville's history, the cultural center of the community was the Eseeola Lodge (Cherokee for "cliffy river"), and its golf course, Linville Golf Club, the one Alan had already mentioned as being one of the Big Four. According to the paper, the eighteen-hole championship course was designed in 1924 by Donald Ross, one of America's greatest golf course architects. It was supposed to be Ross's finest mountain design, and I hoped to see it for myself before too long. Ross, by the way, also designed Pinehurst No. 2 and the Cape Fear Country Club course. Another famous landmark in Linville, according to the article, was the All Saints' Episcopal Church, a rustic mountain chapel designed by Henry Bacon, architect of the Lincoln Memorial in Washington, D.C.

I could understand why Elaine had accepted the newspaper job there. Linville seemed like heaven on earth, even to a dyed-in-the-wool South Brunswick Islands girl like me. For the first time since my frightful flight across the state two days earlier, I began to feel as if I had found some important links between the person I had been back home and this new me, this stranger lost in the dark who was anxiously awaiting her debut, her day in the sun on top of the world.

EIGHT

Aunt Elaine eventually got off the telephone and gave us our orders, to take her Sony digital camera down to Edgemont and Mortimer—where Alan had taken Bo and me on Saturday—and for us to get pictures of people enjoying the outdoors, whether they were campers or picnickers, backpackers or mountain bikers, or outdoorsmen of any sort, she instructed.

"We need to show how people use that area down there since the Fourth is only a couple weeks away," she said, "but especially because it might be designated as wilderness. Some people think that if the government makes it an official wilderness area, motor vehicles won't be allowed in there at all. So if you can get pictures of people on motorcycles or four-wheelers or even in Jeeps, that's what we need. And if you can get an American flag in the picture, too, that's gravy."

"By the way, Mom," Alan began, picking up on her food metaphor, "which diet are we on now? We noticed the powdered milk in the fridge this morning. Is it the Milk-Busters Diet this time or what?" Before she could answer, he quickly added, "You know, Mom, I'm waiting for you to go on the Mellow Mushroom Diet, but all you eat are those darn portobellos Sonny always grills instead of hamburgers." The Mellow Mushroom, by the way, was my cousin's favorite pizza parlor near campus.

Elaine patted her son on the shoulder. "Don't worry, honey," she said. "Going on a little diet for a couple weeks isn't going to stunt your growth. Actually, I think you'll like this one, because Sonny and I came up with it ourselves by taking what's worked from all the other diets we've tried. The key to it is getting some exercise every couple days, like playing tennis or walking—or playing a round of golf, Val. Alan, you're probably overdosing on exercise as it is. But another key is eating right—the *right* foods."

"Such as?" Alan prompted.

Elaine held up an index finger, indicating for us to wait while she opened a desk drawer and lifted out a brown plastic grocery bag half-filled with what appeared to be fruit. "The Gala apple," she announced, handing both of us a shiny red-and-yellow splotched apple. "This is the real key to our diet—and drinking plenty of water, of course."

"Any particular kind?" Alan asked half-seriously. "Evian? Aquavita? Dasani? Deer Park? How 'bout Perrier? Perrier OK?"

"Sonny *does* drink a lot of Perrier," she replied, "but we decided we'd give up all carbonated beverages, even naturally carbonated ones, and stick to just plain old water. I think Sonny likes Table Rock Wilderness Water the best—you know, the one that comes from a spring not far from the Barkhouse and Gingercake."

I couldn't help but ask why Sonny didn't just fill up a bottle from his own faucet, if his favorite bottled water came from so close by anyhow. That's what we used to do back home at Village Point, where the drinking water *did* taste salty and bad before the county ran a water line past our house. At least once a week we would ride over to the county water system's big tower-tank and fill gallon milk jugs with fresher-tasting, chlorine-treated, county water. Elaine said she didn't know why Sonny preferred bottled water over that from the spring on the hill behind the Barkhouse.

"You'll just have to ask him yourself," Elaine said. "On your way back home, I'd like you to come back through Jonas Ridge and pick up Sonny's column at the lodge. You won't mind, will you, Alan?" Though she was talking to her son, she winked knowingly at me. "You can drive up Mortimer Road. It comes out there at the Jonas Ridge Post Office."

"I know, Mom," Alan said. "I've been down in there more than you have." He was starting to get annoyed—or maybe just hungrier—and he motioned for me to head toward the lobby. "So what you got planned for dinner tonight, Mom? Apples again? How about apple pie? *A la mode* maybe?"

She smiled. "You guys can run over to MacGregor's when you get back and get a vegetable plate—but no starchy foods; we're not eating starches or sugars anymore," she said. "I'll give you money. I have to go to a special commissioners meeting in Newland tonight, and I don't know how long it'll last. The board's working on the county budget—it has to be adopted by July 1—and I think some Jonas Ridge people are concerned about some budget items and also about those wilderness study areas at Lost Cove and Harper Creek, where you guys went joy-riding Saturday and where you're taking pictures today. I think they're coming to the meeting tonight."

"But Jonas Ridge isn't in Avery County," Alan noted, overlooking her "joy-riding" remark. "It's in Burke County, isn't it?"

"Yes, you're right," Aunt Elaine said. "Most of what's considered Jonas Ridge *is* in Burke County, but some of it's in Avery County and some's in Caldwell County, too. Sometimes it's hard to figure out who to call when there's an emergency. Even I get confused."

"Yeah," Alan agreed. "Those three counties—Avery, Burke and Caldwell—come together on the top of Chestnut Mountain." For my benefit, he added, "That's the one next to Brown Mountain, Val. I noticed it last night when I was looking at a trail map."

Uh-oh, I thought. It certainly sounded to me as if Alan had already started planning a Brown Mountain Light expedition for us to go on. I was hoping—praying, really—that he hadn't planned it for that very night. I certainly wasn't prepared for an adventure of that type right then.

As we were leaving the newspaper building, Elaine followed us to the front door and called across the *Ledger*'s narrow but well-manicured lawn to the Blazer. "Now, Alan, don't spend too much time talking to Lacey," Elaine said. "You need to take those pictures and get the camera back to me before I leave for my meeting. I'll be here until six o'clock, and then I'll have to hurry over to Newland. So you be back here by six, OK?"

"OK, Mom," Alan replied. "We'll be back by six." He rolled down his window and threw up his left hand as we roared out of the parking lot and then took a left toward the heart of the old village. We passed the chestnut shingle-sided Eseeola Lodge on the left, then made a left turn onto Roseborough Road near a set of green-fenced, green clay-surfaced tennis courts. "Is that where Aunt Elaine and Sonny play tennis?" I asked.

"Maybe, but I'm not really sure," Alan replied. "I think those courts back there are connected somehow with the Linville Golf Club—over there."

Looking to the right, I saw what to me might as well have been the Pearly Gates themselves. It was the golf club's front entrance—twin ten-foot-high rock columns, each bearing a small bronze plaque that simply read "Linville Golf Club" in almost unreadably small lettering. Beyond the asphalt parking lot stood an imposing Tudor-style clubhouse, two stories tall, with its attractive wood-and-stucco exterior adorned by huge boxes and beds of colorful dahlias. I could hear the angels singing, though mere mortals might have mistaken the thwacking sound for that of golf balls being driven one after another on a practice range nearby. Sure enough, the club's range was on the left side of Roseborough Road and immediately across from the club entrance. I craned my neck to look through the Blazer's back glass at the range's teeing ground, which, like the clubhouse, was tastefully decorated with flower boxes bursting with all the colors of the rainbow. It wasn't the B.J., that was for sure.

"Nice, huh?" Alan asked, as we continued up the road, passing a couple of gated driveways and a blossom-adorned arbor gate leading to a walkway up the wooded hillside, all on the left side of the road. To the right, the terrain dropped away at an alarming rate, into what I later recognized as the Lost Cove and Harper Creek Wilderness Study Areas, where we had been two days earlier, as Elaine had noted. Not seeing that I had nodded in agreement, Alan repeated, "That sure was a nice-looking club, wasn't it?" We came to a stop at an intersection with the Blue Ridge Parkway. He looked left for approaching cars, then right and caught my eye as he checked for northbound traffic. "Wasn't it?"

"Heck yes," I said. "Is Sonny a member there?"

Alan shrugged as he gunned the Blazer across the Parkway onto Roseborough Road's unpaved continuation. "I'm not sure if he's a member or if he has some other connection, but I do think he's played there before. If you aren't a member or a guest of one, about the only way you can play that course is to stay at the Eseeola. I've heard you can play a round of golf for every night you stay there." He paused to gear down as the road surface abruptly turned from packed clay to loose gravel. The rocky road wound around a couple of blind curves before beginning its steep descent into the valley.

"You know what's funny?" Alan continued. "There's a big pond, well, a lake at the far end of the golf course. They call it Lake Kawana, like the place down on Harper Creek near where Lacey and her granddad live."

"Yeah, I saw something in the paper about a group called the Kawana Fishing Club or something," I said, "but I didn't read the whole article. I was going to ask you about it. So it's not the same Kawana?"

Alan shook his head. "Nah. Kawana's another one of those Indian names. I think it means 'duck' or something."

"You mean like, 'you'd better *duck*'?" I asked, "or 'quack-quack, it's a *duck*'?" I would have thrown in a Donald Duck laugh for good measure, but it was Bo who could do that, as well as decent Bugs Bunny, Elmer Fudd and Porky Pig impressions. Alan, of course, did Yogi Bear and, when he was in a particularly silly mood, Popeye and Wimpy. Then he would call me Olive Oyl until I slapped him. It was from watching too much cable TV—something else we didn't have at Grandpa's house. The only impersonation I had been able to do lately was of me, and I hadn't been doing it very well.

"A duck," Alan said. "Like with two wings. You know, *a l'orange*."

I laughed. "What is it with all these French terms?" I said. "But, really, how would Aunt Elaine and Sonny play tennis at the club if Sonny *isn't* a member?"

"I don't know that they do play there," Alan repeated.

I was determined to learn that Sonny was a club member and that he could open those Pearly Gates and lead me to the Promised Land, even if he *had* made a bad first impression on me the day before. Having not played a real round of golf in what seemed like ages, I wanted—no, I *needed*—someone, even someone with a questionable fashion sense like Sonny, to save me from this sorry state that I was in. No, not North Carolina, the greatest state in the whole U.S. of A. I was in a state of, oh, I don't know, confusion, maybe, or maybe it was shock, over what I had experienced my whole life.

Golf had redeemed my sense of self-worth back after Grandpa passed away, but then Grandma got sick, and I couldn't take the time away from her to play, especially when I needed to go to school and do homework and keep up the house and all. I had back-sliden, as far as playing golf was concerned, and no one had condemned me for it—not even Billy Joe. But now I had been set free and I had stood on the banks of the River Linville, and—yes, Lord!—I had seen the Land of Par and Birdie, where the big bad Bogeyman had been cast into Lake Kawana for a thousand years. Yes, I was in desperate need of salvation, and I knew my savior's name. It was Sonny. Of that I was sure. Or fairly sure, anyway.

Roseborough Road, the curvey graveled route we were taking down the mountain to Edgemont, was in good shape until we reached the actual Roseborough community about four miles from Linville. Then the way began to more closely resemble a rocky but well-traveled logging road, forcing us to slow down, especially for washouts and, in a couple of spots, fallen trees. According to a Wilson Creek Area map that Alan handed me, since leaving the pavement we had traveled along Rattlesnake Cliffs, around Sassafras Knob, and past Ned Mountain and Bee Mountain before running alongside Webb Creek to its confluence with Gragg Prong at Roseborough. The community appeared to be little more than a few summer cabins, some fishing shacks and a bit of pastureland but mainly just primitive camp sites.

Coming down the mountain we had caught glimpses through the dense foliage of two sets of spectacular cliffs across Lost Cove. When we reached a good pulloff spot, Alan parked so we could eat our apples and check the map.

Pointing at the map's topographic lines, he tried to show me that Lost Cove was basically a three-sided area formed by three long ridgelines. If the dark cove was seen as a triangle, its tips would point more or less toward Jonas Ridge to the southwest; Grandmother Mountain, with its huge blinking television transmission tower on the crest, to the northwest; and Brown Mountain to the southeast. The triangle's northeasterly face, with the Big Lost Cove Cliffs and Little Lost Cove Cliffs at the ends of their respective ridges, opened toward Grandfather Mountain, by far the highest peak within a ten-mile radius of where we sat there near Roseborough. Like the two sets of cliffs, there were two main bodies of water through the triangular cove—Lost Cove Creek and Little Lost Cove Creek. Those two creeks, along with the other creeks, branches and prongs in the larger area, ran into Wilson Creek at Edgemont, where we were headed, and then flowed past Mortimer and finally into the muddy John's River, Alan explained.

He said he had backpacked, biked and kayaked most of the Wilson Creek Area, and that Edgemont was his favorite place of all. When we got there a few minutes later, I saw why. Have you ever heard the word "glade" before? I looked it up in the dictionary when Alan and I finally got home that day, and that word best describes Edgemont, at least on the warm sunny day that I visited the isolated but inviting mountain community. Aunt Elaine's *American Heritage Dictionary* said "glade" means "an open space in a forest" and comes from the Middle English word for "glad" or "shining." That's Edgemont.

After creeping down and around all the rocky curves on Roseborough Road, with the roadbed cut into mountainsides and through tunnels of overhanging trees and rhododendron, suddenly seeing Edgemont with its wide sparkling creeks, acres of open pastureland and quaint frame buildings would make any weary traveler glad—mentally, physically and even spiritually glad—to have finally arrived at this remote place that looks every bit like civilization, right down to the small charcoal gray satellite TV dishes sprouting from the gutters and porch rails of tidy vacation cottages. Even on Alan's Wilson Creek Area map, Edgemont appeared to be an oasis within the Pisgah National Forest, as the hundred-year-old community's privately-owned lands were shown in white surrounded by the darker-tinted federal forestland.

Edgemont apparently existed where it did because of its location at the confluence of two—actually, three—good-sized creeks. From the road we could see where Rockhouse Creek ran into Lost Cove Creek less than a half mile before it flowed into the much larger Wilson Creek in the middle of Edgemont proper. Judging from the number of anglers we had photographed on the rocky creek banks along the way, Edgemont must have been a trout fisherman's paradise. Edgemont probably was a haven for hunters, too. We saw no hunters that day, as it was June 23 and hunting would not be in season for months; however, we *had* seen several deer—a buck and two does, I think—and even a red-gray fox, though it hadn't been nearly sly enough to avoid becoming fly-infested roadkill.

"Where we going now?" I asked. "Mortimer?"

"Not just yet," Alan replied. "I wanna stop at Coffey's Store. They've got all sorts of old pictures and historical stuff. And we can get something else to eat. That apple's already worn off."

Coffey's Store was less than a hundred yards ahead on the left, around enough of a curve to hide the two-story white frame building. A couple of cottages sat next to the store, and across the gravel road was a picnic area with shelters and tables along the rushing creek. "It *is* nice here," I said. "Where does this road go? Mortimer?"

"You've got the map, Sacagawea," Alan quipped. "No, Mortimer's back the other direction. If you keep going this way, you end up at a place called Gragg right below Grandfather Mountain. Why are you in such a hurry to get to Mortimer?"

"I didn't think I was," I said, folding the map as we parked directly in front of the store, which sat only about ten feet off the road. Its banner-like tin sign, appearing to be held up by a big red Coca-Cola cap on each end, stood high above the wooden double-doored entrance. "Want me to roll up my window and lock the door?" I asked.

There was only one other vehicle, a white Ford Explorer, in the small parking area along the road in front of the building. A pleasant-looking older gentleman sat on the porch bench, reading a newspaper and soaking up the sun's warmth. He lowered the paper and nodded to us as we got out of the Blazer.

Alan waved back. "No need to lock up," he told me. "We'll only be a minute. Come on." He skipped up the cement block steps to the uncovered front porch, then pushed open the side of the double doors that was already slightly ajar. Inside, I found that the store was something of a museum, filled mainly with artifacts from times past, including farm implements and a model whiskey still.

Alan pointed me toward a wall full of black-and-white photographs of Edgemont and Mortimer in their pre-Depression heydays. There were yellowed eight-by-ten pictures of trains and one huge trestle on that section of the Carolina & Northwestern Railroad line (sometimes called the Caldwell & Northern Railway), which had carried passengers to and from the inns in the resort area, as well as timber and supplies to and from Ritter Lumber Company, once the largest employer in the Wilson Creek area. Other photos were of the Depression-era Civilian Conservation Corps camp and the cotton mill, both at Mortimer; the Edgemont Inn and Mortimer's Laurel Inn; the most popular Wilson Creek swimming hole, called Crystal Pool; and, of course, flood photos from both 1916 and 1940. Apparently, what the earlier flood didn't destroy, the later one did.

"I heard that this building even got washed down the creek in the Forty flood," Alan explained, "but Mr. Coffey hauled it back so folks here would have their store and post office." He gestured toward the rear of the store, where an iron-barred postal window and no more than maybe forty mailboxes had been installed in the back wall. "I read that the train brought mail to Edgemont every other day until the train quit running around 1940," Alan added. "The old depot building is just up the road."

For sale in the store were soft drinks in a red three-foot-high, five-foot-long Coca-Cola ice chest and assorted snacks in display boxes on the counter next to the ancient brass-plated cash register. Alan had pulled a couple of Diet Snapple Lime Green Tea bottles from the refrigerated box and snatched up two packs of sunflower seeds. He paid for everything, then led me outside. As the door closed behind us, he apparently remembered his other reason for stopping at the store.

"Excuse me, sir," Alan addressed the man still seated on the porch bench. "Do you live around here?"

The man looked up from his reading. "In the summertime, I do," he said. "They anything I can help you with? You need directions somewhere?"

"No, we were just wondering about something," Alan said, hesitating a second. "We were wondering, have you ever seen the Brown Mountain Lights?"

The old gent smiled. "Oh, no, I never have, even though you hear a lot about them. And a lot of people sure do come around looking for them even yet. They was even some folks from Hollywood here not too long ago, to do a TV show. You're always hearing stories about the Lights and things folks has seen over that way, and some of them get pretty wild. But, no, I've never seen them myself. I think folks is just seeing things."

"TV show?" I asked, perking up. "Which one?"

"I'm not sure what its name was," the man replied, folding his newspaper on his lap. "It was one of them new stories that the kids is always watching, I think. I'm not one for those scary kinda shows. *Wheel of Fortune* and *Jeopardy*'s about all me and my wife watch of an evening. And *Touched by an Angel*, of course—never miss that."

"Well, thank you, sir," Alan said. "We were just curious." We both waved goodbye to the nice man and got back into the Blazer.

A few miles back down the road between Edgemont and Mortimer, Alan pulled over to the shoulder near a three-foot-high river rock sign at the entrance to a church called Greenlee Chapel. The driveway crossed Wilson Creek on a one-lane, plank bridge before disappearing into the distant trees. The sign's display area advertised services for "SUNDAY 11AM 6PM WED 7PM."

"There's a good-sized clearing over there, with a little white church and a cemetery and a pretty meadow," Alan said. "It's what all churches should look like, *I* think. Who needs a big fancy cathedral when you've got all this?" With his left elbow on the open side-window frame, he made a circular motion in the air to indicate the natural beauty that surrounded us.

"Are we going over there?" I asked, assuming that the chapel was the center of some community also hidden in the trees.

"No," he replied. "We don't ha—" He squinted through the side window, then through the windshield. "Did you see that?"

"What?"

"I'm not sure," he said. "Kind of a flash of light down in the creek on down the road. And I don't see another vehicle or anything."

"I didn't see anything," I said, straining to look past my cousin. "Maybe it was just the way the sun was bouncing off the water."

Alan nodded, then put the truck back into gear. "Yeah, you're right," he said. "Remember, that's what scientists say the Lights are—reflected, or, rather, refracted light—lights from Lenoir and Morganton that are bent and bounced around through heat vapors and water vapors." He pulled back onto the road. "But I don't know. That sure did look like something—like somebody was trying to signal us or something, with a mirror." He shook his head.

As we drove slowly on down the road, Alan continued to glance out his window, trying to catch a glimpse of anything in the creek that might have caused a reflection. Suddenly, he laughed out loud and hit the brake pedal a little harder than I thought was necessary. "What're you doing?" I asked, as we skidded to a stop. "Are you seeing things again?"

"Yeah," he replied, still shaking his head, though not in confusion this time. "I don't believe it. That's Lacey's granddad over there—old Buck Green—down in the creek. I think he's fishing, but he's just standing there at the edge of the water looking down at his hunting knife. That must have been the flash I saw."

"So?" I said. "What's so strange about that—I mean, about Mr. Green fishing in the creek?"

Alan shrugged. "Well, for starters, the fishing is just as good, if not better, over where they live—you know, in Harper Creek and both Lost Cove creeks. And the other thing is, it's at least three miles from their cabin to here, and that's as the crow flies. It's hard to believe he'd walk three miles one way just to go fishing here when he could catch bigger trout near his house."

"How do you know he walked?"

"He had to walk," Alan explained. "Lacey takes the truck to work up at the lodge, and I know she wouldn't drive all the way over here to drop him off before she goes in. It's too far out of the way. Besides, how would he get home?"

"Why don't you go ask him?" I said, offering my cousin the camera. "And you can get a picture of him fishing while you're at it."

Alan shook his head. "Huh-uh, not me. Old Buck is kinda like the Amish; he doesn't like to have his picture taken. He made a big stink about it at the lodge a couple months ago when Sonny wanted to take pictures of employees for an ad he was running in the *Ledger*. I think it was something from back when Buck got in trouble with the law for moonshining—you know, back in the day. He said he didn't want the law to have a picture of him."

"You're kidding," I said.

"Nope. And if you don't believe me, why don't *you* go try to take his picture yourself." Alan grinned. "Tell you what. I'll give you my Snapple *and* my bag of sunflower seeds if you can get his picture. Deal?"

"You're on," I replied and hopped out of the vehicle.

"Remember," Alan hissed, as I crossed in front of the truck and walked toward the creekbank. "You gotta get his permission first. That's the *Ledger*'s rules."

I waved him off and kept moving toward old Buck Green, who, as Alan had said, seemed to be preoccupied with his hunting knife, the big folding kind that was generally carried in a sheath on the belt. Though he was standing knee-deep in the creek, Buck appeared to be taller than Alan, probably around six-foot-six. The elderly man was dressed in the green pants and matching green shirt that workmen often preferred, especially yard workers. His clothes hung loosely on him, as if he had recently lost weight. I couldn't see his hair color or length or if, in fact, he had any hair at all, because his head was covered by a green-and-yellow John Deere cap, and he was looking down. But even from where I stood, I could see that his skin was tanned a leathery reddish-brown, apparently from a long hard life of working outdoors.

I could have sworn that Alan had said a couple of days earlier that the old man had wild hair and a wild beard, but Buck obviously was clean-shaven and couldn't have had too much hair under that cap.

"Mr. Green!" I shouted, turning on the digital camera and taking off its lens cover as I waited for his response. He didn't look up. "Mr. Green!" I called again. Still, he didn't acknowledge my presence on the bank, though I couldn't have been more than twenty yards away from him. As Alan had noted, the tall old man was doing something with his knife, and either he couldn't hear me above the rushing stream or he didn't want to let me know that he had heard me.

I was preparing to shout his name a third time and maybe even ask if something was wrong when he abruptly turned his back to me and waded out of the creek. Surprisingly nimble for an elderly fellow, he climbed the bank and lumbered off toward the place where the chapel driveway disappeared into the woods. There, just beyond the treeline, I could see a large cream-and-tan lawn tractor parked to one side of the dirt road.

"Where's he going?" asked Alan, still seated in the truck. "You get his picture?"

"No," I replied, as I walked back to the Blazer. "He wouldn't even look at me."

"Did you ask to take his picture?"

"No," I said, getting back in and buckling up. "I told you, he wouldn't even look at me. It was like we were in two different worlds or something."

Alan snorted. "Well, you should've just spoken up and said, 'Hey, old man, what's the matter with you? You deaf or something? I'm gonna take your picture, OK?' What was he doing, anyway?"

"I don't know. But he wasn't fishing. It looked like he was whittling something or maybe cleaning something with that big knife of his. I couldn't really tell what he was doing in the creek, but I think he's working over at the church back there. And after what you said about him, I was kinda scared to just snap his picture, even if he *is* Lacey's grandpa."

"Yeah, he's a strange bird," Alan said. "But that's OK. We'll run over to Mortimer and get plenty of pictures of people camping and stuff. About the only thing in Mortimer nowadays is a campground run by the park service where the old Civilian Conservation Corps camp used to be. Old folks around here call it the C.C. camp. We should be able to get a bunch of pictures for Mom there."

As the Blazer roared down the gravel road toward Mortimer, Alan and I cracked the tops of our Snapple bottles and bit pour-holes in our long narrow cellophane bags of sunflower seeds. "By the way," I said, "if I *had* gotten that picture, would you have *really* given me your drink?"

My cousin took a long draught of the cool greenish nectar, finishing it with a flourish and then tipping the top of the empty bottle at me. "Sure I would have," he said, with a wink, "but I didn't think you'd get it—the picture, I mean."

"Why not?"

He chuckled. "Because I figured Buck would ignore you, and I figured you'd be too scared to just take the picture anyway, especially not without his permission, which he'd never give you. That's the way he is. About the only people he talks to anymore are Lacey and Miss Faye—you know, Sonny's mom. He won't even talk to me. He just kinda grunts when he can't avoid me altogether. Lacey's afraid it's

Alzheimer's or something like that, but I think he's just a mean old coot and he doesn't like strangers. Sonny told Mom the other day that Buck's getting meaner and meaner when he comes to mow the grass at the campground. And for some reason Buck's started clipping the heads off Sonny' s flowers before they even bloom all the way. And he started mowing off hostas with the push mower. So Sonny won't let him do any trimming anymore. All they let him do is ride that big old mower Sonny keeps at the campground—not the new John Deere Sonny bought last spring; the *old* one that was old Preacher Rose's."

"What kind of mower?" I asked, remembering the lawn tractor parked in the chapel driveway.

Alan shrugged. "I'm not sure. It's kinda brown and white, and it's really big for a riding mower—more like a tractor, I guess. The company's logo is a wild horse, I think, 'cause there's one on the side and on the front, kinda like the horse logo on a Ferrari, you know, a stallion rearing up on its hind legs. Same as on my Iron Horse bike. Know what I mean?"

I nodded. "Yeah, that's a White tractor—the company's name, not the color. Billy Joe—I mean, the golf course where I worked back home—it had one we mowed the fairways with. They aren't fancy, but they're tough."

"Sounds like you know a lot about mowers," Alan said.

"Yeah, I guess," I said. "You know, I think that was the tractor I saw back there in the woods near the church. I'm pretty sure it was a White, like the one you said Sonny has."

"Really? Back there at the church?" Pursing his lips, Alan slowly shook his head as the picture of what Buck was doing became clear. "I don't believe it. Buck must've driven Sonny's mower all the way down the mountain. That's about the only way he could've gotten it down here. It's three miles or so on the trails, but it's probably three times that far by the road. I wonder if Sonny knows what Buck's doing. Probably not."

Alan reached for his cell phone and checked to see if he had service. "Stupid cell phone," he fumed. "May as well not have one. If you have to stand on top of a mountain to get a signal, what good is it?" He tossed the phone down between our seats and then gripped the steering wheel with both hands, still shaking his head. "Man oh man, this is gonna cause a stink," he said finally. "But Sonny—and Lacey—need to know what's going on."

"What's the big deal?" I asked. "So he rode a lawn mower down the mountain to mow the grass at a church."

"Well, number one," Alan began, "he isn't supposed to be going off by himself like that, not without somebody to keep an eye on him—not this far from home, anyway. Number two, I don't think Sonny would have told him he could do it, so he's basically stealing the mower. And, number three, don't you think it's a little crazy to do something like that to begin with? Wouldn't it worry you if your granddad, who was a gazillion years old, rode off on a lawn mower to cut a little patch of grass somewhere way off in the middle of nowhere? It would only take a few minutes to cut the grass around the church, and I bet it took him a couple hours, at least, to ride the mower down here. Now *that's* crazy."

I had no idea why I was sympathizing with old Buck Green, but I couldn't help but defend him. "Maybe not," I said. "We don't know the whole story, Alan. Maybe he got permission, or maybe someone hauled him and the mower down here. Maybe it's all OK, and we just don't know what's going on. Maybe *he's* OK."

Alan glanced at me, then turned his attention back to the road ahead. "*You're* the one who doesn't know what's going on, Val," he said. "Let's take a few pictures at Mortimer and then get back up the mountain to Sonny's. I'm gonna find out what Buck's doing down here. You can bet on that."

As we drove on, I could tell that, for some reason, Alan was in no mood for teasing or even for casual conversation, as he was taking this development with old Buck Green as seriously as I had ever seen him take anything. We followed the graveled road to Mortimer and parked at the old white frame C.C.C. building to take pictures of vacationers in the adjacent federally-managed recreation area, a Spartan campground with pit toilets. Alan was still in a bad mood even then, getting all bent out of shape because someone had just cut the grass around the building but hadn't raked up the long wet grass clippings. He fussed to himself and shook his head as he used a yellowed sheet of newsprint from a nearby garbage can to clean his soggy shoes. It was as if my normally easy-going cousin knew something that I didn't.

NINE

By the time we arrived at the lodge and campground near Jonas Ridge that afternoon, Alan had calmed down a bit—just a bit. He had fallen quiet after only a few minutes back on the road; however, I knew he was still angry with Buck, because he drove the Blazer faster than he should have on the rocky winding road through the dark forest up the mountain, and he didn't bother to point out any interesting waypoints, as was his usual practice.

The roadway we traveled from Mortimer, then back to Edgemont, then up the mountain to Jonas Ridge actually had two names. At Edgemont, it was called Pineola Road, for the larger community situated just beyond Jonas Ridge toward Linville. At Jonas Ridge, where the dusty old graveled thoroughfare T-intersected with the wide smoothly-paved main highway, the road was called Mortimer Road, for what had once been the largest and most prosperous of the several communities in the valleys and coves immediately below. On our way back toward Edgemont and the Pineola Road intersection, Alan had turned at Greenlee Chapel and driven across the creek bridge to the church, but neither Buck nor the tractor had been anywhere to be seen or heard. All that had greeted us there was the sight and scent of freshly-mown grass.

Finally back in Jonas Ridge at least thirty minutes later, we turned left at the post office, then drove past the store on the right, with its large covered front porch sporting wooden picnic tables and rocking chairs for weary motorists and cyclists, and the library down the road on the left. As I've already said, the library—an old school building—was the most impressive edifice in Jonas Ridge, the two-story structure made of fieldstones colored the many shades of brown. It sat back off the main highway beyond a paved parking lot with about a dozen spaces and beyond a tidy green lawn. The lush grass was split by a white concrete walkway encircling a rock monument of some sort at the base of a thirty-foot-tall flagpole proudly flying the Stars 'n' Stripes in the cool mountain breeze.

As Alan drove through the community, I noticed that the homes there came in all shapes, sizes and sidings, from wood, stone and brick to plastic-vinyl, asbestos-shingle and cement-stucco, and that they popped up every so often for a mile or so, until we reached the southeastern end of the ridge. There the white-frame cross-shaped Cold Springs Bible Church with its tall steeple and gray-markered graveyard sat alone on a knoll overlooking the foothills and flatlands off the mountain. For a Monday afternoon in late June, the community was surprisingly quiet, I thought, as we had seen only a couple of vehicles at the post office, maybe one Winnebago and a motorcycle or two at the store, and also a single vehicle—a gold Buick LaSabre—at the library.

Barkhouse Lodge, a two-story chestnut-shingled structure on the crest of a low hill off the highway a couple of miles south of Cold Springs Bible Church, was a smaller version of Linville's Eseeola Lodge—or, at least, that was what Sonny had set out to create several years earlier when he had bought the building and renovated it for year-round tourist lodging. He had considered calling the resort "Jellystone Park" but had decided against it after being told that an old dwelling named the Barkhouse had, in fact, once stood nearby.

The lodge itself stood just beyond the entrance to a fifteen-acre compound which included a paved nine-space parking lot immediately behind the main building; a "Ranger Station" beyond the parking lot; and a modern campground with full hookups and pumping facilities for six recreational vehicles, as well as another dozen campsites for tents and pickup-mounted campers toward the rear of the property. A narrow one-way paved road followed the compound's perimeter, cut-across by one paved street-lighted avenue for the RVs, of course, and by two humble graveled lanes for the other, less-privileged section of the campground.

Though he was in a hurry to see Sonny, Alan drove all the way around the property to give me a quick tour—or to look for Sonny out back, since we hadn't seen his black Mustang parked behind the lodge, just Lacey's little LUV truck. The campground was maybe half full, with all but one RV space taken and five or six tents of different sizes and shapes set up in the netherlands. Alan parked the Blazer in a space next to the Ranger Station, across the lot behind the lodge, and activated the door locks and security system with his keychain fob. He waved for me to follow him into the building. "Come on, Val," he said. "Sonny's probably inside." He headed for a brown-painted metal door marked "Rangers Only" on the far right side of the station.

Sure enough, Sonny was inside the rough-sided forest-green wood-frame building, which served on one end as a maintenance garage for Buck Green, the compound's groundskeeper; in the middle as a bathhouse, restrooms and laundry for campground occupants; and on the other end as a plate-glass-windowed museum of "classic" cars, specifically vehicles that Sonny had personally customized to look like famous autos, mostly from classic television shows. The cars sat behind trios of large display windows on opposite sides of the building's end that was nearest to the entrance driveway into the campground. Since three different cars could be viewed from outdoors on each side, no one but Sonny and his personal guests were allowed inside the showroom.

On the front side as we had driven past, I had immediately recognized the "law and order" theme of the three cars on display there: the 1994 white Ford Bronco that we had seen Sunday; a carefully dinged and dented 1974 Dodge Monaco police cruiser painted and outfitted like the *Bluesmobile* ("On a mission from God"); and, Sonny's pride and joy, an orange-red 1969 Dodge Charger with "01" in black numerals with white trim on each side—yes, a replica of the famed *General Lee*, with its whiplike CB radio antenna and annoying "Dixie" horn, from *The Dukes of Hazzard* TV show.

I had a more difficult time seeing the pop-culture connections in the cars on the opposite side until I read the information signs next to them: in the first bay, the red-and-white 1960 Chevrolet Corvette Shark from *Route 66*; in the next space, Sonny's black Mustang convertible, incorrectly identified as the 1971 Dodge Challenger convertible from *The Mod Squad*; and, finally, Aunt Elaine's 1963 sunroof-model VW Beetle. The sign next to the Beetle identified it as *Herbie the Love Bug*. As soon as I saw that sign, I could feel my neck and face starting to flush. *Herbie the Love Bug*?

In the middle of taping the windows and chrome so that he could paint the car white, install "53" decals on the doors and hood, along with a red-white-and-blue racing stripe, Sonny didn't bother to stop when we walked in, as if he were in a big hurry to finish. He was wearing bluejeans and a black "Dale Earnhardt" T-shirt, a contradiction I found hard to fathom, since Earnhardt had driven a Chevy and Sonny had given every indication of being a Ford man. "Howdy, guys," Sonny greeted. "What'd ya think—about *Herbie*?"

I chose to ignore the question, as I was still a bit miffed over Sonny getting *my* car from Aunt Elaine. My cousin, however, spoke right up. "Looking good, Sonny," Alan replied. "Mom really likes driving the Challenger. Says it makes her feel cool, like Julie Barnes. I think the word she used was 'groovy.'"

"Julie Barnes?" I asked. "Who's she?"

Sonny laughed. "You know," he said. "Julie—Peggy Lipton—on *Mod Squad*. Oh, I don't guess you've ever seen that old show, huh? That was back before you were even born—back when Elaine and I were kids." He laughed again. "Alan, I guess that makes you Pete, the spoiled rich boy, and your buddy, Lionel, is Linc Hayes. And you could be Julie, Val. So what *case* are you on today, guys?"

"Well, as a matter of fact," Alan began, "we were wondering if you're missing anything—like a lawn mower, maybe? We were just down at Edgemont and Mortimer getting some pictures for the paper, and we saw Buck Green down there with a tractor that looked like yours—you know, the White. I didn't see it; Val did. But her description sounded like it was yours."

"Yeah, that was mine," Sonny confirmed. "I was wondering where he went off to on it. Dang! Near Edgemont?"

"Yeah," Alan said, "he was mowing over at Greenlee Chapel—well, actually, he was standing in the creek working on something with his knife when we saw him, but Val saw the mower over near the church and the grass had been mowed. You gonna go after him?"

Sonny shook his head. "I don't *think* so. Old Buck may be old, but he'd kick my butt all over creation if we ran into each other right now—after what happened this morning. He was so aggravated with me that I wasn't about to stop him when he rode off on the tractor. I just figured he'd ride up the road a ways—maybe up to Mama's house on Gingercake—and come back later on after I go into town for the commissioners meeting. Lacey said she'll hold things down until I get back tonight, and, anyway, she's Buck's ride home since he can't drive. But dang! Edgemont, you say? I wonder where he got the gas to get that far—unless he used some of his moonshine."

"Wait a second," Alan interjected. "You're going to the meeting tonight?" I could see the wheels spinning in my cousin's head as he came up with an alternative plan to the one Elaine had given us. "Mom wanted us to pick up your column and save you a trip to the office, but since you're going in anyway, you can give it to her when you see her at the meeting, and we can hang around here and help Lacey watch the place. OK?"

With a knowing smile, Sonny agreed. "Sure," he said, "and I'll take the camera to your mama for you, too. We talked a while ago, and she figured you'd be in a *helpful* mood when you heard Lacey was gonna be here by herself." Alan blushed a bit but didn't seem to mind too much that his intentions had been so transparent. "And, Valerie, I've got a favor to ask of you, too," Sonny continued. "Elaine said you'd probably be glad to help me out." He hesitated and glanced at Alan, as if his request were somewhat sensitive.

"What?" I asked. "What you need?" I didn't like being called Valerie, but I didn't correct him.

"Well," Sonny said, "I need someone to stay with Mama tonight while I'm away. She's over at the library now, but after closing she'd be home by herself 'til I get back from the meeting, and I don't really want her to be alone—not tonight, anyway."

"Why not?" Alan said. "Is it Buck? You worried about Buck bothering Miss Faye?"

This time it was Sonny who blushed. "Well, matter of fact, yeah, I am," he admitted, "after our little to-do this morning." He paused, this time to glance out a window toward the lodge where Lacey was on duty in the office area, which doubled as the camp store. "Lacey dropped him off here this morning on her way into town—she was going into town to pick up some things for me—and Buck was piddling around here, waiting for her to get back and take him home for lunch. Well, I made the mistake of asking him to sit in the office and call me on the two-way radio if anybody came in and needed something. Just sit in the office and call me—that's all he had to do."

Sonny finished with the last strip of tape on the VW and then started picking up his tools and trash from the showroom floor as he finished his story. "Well, it wasn't ten minutes, and here comes this old lady running out of the office just screaming and yelling about some wild man in the store. She and her old man were in the big purple bus that *was* parked down on the end of the lane there—until this morning."

At this point, Alan started chuckling, as he apparently had figured out the end of Sonny's tale. "Yes indeedy," Sonny said, "old Buck had scared the ever-livin' daylights out of that old lady, and they pulled out of here in, I don't know, it must've been five minutes flat. I couldn't get 'em to hang around long enough to sort out what had happened exactly."

"What *did* happen?" I asked.

Sonny shook his head. "Well, apparently, Buck was sitting there in the office—like I'd asked him to—and he was whittling on a piece of wood with that big old knife of his, which is what he's always doing when he's bored. Matter of fact, he whittles all the little knickknacks we sell in the store—all kinds of little animals, gee-haw-whimmy-diddles, stuff like that—and he even whittles golf tees sometimes, Valerie, even though he uses 'em in those little peg-board IQ puzzles—you know, where you jump the pegs until just one's left to show how smart you are?"

When Sonny saw that I had no idea what he was talking about, he continued, "So Buck's sitting there whittling, and the camper lady walks into the store there next to the office, and apparently Buck decides to jump up and see if he could help her find whatever she was looking for." Sonny paused to shake his head again. "Now, just imagine—just picture in your mind—old Buck Green with all that wild hair and that wild beard and those sweaty old work clothes *and that big old knife of his* coming for you. Now, he *tried* to call me on the radio when the lady went into the store; he really did try to do what I asked. But I think what he said over the radio was, 'I'll git her,' and he said it really mean-like and loud, like he wasn't too happy about having his whittling interrupted or something. That must've been what scared the pee-doodie out of that lady, and off she went."

Something, however, about Sonny's story didn't make sense to me. "Wait a second," I said. "I got a pretty good look at Mr. Green down at Edgemont a little white ago, and he didn't have wild hair *or* a beard."

"I *know* he didn't," Sonny explained, "because while I was fussing at him for scaring the wits out of that lady in the store, I kinda lit into him for letting himself go—you know, for looking like such a wild man, like a crazy Moses or John the Baptist or some such wild man like that who just came outta the wilderness or something."

"He *did* just come out of the wilderness," Alan observed. I got the idea that Alan wasn't entirely sympathetic with the position Sonny had taken toward Buck and that Alan had changed his mind about being angry with the old man.

"Yeah, but I can't have him scaring off my customers," Sonny replied. "And, besides, he *has* been acting kinda loony lately—around here, anyway. You know he started cutting the heads off my flowers, and he keeps doing it, even though I tell him and tell him I don't want him to do any trimming. I even lock up the clippers so he can't use them. But he just reaches out and pinches the heads off as he rides by on the mower. Claims it's good for them. But he doesn't do that at Mama's. It's just pure-dee-ole meanness, I think. Or Alzheimer's. That's all I can figure, anyway."

"But he got mad because you fussed at him?" Alan asked.

"No, he got mad because I told him he was gonna clean himself up if he thought he was gonna keep working here," Sonny said, "and if he wanted to keep doing chores over at Mama's house for me. *That* was what really stuck in his craw, I guess, when I said I didn't want some crazy-looking old coot hanging around my mama's house."

I didn't think that was a very nice thing for Sonny to say to Mr. Green, but I certainly understood Sonny's protectiveness of his mother. For that matter, Aunt Elaine had acted the same way with Grandma after Grandpa's death, back when Billy Joe had come around the house at Village Point whenever Elaine happened to be there. "Who cut his hair?" I asked, remembering Mr. Green's cleanshaven appearance when I had seen him in the creek near Edgemont.

"*I* did," Sonny replied matter-of-factly. "When Lacey got back, she got him calmed down long enough for me to go get those old handshears my daddy used to use on me back when I was a boy, back in the Sixties when everybody had a crewcut—back before the Beatles were on *Ed Sullivan*. Lacey can make him behave. So I gave him a good haircut and cut his beard short enough so he could shave the rest off with a safety razor. And when he came out of the restroom there, he sure enough *did* look like a different man, and I guess that's why I said that about not wanting some crazy-looking old coot hanging around Mama's—because he didn't look like a crazy old coot anymore, and I was *glad* he didn't. You know I'm kinda fond of him, the old moonshiner."

"Man, Sonny," Alan said, shaking his head. "You know how he is, though. So that's when he took off?"

"Yeah, he bolted out the door and headed straight for the garage to get the tractor. Like I said, I figured he was headed toward Mama's to mow, since that must've been why he sat still long enough for me to cut his hair. I think he *is* kinda sweet on her. I've never let him drive the mower on the highway; I always haul it over there on the trailer and drop it off on my way wherever I'm going so it'll be waiting when he and Lacey get there later. But I figured it'd be OK, and he'd maybe blow off some steam. And, besides, I knew Mama was over at the library all day, so she wouldn't be at her house for him to bother while he was there mowing. Least, that's what I thought."

"Did he say anything as he was driving off on the mower?" Alan asked.

"Yeah," Sonny said. "I yelled and asked where he thought he was going, and he yelled back, 'Fer me to know and you'uns to find out.' Then when he was a good ways up the road, he turned around and started pointing at his head and yelling something about giving *me* a haircut when he got back. All I could make out were the words 'return the dang favor.' I *think* that was what he kept yelling. I don't know, maybe it was 'return the dang mower.' You know how he sounds without his teeth in. Well, anyway, Lacey said not to worry about him, so I didn't."

"Well, are you worried now?" Alan said. "You want Val and me to take the trailer back down the mountain and look for him? I've got a hitch on the Blazer. We could haul the tractor back up here for you."

Sonny shook his head. "No, you stay here with Lacey and wait for Buck to get back on his own. He's probably on the Greentown Trail, and you wouldn't be able to get close to him, anyway. That's the shortest route between here and Edgemont, not to mention it runs close to Buck's place. I bet the old boy's mowing the grass around his cabin, too, while he's at it—don't you think? Getting the most bang for his buck, I guess." Sonny smiled nervously as he turned to me. "And, Valerie, if it's OK, I'll drop you off at the library on my way to the commissioners meeting. You can ride back to Mama's house with her and wait there 'til I get back. It'll only be a couple hours—I hope. That OK?"

"Sure," I replied. Despite the inconvenience, I was looking forward to talking with Miss Faye, who reminded me more than a bit of Grandma. Miss Faye had seemed nice the day before at the Singing on the Mountain. I certainly didn't mind helping the nice widow lady out, especially if it meant that her son would be in my debt. Then he might feel as if he owed me something. Something like, hmm, maybe a round of golf. At Linville Golf Club, maybe? To answer the inevitable question about my character, no, I wasn't above finagling my way into a place that I had begun to see as nirvana, heaven on earth, my fairway of dreams, my own private Iowa. The golf gods would understand my yearning and bless me for my charitable spirit. I just hoped that Sonny would, too, with a guest tee time at his club.

TEN

I didn't get to see much of the Barkhouse Lodge itself before Sonny took me to the Jonas Ridge Library to stay with Miss Faye, but what I did see there sparked in me a grudging respect for Sonny Rose as a businessman and entrepreneur. He certainly was no Billy Joe, as both the lodge and campground were models of good taste (the *General Lee* notwithstanding) and efficiency. There was little wasted space anywhere on the compound, unless you counted the classic TV car museum, though it effectively served as Sonny's garage, because he regularly drove all of the vehicles, Alan said, especially the white Bronco in the winter.

The floorplan of the lodge proper was a marvel of economy. From the rear parking lot, the back door opened into the camp store, which occupied the middle rear of the chestnut-shingled building. Besides Buck's wooden toys, the store shelves held mainly staple foods for campers; basic camping and backpacking supplies; and trail maps of the area. At the front of the lodge, the store narrowed into an office area, with a long polished reddish-orange pine counter that separated the office from the small lobby just inside the front entrance, a heavy oak door with window panels, and a thick black wrought-iron handle and knocker on the outside.

The lodge contained six units, all with their own bathrooms and all accessed from an interior hall that ran to the left and right off the store and lobby. The units include two fairly large rooms, one at each end of the hallway, each with a queen-sized bed, sitting area and fireplace; three mid-sized rooms with full-sized beds and smaller sitting areas; and one tiny room, not much larger than a walk-in closet, that held only a single bed and small dresser. The only king-sized bed in the lodge was upstairs in Sonny's apartment, which was reached by a stairway that began just beyond the lobby and rose above the shelves on one side of the store.

Alan said he had never seen Sonny's apartment, though Aunt Elaine had told him it was spacious and nicely decorated, unlike what you might expect from an old bachelor. Alan added that Lacey often used the single room in the winter when the roads were too snowy or icy for her to get back home or when Sonny wanted her to work overnight. The only bad thing about the single, Alan said, was that it was the only unit without a color television. I wanted to ask my cousin when he had spent enough time in the room to miss watching television, but I figured I'd better mind my own business. What he and Lacey did was their own affair, so to speak.

It made me wonder, though, if I was being left behind, what with both Alan and Elaine having such close friends with whom to share their lives. I had Bo, but he was busy with music camp and would be going back home—to *my* old home at Village Point—in just a couple of weeks, and, besides, we were just best friends, not lovers, despite what some people assumed when they saw us together. I had to remember to call Bo at nine o'clock that night, as he had asked in the note he had left on the Blazer's windshield that morning at the university. With my luck, he would be out late with some girl and miss my call because he'd have his cell phone turned off.

I didn't speak to Lacey that afternoon at the lodge other than to say a quick "hi." While Sonny was upstairs changing into his Sunday duds, the same outfit he had worn to the Singing, Lacey had her hands full with a couple of potential guests, a handsome young man and his pretty wife, who wanted to check in but were insisting on seeing each of the three available mid-sized rooms before deciding on one to rent for one night. They wanted a room with an unobscured view of Brown Mountain to the east-southeast, I heard the man say. They didn't believe Lacey when she told them none of the rooms faced that direction and that Brown Mountain wasn't visible from the lodge.

Despite the extra trouble, though, Lacey remained polite and patient as she worked with the pair. Alan was the one who appeared aggravated, as if the pushy couple were cutting in on his time with Lacey—which, of course, they *were*. Growing more impatient with each passing minute, Alan was seated near the cash register with his elbows on the counter and his face in his hands when Sonny and I headed out the lodge's back door—the store entrance—toward the garage.

"Alan's got it bad, huh?" Sonny said, with a smile.

I nodded. "Yeah, I guess."

"Guess, nothing," he quipped. "I wouldn't be at all surprised to hear those two were engaged before long."

"You think?" I asked.

"Wouldn't be surprised a bit," Sonny repeated, as we walked across the parking area. "Alan's over here all the time—when Lacey's working, anyway."

"You mind?"

"No, not at all," he replied. "Alan's a good guy, and Lacey's a good girl. I'm fond of both of them. Matter of fact, I kinda think of Lacey almost like a daughter, you know? She's something special, and I'm glad she's found somebody who's crazy about her and treats her right. I hope they get married and have bunches of kids, so I can play grandpa and spoil all of them." He opened the "Rangers Only" door for me, then stepped inside and locked it behind himself.

"Why don't you have kids of your own?" I asked, trying not to sound impudent with what I thought was an obvious question. He seemed to like young people, and he was, after all, a teacher.

Sonny motioned toward the red-and-white Corvette. "That one," he said. "Haven't had it out lately." Like a true gentleman, he opened the car door for me and closed it softly but firmly behind me, seeming to listen carefully to the solid *chunk* the door latch made. "Love that sound," he said. "It's like a good forehand on the tennis court or the sound a golf ball makes when it drops in the cup. You know *that* sound, right?"

I smiled and nodded, though I didn't fail to notice that he had slickly evaded my question about his paternal instincts. Still, I didn't press him for an answer, as he had pushed me the previous day at the Singing when he had asked about my plans for the future.

Pressing a button on his keychain fob, Sonny opened the garage door at the end of the building, then carefully backed the Corvette outside. Though I had ridden in many convertibles, especially those owned by my rich teammates at the beach, I had never been in a 'Vette before, with or without the top down. Sonny, however, handled the sportscar on the winding highway up the mountain as if he were a racer on a superspeedway. Even though I was strapped into my bucket seat,

I couldn't help but tense up all over and clench the seat as we swerved around curves and rocketed up the road toward Jonas Ridge.

Sonny didn't say anything for the first mile; he seemed to be listening intently to the roar of the engine. Then, after a small but satisfied nod, he glanced at me when we reached the summit, where the highway passed Cold Springs Bible Church and straightened for the home stretch through the small community's residential section. "I would've liked to have had kids," he said, apparently assuming I remembered my earlier question, "but it wasn't meant to be."

"Why not?" I asked.

He glanced at me again. "Oh, I don't know," he began. "I thought about adopting, but back when I was seriously thinking about fatherhood—back before Daddy died—it was next to impossible for a single guy to adopt a child."

"Why didn't you get married?" I asked. Now, I know what you're thinking, and, yes, the little voice in my head was saying the same thing right then in answer to my question. But I had learned a long time before that there are just some questions you don't ask someone you don't know all that well—someone you're hoping to be invited to play golf with at his fancy exclusive club.

This time Sonny didn't look over at me before replying. "You really want to know?" he said, turning the question back on me. "I'll tell you—if you really want to know." When I couldn't bring myself to say anything right away, he continued, "I mean, it isn't something I'm ashamed of, Valerie, and it isn't some deep dark secret I'm hiding from everybody. It isn't anything like that. My daddy knew about it before he died. Mama knows about it. So does Elaine—and Alan, too, for that matter."

"That's OK," I said finally. "I'll just talk to them later on."

"Talk to them later on?" he said, acting confused. "If you want to know, why not just let me tell you right now? You aren't afraid to talk about *this kind of thing*, are you?"

"*No*," I said sharply, but for some reason then added, "What kind of thing?"

Sonny laughed. "Human reproduction. You asked me why I don't have kids of my own." By this time we were pulling into a space in the library lot, and I was becoming exasperated with him again, as I had been the previous day, invitation to play golf or not. "So you want to know?" he asked again, making no move to get out of the car.

"Yes," I said evenly. "I want to know."

He grinned, having suckered me into demanding to know the truth. "The mumps," he said, apparently knowing full well what I had been expecting him to say. "I caught the mumps when I was doing my student teaching. I'd got permission to come back home and student teach here at the old elementary school—Mama was still teaching then—and what happens, but I had to go and catch the dang mumps from one of the little rats that didn't have all her shots. Her family wasn't well-off, but still...."

He suddenly grew more serious. "The doctor said it could make me sterile, and so I went and had all the tests, and, yeah, it turned out I couldn't have kids. So I guess that kinda affected my relationships with women—when they found out I couldn't give them babies. Or maybe it was just me. Maybe I let it bother *me* too much, so I didn't give anybody a chance." He had been staring through the windshield at the old school building as he talked, but when he had finished his explanation, he looked me square in the eye. "Is that what you thought I was gonna say, Valerie?"

"Call me Val, Sonny," I said, stalling for time.

"OK, Val-Sonny," he said. "Is that the story you were expecting?"

I just shook my head. "Well, no, not really," I said. "Actually, I thought you were gonna say you're gay." There, I said it. It was out in the open.

To my surprise, he laughed again, this time bigger than before, but it wasn't a joyful laugh; it seemed to be more of bemusement. "Val, I never said I was or wasn't, 'cause it really doesn't matter, does it? I mean, good gracious, I love my mama and take good care of her, and I love my friends and most of my students—except the snotty ones who call me a 'fag' under their breath the first time they get mad about a grade or something. That's the first thing out of their dirty mouths. And I try my best, my dead-level best, to be a good person. I love to sing for folks, and I love being a good Christian and giving out Bibles and leading the singing at church. And I love writing my column and playing tennis with your aunt and running the lodge and doing every dad-gum thing I do.

"And, most of all, I try not to hurt *anybody*, even though I know I stick my foot in my mouth a lot of times. I mean, I don't just wear one of those little bracelets that say, 'What Would Jesus Do?'; I ask myself that question *constantly*, and I try my very best to live by the answer I hear." He paused to catch his breath. "So what possible difference could it make whether I'm gay or not? Surely you don't really care."

I said nothing at first. We just kind of looked at each other as we sat there in that beautiful car on that cool mountain afternoon. He was waiting for me to get out so he could continue on up the road to Linville for dinner with Elaine and then to Newland, where the commissioners meeting was to be held that evening, but I just sat there. In the middle of Sonny's soliloquy, Miss Faye had come to the library door and was standing there waiting for me to join her. Sonny had waved cordially to her without slowing his speech one bit. I guess it was a speech he was accustomed to giving to nosy friends and overbearing family members.

"Surely you don't care," Sonny repeated. "Surely not." The pleading look on his face was one I had seen before. I'd seen it on Billy Joe, whenever he was disappointed in my behavior for whatever reason, and on Grandpa's face, whenever, not just me, but any of us—me or Alan or Aunt Elaine or even Grandma—failed to measure up to his high expectations. I got the impression that a lot of people disappointed Sonny. And I think that was when I started to fall in love with him, in the same way that all of his other friends—or anyone who truly knew him—seemed to love him, despite his foibles. "Surely you don't care," he said again in that questioning way of his.

As it turned out, my eventual answer to his "question" surprised him as much as it did me—not to mention his mother, still watching from the library door. "You're OK, Sonny," I said, at the same time leaning over and giving him an uncharacteristic peck on the cheek. As an afterthought, I added, "But don't call me 'Shirley.'" I jumped out of the car and hurried up the walk toward the building. I could still hear Sonny's laughter as Miss Faye beckoned me inside and waved again to her son before letting the door close behind us.

ELEVEN

I enjoyed spending time that afternoon at the Jonas Ridge Library with Miss Faye. She was a truly nice lady, much like Grandma, who could be gruff at times but never let you doubt her concern for you. I had been at the library only about an hour before Miss Faye started straightening up and preparing to close for the day. It wasn't as if she had to run anyone out of the building, though, because no one else was there while I was with her. She claimed she had been "really, really busy" right after lunch, but I wondered if that only meant that a couple of cyclists had stopped off at the library to use its free Internet access to check their email or to scan the weather radar for approaching thundershowers.

Alan had told me that it had been an exceptionally wet spring and early summer—so wet, in fact, that he had seen more varieties of mushrooms while hiking and biking that year than he had ever seen in his whole life. Alan had gone on and on to Bo and me—this was Saturday on the way home from the airport—about all of the amazing mushrooms he had found and photographed and collected and even eaten around Lost Cove and Harper Creek. *Mushrooms?* I had thought. *My cousin likes stars and mushrooms? Boy, has* he *turned into a real fun-guy!* (That's one of Billy Joe's jokes.) I also couldn't help but notice the irony in that Alan's favorite things—stars and mushrooms—both thrived, as it were, in the dark, while I couldn't go to sleep in my own bedroom without my beacon-shaped night light burning nearby.

But corny jokes and oddball observations aside, as I helped Miss Faye reshelve some reference books that had been used over the past couple of days, I ran across a thick hardcover volume entitled *Mushrooms Demystified: A Comprehensive Guide to the Fleshy Fungi* by David Arora. Several pages had been marked with bits of newsprint, and when I opened the book to remove the paper for Miss Faye, I saw that the recent reader—maybe Alan himself or some visiting mushroom hunter—had marked the pages for three distinctive mushrooms commonly found in the region: the hallucinogenic Fly Agaric (*Amanita muscaria*), the deadly Destroying Angel (*Amanita virosa*) and the edible Black Trumpet (*Craterellus cornucopioides*).

I hoped it hadn't been Alan who was looking up that information, because it bothered me to think he might be foolishly dabbling in fungi. Billy Joe had cautioned me *never* to pick and eat *any* mushroom while I was working on the golf course—or when I was anywhere else, for that matter. "Them things'll kill ya deader'n a doorknob," my old pro had warned, and I had taken his wise words to heart.

"I'm glad you came to see me today, Valerie," Miss Faye said, as she locked the library door and walked with me toward her car. "It was nice to have some help."

I nodded. "I've always liked libraries," I replied. "Back home—I mean, where I used to live—I was always going to the library in Shallotte. That's the town near Village Point, where our house was—is, I mean." I was starting to get frustrated with myself for stumbling through such a simple explanation about something in my former life. It was happening to me more and more frequently, the longer I was away from my old home.

But Miss Faye seemed to understand my trouble. "You must be—oh, what's the word?—*discombobulated*—that's it—discombobulated, to be living up here in these hills with Elaine and

Alan, after living your whole life down there at the beach," the nice lady observed. "I know that's how I certainly would feel, if I ever had to move way down there after spending my whole life up here." Fumbling in her huge black leather purse for her keys, she finally located them and unlocked the passenger-side door of her dark gold Buick sedan. It was definitely a car that an older person would drive, with its subdued metallic paintjob, four doors and plain interior. However, like Alan's fancy yellow Blazer, Miss Faye's ride *did* have a CD-cassette-AM/FM six-speaker stereo system and an OnStar telephone (though Miss Faye said she had never used either device in the almost two years she had owned the car).

"Do you drive, Valerie?" Miss Faye asked, as she slid behind the steering wheel. She posed the question as if she actually were considering letting me drive to her house, which was only a couple of miles away on Gingercake Mountain between the church and lodge.

"No, ma'am," I said. I was more than a bit embarrassed about not having a driver's license—and not just because I was eighteen and still couldn't legally drive myself anywhere. It was because the State of North Carolina back then tied a teen-ager's academic achievement to her ability to obtain a valid operator's license. In other words, if you didn't complete enough classes in high school, you couldn't take driver's education and then get your learner's permit and your license and then drive a car legally and start getting speeding tickets and such (like my daredevil cousin Alan, by the way). That was what happened to me, sort of—not getting things together in time to get my driver's license at age sixteen, like your average Tarheel teen-ager.

When Grandpa died right before I started high school, something in me kind of snapped, as far as me wanting to do well in school was concerned. I was much more interested in playing on the golf team and working at Billy Joe's than I was in reading boring books and working silly math problems. I couldn't see how I would ever use any of that later in my life.

Now, before you get the wrong idea, I wasn't a behavior problem in school, and I really did love reading and going to the library, as I've said; however, I wanted to pick my own reading list, not read what my teachers assigned me. I mean, exactly how in touch with the realities of modern life *is* Shakespeare, anyway? To be or not to be boring? *That* was the dang question, and I had the answer before I even opened the book. The only things I didn't mind reading in English class were *Huckleberry Finn*, because I could understand what Huck was saying, and one story about golf by the guy who wrote that *Gatsby* book. And—oh, yeah—another kind of long story about a lady newspaper reporter who was in love with a soldier who got killed in the war, because it reminded me of Aunt Elaine and Uncle Lance.

I had a problem with fiction, in general, back then. I saw reading make-believe stories as nothing but a waste of time. My favorite "literary works" in those days were *The Rules of Golf*, a 156-page stapled paperback booklet I carried in the back pocket of my jeans, both on and off the course, and *Down the Fairway* by Robert T. Jones, Jr., better known as the great Bobby Jones, Grand Slam golf champion and designer and builder of the hallowed Augusta National Golf Course, where the Masters has been played every spring since 1934, except for three years during World War II. The second spring I worked for Billy Joe, he took me to Augusta to watch some practice rounds, and I got Tiger's autograph and had my picture taken next to the Arnold Palmer and Jack Nicklaus plaques. And then Billy Joe bought me my hardback copy of *Down the Fairway* in an Augusta gift shop. He said I should read it for him and then fill him in on all the important parts. I was happy to.

After what I'd already experienced in life, with the deaths of my parents and then my grandpa, I didn't feel that making A's in school was all that important. Besides, neither Grandpa nor Grandma finished high school, and they did OK for themselves, I figured. So, since the high school golf season was in the spring, I would do just well enough in my classes fall semester to be eligible to play; then my classroom motivation would duckhook out of bounds spring semester while I was actually on the golf team. I never officially failed a class, but I did get one or sometimes two incompletes each spring that I'd have to make up. Grandma always saw to that. Luckily for me, I could take a mulligan—a "do-over," that is—in summer school and then start over with a more or less clean scorecard the next fall.

However, since I moved away at the start of that summer after my senior year, I couldn't make up the two classes I hadn't completed the previous spring (English, of course, and social studies). Miss Carman, the nice senior sponsor, let me "walk the line," as she called it, to keep me from losing my self-esteem, she said. I think she just felt sorry for me after Grandma died that spring. But the black leather-look diploma cover that Mr. Birch, the principal, handed me at commencement held only a copy of my transcript and a summer school application, not an actual high school diploma. And, of course, driver's education class also had somehow gotten lost in the shuffle. So that's the long and short of why I didn't have a driver's license yet. Now you know.

Miss Faye just smiled pleasantly and nodded when I didn't offer her the explanation I just gave you. She seemed to know my life story already, though she apparently wanted *me* to tell it instead of relying on the second-hand stuff she had been hearing—from Sonny, I guess, and from Aunt Elaine, too. "Well, then, do we slip into town for a bite of dinner at Duffy's place," she asked, "or do we go on home and whip something up ourselves? I bet you're a good cook, aren't you?"

"No, ma'am, not especially," I admitted. "I can boil shrimp and fix a clambake pretty good. But I don't really cook--just enough to get by. Aunt Elaine got us one of those little microwaves when Grandma got sick, and that's how I heated up her meals, the ones the county brought us."

After turning left onto the highway and slowly accelerating, Miss Faye gripped the wheel and peered through the windshield at the road ahead as if driving the Buick were a matter of life and death, which, in her case, it might have been, for all I knew. "Well, we'll just go on to the house then," she said. "There's no sense wasting money when there's *plenty* of perfectly good food just going to waste in the Kelvinator." I knew she was referring to her refrigerator, because Grandma always used the same expression, even after we had replaced our old fridge with a Hotpoint (another one of those names that didn't make sense to my young mind when I was a child).

"Well, maybe I can show you a trick or two," Miss Faye added. "I fix things *pretty well* when I want to."

"Excuse me?" I said, no longer quite following her line of thinking.

"Cooking," she explained, smiling at my confused response. "Maybe I can show you how an old widow woman cooks on a woodstove. I've used a woodstove ever since Preacher Rose—that's what everyone called him—ever since Preacher Rose and I set up housekeeping back in 1947."

"Really?" I said. "I mean, do you really use a woodstove in the summertime? It's not too hot?"

She shook her head but kept her eyes on the road. "Well," she began slowly, "the temperature in my little old house is down in the forties first thing of a morning—in the summer, I'm talking about—so I light my stove first thing and get the house warm before I go to the library. I bake Sonny a pan of buttermilk biscuits in the oven, and he stops by for biscuits and honey on his way to town. He hasn't stopped by the past few days, though. It must be that diet he's on."

"But doesn't the woodstove make it too hot during the day?" I asked again.

"Well," she said, "Preacher Rose always claimed there was no heat as comfortable as wood heat, even in the summertime up here. We can just open up the doors and windows and let the mountain breezes blow through the house on the warmest summer day, and it's just as comfortable as can be."

Even before we had left the library, I had noticed Miss Faye's tendency to avoid answering my questions directly, and I couldn't really figure out why she was being that way—why a simple "yes" or "no" didn't suffice. Still, I knew that everyone has her own unique speech pattern and that "heeing and hawing," as Billy Joe put it, wasn't a federal offense by any means. And, to be honest, it was nice to talk to someone who had more to say than a simple "yes" or "no," neither of which is ever all that simple when you get right down to it. Nothing is simple.

Miss Faye's house on Gingercake Mountain—a tidy white cottage, actually—was pretty much what I expected, even though many of the newer houses in the mountain community looked more like Swiss ski chalets, Bavarian hunting lodges and down-sized Frank Lloyd Wright knockoffs than vacation homes. It appeared to me that Miss Faye's cottage must have been built in the years before the big influx of vacation-home builders, not only because of her house's comparatively modest design but also because it stood alone at the end of a long, almost-hidden, dirt driveway near the southern crest of the mountain.

With a one-car garage out back, the single-story frame house was surrounded by what anyone other than Miss Faye probably would have described as a cottage garden. Flower beds bursting with all the colors of the rainbow, flowering shrubs of pink and red, and trees with leaves or blossoms of green, red, white or purple filled the yard. When I asked Miss Faye about her garden, she just laughed, "This little old yard would be an absolute mess, Valerie, if I tended it. Oren's the one with the green thumb. He does absolute wonders here."

"Oren?" I asked.

"Yes," she replied. "Oren. Oren Green. Lacey Green's grandfather. You *have* met Lacey, haven't you? She works for Sonny at the lodge, and Oren works there, too—and here, when Sonny lets him."

I nodded. "Oh, yeah," I said. "*Buck* Green. Yeah, Alan and I saw Mr. Green just this afternoon down near Edgemont. We were down there taking pictures for the paper."

"Yes, I remember, you told me that earlier—that you had been taking photographs with that rascal Alan," she said, with twinkling blue eyes. "I didn't know, though, that you two ran into Oren. What did he have to allow?"

"Excuse me?" I said again, having never heard that expression before. "What did he have to allow? I don't know what you mean."

Miss Faye smiled patiently. "Did Oren have anything to *say*? Maybe I shouldn't be talking out of school, but Sonny had a little run-in with Oren this morning, and I feel just terrible about it. It was all my fault."

"How was it all your fault, Miss Faye?" I said. "Sonny told us about it, and he said it had to do with Mr. Green scaring a lady at the campground." I gave her the short version of Sonny's tale about Buck and the camper he had frightened in the lodge and about Sonny giving Buck a shave and a haircut.

"Well, that might be the story Sonny *wants* you to believe," she began, "but it isn't the *whole* story by any means. Mercy, no. This goes back about three years, I guess, to when Sonny asked Oren to come mow my yard the first time.

"Just between us girls," she continued, "Oren Green has always been sort of sweet on me, ever since I was a schoolgirl. As a matter of fact, he used to follow me to school and throw rocks at me and my girlfriends when we'd turn around and tell him to get on back home and leave us alone. You see, he didn't go to school. He was too old—and too mean, too. He was a regular scamp and mean as a snake most of the time, that tall skinny little boy was. But I knew he liked me and was just trying to get my attention all those times he'd get after us along the road to school.

"He even came to church a time or two, just so he could sit on the back pew and look at me up in the choir all through the service. He'd sit back there and make goo-goo eyes at me until I started giggling, and then Georgie—Preacher Rose, back when he was a young man—George would turn around and give Oren a look that could melt a block of ice on the coldest day of the year. Then after church it would be all I could do to keep the two of them from going up to the Indian Bald Ground on the mountain—that's on the top of Jonas Ridge, where the Indians used to play their ballgames, which is why people think it's the *ball* ground, B-A-L-L, but it isn't. Anyway, those two boys were going to go up there and have it out, but I stopped them from fighting over me. I did. I said I wouldn't have *either* of them if they got involved in that kind of foolishness. Georgie *was* kind of high-tempered back in those days, and I'm just glad the two of them finally made their peace eventually.

"So Georgie married me and built this house, and we eventually had Sonny—not right away, after a few years of trying to start a family but not having any luck. And Oren, he married Beulah—she was from over Linville way—and they started having children right away, the first one not even a year after they were married. I don't know how poor Beulah stood it. And they had the worst luck. One or two of their little ones died of scarlet fever, I think it was, and then one of Oren's little boys was playing in the water at the top of Harper Creek Falls, the pretty falls there near Kawana, and he slipped on a slick rock and fell all the way down into the pool at the bottom."

"Did he die?" I asked.

"Well," Miss Faye said, "as I recall, he was hurt really badly, and Oren had a really hard time getting him up the mountain to the hospital at Crossnore. That boy broke every bone in his little body. Yes, I think he died five or six years ago."

Huh? I thought, but said, "He didn't die in the fall?" Well, it took her about three or four more minutes to explain that, no, the boy hadn't been killed in the fall from the top of Harper Creek Falls but had recovered and had grown up, gotten his driver's license, gotten married, had a family of his own, then had gone out drinking one Saturday night and gotten into a fatal head-on collision with a tree on the road coming up the mountain from Morganton, at a place called the S Curves, not too far south of the Brown Mountain Overlook, and *that's* how he died, Miss Faye said.

I must admit, Miss Faye's unique speech pattern was starting to wear me down, but I wasn't rude enough—yet—to let her know it. She did possess, after all, a wealth of information about Jonas Ridge, and I was determined to mine her memory banks for all they were worth—starting with what she knew about the Brown Mountain Light.

As it turned out, the Light was one of Miss Faye's pet topics. Since it was still light out and would be for at least another hour after our dinner of microwaved soup (to keep from heating up the house with the woodstove, she said), she led me down a well-worn trail through the woods behind her house to a rock formation that she called the Devil's Cap. It was a huge boulder about twenty feet high, fifteen feet long and ten feet wide, with a smaller boulder perched precariously on top at the south-facing end of the larger rock. She said there was a folk tale claiming that the devil had placed the one rock on top of the other, and that if anyone climbed up there and tried to push the smaller rock off the larger one, a thunderstorm would immediately come up—even on a clear day—and send a thunderbolt from the blue to strike the man stone dead.

In more recent years, tourists had started calling the rock formation Sitting Bear, because that's what it kind of looked like from the highway over on the next ridge near the Brown Mountain Overlook, she added. After we walked around the rock a couple of times, Miss Faye pointed to the east-southeast at a long low bluish ridge which she identified as Brown Mountain itself. "You can see the Light really well from here," she claimed.

"Have you really seen it?" I asked.

"Well," she began, "my husband always said—"

"Have *you* seen the Light, Miss Faye?" I interrupted, not wanting to spend five minutes waiting for a simple "yes" or "no."

"Well," she said again, "yes—and no. My husband always said it was just the devil up to no good over there on that ridge. Moonshiners, in other words. He said he knew there were more illegal moonshine stills over there on Brown Mountain than you could shake a stick at, and that's all we were seeing on those clear nights when we'd be running around all over creation and we'd start seeing lights popping up all over that mountain over there. But I don't know. I've seen some pretty odd-looking things in all the years I've lived up here. Some of the things I've seen *couldn't* have been moonshiners.

"Once, for instance, I saw something that looked like a Roman candle go up from a spot on the north end of the mountain, and then it jumped down the ridge and kept right on flaring up longer than any Roman candle *I've* ever seen. And that's just one of the lights I've seen over there. They look different at different times of the year. I think it all depends on the weather and on the phase of the moon, too, I think. If you want, Valerie, we could come back over here after dark and see what we can see, if we leave Sonny a note. I doubt he'll be back from the meeting before dark. What do you say?"

I wasn't sure I wanted to see the Light that badly—to go out in the dark with this old woman, as nice as she was, to a place called the Devil's Cap. The name Sitting Bear, by the way, didn't sit much better with me. This, after all, was Alan's little pet project. And Bo's. Not mine. Right then I felt that I could be perfectly happy to spend the rest of my life without seeing for myself what the Brown Mountain Light looked like, whether like a Roman candle or like red, orange and yellow circles of light flashing from crevices or like the man in the moon, for all I cared. Not to mention there was a wild man on the loose on a stolen lawn tractor. "Can we see the mountain from your house?" I asked.

"No," Miss Faye replied, "the trees are too tall. You have to come over here to the rock—or, at least, somewhere near here where you can see across that ridge where the highway runs. As a matter of fact, this trail here runs on down the hill a ways to Table Rock Road, and if you turn left and then back to the right, you eventually come out over on the highway near the Brown Mountain overlook. It's kind of a shortcut that some folks take to get over here. Oren comes that way, when he comes just to visit."

"Oren?" I knew that she was referring to Buck, but I was surprised to hear that the old guy was making social calls on Miss Faye—though that possibly explained, finally, how the run-in between Buck and Sonny that morning might have been all her fault.

"Yes," she said. "He comes to see me at least once a week—other than when Sonny or Lacey brings him here to mow my yard. We sit and talk and just have the best time. It's usually an evening when Sonny is gone to a meeting. Like tonight. We just sit out in the yard and look at the stars and talk over old times. To have been such a mean little boy, he has grown up to become a nice old gentleman—when he wants to be. He's nice to *me*, anyway." She smiled as she spoke of her old friend.

I wished I could think of him as fondly as she apparently did, but that wasn't really possible right then, not with darkness falling soon. Ordinarily, I might have asked her to explain how Buck got to her house on his own if he couldn't drive. Did he walk all that way? Did he ride the mower in the dark? Did he harness a Brown Mountain Light and fly there? Instead, I asked, "Miss Faye, could we start heading on back to your house? I just remembered I need to call my friend Bo. Remember, my friend that you met yesterday at the Singing?"

"Oh, yes," she said. "The little colored boy. He was so sweet, but I was so surprised at how quiet he was." I was about to ask her to explain that last remark when she added as an afterthought, "Oh, that's right, you're afraid of the dark. I almost forgot that. Well, we'll go back now. Let's hurry back to the house before it gets dark."

Daylight was fading fast as we headed back to the house. In the distance, off toward Brown Mountain, came a sound I hadn't expected to hear that evening, even though it was a familiar enough sound—a tune, actually—and, in hindsight, was thoroughly appropriate for the time and place I heard it. It was the lonely far-off sound of a bugle, echoing through the hollows and off the cliffs of Miss Faye's mountains. The bugler was playing "Taps," that mournful call to signal sunset, day's end, lights out, death. I had heard that call a week earlier, and I didn't care to hear it ever again. "Who's doing that, Miss Faye?" I asked.

"Doing what?"

"Don't you hear it?" I said. "The bugle."

"Oh," she began, "that's Oren. That's how he tells me 'good night' from all the way down at his house beyond Harper Creek. Instead of calling on the phone—since he doesn't have one—he just steps out on his porch and blows that old horn of his. He has another call he blows when he's coming to see me and one for just about every occasion—getting up in the morning, coming to dinner, everything. He was a bugler back in his younger days. I hear that 'I'm coming to see you' bugle tune, and then about thirty minutes later here comes Oren on his old horse up the trail from the Devil's Cap, just like a knight on his charger. If he isn't coming to mow my yard, he rides old Niblick—that's the horse's name—he rides him all the way from Harper Creek. Oren says old Niblick knows all the trails from way back when they were in another line of work, and he could probably run from one place to the next blindfolded, he's so smart. But, Valerie, don't you tell Sonny any of this. It's our little secret, Oren and mine, just like you and that little colored boy must have secrets, too, I'm sure." She giggled like a schoolgirl.

Apparently, Sonny's foot-in-mouth disease was an inherited trait—or else it was communicable. But as long as Miss Faye led me back up the trail to her house and kept the lights on inside—with or without the woodstove burning—I knew I'd be OK. If I was still with her at nine o'clock, I'd borrow Miss Faye's phone and call Bo from there. Or if Sonny was back from the meeting and we were on the road at nine, I'd borrow either Sonny's or Alan's cell phone to make the call. Like Miss Faye, I enjoyed having a friend with whom I could share my memories and hopes and dreams, and I didn't want another person's thoughtlessness to come between my friend and me. Not Miss Faye. Not Sonny. Not Alan or Aunt Elaine. Not nobody.

When I finally got him to answer his cell phone, Bo acted as if my call were a major inconvenience. For whatever reason he didn't bother to explain, he seemed in a really bad mood, and he sounded determined to get me off the phone as soon as possible. Luckily, the telephone I used at Miss Faye's house was the one in her bedroom; she had sent me there so I could have some privacy, she had said as she snapped on the bedside lamp before I would enter the dark room. So Miss Faye didn't hear my side of a conversation that left me feeling somewhat empty and hurt. I don't think Bo knew how his moodiness struck me that night. He might have just been acting like his idol, Miles Davis, but *I* was the one who was becoming kind of blue.

"What?!" Bo had huffed, after answering on the fourth ring.

"Bo?"

"What?" he said again. "What do you want?" I had to listen carefully to understand what he was saying, his voice was so low.

"It's Val. You said to call at nine."

"It's five till."

"I'm sorry," I said. "I'm at Miss Faye Rose's house, and her clock's a little fast, I guess."

There was a moment of silence. "Well?" Bo whispered. "What do you want?"

This wasn't like him at all, I thought, not even the way he had been lately. Surely Bo remembered that *he* had left the note on Alan's car and had said for *me* to call him then, even if I was five minutes off. "What's wrong?" I asked. "Can't you talk?"

Again, more silence. "Nothing," he replied, pausing again. "Can I call you back later?"

"Sure. But I might not be at Aunt Elaine's for another hour. I might be on the road when you call."

"Not tonight," he said. "Tomorrow. I'll talk to you tomorrow."

"OK," I said, then tried to continue. But I could tell he had already ended the call, either right after his last word or as soon as I said "OK." I would have to wait until the next day to find out what he had learned about Agnes Morton and the Brown Mountain Light, and to tell him what all I had learned in my long day with Alan and Miss Faye.

There were, however, some encouraging developments in my social life that night, as if what I had going for myself could be called a social life. Sonny finally got back from the county commissioners meeting and picked me up at Miss Faye's, to take me back to the lodge so that I could catch my ride home with Alan. After giving his mother a quick but animated rundown of the meeting, Sonny and I left in the Corvette. He had put the top up to shield us from the brisk night air and had turned on the defroster to keep the windshield unfogged, though I still felt chilled to the bone in my T-shirt and shorts.

"You'll have to dress different up here," Sonny said, apparently noticing I was shivering. "It's chilly even in the summertime—at night and in the morning, it is. But that's why I like it up here. You don't need air-conditioning like you do everywhere else down South. I mean, can you just imagine how much it'd cost to air-condition the lodge? All those Floridians would crank up the A/C, and my light bill would go through the roof. Through the dang roof, you know?"

"Yeah, I guess," I replied, wondering if his question really called for an answer.

"I talked to Elaine," he said, "and she had a good idea." He hesitated as if I were supposed to guess what he and Elaine had discussed. I didn't know what he was referring to. Something related to the meeting? His weekly newspaper column? My poor clothing choices? The price of putters in Japan? When I didn't say anything, Sonny continued, "She said since I turned in my column on time for a change and don't have a blessed thing to do tomorrow morning, I need to come pick you up at the paper and go do something neither one of us has done in a *long* time." Again, he paused, waiting for me to say *Do what?* I guess. I was starting to get annoyed.

"Do what?" I said.

"Guess," he replied. "Guess what we're gonna do tomorrow morning."

Now, in the first place, I seriously doubted that this man—busy as he was always supposed to be with his various vocations, avocations and sundry projects—had absitively, posolutely nothing else to do on a Tuesday morning. So, if that *were* the case—that Elaine had suggested to him that he do something with me—then *I* must have been the *project du jour*, as Alan might have said. "I don't know," I said. "I have no idea."

Sonny slapped my left thigh lightly. "We're gonna go play golf, silly," he said. "You bring your clubs to the office, and I'll pick you up there at nine sharp. We'll head over to the course and get nine in before lunch. Then if we want to play nine more after lunch, we can. How's that sound?"

My spirit soared at the thought of playing that heavenly course in Linville. Just imagine, spending an entire day on those ethereal links designed by American golf god Donald Ross. "That sounds like a winner!" I replied. "I can't wait!"

For that matter, it was all I could do to sit still long enough to get back to the lodge where Alan waited and then get back home with him to thank Aunt Elaine for coming up with such a great idea. For the time being, I forgot all about Buck Green's craziness and my friend Bo's moodiness and even my own fears of this, that and the other thing. At least for that one night, I had a definite reason to live.

TWELVE

Despite what Alan had told me about all the rain in the mountains that spring, the High Country's weather had been glorious since I had lived there. All three days. Well, maybe there was a trace of rain on Saturday as we were on our way up the mountain—an afternoon shower, maybe—but I had no complaints, after having lived through all those hurricanes and tropical storms on the coast since I moved in with Grandpa and Grandma after the wreck that killed my folks.

I even remembered Hurricane Hugo like it was yesterday. That was the one that scared Grandpa so bad he sailed *The Lady of Shallotte* all the way up the Lockwood's Folly River to ride out the hurricane inland, away from the damage the storm surge would do near Village Point where we lived and kept our dock. I wanted to go with him, but he wouldn't let me. He said it was too dangerous and that, besides, I needed to stay with Grandma and take care of her for him while he was away. Somebody needed to take care of her, he said. So that's why I stayed with Grandma, and we went to the shelter at the high school together and didn't leave until we got word through the ham radio guys that Grandpa was OK and that he had sailed back to our house in *The Lady*. We were so glad to see him when we got back home, and he almost danced a jig out on the dock when we got out of

Billy Joe's car. Billy Joe had stayed in the shelter, too, and had given us a ride home. So I barely noticed a little thundershower after I moved to the mountains. I'd been through a lot worse.

That Tuesday morning when Sonny picked me up at the *Ledger* office, the forecast for Linville called for partly to mostly sunny skies, with a high temperature in the low to mid seventies and a low temperature in the upper forties to around fifty—perfect golf weather. I knew the forecast by heart, because I had been listening to the local radio station almost constantly since I had gotten out of bed. Driving us from Aho to Linville via the foggy Blue Ridge Parkway across the slopes of Grandfather Mountain, Aunt Elaine had come close to snapping at me as I tried to tune in the Boone station on the Challenger's staticky AM radio. Her nerves always were frayed on Tuesdays, she said, because it was deadline day, when she would be doing the bulk of her writing and editing for that week's edition.

Though the *Ledger* wasn't actually printed until Wednesday around noon and didn't hit the newsstands until Wednesday afternoon, the morning of press day had to be spent laying out and pasting up on computer the paper's sixteen or so pages so that metal plates could be photographed and run on the big offset press with its racks of rollers and web-like newsprint. As the paper's only full-time writer, Elaine also often had to cover any local board meeting that popped up on a Tuesday night and then write it up first thing Wednesday morning.

I didn't complain that morning when she told me to "pick a station" on the car radio. She used to say the same thing to Alan back when they lived near us on the coast and I'd be over at their house watching television. In those days they could afford cable TV, but no longer. With only two over-the-air stations from which to choose and bad reception to boot, Alan now used the remote only to turn the set on and off and to adjust the volume most nights when we were sitting around watching TV, which wasn't very often.

That probably was another reason Alan spent so much time at the Barkhouse with Lacey, because the lodge had a satellite dish, and Alan could catch up on the *Cartoon Network*. No, I'm just kidding. He liked the *Discovery Channel* best, he claimed. My favorite channel to watch at Sonny's place was *The Golf Channel*, of course—golf and more golf, 24/7—Tiger, Annika, the Golden Bear. But that came later, after I had gotten to know Sonny better. And after that Tuesday morning when he and I played golf together for the first time.

I had spent at least an hour before bedtime the night before literally dusting off my golf clubs. Since the Linville Golf Club was among the *creme-de-la-creme* of courses in the Carolinas, I wanted to make sure my mismatched clubs and inexpensive bag didn't look too cruddy—or like the "cream-*della*-crap," as someone used to say.

I had long since discarded that old Wilson Sunday bag I once used. I now carried my clubs in a black nylon-covered Knight Golf carry bag. I wasn't particularly proud of the bag, but it was fairly light and nondescript and had been cheap enough for me to afford. Well, actually, the rude father of one of my high school teammates had given me a hundred bucks and had told me to go buy myself a real bag because I was embarrassing the rest of the team with my "shitty" equipment—that was *his* word, not mine.

When I told Billy Joe what the man had said, Billy Joe came really close to driving over to that guy's office to kick his butt and teach him some manners, but I talked him out of it. I said it would just make things worse for me. Billy Joe told me I should just pocket the man's money and keep using the Sunday bag, but I felt kind of the same way about my stuff that the man—and apparently his son—did. I guess I *was* embarrassed that I didn't have all the nicest and latest equipment and sportswear, and that I was frequently referred to as "that poor girl" by opposing teams who didn't know my name. So I got Billy Joe to take me over to Wal-Mart that evening, and I bought that black Knight bag, because it was the cheapest nice one I could find. And *then* I pocketed the sixty bucks left over.

Well, no, I didn't actually pocket the money; I gave it to Grandma to pay some bills, though I didn't tell her where the money had come from, for fear that she *would* have gone and kicked the man's butt no matter what I said to dissuade her. I just explained the extra cash by saying someone had given me a "tip" on the course. That was close enough to the truth, I figured, because I knew I'd never forget what that man said to me that day. And I never have.

But I'm getting sidetracked here. When crazy Sonny pulled up in front of the *Ledger* in, of all things, his *Bluesmobile*, my clubs and I were waiting on the building's front stoop—my shiny mostly-silver clubs in their neat black bag, and me in my gray cargo shorts, which Elaine had let me wash the night before, the black Hootie & the Blowfish Ninth Annual Monday After The Masters Celebrity Pro-Am Golf Tournament golf shirt that Bo and his mom had given me on my last birthday, white footies, my freshly-polished shoes and, of course, my white Nike cap. If I'd had some money to blow and the time to blow it, I might have run out and bought some black Nike footies and one of Tiger's black Nike caps to match the rest of my outfit before playing with Sonny that day. But I was more of a mismatched kind of person back then and probably still am. My clubs certainly were, as I've mentioned before.

Even though fourteen clubs make a complete set, I carried my own full complement of twelve mismatched sticks—my driver and number three metal-wood; irons three through nine (including my Hogan six-iron); my Yonex pitching wedge; the Wilson sand wedge Billy Joe had given me as a going-away present; and my Ping putter, with its dull gold-colored head. Those twelve clubs, six optic-yellow Top-Flite balls, six red wooden tees, my Nike golf glove and *The Rules of Golf* were all my bag held, even though it had plenty of pockets that could have been stuffed with all sorts of golf aids, gadgets and souvenirs if I had had the money, time and inclination to collect them.

I fully expected Sonny's bag, though it remained out of sight in the *Bluesmobile*'s trunk, to be like the one used by comedian Rodney Dangerfield's character in the first *Caddyshack* movie—super-sized, gaudily-colored and containing everything from a stereo system and color TV to a dorm-sized refrigerator and rolling wet bar. I didn't get to see Sonny's bag right away, though, because he had me stow mine on the back seat so he wouldn't have to get out of the car and open the trunk, where his clubs were.

But that didn't make me want to get out there on that gorgeous tree-lined Ross-designed Linville course any less. It would have been my first time playing a course laid out by the Michelangelo of American golf courses. Yeah, that's right—*would have been*. Because when Sonny pulled out of the *Ledger*'s lot, he turned right toward Foscoe, not left toward Linville.

"Where we going?" I asked, still fumbling with the *Bluesmobile*'s antique seat belt. Though I was disappointed that it looked as if we weren't going to play Linville after all, I sheltered a flickering hope either that Sonny just needed to run a quick errand before hitting the links or that we were at least going to play the Hawksnest course near the college. That wouldn't have been bad either, I figured, even though it wasn't my dream come true.

Sonny—who, by the way, was dressed rather oddly for golf—smiled and replied, "Why, to play golf, silly. Where'd you *think* we were going? To the House of Blues?" He had noticed the House of Blues' Sacred Heart logo on my Hootie shirt. "Really cool blouse!" he added. "How'd you know I was driving the *Bluesmobile* today? I didn't tell Elaine."

I should point out here that what was odd about his dress was that it matched the car. He looked something like one of the Blues Brothers, except that instead of a dark suit, Sonny wore black Dockers slacks and a black Members Only windbreaker over a white knit golf shirt and a skinny black necktie. He also sported a black-painted fedora-like straw hat with a black silk band, black Wayfarer sunglasses and black FootJoy golf shoes with white socks. He was a real sight.

"I didn't know," I said, referring to the decommissioned Dodge Monaco police cruiser with its "Mt. Prospect PD" and "On a mission from God" decals, and its fake BDR-529 "Land of Lincoln" front license tag (the rear tag was the official "First in Flight" North Carolina plate). "I never would've guessed."

He checked the rear-view mirror, apparently to make sure there wasn't a *real* police cruiser on our tail, though it would have been either a county sheriff's department or state highway patrol car, since neither Linville nor Foscoe had a police department. "I take turns driving all my cars so they keep running good," Sonny explained. "You know what they say—use it or lose it. When you get my age, that's true about a lot of things." He chuckled, glancing over to see if his banter amused me.

I nodded and smiled. "That's what my old boss Billy Joe used to say, too," I offered. "He was always saying goofy things, because he'd always mess them up somehow."

"What you mean? He have a speech defect or something?" Sonny checked his mirror again and this time did a double-take as he apparently spotted something.

"No," I replied, turning my head to see what Sonny had noticed behind us. All I saw was a small green pickup about a quarter-mile back, but it disappeared from sight as we rounded the next curve. "Is somebody following us?"

He checked the mirror one more time. "No," he said finally. "I thought so at first, but I guess they turned off."

I was starting to worry. "Who was it?"

"Well, to tell you the truth, I thought at first it might be Buck Green," he replied. "He keeps sneaking off on my mower, and we're worried he might work his way up to taking his truck out on the road again—you know, the one Lacey drives—even though he doesn't have his license anymore."

Breathing easier, Sonny continued, "But you were telling me about your old boss, the one that couldn't say anything right."

"Well, no, it wasn't that Billy Joe didn't say stuff *right*," I explained. "It was more like he changed old sayings a little, but they still got the right point across. Like, what you just said—you know—use it or lose it? Billy Joe would say, 'Use it or abuse it'—something like that."

Sonny smiled. "Kinda like Yogi Berra's malapropisms," he said. "You know, words or phrases that get mangled in a funny way."

"Yogi Bear?" I asked, confused. I didn't remember Alan's Yogi Bear impressions having anything to do with messed-up words or phrases.

"No, Yogi Berra," Sonny said. "Ber-ra. You know, the old baseball player. I think he's in an American Express commercial on TV now—you know, the one with that tall Chinese basketball player?"

"Yow?"

"Huh?" Sonny said, his blond eyebrows scrunching up. "Something wrong?"

"Yow."

"I don't understand," he said. "I was saying, Yogi's in the commercial with that tall Chinese basketball player."

I nodded. "Yow."

"Who? What?" he said, his voice rising a bit on the second word as if he still hadn't caught on to my little joke. "I don't know what you're saying." Instead, he just shook his head in puzzlement and stared out the windshield at the road ahead. I could almost see the wheels spinning in his brain. After a few seconds of slightly strained silence, he stated, "No. *Who*'s on first, *what*'s on second, and *I-don't-know*'s on third. Right?"

We both burst out laughing at that. That was when I figured out that Sonny Rose, for all of his goofiness, was one sharp fellow. But it also made me wonder if maybe he had been playing along with my little joke all along and that the joke was really on *me*. I wondered if he could have been that good of an actor to have fooled me into thinking I was fooling him. Still, about the time we passed the turn-offs to Skyland Tech and Hawksnest and then continued on up the highway toward Boone, I really didn't care if Sonny had been acting or not. I wanted to know where he was taking me, and I asked him.

"My favorite course," he replied. "Willow Creek."

My spirits sank. "The par three?"

"Well, yeah," he said, picking up on the disappointment in my voice. "What's wrong with a par three? I thought you haven't played in a while."

"I haven't—not since Grandma got so sick."

Sonny shrugged. "Well, then this oughta be a good practice round for you, instead of going out on a big course right off the bat, don't you think? And, besides, that place you used to work at was a par three, wasn't it? That guy's place? Billy Joe, wasn't it?"

"Yeah, but…," I began. Right then I felt like a spoiled brat who had just had her big red lollipop taken away before suppertime.

Now Sonny *was* starting to get annoyed. "Yeah, but *what*?" By now he was turning onto a side road into the development that surrounded the golf course. "This is a nice little course. It really is. And it's not expensive to play, like a big course would be. Where did you think I was gonna take you—Linville?" I'm sure he could tell from the way I avoided his eyes that he had me pegged. "That *is* where you thought we were going to play, isn't it?"

"Well, you're a member there, aren't you?" I said accusingly, as if he might have thought I wasn't good enough to be his guest on the Linville course.

"Where did you get *that* idea?" he asked.

"Well, don't you play tennis in Linville with Aunt Elaine," I shot back, "and with Duffy and Miss Kitty?"

"Yes," he said, "but not at the club." Sonny relaxed a bit now that he understood why I was getting so bent out of shape. "Duffy and Kitty are both members, I think, but we play at Duffy's house. He has his own tennis court—a real nice one, too. You know, the big joke around town is that the *Ledger* holds its staff meetings during the changeovers in our matches, and that Elaine decides how much to edit all our columns based on whether we're ahead or not. But, no, I'm not a member of the golf club or tennis club. Matter of fact, I've never been on that course—not with a golf club in my hand, anyway."

"What do you mean?"

He smiled. "Oh, when I was a kid, I used to come into Linville with my daddy when he'd be out visiting folks," Sonny explained, "and while he was sitting in their living rooms witnessing to them, I'd be out running around like a little pixie, giving folks reasons to *lose* their Christianity. And I mighta found my way onto the golf course, I don't know. I did get myself into a heckuva lot of trouble sometimes, so much that Daddy eventually stopped taking me on visitation with him. That's what he called it. Visitation."

We were parked in the golf course lot at Willow Creek's small clubhouse with its basement pro shop and adjoining cart shed, where a whole fleet of nice-looking carts were available for use. I could see the practice green behind the building and the club's swimming pool up the hill between a couple of surprisingly lush fairways. Townhouse buildings adorned the hillsides within and around the course. The putting greens I could see appeared velvet-smooth like the tops of billiard tables. And there wasn't any trash lying around. No beer bottles or cellophane peanut wrappers or discarded cardboard golf ball sleeves. As a matter of fact, the whole place looked nice, I thought—a lot nicer than Billy Joe's par three, that was for sure. And Sonny was right; I *did* need to start back slowly with an easy practice round before knocking out the pegs on a big old eighteen-hole championship course.

But, doggone it, I *was* going to play that old Linville course. One way or another. With or without anyone's help.

THIRTEEN

Willow Creek had no driving range, just a medium-sized practice green where a golfer could test the speed of a representative bentgrass putting surface before heading out onto the hilly nine-hole course with its small but undulating greens. I *always* spent at least ten minutes on the practice green before a round, even longer on an unfamiliar course. Sonny, on the other hand, remarked that his "diuretic just kicked in" and disappeared into the clubhouse while I tried to get a feel for the practice green. I stayed there until I knocked in three straight putts of at least six feet; then I picked up my bag and headed for the bench next to the first tee.

In looking over the scorecard as I waited for Sonny to get back from the restroom, I noted that the longest hole, at 218 yards from the back tee box, was number nine, which Sonny later identified as Willow Creek's signature hole, the "Little Green Monster." A course diagram on the back of the simple green scorecard showed that the ninth fairway ran straight as a shot along the road to a green that was protected on the front, left and rear by a large wraparound pond and on the right by two sandtraps. The third hole was almost as long as nine, though number three didn't appear to have water anywhere close to its green, just another pond immediately off the tees. The two shortest holes were number six at 130 yards and number one at 162 yards. From where I sat, I couldn't see number six and, therefore, had no idea of the hole's topography or what it looked like, though I saw on the scorecard's handicap ratings that it was the easiest hole on the course (it was rated "9," as in the ninth most difficult hole).

But the challenge of number one, despite its "8" handicap rating, was right before my eyes, as yet another pond fronted the tee box and ran along the fairway to the right all the way to the green. That opening hole was a piece of cake for any golfer who didn't have a slice—that is, a tee shot that veers off to the right. However, without having had a practice range to warm up on, I knew that chili-dipping or skulling my first shot into the pond immediately in front of the tee would be a definite possibility, no matter how short the hole was or how easy it was supposed to be.

By the way, according to the handicap ratings, the two hardest holes were number nine and the 193-yard number four, which appeared to be the only true dogleg on the course. I had been playing golf long enough to know that length really didn't matter, even when every hole was par three. There was no single green on that course that I couldn't have driven with a well-struck tee shot. But I knew there were other factors at play on every hole other than the three most obvious elements of nature's Big Four—earth, wind and water. I was well aware that the fourth element of nature was inside me—whether that fire was in the form of fear or desire—and that it could be the most devastating or most inspiring factor of all. It was what made me tick.

"Ready to go?" Sonny asked, as he walked up behind me. He carried a black Wilson Sunday bag exactly like the one I had once used before giving in to fashion and buying my Knight bag. Sonny's bag bore only four clubs: a new King Snake seven-wood, an old MacGregor seven-iron, a battered Wilson lob wedge and a scuffed gray L-shaped Walter Hagen Black Jack putter. He also carried a multi-colored golf umbrella and a yellow-headed ball retriever, which he said was his "most valuable club." The seven-wood—a counterfeit of the King Cobra fairway metal, by the way—was the only club of Sonny's in good shape, only because he had bought it that morning especially for our outing, he said. His other clubs showed their age with dinged heads, rust-flecked shafts and cracked grips. "Ready?" he asked again.

"Ready as I'll ever be," I replied, rising from the bench and pulling my five-wood from my bag. I headed toward the back tee box, marked by two grapefruit-sized black ceramic balls stuck in the ground. I figured we could take some practice swings and then decide who got the honor of teeing off first.

"Hold on, hold on," Sonny said. "Where you going, girl? We play the white tees where I come from. You want me to get a hernia or something?" And then he added as an afterthought, "And we play 'ready golf' here. So you *ready*?"

"Huh? Uh, OK," I replied, actually in reference to his remark about the tees. I took out my scorecard and checked the white tee's shorter distance to the center of the green. It was only 128 yards, which I knew I could easily hit with my six-iron. I switched clubs and moved toward the tee box for my swings while Sonny fussed with retying his shoes and adjusting his glove. "Ready to flip for honors," I asked when he finally joined me. I held up a red wooden tee point-first for him to see and prepared to flip it like a coin into the air with my thumb.

"Don't bother," he said. "Your choice. You go first if you're ready—or I will, if you're nervous about hitting first."

I shrugged. "Whatever," I said, "but the rulebook says it's supposed to be decided 'by lot.' You know?" Even though deciding who went first was no big deal to most duffers, I was ready to pull out my copy of *The Rules of Golf*, turn to page thirty and show Sonny that blind chance, not personal preference, was supposed to decide the honor at the first teeing ground, by gosh.

Sonny smiled. "Sure, that's fine," he said. "Flip away." I tossed the tee into the air, and it came down pointing toward Sonny. "Okey doke," he said. "I'll go first then." He drew his seven-iron from his bag resting against the bench, took a couple of practice swings, then planted a bright-white ball into the ground on a low tee and prepared to drive the dimpled orb over the pond toward the not-so-distant green. "Beautiful day, ain't it, Val?" he said, looking around the course. "And we have all this to ourselves, it looks like. Can you believe it? Guess we're the dawn patrol—even though it's nine o'clock."

I looked around, too, and, sure enough, it *did* seem as if we were the only golfers or at least the first ones on the course, though there were a few other vehicles parked in the clubhouse lot around the *Bluesmobile*. "Yeah, this is nice," I replied. "The courses down at the beach are always crowded, even this time of year—you know, in the off-season."

"Off-season?" Sonny said. "Dang. Summer is *in*-season here in the mountains, when it's so nice and cool. Yeah, I guess it *would* be kinda miserable to be playing golf out in the hot summer sun down there. When I go to the beach in the summertime, golf is the *last* thing on my mind, you know?" He kept talking as he waggled his club over the ball.

When I didn't answer him—trying to be polite *and* to follow the rules—he stopped waggling and looked back at me. "You know what I mean?" he asked again. I nodded, which apparently satisfied him enough to go ahead with his tee shot.

I don't really know what I was expecting from him, but Sonny's swing turned out to be something from an instructional video—a flawlessly fluid motion that slowly cocked and then uncoiled into the ball with unbridled grace and controlled force like nothing else on earth. It was the perfect marriage of man and machine, that seven-iron in Sonny's hands.

The ball rose on a high gleaming arc toward the flagstick, the sphere's trajectory carrying it into the blinding morning sun, then down softly onto the velvety "dance floor," as old golfers liked to call the putting green. Actually, the ball landed about six feet beyond the pin; however, the backspin imparted by Sonny's seven-iron jerked the ball like a yo-yo back toward the front of the green. Missing the hole by inches, the ball came to a stop just barely on the fringe, the slightly higher cut of grass that encircles the putting surface but is not considered part of it. Still only six feet from the hole, Sonny could either putt or try to chip in, with a reasonable chance of sinking the shot either way, assuming his short game looked anything like what I had just seen of him off the tee.

After snatching up his tee, Sonny looked at me and smiled again. "That felt *good*," he said. "Almost good enough for a cigarette—if I still smoked, which I don't." He chuckled and shook his head as he walked back to the bench for his bag.

"Dad-gum, Sonny," I said. "How long has it been since you played?"

"I don't know," he replied. "About a year, maybe? I used to play a lot more, back before Elaine and I started playing so much tennis together. I was a regular golf addict, I guess you could say."

He didn't seem to be in any hurry to see me tee off, and, to be perfectly honest, I *was* getting a bit nervous about showing him my mostly self-taught swing, which Roy McAvoy—Kevin Costner's character in *Tin Cup*—would have described as looking like an "unfolding lawnchair." I rarely felt that "tuning fork" go off in my loins with a well-struck golf shot on the first tee like the one I had just witnessed. I was a slow starter and knew it. I needed to tune up with at least one small bucket of balls on a practice range in order to start off on anything other than a sour note. But there I was at the tee, with Sonny sitting on the bench behind me and his ball lying less than six feet from the hole on the apron of the green, whose nearest edge was over a football field away from where I stood.

"Just relax, Val," Sonny said. "Just pretend that pond ain't even there." Hmmm. Now I really *was* thinking about the water, and I was even visualizing my little yellow Top-Flite splashing down in the middle of the darkish tarn. I backed away from my ball and took two more practice swings. "That's a little too much club, ain't it, Val?" he asked, after noticing the Hogan six-iron in my hands.

I hadn't told him that the Hogan was my go-to iron, my most dependable club, in fact, when I was nervous or out of practice or, in this case, both. I shot him a look that said, *Check page twenty-eight, buddy, page twenty-eight!* ("During a *stipulated round*, a player shall not give *advice* to anyone in the competition except his *partner* and may ask for *advice* only from his *partner* or either of their *caddies*.") Sonny just smiled at me and leaned back on the bench, turning his face to the sun as if he had all day for me to tee off—or get teed off, as the case might have been.

My tee shot, when I finally hit it, was neither awe-inspiring nor humiliating. It was yawn-inspiring at best. Just kind of ho-hum. The story of my life. My six-iron would, in fact, have been too much club for the shot under ordinary circumstances; however, my cautious approach to the hole and my overly-tentative swing resulted in a shot that landed well short of the green and stopped rolling a good six or seven feet in front of the fringe. Sonny's white ball—a Titleist, maybe?—lay directly between my yellow Top-Flite and the hole. At least I had hit the ball straight, if not high and long.

Once my ball had landed, Sonny rose with his bag and strolled down the fairway toward the green. "That's do-able, Val," he said. "That's do-able. I'll go first and get out of your way."

"I'm *away*," I corrected, as if he were an idiot for not knowing that the player farthest from the hole hits first until everyone is on the green. "You can mark your ball so I don't hit it."

Sonny gave me a puzzled look, as if he didn't know that under certain circumstances a golfer can mark a ball off the green. He just shrugged and walked on, shaking his head a bit and mouthing something, though I couldn't hear what he was saying to himself *or* to me.

When I reached my ball, I pulled my pitching wedge, dropped my bag behind me and took two practice swings as I waited for Sonny to lay his bag to the side after selecting his wedge, then for him to mark and lift his Titleist. He also went ahead and removed the flagstick, since we both were close enough to the hole to see its location clearly. As I took my chipping stance by my ball and glanced up toward the hole, though, I saw something glinting in the sunlight—something that had to be Sonny's marker. It appeared to be a silver coin or token of some sort and looked to be thicker than the thin plastic ball markers most golfers use on the green itself. At least he hadn't used a wooden tee as his marker. "What *is* that, Sonny?" I asked.

"What?" He looked confused again.

"*That*," I said. "Your marker."

"Oh, it's my lucky three-cent piece."

"Huh? *Three*-cent piece?"

"Yeah," he said. "An 1857 silver three-cent piece. My daddy used to find all sorts of neat coins in the collection plate at church. Somebody even dropped *that* one in the plate not long before Daddy got sick. He gave it to me when he saw it was pre-Civil War. He said it'd bring me good luck. I wish he'd kept it."

"Isn't it worth a lot?" I asked.

"Just its sentimental value," he replied. "I think it's really worth about—oh, I don't know—maybe ten bucks or so. Don't worry. You ain't gonna hurt it."

I really wasn't worried about damaging the coin; I just didn't want the coin to deflect my chip shot, as Sonny's marker rested on the apron directly between my ball and the hole. Since the pin was so close to the front of the green, I intended to pitch my yellow Top-Flite onto the slightly longer cut of the fringe in order to slow the ball just a bit before it reached the faster putting surface. I knew that if my ball struck the coin, then I would have an even slimmer chance than usual of chipping in for a birdie (one stroke less than par) and I would probably end up with a longer-than-necessary par putt. So I asked Sonny to move his marker—which, according to *Rule 22*, I had every right to do.

"No problem," he said. "I thought you were ready to hit."

"Well, I'm not," I replied. "Not just yet."

Before I realized what he was doing—because I had turned my back to him to take a few more practice swings—Sonny had replaced his ball on the fringe and chipped it into the cup! Well, actually, I didn't *see* him chip it in, but I did *hear* the distinctive sound of his wedge clipping the ball, then that unmistakable hollow rattle of a golf ball dropping into the cup. When I turned to see what had just happened, I saw Sonny's backside as he bent over to retrieve his Titleist. And he did still have the lob wedge in his hand. "OK," he said with a grin. "Marker's moved. Now just let *me* get out of the way." He stepped gingerly off the green to where the flagstick lay.

Now I was the one shaking my head and muttering to myself. I was so distracted by Sonny's apparent flouting of the rules and etiquette of golf (*Rule 10—Order of Play*) that I didn't take enough time with my own chip-in attempt, bladed the ball thinly and sent it skidding across and off the green. It came to rest at least three feet beyond the far fringe. "You're all right," Sonny remarked when he saw how aggravated I was becoming. "If you don't chip in, you can still get up and down for bogey. It's just the first hole. You can make it up on the next one."

This time I didn't rush myself and was careful to take a couple of practice swings that approximated the actual shot I was preparing to execute, instead of taking one or two routine swipes through the air for show. I tried my best to quiet my mind and to focus it on the ball instead of on Sonny. And though I wasn't on the green yet, I was even ready to *be* the ball, if that would have helped me sink the shot for par.

Evidently, the same idea popped into Sonny's head at the same time. "*NN-NN Nn-Nn nn-nn*," he intoned, as I addressed the ball.

"Do you mind?" I asked, looking up. Now he really *was* getting on my nerves.

"*NN-nn Nn-Nn nn*-not at all," he replied, still chanting like Chevy Chase's Zen-golfer character on the putting green in *Caddyshack*. "Sorry, Val. Just trying to lighten things up a little, you know?" He grinned again.

I backed away from my ball to refocus and ended up walking back to my bag to change clubs. Though I had never chipped with it before, I decided to go ahead and take a chance with my new sand wedge, to put just a tad more spin and loft on my shot. I had wanted to try it out first on a practice chipping area somewhere before using it on a real course, but I figured there was no time like the present to give it a test drive—or chip, as it were. After all, my new favorite short iron felt just right in my loving hands; it was the perfect weight, had the perfect grip and had been a parting gift from my old pro. Be the ball? By gosh, I was gonna be the dang club and put that ball where the sun didn't shine, if I heard any more *NN-NN Nn-Nn nn-nn*s out of one Sonny Rose.

Luckily for me, my yellow Top-Flite was sitting up nicely on the seldomly-trod grass behind the green. Again using my putting stroke but with a bit more backswing, I clipped the rich turf as I bumped the ball and popped it about a foot into the air straight at the dark hole. The ball touched down once on the fringe and again on the green itself before landing and rolling across the smooth surface at a speed that at first seemed too slow, especially as I noticed that the ball was gathering moisture from the morning dew and, therefore, growing heavier with each revolution. I was afraid that the ball would stop way short and leave me a difficult bogey putt. However, the yellow sphere kept rolling and rolling and rolling on across the green all the way to the brink of the cup, with Sonny, flagstick in hand, standing a couple of paces to the right. There, on the edge of the drop, the ball paused, like a hesitant child peering down into the pool from the end of the high dive. I glanced up at Sonny and saw that he was still staring at the ball, as if he still fully expected it to drop into the hole from the lip.

What's holding it? I wondered, moving toward the ball without bothering to get my putter. "Come on, baby," I intoned, then said with more urgency, "Get in the hole!" I said it, even though it annoys me to hear guys in the gallery shout that at Tiger's putts or chips during televised matches. I wondered if my approaching footsteps would be enough to jolt the ball off its perch. But it just hung there, taunting me. Still, I wasn't ready to give up on my par. "Get In The Hole!" I scolded. Nothing. So I gave it one last shot, this time throwing up my hands in despair as I commanded, "GET IN THE HOLE!"

Maybe it was the power of positive thinking at work. Maybe it was good karma or mojo or maybe even a little of that old black magic. Maybe it was the force of the breath that I expelled in issuing my order. Or maybe it was just sheer coincidence. But whatever caused it to happen right then, my ball dropped into the cup with a satisfying rattle.

Shaking my head in disbelief, I fished the ball out of the hole and looked up at Sonny with a weak grin. "First time *that's* ever happened to me," I said. "Unbelievable, huh?"

Sonny replaced the flag and started walking toward the second tee. "I've seen balls drop like that a few times," he replied, then added, "You keeping score for us, or you just wanna play and not worry about it?"

I laughed. "Naw, we *gotta* keep score," I said, "especially after *that* shot. That's the toughest par I've ever made."

"Par?" Sonny said. He gave me a quizzical look.

"Well, yeah," I said, wondering what he was up to now.

"How do you figure that?" he asked. "I mean, we *are* playing by the rules, aren't we?" He didn't appear to be upset with me, but he did seem to be in a strange mood.

"Sure," I said. "I *always* play by the rules. I had a three on that hole—the six-iron off the tee, the chip shot I sculled with my pitching wedge, and then the chip with the sand wedge that went in. That's three. Par. Right?"

"No," he corrected, "that was *four*. If we're playing by the rules, *all* the rules, then we gotta go by the one that says a ball hanging on the lip of the hole has to drop within ten seconds after the player reaches it or else you count the ball dropping as a stroke, basically. I counted, and your ball hung there on the lip for at least fifteen to twenty seconds, the whole time you were telling it to get in the hole. Right?"

"Oh, come on," I said. "Ten seconds? I've read *The Rules of Golf*, and I don't remember seeing *that* rule. And, besides, you broke the rules when you went ahead and hit out of turn back there. I could ask you to hit over, if I wanted to."

Sonny shook his head. "I didn't break any rule by hitting ahead of you. I was ready to hit, and you weren't. Remember, we agreed to play 'ready golf'—which means you hit when you're ready. It's kinda like the continuous putting rule. And, yeah, there *is* a ten-second rule on putts dropping."

By this time I felt my face turning red. "Yeah, well, I've got the rulebook right here, and if you can show me that rule, I'll, uh, I'll pay you for a lesson. Twenty bucks, that's the going rate for a lesson down at Billy Joe's where I worked." I dug the booklet out of my bag and handed it to him.

"OK," Sonny said, thumbing through the pages. "OK, here it is—sixteen-dash-two. 'Ball Overhanging Hole. When any part of the ball overhangs the lip of the *hole*, the player is allowed enough time to reach the *hole* without unreasonable delay and an additional ten seconds to determine whether the ball is at rest. If by then the ball has not fallen into the *hole*, it is deemed to be at rest. If the ball subsequently falls into the *hole*, the player is deemed to have *holed* out with his last *stroke*, and he shall add a *penalty stroke* to his score for the hole; otherwise, there is no penalty under this *Rule*.'" He closed the booklet and handed it back to me. "Rule sixteen-dash-two. See for yourself."

I flipped to that page and reread the rule. I saw for myself that Sonny had read it word for word. He was right. I was wrong. I owed him twenty bucks. "So are we playing by the rules, or are we just playing a nice easy practice round between two friends?" he asked, smiling and holding out his ungloved right hand to me.

"A nice easy practice round," I replied, noting his gentle but firm grip as I shook his hand. "But how about if we play number nine for real? That's the toughest hole, isn't it?"

"The Little Green Monster?"

"Yeah. Number nine."

"Sure," he said, "and whoever *slays* him buys the Mountain Dews after the round. Deal?"

"Deal," I agreed, as we arrived at the second tee and got ready to begin the process all over again, from tee to green to hole, encountering the occasional fairway, rough or hazard along the way when things didn't work out as planned. From then on, it was just another day on the links. Well, sort of.

FOURTEEN

Sonny and I decided that nine holes of golf, even on the Willow Creek par three, would be enough for one day. That was once around the nine-hole course, and neither he nor I felt the need to replay any of the holes, not even number nine, the most challenging one by a long shot. Sonny didn't need to go around again, because he had played about as well as anyone could expect him to, especially after having taken a year off from golf to play tennis with Elaine.

That morning at Willow Creek, he birdied the three easiest holes, parred the three middle-rated holes, and bogeyed two of the three most difficult holes. The other difficult hole—the one he didn't bogey—was number nine, yes, the Little Green Monster, which, as unbelievable as it sounds, Sonny aced. A hole-in-one. No kidding. It was a seven-wood shot to the Monster's heart, unlike anything I had ever seen before. Sonny couldn't believe it either. When the ball rolled into the hole, Sonny did a little victory dance around the tee area and sheathed the seven-wood in his belt as if he were Sir Chi-Chi Rodriquez on the putting green.

So while Sonny finished at three strokes under par, I closed out the round at, oh, at least nine over par—at least one extra stroke per hole. How did I play on number nine? Well, let's just say that when Sonny and I loaded ourselves back into the *Bluesmobile* to leave Willow Creek, I was singing the "Double-Bogey Blues." My main problem had been my putting; I had lost my touch and didn't find it over the nine holes we played. Sonny said it was my putter, that it wasn't the right style for my putting stroke. By the time I three-putted the Monster, I was ready to agree that I needed to replace my Ping putter whether it was one of my favorite clubs or not.

Around noon, the day was still beautiful—a heartbreakingly blue sky with a white cottony cloud here and there, and the temperature in the mid-seventies—when Sonny decided I needed to tour Valle Crucis, the little farm village near Willow Creek. Besides the old elementary school with its gray stone facade, a hundred-year-old general store—a huge white frame structure much like Coffey's Store at Edgemont but larger—was the true center of the community. The two-story Mast General Store sat imposingly on the shoulder of the two-lane highway through Valle Crucis, so named because the valley appeared to be cross-shaped from the three streams and their coves that came together there.

We parked behind the store, walked up the back steps and past the rockers and benches on the back porch. Sonny held open the screen door, tethered by a long tight spring and adorned by a red metal Coca-Cola sign. Entering the store itself was like stepping back seventy-five years in time. Canned goods of all types, some even in glass Mason jars, lined the high shelves. Larger items, like baskets and tubs and sleds, hung from the ceiling. One section of the store toward the front door still served as a post office, with a wall of numbered bronze mail boxes surrounding a little barred window for the clerk to do business through.

Sonny nodded toward a low red Coke icebox. "Grab us a couple o' cold Mountain Dews, Val," he said. "Be careful when you take the tops off. Opener's on the side."

I slid open the refrigerated box's lid and reached into the chilly wet interior for two of the easily distinguishable Mountain Dew longnecks of green glass with crimped metal tops. Even though I had heard Sonny's warning, I was in too much of a hurry with the built-in bottle opener on the side of the drink box, and the first bottle spewed a few drops of its sweet yellow froth over my fist before I could clamp the open top with my free hand. "Woh, girl!" Sonny laughed. "I told you it was tricky."

"My bad," I said, taking more care with the second bottle, then carrying both to the counter, adorned by a huge brass cash register.

Sonny paid for the drinks, handing three bills to the cashier, a pretty college-aged girl. "You just keep the change, honey," Sonny told the clerk, who smiled and thanked him.

Back in the *Bluesmobile*, Sonny tilted the bottle to his lips as he waited for the traffic to thin on the highway. "Ummm," he murmured, tasting the nectar. "I do *love* Mountain Dew." Then he added, "Now, don't you go and tell Elaine I had this, 'cause it ain't on our diet. She'll skin me alive if she finds out I'm drinking Mountain Dews and she's drinking nothing but water." He handed me his bottle so he could wheel the car out onto the road, turning right instead of left as I expected.

"Where we going?" I asked, giving him back his drink.

"I want to show you one of the prettiest little churches around here," he replied. "It's at the head of the valley's cross, I guess you could say."

We followed the paved highway for what must have been a couple of miles, then turned onto one graveled road after another along the Watauga River. Finally, we pulled into a small parking area along the fence that enclosed the church about which Sonny had spoken. Like Greenlee Chapel near Edgemont, this church was a tiny white frame building with a graveyard to one side. The main difference between the two churches was that this one was perched on a hill, while Greenlee Chapel sat in bottomland. Also, a six-foot-tall gray granite Celtic cross standing in this churchyard greeted visitors here, unlike the humble river-rock sign marking the entrance to the chapel off the mountain.

"What kind of church is this?" I asked. "Baptist?"

Sonny smiled. "No, it's an Episcopal church," he corrected. "Valle Crucis was settled by Episcopalian missionaries back in the 1800s—monks, actually. It's so peaceful I like to come over here and just sit sometimes."

Though we stayed in the car next to the churchyard, we could easily look out over the picture-postcard valley, with its green and yellow blocks of farmland beneath the blue and white late-June sky. Neither of us spoke for a few minutes. Then, as usual, Sonny broke the silence and gestured toward the cemetery. "See that tombstone over there?" he asked, pointing to a grave at the front.

"The one that's off by itself?" I said.

"Yeah, that one," Sonny replied. "That's the preacher's grave—the preacher who some silly people say haunts this church." He gave me one of those phony wide-eyed spooky looks, arching his eyebrows as if he were Vincent Price or Bela Lugosi or somebody.

"Oh, come on," I said, though I caught myself looking around uneasily to make sure nothing was sneaking up on us.

"No, really," he said. "That's the story you hear all the time around here, how the old preacher hung himself in the church—which he didn't do, by the way—and then how on certain nights he and his whole congregation rise from their graves and walk down there right into the river—for a ghostly baptismal service, I guess. Even though they all *were* Episcopalians and not Baptists."

With a chuckle, Sonny shook his head. "It just goes to show you how silly people can be, what with all the ghost stories about this place. I've been coming here for years, ever since I was a teen-ager, and I've *never* seen or heard anything that couldn't be explained later."

I wanted to agree with him. However, his explanation still didn't explain why the preacher's grave was by itself, away from the other graves in the cemetery. That really *was* odd, I said. "Well, yeah," Sonny replied, "but why does it have to mean something spooky, something supernatural? Why couldn't the explanation be just that the preacher's grave was one of the first one's here—it *was* moved here, by the way? That's easier to believe than some ghost tale, ain't it?"

I nodded. "Yeah, I guess so," I conceded, "but it isn't nearly as much fun—kinda like all those stories about the Brown Mountain Light. Right?"

Sonny eyed me suspiciously. "Oh, so Alan's hooked you, too," he said, with a smile. "I swear, that boy is determined to figure out the story behind those Lights, even though they've been around for centuries and nobody's been able to explain them. Not really, anyway."

"Have you ever seen it—the Light, I mean?"

"Maybe, maybe not," he said. "I think I have, but I'm kinda like Alan. I think there's got to be some explanation everybody's been missing all these years. I think if a person looked hard enough, he'd be able to find the proof. Now, of course, the explanation *could* end up being supernatural, 'cause you know the Bible does talk about spirits and demons and witches and stuff, so they *do* exist. I just don't see why that's the *first* thing people come up with to explain something they don't understand.

"It's kinda like that fairy ring over there," he continued, pointing at a circle of golf ball-sized mushrooms growing in the churchyard near the preacher's grave. "Fairies—*the little people*—have absolutely nothing to do with those rings, but that's how folks started explaining them, 'cause they didn't understand how certain fungi spread and grow. Believe it or not, there's even a theory that the Brown Mountain Light is caused by an underground fungus. My daddy always thought the Light—or Lights—were moonshine stills. Now, he *did* believe in spirits and demons and such—he certainly believed in angels, for instance—but he didn't think they were what was making those lights."

"Yeah, your mom was telling me that last night," I said. "But she said she's seen some really weird stuff—stuff that couldn't have been moonshiners."

"That's right. She has. And *I've* seen some unusual things there, too. But as far as I'm concerned, the jury's still out on the Brown Mountain Light—until Alan or somebody else brings in the evidence to prove or disprove it. Besides, that mystery's just too good for business for me to go one way or the other on it. I mean, I don't want to say I *don't* believe it, and I don't want to say exactly what I *have* seen, 'cause then what other folks think *they* see might not be the same thing I saw, and then they might not let their imaginations run away with them quite as much. That make sense?"

"Yeah, I guess so," I replied, though I was actually having a difficult time following his line of reasoning. Why couldn't it be a black-and-white kind of thing? Either you believed in the Brown Mountain Light or you didn't. Why did everything have to be a shade of gray? "But can't you tell *me* what it looked like? You've told Alan and Elaine, haven't you?"

He shook his head. "Actually, no, I haven't." He paused, as if to decide whether or not he should go ahead and reveal some deep dark secret. "The way I figure it, everybody needs to see it for themself—or *not* see it, as the case may be. I know some folks who's parked at the Brown Mountain Overlook for *years* and haven't seen the first thing that's anything close to the Light. And I know other folks who's gone there once and seen a porchlight come on in the valley, and then they go running around swearing to everybody they saw the Brown Mountain Light. But like I said, I think everybody's got to make up their mind for themself."

He had long since finished his Mountain Dew, but he continued to tilt the bottle up every so often to let every last sweet drop of the soda drip onto his tongue. I still had half my bottle left. "Course, I could make you a little deal," Sonny continued, giving me a sly look out the corner of his eye. "I could tell you what I saw, if you do me a favor—and promise never to tell anybody."

"About what?" I was starting to get uneasy about being alone with him, wondering if maybe I had misjudged Sonny's motives in taking me on this outing. I had been asked to do favors before *and* to keep secrets, and those situations had never turned out well, for me or the one who asked for the favors, whether it had been a teammate or a coach or a teacher or even a so-called friend. I never ceased to be amazed at how bold—and at the same time how timid—some guys could be, to think they could trick me somehow into agreeing to do what they wanted. "What shouldn't I say anything about?"

Sonny seemed confused. "About what I saw—about the Light," he said, then suddenly seemed to understand my question. "And, yeah, I wouldn't want you to tell Alan or Elaine about it—or about our deal. It would have to be our little secret—the truth about what the Brown Mountain Light really looks like."

I felt he was making just a bit too much out of the whole thing, but I decided to keep playing along, to see what the terms of his little deal were, to see what kind of man he really was before I put him in his place. "What do I have to do?" I asked.

Like a snake who had just swallowed its mousey lunch whole, Sonny smiled. "Oh, nothing much," he began. "Just come see me every day for a few weeks, spend a little time with me and then go stay with Mama for a couple hours. That's all. Elaine could drop you off at the college on her way through Foscoe every morning. It wouldn't be much out of her way. I could drop you at the library in Jonas Ridge on my way back to the lodge. And then Mama could run you in to Linville when the library closes."

"I thought you didn't have to teach school this summer," I asked. "Why would you want me to meet you there?"

He smiled again. "That's where my books and videos are."

"Huh?"

Chuckling this time, he continued, "Because if I'm going to help you make up your incomplete in social studies, I need to have my books and videos and maps and stuff, and I don't want to haul everything home. Mama can work with you at the library. There's plenty of books to read there. We figure you can make up both incompletes in about three weeks, if you keep your nose to the grindstone and take it seriously. And, by the way, Mama's the type of old English teacher who'll see that you do. But you'll learn a lot, and you'll have fun helping her out around the library. Maybe even make a little money, so you can pay me the twenty bucks you owe and the hundred bucks the county's charging you for this little summer school we're gonna be running just for you."

"What!?"

"That was the deal, wasn't it?" he said, with a laugh. "If I remember correctly, you said you'd pay me for a lesson if I was right about that ten-second rule. And I *was* right, wasn't I?"

"Yeah, you were right. OK, OK, I'll pay up." I knew when someone had me dead to rights. "And I'll do the summer school thing, since it looks like everybody's already made all these plans for me. What day do we start?"

"No time like today," Sonny said, reaching down to crank the *Bluesmobile*. "After we get a bite to eat, I'll drop you off at the library, and Mama can get started with her assignments for you. I've already made mine."

"Huh? What assignments?"

"Assign-*ment*, actually—singular," he replied. "Let's see. What'll we call this research project you're gonna do for us? Hmmm.

OK, how about this?" He paused with his hand on the *Bluesmobile*'s steering wheel and gazed up into the sky for a second, then looked over at the colorful embroidery on the left breast of my golf shirt. "How about 'Golf, the Blues, and the Brown Mountain Light: What These Three Things Have in Common,' or something like that? You probably oughta write that down before I forget it. You still got that scorecard and pencil in your pocket? If you don't, I can probably find something in the floorboard to write on."

"You're kidding."

Sonny threw the car into gear and wheeled it around to head back down the road. "Nope," he replied. "I think that'd make a *great* research project. And I'll let you decide how you want to present your findings—a twenty-page *typed and single-spaced* paper, maybe, or a Powerpoint presentation with—oh, I don't know—at least fifty or sixty slides, or maybe an article in the *Ledger*. A series of guest columns on the op-ed page across from *my* column. Yeah, now that I think about it, that'd be a good way to present your findings. And then everybody could learn from what *you* learn this summer."

"Gee whiz, Sonny," I said. "Why don't I just write you a dang book?"

"Or you could do *that*," he quipped. "But I don't think you'll have time to write a whole book this summer, busy as you're gonna be. And then in the fall, we're thinking you'll probably want to enroll at Skyland if you can't find a job you like right off. Matter of fact, we could probably find you a part-time job somewhere, maybe even at the lodge. But writing a book—I like that idea. Maybe you can do that later on, after you get a little experience under your belt. I've even thought about writing one myself."

Ordinarily, I might have gotten upset that everyone obviously was making plans for me and that they were deciding the direction of my life without giving me any input. At first I didn't appreciate their apparent forwardness, but then it occurred to me that I hadn't been doing a very good job figuring out what to do with myself, if mowing grass at a golf course for the rest of my life was the best plan that I could come up with on my own. I decided that I *needed* help from somebody, as I hadn't been getting anywhere by myself.

Even my friend Bo was letting me down. I tried to call him from the *Bluesmobile*, as Sonny and I headed back toward Linville. Sonny even stopped at the golf store on the way and went inside to give me some privacy while I tried to reach Bo. But my best friend didn't have his cell phone turned on, and he apparently had disabled both his voicemail and text messaging. I guessed he had forgotten that the previous night he had told me to call him the next day, or maybe he had said he would *talk* to me the next day—that, I guess, was what he had said. Anyway, as it turned out, I couldn't get ahold of Bo, and he didn't bother calling me that day, either, for whatever reason.

It wasn't like Bo to be so undependable. I figured his feelings were still hurt over that CD of Sonny's, and I hoped Bo would get back to being himself before long. Maybe if he got to know Sonny as I was getting to know him, then Bo would see that Sonny hadn't meant anything by that Rebel flag stuff.

When Sonny emerged from the golf shop, he carried a new putter over his shoulder—well, not a *new* club, actually, but one he had just purchased from the store's assortment of used equipment. "Here you go," he said, handing me the putter head-first as he got back into the car. "A little going-back-to-school present."

Taking the club by its steel shaft, I saw it was a vintage Walter Hagen Silver Star putter, with a simple blade-shaped brass head and its original perforated leather grip. "This is what you need, and it didn't cost anywhere near as much as that Ping of yours," Sonny said. "Don't worry about paying me back right away. I'll put you on my easy-payment plan. And if you make up those two incompletes before the end of the summer, this'll be a graduation present, too. Deal?"

"Deal," I agreed.

"And Tuesday will be *our* day, our golf day—OK, Val?" Sonny said, as he cranked the car to go. "We'll play a round every Tuesday if you keep up with the assignments Mama and me give you. Deal?"

"Deal," I said again, then thought to ask, "Where? Where will we play? Willow Creek? Or Hawksnest?" I would have been happy with either course, but there was one paradise whose name I dared not mention, for fear that all hope of playing there would be extinguished.

Sonny smiled. "Who knows," he replied. "Play your cards right, babe, and we might even find a way to play a round at Linville." Sly old Sonny sure did know how to sweet-talk a girl like me. He knew exactly what to say and exactly what I wanted to hear. I just hoped the promises he whispered in my ear weren't sweet nothings.

FIFTEEN

Early the next morning—Wednesday, the day the *Ledger* would be printed and put in racks—Aunt Elaine dropped me off at Skyland Tech on her way through Foscoe to Linville. On any other morning she might have stopped for breakfast at the Grandview Restaurant, one of Foscoe's most popular eating places among locals and tourists alike, with its grandiose view of Grandfather Mountain out the building's row of picture windows and its even grander orders of steaming hot biscuits fresh from the oven and creamy sausage gravy and buttermilk pancakes and homemade apple butter. But Elaine was still on that darn diet of hers, and she was in such a hurry to get to the paper that she barely said goodbye before setting me out in front of Sonny's building. She *did* think to remind me that she would be taking a late lunch that day, after the paper went to press, so I might want to get something to eat in the campus "canteen" before leaving Skyland.

At seven o'clock, with Sonny not scheduled to arrive for at least another hour and a half or so, I figured I'd wander around the deserted campus and find the snack bar, though I doubted it would have anything close to the Grandview's sumptuous fare. And I was right. I eventually found the canteen in the basement of the administration building and breakfasted on half a Diet Dew and a pack of Lance cheese-on-wheat crackers.

I could have purchased a Gala apple from one of the vending machines, but I decided to save my remaining fifty cents for another "pack o' nabs" at lunch. The jingling of the two quarters in my shorts pocket annoyed me as I killed time walking around the tiny campus, but at least it was a reminder that I wasn't totally broke, as had often been the case back after Grandma got sick and I was trying to pay for her medicine with my meager paycheck from Billy Joe's.

I was sitting on the front steps of Sonny's building around 8:45 when I saw his black Mustang turn off the main highway, pull up the long and winding driveway, and roll into a faculty slot in the parking lot. Sonny spotted me right away, smiling and throwing up his hand in greeting. I waved back but with considerably less enthusiasm.

"Ready to get started for real?" Sonny asked as he approached me. He was carrying his full set of golf clubs and was wearing his "working-class" uniform of blue jeans, T-shirt and sandals.

"Guess so," I replied, rising from my seat on the steps and taking the big golf bag from him as he passed. "We playing today?"

He shook his head. "No. I figured you could clean my clubs for me as a little warm-up," he said, "before you get down to business on your research—you know, since your project's about golf and the blues and all." He gave me what Billy Joe would have called a "grit-eatin' grin," then added, "How'd things go with Mama yesterday?" I could tell he had already heard about my afternoon at the library.

"Fine," I said, as we entered the building and headed through the lobby toward the twin elevators. A couple of students loitering down the hallway outside a first-floor classroom called out to Sonny and waved to him as if he were their favorite teacher. He waved back, then punched the up-arrow button on the wall panel between the sets of doors.

I could hear the elevator car begin to descend from above, and we both looked up to see its progress displayed in the green electronic numerals that flashed in the small dark LED screen above the metal doors before us: *4...3...2...L.* The car came to a mechanical stop behind the shiny metal barrier. There was a pause before the mirror-like doors slid open to reveal the empty compartment awaiting our entry. It was a plain elevator car, decorated with only the requisite inspection certificate and safety reminders. The carpet, though appearing relatively new and freshly vacuumed, was an uninspiring pattern of various shades of gray; the three solid walls were painted a lighter gray. The ceiling was a square grillwork of opaque plastic backed by three bright fluorescent tubes that lit the compartment more brightly than I thought necessary.

Once inside the elevator, Sonny punched the "4" button on the wall panel, then stood back with me to watch the numbers change on the screen. "Fine, huh?" he said presently. "That's not what Elaine told me."

"When did you talk to her?" I asked.

"This morning. She called me after she got to the office. Caught me on my way out the door. Said there was a little problem with my column, and she wanted to check with me before she cut it."

"Problem?" The elevator doors opened at the fourth floor, and we stepped out into the hallway. I let Sonny take the lead, as I had never been to his office before.

He nodded. "Yeah," he replied. "She said it was a few inches too long, and she wanted to know which part I wouldn't mind leaving off until next week. You know, some editors wouldn't even bother asking the writer; they'd just lop part of the column off. Elaine isn't like that, though."

We stopped at his office door and waited as he fumbled with the guitar case, then finally managed to fish out his keys to unlock the door. Knowing Sonny even as well as I did at that point, I was expecting something that was at least a bit on the plush side—maybe, at the very least, a Western theme with bull horns and cowboy movie posters—but his office was nothing special, just three walls of shelves jam-packed with boringly-titled history books and a budget-model desk holding what appeared to be a five- or six-year-old computer and nothing else but a Carolina-blue plastic Tarheels drink cup filled with pens and pencils. There wasn't even a window. His rolling desk chair didn't look comfortable at all, with no arms and no extra padding; neither did the metal folding chair sitting next to the desk which presumably was meant to be the seat for any visitor to the office. That chair, however, was filled with a stack of books that Sonny nodded toward.

"There's some books you won't find at Mama's library that might help you out," he said. "You can start looking through them after you finish with my clubs. There's notecards in the top right drawer. You *do* know how to take notes, don't you?"

I frowned. "Well, yeah," I replied. "I'm not a complete idiot."

He smiled. "I know you're not, Val. But, listen, I need to run into town for a couple hours, and then I'll be back, probably around eleven or so, and we'll go over some things—like, maybe, what you think of that top book there." He nodded again toward the stack in the chair, specifically at the top book, a small blue paperback entitled *Lost in the Cosmos: The Last Self-Help Book* in big white lettering. It was by some guy named Walker Percy. His name was in big letters, too, higher on the page than the book's title, so I figured he was some big writer or somebody, even though I had never heard of him.

"You're kidding," I said. "Two hours to read a book?"

He just smiled again. "To *skim* a book—and clean a set of clubs," he corrected. "Besides, I might not get back until noon. I'm not sure how long this'll take. I'll leave the door unlocked, just in case you need to go to the restroom or somewhere. I wouldn't want you to get locked out. And, oh, there's some cleaner and paper towels in the right bottom drawer there." He took a second to fix the door so it wouldn't lock, then started to leave.

"Mind if I use your computer?" I asked.

"No, I'd rather you *not* mess with it, if you don't mind," he said, shaking his head. "Not that I don't trust you. It's just I think we've got too many computers in our lives now as it is, and there ain't no sense in using them if you don't have to. You can find everything you need to know in that book there—everything you need to know today, anyway. OK? Besides, they unhooked it at the end of spring quarter, and I'm not sure exactly how to hook it back up." Before I could offer to hook the computer back up for him, he nodded again and made his getaway. I could hear his Birkenstocks flip-flapping on the tile floor as he beat a hasty retreat toward the elevators.

"Well, crap," I muttered to myself. I plopped down into Sonny's seat and rolled it under the desk, then leaned over to check out the other titles in the stack on the folding chair. "Crap," I repeated, as I saw nothing I had already read and the names of only a few authors with whom I was at all familiar.

Sonny's other assigned books included *Driver's Handbook* by the North Carolina Division of Motor Vehicles (Sonny said I *would* get my driver's license that summer, even if I didn't have a car to drive yet); *Six American Poets*, an anthology edited by Joel Conarroe, with poems by Walt Whitman, Emily Dickinson, Wallace Stevens, William Carlos Williams, Robert Frost and Langston Hughes (I had heard of Whitman, Dickinson and Frost, but not the other three); *The Amen Corner* by James Baldwin; *The Soul of Golf* by a man named William Hallberg; *Singin' and Swingin' and Gettin' Merry Like Christmas* by Maya Angelou; *Blues for All the Changes* by Nikki Giovanni; *Mexico City Blues* by Jack Kerouac; and *Perfect Lies: A Century of Great Golf Stories* by that Hallberg guy again, who must have been Sonny's favorite author, because Sonny had yet another golf book by the same man on the shelf just above his desk, a paperback novel called *The Rub of the Green*. I wondered why Sonny hadn't assigned me to read that one, too. Probably because it might be a good book that I might enjoy reading without having to think too awful much—even though I didn't like fiction because make-believe stories were a waste of time, as far as I was concerned.

The previous afternoon at the Jonas Ridge Library, Miss Faye had given me her own "pile" of books to read—ten books that *she* said contained almost everything I needed to know. Actually, what she gave me was a hand-printed and numbered list of titles and authors on a single sheet of college-ruled notebook paper. She said I should learn to find the individual volumes myself in the library's stacks. "Do for yourself, young lady," she said, though she *did* help me find the first book on her list.

Miss Faye's assignments included, in the strict order that she said I should read them, *A Wonder-Book and Tanglewood Tales* by Nathaniel Hawthorne (yes, the same guy who wrote *The Scarlet Letter*); *American Folk Tales and Songs* by Richard Chase (who Miss Faye said used to live near there); *Harbrace College Handbook* by

John C. Hodges; Alfred, Lord Tennyson's *In Memoriam, The Princess, and Maud*, edited by John C. Collins; *Twelfth Night* by William F. Shakespeare (I added the F myself, partly because that was the grade I usually got on Shakespeare assignments in school); *Listening for the Crack of Dawn* by Donald Davis; *Pudd'nhead Wilson* by Mark Twain (finally, someone whose books I liked); *In the Clearing* by Robert Frost; *Honey and Salt* by Carl Sandburg; and *Grandfather Tales* by Mr. Chase again. When Miss Faye gave me her reading list, she laughed and said I was lucky that Preacher Rose, rest his soul, hadn't made the assignment. He would have handed me just one book, she said—the King James Bible, by God.

"We're so fortunate nowadays," Miss Faye added. "Back when I was teaching, country schools were so poor that the only thing even close to a literature textbook that most students ever had was a little book called *101 Famous Poems*, and we had to hold fund-raisers year after year to buy copies for each child. The children picked up bottles for the deposits and begged for donations and such as that. It was shameful what we had to do just to put books in our children's hands, but—I tell you what—my students *cherished* their books when they finally got them, and some of them come back even now as grown-up men and women, and they tell me they *still* read from their little poetry books—what poems I didn't make them memorize and recite in front of the class, that is."

Jeez, I hoped Miss Faye wasn't going to make *me* do that—memorize poetry and recite it in front of people. And what with all this heavy reading that she and Sonny expected me to do over the next few weeks, I couldn't imagine when I'd have time to actually *write* anything, especially some stupid research paper about golf and the blues and the Brown Mountain Light and what they all had in common. And since none of the books from either Sonny or Miss Faye apparently mentioned the Light, I figured I was expected to find out about *that* by myself, even though I knew I could get some help from Alan and maybe from Bo, if he wasn't still in a bad mood.

Before getting started on that "self-help" book that I had only a couple of hours to read, I took down the Hallberg golf novel that Sonny *hadn't* assigned and looked it over. That was the way I was back then: I could always find something else that interested me more than whatever it was I was supposed to be doing at any given time. Grandpa used to fuss at me a little bit about that, especially after I'd beg and beg to go out with him on *The Lady of Shallotte* and then spend the whole day asking how much longer it would be before we could go back home. I think he understood I just wanted to be with him but that I didn't particularly care about shrimping. He knew he was my hero and that I loved him more than anybody in the whole wide world then, after my folks passed away, and that I liked nothing more than listening to him tell all his old sea stories over and over again. But the front porch of our big old house there at Village Point was a lot more comfortable and considerably less fishy-smelling than the deck of *The Lady* when the shrimping was good.

The Rub of the Green had an interesting cover—a painting of a lone golfer driving the ball up the most gorgeous fairway imaginable toward an elevated green backed by dark leafy hardwoods and beneath gathering storm clouds in an otherwise blue sky. I could see the pin's little red triangular flag on the distant green; however, I couldn't find the ball itself anywhere in the picture, even though the golfer's pose, caught at the butt end of his swing, indicated that he had just driven the ball off the grassy tee and was watching it soar straight toward its mark. The painter had made the topography of the hole being played—with its undulations and swales—look like the body of a woman in a subliminal sort of way.

I flipped the book over in my hands to read the blurb on the back cover and was surprised to see that, of all people, "bestselling author Walker Percy" (the guy whose book I was supposed to be reading right then) had called *The Rub of the Green* a "brilliant" book. He said it was like "hitting the sweet spot" in golf. This was the one I wanted to read first, not some "self-help" book by an old man, bestselling author or not, who would probably much rather read my first choice than Sonny's—or Miss Faye's first choice, too, for that matter. That's what had happened the afternoon before, or, rather, how the whole thing with the old lady started.

After Miss Faye had given me those ten books and had said I should begin with the Hawthorne, I had muttered something about wasting my time reading "baby books." That was when I got to see another side of sweet old Miss Faye.

She didn't say anything to me right off, but I could tell she was hurt, apparently because *A Wonder-Book and Tanglewood Tales* had been her favorite book when she was a girl, she had said. I looked at its table of contents and saw nothing that struck my fancy. Then when I fairly tossed the old book (a rebound 1923 edition with yellowed dog-eared pages) aside and went back to the mushroom reference I had been reading, Miss Faye went ballistic. And this time she got right to the point.

"Young lady!" she had shrieked. "Don't you ever, *ever*, handle one of my books in that careless manner again! This is a library, not a playground!"

"I'm sorry, Miss Faye," I said, "but I saw some mushrooms this morning with Sonny, and I was wanting to see what kind they were." Assuming my apology was sufficient, I had continued thumbing through *Mushrooms Demystified: A Comprehensive Guide to the Fleshy Fungi*, the book I had found the first afternoon I had spent at the library with Miss Faye. But I was wrong.

"Miss Galloway," Miss Faye said firmly. "While you're here in *my* library, you will abide by *my* rules. If you wish to complete your course of study in a timely manner, then I advise you to follow the rules I set down, as well as my instructions for your education. By the way, you *did* make an agreement with my son today regarding the completion of your assignments, did you not?"

"Yeah—I mean, yes, ma'am," I replied. "He said we'd play golf on Tuesdays if I keep my work up."

Miss Faye gave me one of those schoolmarmy looks I used to hate—the look of knowing she had me backed into a tight corner and that I probably wasn't bold enough to do anything to get out of it. She knew I wanted to play golf with Sonny and that I would do whatever I had to do for that privilege, especially if it meant eventually getting to play at Linville Golf Club.

"Somewhere along the way, young lady," Miss Faye continued, "we Americans got the wrong idea about education—the *wrong* idea. And a lot of wrong ideas about a lot of other things, too, for that matter. Somewhere somebody got the idea that everything we do is supposed to be *fun* and that we deserve some kind of *reward* for doing things we really don't want to do. Well, my dear young lady, you need to learn right here and now that *I* don't ascribe to that liberal philosophy, especially where one's schoolwork is concerned. Yes, you heard me correctly; it's called school-*work*, not school-*play*. And however liberal my son has become over there at that fancy new college of his, bribing students to do their work and trying to make sure they all have *fun*, I still believe that learning is its own reward and that reading *is* *fun*-damental, as the saying goes."

She paused a moment to catch her breath and to study my reaction to her lecture before continuing, "So you *shall* read the books I assign, in the order I assign them, and you shall *not* handle any of my books in a careless manner ever again. Books are our friends, sometimes the only ones we have. Is that clear?"

"Crystal," I answered, figuring she hadn't seen *A Few Good Men* and wouldn't recognize my allusion to the similar exchange between Tom Cruise's cool-guy character and Jack Nicholson's uptight Marine colonel character. Again, I was probably wrong.

"And no more of your smart mouth," Miss Faye scolded. "I want to be liked as much as Sonny does. But, Valerie, I refuse to compromise my principles when so much is at stake."

"What's at stake?" I asked, then quickly added, "No, Miss Faye, I'm serious. What do you think's at stake?" I wanted to know if she knew more about me than I thought she did—or possibly should.

She merely shook her head and jabbed her finger at the next book in the stack, *American Folk Tales and Songs*, taking my mushroom book and the Hawthorne volume as she walked back toward the circulation desk near the front entrance. "On second thought, just never you mind then about the Hawthorne," she said. "It's much too fragile. But you be careful with Mr. Chase's book, too. It's autographed." I looked inside, and, sure enough, the author had scrawled a brief personal message in red felt-tip pen on the dedication page. "Have fun! Uncle Dick," the undated inscription read.

About thirty minutes before closing time, Miss Faye returned and started quizzing me about the book's contents, as if I had actually been paying attention as I was looking through its stories about that silly Jack character that hillbillies seem to like so much. To tell the truth, I had only read maybe one Jack tale and then had gotten sidetracked with a real children's book—a picture book, even—called *The Green Man* that someone had left on the other end of the table where I was sitting. The author was Gail E. Hailey, who had written another Jack tales book called *Mountain Jack Tales* (which I looked at, too, and liked a lot more than Mr. Chase's book, actually), so I figured Miss Faye wouldn't mind too much if I made the substitution. And, to be honest, I kind of enjoyed reading *The Green Man* story and looking at all the pictures.

But Miss Faye *did* mind. "Did you not take notes?" she asked incredulously when I couldn't tell her much about the Chase book. My negative response to her question won me a mini-lesson on note-taking, as well as a pack of four-by-six notecards from the library storeroom, a half-used Black Warrior number-two pencil and a black capless BIC Cristal ball-point pen that had about an inch of ink left in its clear barrel and looked to be at least as old as I was then. I asked for a new pen, but Miss Faye said, "Well, beggers can't be choosers," and didn't seem to care if I took offense or not, seeing as how I *was* kind of impoverished at that time in my life.

She then closed the library and drove us to Linville so I could catch a ride back home with Aunt Elaine. The old lady even parked her car and followed me into the *Ledger* office to tell Elaine about my "behavior." Through her open office door, Elaine glanced at me sitting in the lobby a time or two as Miss Faye fussed and fumed, saying Valerie *this* and Valerie *that*. She—Aunt Elaine, I mean—even smiled weakly at me once when the old lady wasn't looking, so I figured I was OK with her.

But, boy, was *I* ever wrong, again. I found out on the way home, when we stopped at MacRae Meadows to walk the cinder track for a few minutes so that Elaine could unwind a bit from what must have been a trying day at work, judging from her harried look and quiet bearing since leaving the office. I just hoped *I* wasn't her entire problem that day and that there was something else on her mind.

Figuring Aunt Elaine should hear my side of the story, too, I fussed and fumed myself about all the books Miss Faye was assigning me to read and how most of them looked like children's books; about how it was crazy to make me read all that stuff and then expect me to write some silly research paper about some stupid topic that Miss Faye and Sonny had thought up; and about how it was all a big waste of time, but I'd do it just to keep everybody happy, even if they *weren't* anything to me. I didn't want to cause trouble between Elaine and Sonny and his mom, I said. I'd *try* to read all those books and *try* to write the darn research paper, I said.

It took me almost a complete circuit of the track to finish my ranting, and we were literally walking down the home stretch, about even with the memorial cairn on the hillside above us, when Elaine evidently decided she couldn't let things stand as they did right then—in other words, let me think I was going to sleepwalk my way through my summer school studies just so I could play a little golf, as I had done in my regular high school courses to begin with.

"Let's get something straight, Val," Elaine had said. "I don't want to upset you or say anything that might give you the idea I don't love you dearly, because I *do* love you very, very much. Alan and I both love you. And Sonny and Miss Faye think a lot of you, too, already. But—"

"Sonny, maybe," I said, cutting her off, "but there's something wrong with his mother, because she's sweet as can be one minute and mean as a witch the next. All I did was slide a book across the table, for Pete's sake."

"That wasn't what upset her," Elaine countered. "She thinks the next three weeks *would* be a waste of time, because you're not taking your education seriously and you don't seem to appreciate what she and Sonny are trying to do for you—or what *I'm* trying to do for you."

"What?" Now I was the one whose feelings were hurt.

Elaine lay her hand on my shoulder and squeezed gently. "Like I said, Val, I don't want to upset you or give you the wrong idea. But I've been thinking about it, and Sonny was right the other day—you know, at the Singing—and Miss Faye is right now. You really do need to start taking your education seriously and start thinking about your future, about what you're going to do with your life."

"But Aunt Elaine, I—I can't...," I began, not knowing how to finish my thought, not knowing exactly what my thought was.

"I know, I know," she said tenderly. "The past year has been a really bad time for you. I understand. Believe me, I do. And I know you've had problems with everything you've been through ever since you were a little girl. God knows our family has had more to deal with over the past ten years than most families *ever* deal with, and *you've* had to bear the brunt of it." She patted my shoulder, then pulled me close and wrapped her arms around me for a couple of seconds before giving me some space again.

With both hands on my shoulders and looking me squarely in the eyes, she continued, "You need to do a good job for Miss Faye and for Sonny the next three weeks, and you need to do everything they tell you to do and not complain one bit, even if you don't understand why they're asking you to do it. You need to trust them, both of them, because they really do have your best interests at heart. I know it's hard for you to trust anyone now. But you have to start trusting people again."

"I *do* trust people," I said. "I trust you and Alan. And Bo. And I was *starting* to like Sonny, but…." I looked away and kind of shook my head, again not knowing what I was really thinking.

"No 'buts' about it," Elaine said, once she decided I wasn't going to finish my sentence. "Sonny Rose is a good person, and Faye Rose is a good person. They're both good people, and they want to help you. We *all* want to help you. But you have to let us."

She hesitated again but finally got up the courage to finish what she had started. "It's kind of like this, Val. You really do have to make up your mind about school or work or *whatever* by the end of the summer—by the end of July, actually—because right now things aren't looking too good for us, for all of us—you, me and Alan, I mean. It's gotten to the point where I can't keep making the house payments and keep paying all the other bills, too—maybe for one more month, but then the car insurance comes due and Alan's tuition for next semester, and…." She was starting to break down, and I saw that it was now my turn to offer a comforting hand.

"I'll get a job, Aunt Elaine," I said. "I'll start looking tomorrow if you want me to. I don't need to waste time with school."

She shook her head. "No, it wouldn't really matter," she said. "Well, it would help a little but not enough to keep us from losing the house. You need to be prepared to take care of yourself, because I don't know if *I'll* be able to much longer. Lance called this afternoon and said—well—he said he has proof that I'm—well—that I'm an unfit mother…. He's going to use it to—to cut off the child support he's been sending, cut it off a year or so earlier than he would have, anyway, when Alan turns twenty-one."

"What proof? Did he say?"

"No," she replied, shaking her head again, "but I'm guessing it has something to do with Sonny, because of all the time we spend together. It looks like we're dating or something, but we really aren't—we're just good friends. Lance's probably just jealous, and he's just doing this to get even with me—even though *he's* had girlfriends since *before* we split up. That's *why* we split up—because he couldn't behave himself and be married at the same time. That's no secret. And he and I never were good friends. We only got married because we *had* to."

This time I didn't know what to say or ask, because that little revelation *was* a secret, at least as far as Alan and I had been concerned. Never before in my life had I ever heard anyone even hint that Alan had been an "oops" baby.

Aunt Elaine must have sensed my confusion, because she added, "We lied about our wedding date—that's why no one figured it out. We told everyone that we'd run off and gotten married a month before we really did, after I found out I was pregnant. And since we were both off at school, nobody knew for sure whether our story was true or not. Things were different back then, and I was afraid Daddy would kill Lance if everything didn't look right and proper. I was Daddy's little girl, and he didn't always keep his cool about things where I was concerned. You know how he was."

"Yeah." I took her hand as we continued our stroll on the track. "Can't Sonny help you out? He has the money, doesn't he?"

"Yes, I guess so," she said. "But I wouldn't dare ask for *that* kind of help—from him or anybody else, especially with whatever Lance has up his sleeve."

Despite the seriousness of the previous few minutes, I couldn't help but smile and comment, "Now *you* sound like the one who doesn't trust people."

Elaine nodded sadly. "Sometimes I don't, especially people who prove they don't deserve my trust. But that's not why I won't ask Sonny for help. It's just that as good a person as he is, I'm afraid it would end up coming between us and ruin our friendship *and* our working relationship. How would *that* look—the boss owing a bunch of money to one of her employees?"

"Well, you aren't *really* Sonny's boss," I observed. "He doesn't *really* work at the *Ledger*."

"It just isn't a good idea for friends to loan money to each other," she stated. As we left the track and headed through the grass toward where the Challenger was parked near the highway, the thought must have occurred to her that she had already accepted help from Sonny—the car itself. "And the deal we made on the cars is that Sonny doesn't pay me one red cent for the Beetle until I return the convertible to him. He didn't want to do it that way, but I insisted. So I guess that's one more thing I'll need to handle before the month's out—getting a cheap car so I can accept Sonny's money for the Beetle and use it on the house for one more month, I guess."

She almost started crying again. "You know, Val, sometimes everything just gets to be almost too much for a person to bear." She sniffed and managed to fight back the tears. "But we have to stay strong and not let those…those…*men* win."

"You mean Uncle Lance?" I asked.

"Not just him," she replied. "That other guy, too. The one *you're* afraid of."

It was something about which I didn't want to be reminded. "I'm not afraid of anyone," I said stiffly.

By now we were back in the car, and Elaine was rolling down the driver's-side window to let the cool mountain air inside the solar-heated compartment. "You still don't want to talk about it?" she asked.

This time I turned and looked her in the eyes. "Talk about what?" I said.

"Nothing," she replied, and cranked the motor to leave.

We rode in silence all the way back to the Aho house, and when we got there, I went straight to my room and didn't come out, even for supper. I'm merely assuming that Elaine had supper, because she didn't call me to the supper table at the usual time. Alan didn't come in until late; he had been hanging out with Lacey at the lodge and had eaten there, I figured.

He and Lacey must have gone somewhere after she got off work, too, because he didn't get home until after midnight. I knew what time it was, because I was still awake when I heard the garage door roll up and his Blazer pull into the empty bay next to the Challenger. I was still awake an hour later after I heard him turn off the TV set in the living room and clomp up the stairs to his bedroom—and an hour later when I heard someone—Aunt Elaine, I guessed—flush a toilet and then turn on water in one of the upstairs bathrooms. Even with my little lighthouse burning in the outlet on the wall next to my bed, I was trembling way too much to fall asleep before dawn.

SIXTEEN

Alone with those books in Sonny's office at Skyland Tech, I thought that first morning of "summer school" would never end. Oddly enough, cleaning his golf clubs was what I expected to be the most enjoyable part of the morning, but even *that* kind of fun couldn't last forever. I eventually had to get down to reading—excuse me, skimming—that first book Sonny had assigned: Walker Percy's *Lost in the Cosmos: The Last Self-Help Book.*

Well, actually, there *were* some interesting sections of the book, a little paperback edition. According to the "Books by Walker Percy" blurb on the second page, Mr. Percy also had written a book called *The Second Coming*, which sounded to me like a religious book of some kind. The immature guys on the golf team would have snickered and made rude remarks about the title.

Anyway, I started turning through the book and discovered that it was some kind of multiple-choice test and that it started with "A Preliminary Short Quiz" to determine whether or not I needed to take the "Twenty-Question Self-Help Quiz," which pretty much made up the rest of the 256-page volume. The short quiz was eight pages of big words about looking at stars and at planets and at yourself in a mirror and in storefront windows and recognizing this and that about yourself, and asking you what kind of "self" you are. Jeez. It included five multiple-choice questions that really had no wrong answers and then eleven different types of "self" to choose from in identifying yourself.

I answered the five questions and easily recognized myself as "6g: The Lost Self," which was just my luck, because the very last paragraph of the short quiz stated that if I could answer all five questions but *didn't* check the "6g" box, then I probably didn't need to take the Twenty-Question Quiz. Like I said, just my luck. I thumbed through the rest of the book, looking for more information on myself—The Lost Self—but I couldn't find anything specific, just three sections on "The Fearful Self" and two sections on "The Lonely Self," either of which I might have checked in the short quiz if those two classifications had been listed as choices, which they weren't. I never was any good at taking tests.

When Sonny finally got back, around a quarter to twelve, I was more than ready to go somewhere else, anywhere else, as long as I didn't have to keep sitting in that windowless room all by myself and keep reading books about my "self." After that morning of solitary confinement, I even looked forward to spending the afternoon at the library with Miss Faye, partly because I wanted the opportunity to set things right with her and partly because the library's windows opened out onto gorgeous views of the mountains. I basically liked Miss Faye, and I hoped she hadn't given up on me yet. And I truly hoped she wasn't going off the deep end like old Buck Green, because I couldn't think of a worse thing to happen to a person—to become so confused you don't even know who you are anymore. I had seen elderly people like that back home when I stayed with Grandma at the hospital, and it was a pitiful sight.

Sonny quickly checked his clubs to see that I had cleaned them properly, then shouldered the big bag and told me we were "callin' it a morning." I started to pick up the stack of books, but he said I could take only one book from his office per day—my choice—and that I had to bring it back the next morning. I'm sure he thought I'd pick one from my stack, but I surprised him by picking *The Rub of the Green*, the book I had found on his shelf, one he *hadn't* assigned. He just shrugged when he saw my choice and motioned for me to follow him back to the car so he could take me to Jonas Ridge for my afternoon with his mother. Once we were back in the Mustang and on the road, the real questioning began.

"Do you have money for lunch?" Sonny asked, glancing over at me as we neared the intersection with McDonald's on the corner.

"Well, no," I replied, even though I *did* have the fifty cents left that I hadn't spent on crackers after all, since I hadn't left Sonny's office all morning. But fifty cents wouldn't buy much, if anything.

"That's OK. Mama'll have something for you at the library. It won't be a hamburger or pizza or whatever else it is you young'uns like to eat, but it'll be good enough, and it'll be filling. Lord, I can't believe the way kids eat these days, nothing but potato chips and candy bars and sugary crap. It's no wonder your brains are turning into Styrofoam."

"I don't eat that stuff."

"You don't? Why not?"

I turned my head to look out my window at the green mountains. "Just never did. We didn't have money for stuff like that. The only kind of candy Grandpa liked were those big orange peanut-shaped marshmellowly things—I think he called it 'banana candy.' But he wouldn't spend money on anything else."

Sonny chuckled. "Yeah, my daddy used to buy that kind of candy, too. He said when he was little, that would be all he'd get for Christmas—that and peppermint sticks and an orange. Funny how we latch onto something when we're little and hold onto it the rest of our lives, ain't it? Kinda like my Mountain Dews, which, by the way, my daddy thought was liquor, the first time I asked could I buy one. All I ever remember him drinking was springwater and black coffee that was strong enough to walk and talk all by itself."

"Yeah," I mused, "that's how Grandpa was. But Grandma said he used to drink other things, too. She said he used to have a drinking problem, but she didn't like to talk much about it. He never drank when I lived with them, not a drop. It was back when he was a young man when he had a problem."

"Yeah," Sonny said. "Elaine's told me about it." We both were silent for a mile or so before Sonny's questioning continued. "So, what did you think about the book?" he asked.

"What book?"

"You know, the one I asked you to look at," he replied. "The Walker Percy book."

"It was OK."

"Just OK?"

"Well, yeah."

"Did you take notes?"

"Notes?"

"Yeah, notes. Didn't Mama show you how to take notes yesterday?"

"Yes."

"So did you?"

"Take notes?"

"Yes."

"This morning?"

"Yes."

"No."

"Why not?"

"I don't know."

"Did you even *read* the book?"

"I told you I can't read a big book like that in only a couple hours."

"But did you look it over?"

"Yes, I did."

"Well, then tell me what you read," Sonny said. "Let's talk about it."

I thought for a second, wondering where to begin. "Well, I remember that the same guy wrote a book called *The Second Coming*. What kind of book is that? About God or something?"

Sonny smiled. "Yeah," he replied, "it's about God—or something. But it's also about golf. An excerpt from it is in one of the other books you'll be reading—*Perfect Lies*. It's edited by Bill Hallberg, the man who wrote that book you have there, *Rub of the Green*. He picked a bunch of golf stories by Percy, Updike, Fitzgerald, a lot of good stuff about golf—or something. I think you'll enjoy reading them."

"He your favorite writer?" I asked.

"Who?"

"Hallberg."

"I don't know if I have one favorite writer anymore," Sonny said. "There are just so many good books out there that I'll never get around to reading them all. I used to like Leon Garfield the best when I was little, especially *Black Jack*. You ever read Garfield?"

"Just in the funny pages," I said, trying to be cute.

"Ha, ha. I'll take that as a *no*."

"If it's a kiddie book, I bet your mother will make me read it."

"Good," Sonny said. "It's a great book. You'd enjoy it."

I shook my head a bit. "I'd rather wait for the movie."

"Why? Why limit yourself to what some Hollywood producer or director or somebody decides you should see? It's usually such crap. You know most of them try to appeal to the lowest common denominator. You know that, don't you? Same thing on TV—it's usually just the lowest common denominator so they can make a bunch of money and sell a bunch of crap. I know, 'cause I used to work out there around those people all the time. There are exceptions, but they aren't the rule anymore."

"Same thing happens with books, doesn't it?"

He thought for a moment. "Well, yeah, I guess so, to a certain extent. But it isn't *really* the same thing, especially when you think about all the old stuff that was written back before this so-called Information Age started—the classics and all the other great stories and novels and poems and songs and plays. It just goes on and on."

"Like all that stuff your mom's making me read."

"Right! That's the best stuff in the world, and you should enjoy studying it with her. What did you read yesterday?"

I shook my head. "I don't know."

By this time, we were traveling past the entrances to Grandfather Golf & Country Club on the left and Linville Ridge Golf

Club on the right, and I was more interested in catching a peek of the Grandfather course than in answering all of Sonny's questions. "Come on, Val," Sonny goaded. "What did Mama want you to read first yesterday?"

"I don't remember," I began. "I think it was—oh, yeah, it was something by the guy who wrote *The Scarlet Letter*. But she took it away from me and gave me another one."

"Was it *A Wonder-Book and Tanglewood Tales*? Nathaniel Hawthorne?"

"Yeah, that's it—a bunch of old stories, like King Midas and Pandora's Box and Jason and the Golden Fleece, I think. It looked like a children's book."

"So?" Sonny said. "You need to trust her—and me. We've both been teaching stubborn young'uns like you for a long time, Mama especially. You're lucky she didn't hand you *The Blue Fairy Book*, too. She made me read that *and* all those Hawthorne stories when I was about your age." He pushed down the turn-signal lever to indicate we were turning left onto a graveled side road before we got to Linville. "Here, let me show you something. I haven't been up here in a while."

The road dropped steeply and curved to the right, then bent back to the left and ran across the river and into the trees. The dark, wooded drive climbed gradually up the hill above the river before turning sharply to the right and dead-ending at the gated and locked entrance to a cemetery occupying a football field-sized clearing bordered on three sides by dense forest, like a verdant terrace perched above the rocky river gorge below.

After turning off the motor, Sonny remained seated for a minute, as if he weren't sure he really wanted to get out after all. "This is Tanglewood Cemetery," he said. "It's for people who live in Linville. Daddy's buried over there. His mama's folks—my grandmother's people—lived here. And I think Lacey Green's great-grandparents—Buck's in-laws—are over that way. Old Buck met his wife when he was working up here, when he wasn't in jail." Sonny pointed to a densely-populated section to the left of us.

"Must be somebody important over there," I commented, pointing to several large monuments ahead and to our right, in a section of the cemetery with relatively few graves. In fact, the open grassy area to our immediate right beyond the chain-link fence held no graves at all and was so lush that it looked like a golf course fairway. The largest stone, standing beneath a spreading chestnut, was an eight-foot-tall Celtic cross with "MacRae" chiseled in the granite. "Is that the lady who has the monument at MacRae Meadows? What's it called? A cairn?"

Sonny shook his head. "No, I don't think so. I think she and her husband have a marker straight ahead, just beyond the flagpole up there. Let's go see." He unhooked his seatbelt and opened the door to get out, then stopped halfway and nodded toward the back seat. "Hey, Val, reach back there and grab a club out of my bag, just in case we run into a snake or something. You never know when a big old copperhead might decide to get himself a little sun."

"Sure," I said, as I pulled Sonny's Hagen putter from the Sunday bag. From having just cleaned it, I knew that the old Black Jack putter was so dented and dinged that killing a snake couldn't hurt the club anymore than its decades of use already had.

As we entered the cemetery through an unlocked pedestrian gate in the chest-high steel fence, I noticed that the thirty-foot-tall pole with its regular-sized American flag stood in the exact center of a perfectly-round platform that was about ten feet in diameter, about a foot off the ground, and rimmed by a brown river-rock wall. Along with some wildflowers and blossoming shrubs, the area around the pole bore a foot-wide grass strip that was there to allow easier access to the pole itself. The turf there was closely-cropped, like that of a putting green.

With the Hagen putter in hand, I paused at the edge of the flagpole platform to see if I could read the strip's grain, as it were, even plumb-bobbing the pole itself with the putter's chromium shaft.

Sonny laughed. "Want me to mind the flag?" he quipped, then added in a surprised tone, "Well, Val, right there's your ball—over there against the rock wall, down in that crevice. See it?"

I looked up, and, sure enough, there lay what appeared to be a brand spanking new Top-Flite Infinity 0 (the numeral indicating that the ball had originally come from a package of five three-ball sleeves, not the usual four sleeves). I walked around the "green" to retrieve the ball and found that its owner had marked it with a *pi* symbol, to distinguish it from other Top-Flite Infinity 0's. Ironically, that was the same identifying mark Billy Joe always used—which would give him the opportunity to say, "*Pi* are round, cornbread are square," when he drew the symbol with the Sharpie he always borrowed from me.

Now, with putter *and* ball in hand, I looked over at Sonny and couldn't help but smile and lift my eyebrows to ask his permission.

"Go ahead," he said. "I won't tell anybody." Then, looking around, he added, "And I don't think anyone else here will tell. Matter of fact, Mr. Julian Morton over there is the man who built the Linville course—*built* it, I'm saying. Donald Ross designed it, but Mr. Morton was the one who actually built it. And there are a number of old caddies buried up here, too. And right over there's Mr. Castleman D. Chesley, the man who put college sports on TV back in the 50s—you know, the 'sail with the pilot' guy from Pilot Life Insurance Company.

You aren't old enough to remember that, but he was one of *my* heroes. And over there's Mr. Joe Hartley. He's my hero, too. He started the Singing on the Mountain. Just goes to show you, everybody takes a different path from tee to green, some of us walk and some of us ride, but we all end up at the same hole. So go ahead. I don't think anyone will mind one bit.

"Here," Sonny said, reaching into his pants pocket as I stepped up onto the "green" and dropped the ball to the turf. "You can even use my lucky three-cent piece for your marker." He tossed me the dime-sized silver coin, which I caught in my right hand and dropped into my shorts pocket with my two quarters. Right then, I felt as rich as the wealthiest person in that cemetery had been. Money had nothing to do with it. Just standing over a ball on a putting green with a putter in hand made me feel that way.

With the flagpole itself as my target, I knelt behind the ball to read the line of this niggling four-footer that would finally win me my first Masters championship, the first ever claimed by a woman. This almost gimme of a putt would complete my first Grand Slam, following up my U.S. Open, British Open and PGA Championship titles last year. I rose, reached into my pocket for my marker, then bent over and slid the coin behind the ball, snatching up the sphere to check it for even a grain of sand that might divert the ball from its appointed route to the hole.

Replacing the ball and taking up the coin in one fluid motion, I stepped to the left of the ball and took my putting stance, my eyes looking straight down at the *pi* symbol on the field of dimpled white. I took a half step back, still in my stance, and made two phantom swings with the surprisingly well-balanced Hagan, the top of its mallet-shaped head scored perpendicularly with two red lines to help guide the stroke. I stepped back up over the ball and let my eyes follow what would be the ball's line to the hole, checking for any twigs or leaf fragments that I could remove without penalty. There were none.

In the background, I could hear my caddie, Bill Murray's character in *Caddyshack*, muttering, "This crowd has gone deadly silent; it's a Cinderella story outta nowhere…," under his breath. I tried to block his voice out of my mind. With my arms and shoulders forming a triangular pendulum, I carefully drew the putter back not even a foot, then guided it ever so smoothly forward into the ball, taking care not to follow the ball's path by turning my head. Instead, I watched the ball out of the corner of my eye and listened for the metallic ringing of the ball striking the pole. *Ping*. There it was!

If I hadn't been standing beside a flagpole in a town cemetery, I would have hoisted my putter—Sonny's putter, I mean—into the air and then fallen down to my knees to kiss the ground, a little show for the TV cameras up the hill there, before accepting my junior missy green jacket from the other champions waiting for me to join them over in the Butler Cabin. I could almost hear the muffled roar from the throng surrounding us there on the Tanglewood green.

"Good roll, Val," Sonny said, giving me a soft golf clap. "Too bad it wouldn't count."

"Why not?" I stepped toward the ball to pick it up, but Sonny got to it first and deposited it in his pocket. I'd have to ask him for it later, because I intended to use that baby on the *real* course when I finally got on it. Not only was it a Top-Flite Infinity; it was an Awesome Distance Infinity, "the ball you play, if you live for distance," according to the advertisement for that particular ball. By gosh, I intended to give that ball the ride of its life when the time finally came, even if I didn't have one of those super-expensive space-age titanium drivers. Instead, I had a humble Hogan persimmon three-wood.

"Rulebook says if you don't pull the flagstick and then you hit it with your putt, there's a two-stroke penalty and you gotta play it as it lays," Sonny stated, coming close to reciting *Rule 17-3c*. "Them's the rules, toots. Sorry."

I laughed. "Pull the flagstick? It's a dad-gum flagpole!"

"Flagstick, flagpole, what's the difference?" he quipped. "You ain't gonna win this one, babe, so don't even try. But I tell you what. You get today's consolation prize—an 1857 silver three-cent piece. Keep it. It's yours." He chucked my shoulder and turned to walk back to the Mustang.

"Aren't you gonna go see your dad?" I asked.

He shook his head. "No," he replied, smiling warily. "That ain't Daddy."

"Huh?"

"He ain't here," Sonny continued. "I'm saying, what's buried over there is just the, the—I don't know—the *shell* he inhabited while he was here. That's what *he* would have said, too. This body ain't what makes us *us*. You know what I mean?"

I nodded. "Yeah, I know, Sonny. That's how I feel, too. Four of the five people I've loved the most in my life are buried at my church at Village Point, and the fifth one was cremated so I could spread his ashes on his golf course. And, you know, I feel his spirit just as strong as I feel the other four."

Sonny slipped his arm around my shoulders as we walked. "You're talking about your folks and your granddaddy and grandma, right? And that man you worked for? Billy Joe?"

"Yes." I could feel tears starting to well in my eyes, as I thought about the last time I saw my boss, my old pro, my friend Billy Joe Pearlman, who had come closer than anyone else to filling the void caused in my life by the death of my grandpa. Occurring so soon after Grandma's passing, Billy Joe's loss was more than I could handle, even though I was moving to the mountains, anyway, and wouldn't have been able to see him except every now and then.

Sonny stopped us before we reached the car, and he gave me a hug. "You don't have to talk about it, little girl," he said. "I know *exactly* how you feel. There's so much goes on in this crazy world that just doesn't make a bit of sense, I want to scream sometimes. But just give it time, and those old wounds'll heal. You know what they say."

Yes, I knew good and well what *they* said—what they *always* said to me my whole life whenever I lost someone I loved. And I was sick to death of hearing it. And, yes, wounds do heal eventually. But what about all the scars that remain?

My afternoon at the library with Miss Faye went much better than my experiences with her the previous day had. As Sonny had predicted, his mother had lunch waiting for us when we arrived—homemade vegetable soup, always good on a cool mountain day, and toasted cheese sandwiches. I was surprised that Miss Faye had even fixed a meal that agreed with Sonny's diet, as the soup had no starchy potatoes and the sandwiches were made with whole-wheat bread. We drank ice-cold springwater from the library kitchen's faucet. Dessert for each of us consisted of a single crisp Gala apple. She had remembered what he could and could not eat.

So when Sonny left us in order to work Lacey's lunchhour at the lodge, he appeared to be a contented man indeed, as his tummy was full of agreeable food and his mind was at least temporarily at ease over my student-teacher relationship with Miss Faye. I'm sure he had been at least a bit worried about whether or not she and I would get along after our rocky start the day before. He probably also had been worried about Miss Faye, in general, seeing as how she was alone and getting on up in years.

The book I looked over for her that afternoon was *Harbrace College Handbook*, a grammar book that Miss Faye herself had used in college, according to the inscriptions and date that "Ola Faye Morgan" had printed neatly sometime during "Fall 1944" inside the blue cloth-bound cover. I even took notes—after she reminded me to.

SEVENTEEN

On Thursday morning, the day the *Ledger* hit the racks, Aunt Elaine invited me to accompany her and Sonny for their weekly tennis doubles with Kitty and Duffy. It was Elaine's morning off, and I'm sure she didn't want to have to worry about carting me from one place to the next when she could be unwinding on that soft clay court at Duffy's house up the road from the newspaper office. Besides, I could sit and read one of Sonny's books there in Linville as easily as I could at the college, even though the only book I had with me was *The Rub of the Green*, the book Sonny *hadn't* assigned. Or had he?

Because she didn't have to drop me off in Foscoe, Elaine drove to Linville on the Blue Ridge Parkway, her preferred route to work due to its scenic splendor. It was a beautiful morning, with only a few puffy white clouds dotting the blue sky and the temperature in the low sixties—warm for the High Country. As we cruised the Parkway with the Challenger's top down (Elaine's idea, not mine, because she was wearing her Prince warmup suit, while I had on my usual shorts and T-shirt), my aunt made a point of pulling into every overlook along the way to show me the sights off the mountain. Even though I was chilled to the bone, I kind of enjoyed the guided tour and getting to see the spectacular views. The sun already had been up for a couple of hours, so it wasn't the sunrise that was the spectacle; it was the sight of misty fingers of fog rising from the creases in "God's green carpet," which is what Elaine said Grandpa called the view the first and only time he visited the mountains on a family outing when Elaine was a girl.

After mentioning Grandpa at the Thunder Hill Overlook, she didn't stop again or say anything else until we reached the Wilson's Creek Valley Overlook on the slopes of Grandfather Mountain. I assumed we stopped there because it was the best and highest overlook on that section of the Parkway. My aunt had something else on her mind, as she killed the motor and clued me in on why she had been in such a quiet mood the past few minutes.

"It was all we could do to get Daddy to leave Village Point, even for one night," Elaine recalled, gazing off the mountain to the east. "I had been whining for days about how we never went on vacation and how all my friends went places in the summer. So way before sunrise one morning right before the Fourth—I don't know, it could've been today—Daddy loaded us all up in the car. It was him and Mama and me and Thane, your dad, in that old light blue Ford sedan that was always overheating, and we started driving west. I asked Daddy where we were going, and all he'd say was, 'To the mountains.' That's all. I don't think *he* knew where we'd end up.

"Well, when we got to Morganton—and it was really late in the morning, I think—we stopped at an old Esso service station for gas and water and sandwiches and drinks, and then we headed up the highway to Jonas Ridge, where you can get on the Parkway. I remember we stopped at the Lost Cove Overlook to eat our lunch—there was a picnic table there—and Thane kept begging Daddy to let him drive the car on the Parkway. Thane wasn't sixteen yet and didn't have his license, but Daddy let him drive, anyway. And I remember sitting in the back seat, closing my eyes and holding my breath every time we even came close to an overlook, even though the Parkway didn't run up here on Grandfather like it does now. I remember driving past the Grandfather Mountain entrance and begging Daddy to make Thane stop, but Daddy said we didn't have the money.

"Well, finally, back on the Parkway, after we'd gone winding through these mountains and I was sick as a dog—carsick from Thane's driving—Daddy made him pull off the Parkway—it was back at the Thunder Hill Overlook—so Daddy could look over the road map he'd got at the service station. He wanted to plot a route back home without having to backtrack too much. We even had time to walk up on the hill while Daddy looked at his map on the hood of the Ford and checked the water and oil and whatever else. Well, when we all got back to the car, Daddy drove us down the Parkway a little ways and Aho Road back to Blowing Rock and then down the mountain to Lenoir and back home from there.

"I remember passing the Green Park Inn there by the highway right before we started down the mountain. That's where Lance and I spent our honeymoon, you know—at the Green Park. I begged Daddy to spend the night there, and he said we didn't have enough money again. And then I begged for him to go back to the Pixie Motel in Linville. I'd seen some billboards for it, and it sounded like a fun place to stay. But he said 'no' again—that we needed to get on home, 'cause he had things to take care of.

"And *that*, Val, was our big family vacation, the only one we ever went on when I was a girl," Elaine concluded. "I'm ashamed of myself for being such a little brat, but you know how children are. They don't know the value of anything, like money grows on trees."

At first, I thought she was referring to me and that she was making a subtle remark about the extra expense of supporting me when her finances were so tight. But then I saw a tear in her eye, and I knew she was thinking about Grandpa and no one else. Aunt Elaine wasn't the type to cry out of self-pity. At the same time, she and Alan both were starting to do things that surprised me, as if I didn't know my aunt and cousin as well as I thought I did—like getting so close to Sonny Rose, for example. Elaine had always been such an independent person when she lived on the coast near us, and now she seemed to be getting more and more dependent upon a man she *couldn't* know all that well. And I never thought Alan would take to someone as he had to Sonny, who was so close to Alan's father's age. But as Grandpa—and Billy Joe—used to say, "Life shore is full of surprises, ain't it?"

While Elaine and her three columnists played tennis, I decided to take a walk around Linville and maybe even tour the golf club, starting with the clubhouse. I approached it from the side, not from the parking area in front. The club's tennis courts were situated just beyond a practice chipping area, the first tee, and a small lawn with a huge shade tree between the south side of the Tudor-styled clubhouse and Linville's main thoroughfare. Sonny had said that the big chestnut was called the Tennis Tree, because it was where spectators always gathered through the years to watch matches, especially on sunny summer days. Tennis, he added for my benefit, actually had an older tradition in Linville than golf did, as the grand Eseeola Inn advertised tennis as an amenity in its earliest brochures dating back to the 1890s. Also, local tennis enthusiasts organized the Linville Lawn Tennis Club in the early years of the resort before the golf club was established. All that might have been true, but I—Valerie Kirsten Galloway—was a golfer to the bone and had no intention of taking up another sport. I *still* couldn't afford to restring a tennis racket.

After looking around out back of the clubhouse for a few minutes, I got up enough courage to wander over to the porch immediately outside the pro shop by the practice green. Nattily-dressed golfers of both genders, chatting about the beautiful weather or the difficulty of a particular hole, came and went through the shop's screen door, and no one seemed even to notice me sitting alone on one of the bent-wood loveseats along the wall. Deciding finally that the worst they would do was throw me out, I waited until I could hear several voices inside the shop, and then I went inside, trying to act as if I belonged there.

I figured the clerk would be less likely to notice me if he was preoccupied with a foursome waiting to get on the course. That might have been the case initially; however, the clerk, a handsome clean-cut fellow not much older than I was, smiled at me when the golfers finally left, and politely asked if he could help me with anything.

"No," I said softly. "I'm just looking."

I was facing a wall display of Linville Golf Club caps, all in tasteful earth-tone colors and with the elegant club logo on the front (a teed-up ball bearing a large italicized *L*)—all the caps but one. The odd cap was the distinct shade of green that groundskeepers and maintenance workers wore, the same green of the workclothes that Buck Green had been wearing when Alan and I had seen him earlier in the week near Edgemont. The cap bore no logo like the other designs, just the year "1892" stitched in plain white numerals on the front and the word "Linville" in small block letters on the back. I picked up one of the caps to look for a price tag before noticing a sign that said all caps were twenty dollars each. As I put the cap back on the shelf, I wondered what the "1892" stood for but didn't have the nerve to ask the clerk.

When I got back to Duffy's house where the doubles match was still going on, I waited for a changeover, then asked Sonny what had happened around Linville in 1892. He was a history teacher, so I figured he'd know, if anybody would. "Oh, that's when the resort was started, I'm pretty sure," he noted. "That has to be it, because there was a big hundredth anniversary celebration for the whole village back in 1992, I think it was. Remember, Duffy?"

Mr. MacGregor, sitting with a white towel draped over his head, nodded but appeared too pooped to comment. Aunt Elaine and Miss Kitty had run into the house for a bathroom break, and Duffy apparently didn't want to waste any energy answering a teen-ager's random questions.

Once the two ladies returned to the court, I didn't see any point in hanging around, so I walked back to the *Ledger*, where both Elaine and Sonny had parked their cars. Walking past Sonny's Mustang, I looked inside and noticed that his golf clubs were still on the back seat. With nothing better to do, I pulled Sonny's sand wedge—a Wilson just like mine—and felt around in the bag for some old balls. The only used ball I could locate in any of the bag's pockets was the nearly-new Top-Flite Infinity 0 with the *pi* mark that Sonny and I had found the previous day at the cemetery. I figured it would have to do.

Behind the *Ledger* building was an open grassy area that my aunt had said was used only once a year for public parking during the four days of the Highland Games at MacRae Meadows. Members of the general public parked their vehicles there in those grassy fields at the bottom of the mountain and rode school buses from Linville up the graveled Yonahlossee Road to the meadow where patrons with special permits were allowed to park, Elaine had explained. The other fifty-one weeks of the year, the parking areas lay largely unused, partly because they were fenced off and the gates were locked. Also, a branch of the river snaked through the field immediately behind the *Ledger* and flooded more often than was comfortable for Elaine and the other newspaper employees. Flash floods in the mountains were nothing to take lightly, she had warned, going on to tell me about drownings that had occurred in floods on area creeks and rivers just since she had been living there and working for the paper.

I climbed over the white wooden board fence that separated the newspaper property from the field and walked to a spot where the grass was especially lush, as inviting as that of any course I had ever played. I would have taken my drop there and hit out over the "fairway," but I was afraid that if I did, I'd lose the ball, my only ball, in the river. The field had been mowed recently, evidently because the Highland Games were scheduled for the week after the Fourth, so it wasn't hard for me to imagine I was walking that old Linville course, anyway, even if I *wasn't* well-off enough to be on the best mountain course that Donald Ross had ever designed, by gosh. I walked along the river and cut through the field until I came to another gate, this one leading into the road Sonny and I had driven up to the cemetery.

I looked off toward the cemetery in the clearing on the wooded hillside where we had been the previous day, and I tried to guesstimate the distance to the "flag." With only a sand wedge in hand, I knew I didn't have nearly enough club to reach the "green," but I decided to give it a shot, anyhow. After all, what did I have to lose, other than a ball that wasn't mine anyway? Measuring three club lengths back from the iron gate, I took my drop, then two practice swings, and then I drilled that ball high and far into the dark woods, careful not to hit toward any houses. It was probably the best wedge shot I had struck in a long, long time.

Amazingly, the little white sphere hit no tree trunks that I could hear during its high-arcing flight, but it did hit *something*, because a second or two after the ball should have landed I heard a shout from the direction of the cemetery and then the sound of an engine roaring to life. Seconds later, to my further surprise, I saw a large lawn tractor descend the road from the cemetery with none other than Buck Green himself aboard. I couldn't tell if my ball had hit him or had just come close, but I didn't hang around to find out. I ran all the way back to the newspaper building and locked myself in Elaine's office, keeping Sonny's sand wedge with me in case I needed to defend myself against crazy old Buck Green. Of course, maybe Buck was just upset that I hadn't yelled, "Fore!" But I doubted it.

While I was hiding—I mean, waiting—in the *Ledger* for Elaine and Sonny to return, I had the chance to look over that week's edition of the paper. I saw the photos Alan and I had taken Monday afternoon, and I read my aunt's story on the commissioners meeting she had attended Monday evening, the meeting in which citizens had expressed concern about the government creating a wilderness area at Lost Cove and Harper Creek. And I read Sonny's column, entitled "A Sincere Apology For My Song."

In his regular spot at the top of the editorial page to the right of the editorial itself, Sonny asked forgiveness for having composed and recorded "The Bold Rebel Flag (Is My Old Rugged Cross)," and he pledged never to sing the song again publicly or privately. He wrote, in part:

> I have always enjoyed singing my songs for the glory of the Lord and for the edification of my friends in Christ. However, it has come to my attention that one of my songs has become a stumbling-block rather than a stepping-stone to brotherhood and understanding.
>
> For that, I am greatly ashamed, and I sincerely apologize.
>
> Being a son of the New South, I have always been proud of my Southern heritage. And yet, the history that we Southerners share bears a scar of which no one should be proud, the scar of slavery and racism.
>
> In composing and recording my song "The Bold Rebel Flag (Is My Old Rugged Cross)," I certainly did not intend any offense to anyone.

But I see now that any glorification of the Confederate battle flag is yet another lash upon the already scarred backs of the descendants of those unfortunate individuals who were enslaved against their wills by Southern slaveholders, whether those reprehensible persons were our actual ancestors or not.

While relatively few African-Americans live in our mountain community and subscribe to this newspaper, I nevertheless beg their forgiveness for my thoughtlessness, as well as the pardon of all who have heard me sing that particular song whether in person or through my recording of it.

I am man enough to admit my mistake and to make an honest attempt to mend my ways.

From this day forward, I want absolutely nothing to do with the perpetuation of the racist attitudes of our Southern past.

The song I shall sing will be one of hope for a brighter future in a more understanding world.

It wasn't going to win a Pulitzer Prize, but Sonny's column was certainly guaranteed to get a lot of attention among the *Ledger*'s readership, both positive and negative, as was usually the case with his weekly editorial comments. The rebel flag controversy was an issue near and dear to many High Country hearts, and Sonny had firmly planted himself on the side opposed by certain locals who would think nothing of teaching the big-mouthed history teacher a lesson or two about Southern heritage. Even I realized that Sonny was taking a big risk by publishing that particular column. But it also made me admire my aunt's best friend more.

In addition, I figured the apology would make a good impression on my own best friend Bo, and I was right on the money. That afternoon at the library, while I was reading and taking notes on Tennyson's *In Memoriam, The Princess, and Maud* for Miss Faye, a telephone call came for me. It was Bo, calling from outside the university library, where he had just read Sonny's *Ledger* column in the periodicals room. Bo said he was sorry for being out of touch all week but that he had been busy with music camp and with his "research." He added that Alan had looked him up that morning and had filled him in on a number of things, including my new summer schedule, Sonny's latest column and Alan's own summer-school project involving the Brown Mountain Light. Also, Alan had invited him to join us that very Friday night as we searched for the Light, said Bo.

"What was that?" I asked. That Alan and I had plans to go Light hunting Friday night was news to me.

"He's got this big plan for you and me to go one place," Bo explained, "and for him and Lacey to go another place, and then we try to pinpoint the lights from different angles. We can kind of triangulate their locations. Dig?"

"I guess so," I replied, "but how would we know we were seeing the same thing?"

Bo snorted. "*I* don't know. You gotta talk to Alan about that. He's the man with the plan. But, anyway, he's gonna pick me up tomorrow afternoon and take me to the lodge that singing guy owns, and we'll leave from there. That's what he told me."

Even though I was worried about the prospect of spending an extended period of time in the dark Friday night with Bo, I was glad he had called to let me know, if indirectly, that he was still my friend. I wondered where Alan would send us, and I wondered what, if anything, we would see there. Maybe it would be something I could use in my own research paper, the one Sonny and Miss Faye had me working on. Maybe I would learn something about the Brown Mountain Light and what it had in common with golf and the blues. Maybe I would learn something about myself. I had already learned something that day about life, in general—that it's made up of a lot of maybes. Or maybe not.

EIGHTEEN

Friday afternoon couldn't come too soon for me, not because I was looking forward to our outing that night, but because I wanted so badly to see Bo and to talk with my best friend about all the things I had done and seen that first week in the mountains. I knew that he, too, would be full of new stories, even if they would be about band camp and the new people he had met there. I wanted to hear Bo tell me what else he had learned about Miles Davis and Doc Watson and all his other musical heroes. I wanted to hear his plans for us to go to Doc's music festival in a couple of weeks to hear him flatpick his guitar like nobody's business.

When Alan had finally gotten home Thursday night from courting his old girlfriend (as Grandpa used to put it), I had gotten *him* to tell me his big plan for getting a fix on the Brown Mountain Light. He said the six of us—me, Bo, Sonny, Aunt Elaine, Lacey and him—would divide up into three pairs and go to three different spots where the Light, if it made an appearance, should be visible from: the Brown Mountain Overlook near Jonas Ridge, somewhere along the opposite ridge near Blowing Rock and, of course, Wiseman's View overlooking the Linville Gorge.

"What about the Lost Cove Cliffs Overlook?" I had asked. "Isn't that where the signs are about the Brown Mountain Light?"

"Yeah," Alan had said, "but you can't even see Brown Mountain from there. It's hidden back behind Big Lost Cove Ridge and Long Ridge. I don't know why the Park Service put up those signs there, at *that* overlook, unless it's because that spot has about the same view of the valley as the other places where the Lights are seen from. I just want us to be able to actually see the mountain itself if we see anything that looks like a Light.

"Lacey and I'll go to Wiseman's View since we have four-wheel-drive; you and Bo can go to the Brown Mountain Overlook, 'cause it's easy to get to; and Mom and Sonny'll be somewhere in Blowing Rock, probably at that restaurant that looks out over the valley. You can see Brown Mountain from there. If we don't see anything from any of those spots tomorrow night, we can go to three different places some other time and try again, maybe even go camping the night of the Fourth and look for the Light after watching all the fireworks everywhere. That sound like a plan, cuz?"

"Except for one thing," I replied. "How are Bo and I supposed to get to the Brown Mountain Overlook and back? Walk? In the dark?"

Alan grinned. "Well, I guess you *could*. It isn't *that* far from the lodge. But, no, I already asked Sonny. He said he'd loan you guys a car."

"Well, Bo'd have to drive it, because you know I don't have a license." I didn't tell Alan that one of my "assignments" that summer was to *get* my driver's license, even though I didn't have a car to drive and probably wouldn't be in a financial position to buy one for a long, long time.

Anyway, I got through Friday the best I could, studying both the handbook and *Six American Poets* in the morning for Sonny and then finishing up the Tennyson volume for Miss Faye. Speaking of the poetry I read that day, I especially liked Tennyson's "The Princess," Langston Hughes' "The Weary Blues" and, surprisingly, Robert Frost's "The Bearer of Evil Tidings," moreso than the more familiar "The Road Not Taken." I liked "The Princess" because it made me think about maybe going off to college myself; "The Weary Blues," because I seemed to remember Bo talking once about a song of the same name; and "The Bearer of Evil Tidings," because the story in the poem reminded me of my own present situation, being a newcomer like the "bearer," who was accepted in a strange new community though he was hiding some bad news from all those around him, even from the one he loved.

Toward the end of the day before Bo arrived, Miss Faye let me look through the books on the "Local Authors" shelf for information on the Brown Mountain Light. It was fairly easy to find mentions of the phenomenon in the local history books, like *Burke: The History of a North Carolina County* by Edward W. Phifer, Jr.; *Western North Carolina Since the Civil War* by Ina W. Van Noppen and John J. Van Noppen; and *A History of Jonas Ridge* by Earline F. Johnson.

The most helpful of those three sources by a long shot was the humble Jonas Ridge history book, even though it appeared to have been typed and published by the Johnson lady herself, who, like Miss Faye, had been a teacher. Mrs. Johnson's book, which was actually a sheaf of stapled-together eight-and-a-half by eleven paper in an orange card-stock cover, stated on its title page that it had been "issued with the assistance of Puddingstone Press, Lees-McRae College, Banner Elk, N.C., 1974":

> Many fascinating tales have been told about the Brown Mountain Lights. One story is that a young Cherokee Indian girl and a Catawba Indian brave met and fell in love while the two tribes were enemies. They were planning to get married, but he had to go off to war. She waited many moons, but he never returned. Finally she went up on a mountain and built a hut. Every night she walked back and forth across the mountain carrying a torch. She thought that if he saw the light, he would return to her, but he never came. People say the Brown Mountain Lights are caused by this Indian maid carrying her torch back and forth to light the way for her lover.
>
> Some people say a lover was lost, and the young man searched every night, carrying a lantern to light the way for his lover. She was never found, so the man still carries the lantern.
>
> Still another explanation, perhaps more scientific, is that the Brown Mountain Lights are caused by a gas from some mineral inside the earth which causes a light to appear at certain times. Like the less scientific explanations, however, little concrete evidence has been found, and the lights remain a mystery to this day.
>
> For generations eerie lights have excited the imaginations of North Carolinians and visitors alike. Different observers say the lights are red, green or yellow, appear in varying numbers, no predictable regularity and disappear quickly. Some say they appear on the side, and others, the top of the mountain. Theories are, they are from St. Elmo's fire, to liquor makers. (St. Elmo's fire is a luminous electrical discharge which bounces off masts, lightning conductors, and similar objects during thunderstorms.)
>
> Everyone has their theory of what causes the Brown Mountain Lights, but there has been no theory proven satisfactorally.

Mrs. Johnson then went on to print the lyrics of the Scotty Wiseman song "The Legend of the Brown Mountain Light," the ballad that Bo had talked about during our ride from the airport with Alan and Lacey.

Other items in the history book also caught my attention, including the legend of "The Devil's Cap" that Miss Faye had told me earlier in the week when she and I had visited the rock formation also called Sitting Bear; an account of a Civil War skirmish fought at a spot called the Winding Stairs near the lodge; and the following story entitled "Mother and Son Murdered":

> One of the oldest settlers is said to have killed his little boy and buried him under an apple tree. About a week later, he killed his wife and dragged her on a sled from his home on Dogwood Knob to the cliffs on the Cole Mountain and put her under a rock on the cliffs. Later he had many bad dreams about chickens, cows, sheep and pigs. One, however, was much worse than the others: a cart with three people in it. The man that killed his wife and dragged her on a sled to Cole Mountain did not live on Dogwood Knob. He set the wood afire when he put his wife under the cliff. Later her skeleton was found....This story comes from the old settlers as told to their children.

The other tidbit I noted from Mrs. Johnson's book was one of the many mountain superstitions she listed: "If you see a light at night, it is a sign someone is going to die." Knowing we were going to be *looking* for lights that very night, I couldn't help but mention the superstition to Miss Faye, to see if she was familiar with it.

"Oh, yes," she replied. "Everybody knows it's bad luck to see a falling star."

"But this doesn't say 'a falling star,'" I remarked. "It says 'a light at night.' That could be *anything*."

"Well," Miss Faye began, "I think it's referring to any odd light in the night sky, like a falling star or a comet—or even the Brown Mountain Light. You know, Halley's Comet caused a really big stir in this community back in 1910. It says so right there in that book. And you know, Valerie, come to think of it, most of those legends you hear about the Brown Mountain Light have to do with death some way or other—the death of a lover or the death of a master or of a faithful slave. I guess that's because death and killing are sad things we'll never really understand, just like those old lights that pop up all around Brown Mountain."

I nodded but said nothing.

"Something else I've noticed," she continued, "is that a lot of times all these old stories get all tangled up over the years until eventually they're something totally different—like the old story about the man here who was meaner than the devil himself."

"Here?" I asked. "He lived here? In Jonas Ridge?"

"Yes, indeedy, a long, long, *long* time ago," she said. "I won't tell you his name, and I won't tell you where he lived, exactly. But they say this feller was so mean, everybody swore the devil himself would have to come get him when his time came. Stories going around had it that he'd killed his wife *and* his little child and that he'd buried them way off in the mountains under a big rock so nobody'd find the bodies.

"Well, finally one day, that mean ol' man got sick and was on his deathbed, but nobody'd go in his house to help him, they were so scared. They just kinda watched and waited for something to happen. And sure enough, 'long about midday of a cold, cold Wednesday in February—Ash Wednesday, I think it was—this evil-looking black cart pulled by two black oxen came rolling down the road from all the way up around the Indian Bald Ground. Now, besides it being all black, what was so odd about it was that nobody was driving it. That team of oxen just pulled the cart down the road as if they knew exactly where they were going, and, sure enough, they stopped right out front of that mean ol' man's house. About then, folks who saw it said this big ball of fire flew out of the cart and into the house and was in there a while, and then it swooshed back out to the cart, and those oxen took off on down the mountain like somebody'd lit a fire under them.

"When folks finally got up enough nerve to go inside the house, they couldn't find hide nor hair of that old man. He was *gone* and never was seen nor heard from again. Folks said that ball of fire was the devil coming after him. And other folks say that's when people started seeing so many lights around Brown Mountain, 'cause that's the direction the black ox cart was headed. Others say the lights were the spirits of that mean man's young wife and little baby, whose bones were found under a great big boulder over near Brown Mountain not long after that old man disappeared with the devil, because that's where the lights would point. But you know, the stories never end. They just go on and on and on."

She was right about that. I had already noticed how certain stories—or story*lines*, rather—and certain characters kept popping up in many of the folk tales I had read in that first book I studied for Miss Faye, the one by Richard Chase. Among other things, he had collected mountain tales that were like Disney cartoons and Bible stories that I had seen and heard as a child, and like stories from Shakespeare and other old authors that I had heard about in high school. I mentioned that to Miss Faye, and she had trouble containing herself, she was so proud of me. She didn't explain why she was so proud, though. I guessed it was because she realized I had learned something from her.

Since she seemed to be in a good mood, I tried to get her to let me read something else next besides that Shakespearean play she had picked, *Twelfth Night*, but she wouldn't budge on it. She said it was the perfect play for me, better than *MacBeth* or *Romeo and Juliet* or even her personal favorite, *King Lear*, which also had parallels in Southern Appalachian folklore, she noted. "It's a comedy—sort of," she added about *Twelfth Night*. "You'll enjoy it *so* much when we read it Monday. And then if you want, we could read another play, one of *your* choice on Tuesday—no, you won't be here on Tuesday, will you?—on Wednesday, then. What do you say to that? It'll be such fun."

I just kind of looked at her. "One day?" I gulped. "I can't read a whole play in one day. That's crazy."

From the way her eyes suddenly narrowed, I could tell Miss Faye wasn't quite so proud of me anymore. "Yes, ma'am, you *shall*," she said pointedly. "If you were watching it on stage or at the movie house or on television, how long would it take to view? Two hours? Three hours? Maybe four? Then why *couldn't* you read the same material in the same length of time? Tell me why you can't."

"Because," I replied, "it just isn't the same. I can't read *anything* straight through in three or four hours—and *remember* it."

"That's why you take notes," she said. "Your pencil is longer than your memory."

Maybe longer than yours, I thought, but didn't say so, especially when I considered the fact that I did, in fact, use a stubby golf pencil to mark my scorecard on the golf links because I, like most duffers, wouldn't be able to keep score entirely in my head if my life depended on it. Sometimes, if I was having a particularly bad day, I could forget how many strokes I had taken even on one hole. "Can I just watch the movie?" I asked. "That's what my English teacher back home did. She'd just show us the movie, and we'd learn just as much—or more, really, because we could understand what was going on better. She said Shakespeare's plays are *supposed* to be watched, anyway. They aren't supposed to be read. Besides, I'm a visual learner."

"No, ma'am," Miss Faye said. "You will not watch a *film* to avoid reading a good book—or play. And you will not listen to all of these books on tape, or whatever they're called, to keep from having to read, not unless you're blind and *can't* read, and even then I'd expect you to learn Braille. If I've said it once, I've said it a hundred times: Reading *is* fundamental. Reading stories, reading plays, reading poems—I just can't impress that upon you enough. And I'm *not* crazy—yet."

"But, Miss Faye, what's wrong with watching a good movie or listening to a good tape? Isn't that how your old mountain storytellers did it—by word of mouth? That's what Mr. Chase was talking about all the time in his book."

"Oh, really?" she said. "Mr. Chase *talks* about that, does he? In his *book*?" I caught the twinkle in her blue eyes. "No, Valerie, there's nothing wrong with watching a good film or listening to a good recording or to a good story or poem. But the oral tradition—the passing down of stories and songs and poems from one generation to the next—has been hurt, badly, by all our fancy gadgets and the way we live now. There are just too many distractions nowadays, too many things people would rather pay attention to than the things we attended to in years past, things that helped us live fuller lives and come to terms with the problems we faced. Things that held families together.

"A good book can give us back that personal touch, that focus. It can help us cut out all those other distractions, because a reader has to concentrate on what she's reading if she wants to understand what's being said. She does have to *hear* it and *see* it and *experience* it—but with her imagination. She has to work her *own* imagination, not the imaginations of others. All those other people want is our money. They don't care about our souls."

"You sound like Sonny," I said. "He said almost the same thing the other day."

She laughed. "Well, good. I'm glad he's learned *something* from me after all these years. I was beginning to think he wasn't paying attention." She hesitated, as if she had something else to say but couldn't quite remember what it was. Then she repeated, "But I'm not crazy—yet. So we *will* read Shakespeare on Monday—and maybe again on Tuesday, too, if I take a notion. I *am* the teacher, and you *are* my student."

Right then, I didn't think it would be wise to point out that we'd already covered that ground, that she had already stated she knew we didn't have class on Tuesdays, as that was Sonny's day off and the day he and I planned to play golf together (if I had completed my assignments satisfactorily). But then, the bothersome thought occurred to me that maybe Miss Faye knew *exactly* what she was saying and that if I didn't finish the play she assigned on Monday, maybe I *wouldn't* be allowed to play golf the next day. Maybe I didn't want to find out.

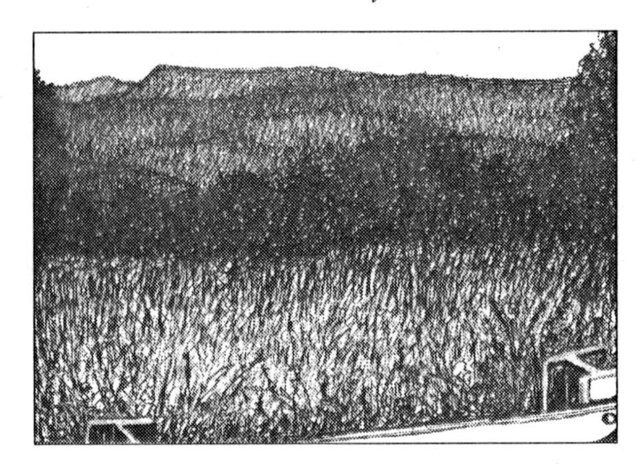

NINETEEN

Alan and Bo arrived at the Barkhouse Lodge no more than a couple of minutes after Miss Faye dropped me off there. Having found no one—neither Sonny nor Lacey—at the front desk inside the lodge, I had just gone out the back door and was crossing the parking area to the Ranger Station, when I heard a car horn toot. I turned to see Alan's Blazer roll into an empty space next to the lodge.

With both front windows rolled down, I could hear old-timey bluegrass music playing on the vehicle's fancy stereo system, and I assumed it had to be something Bo was sharing with Alan, since my cousin's "old-timey" musical tastes were more along the lines of Garth Brooks. Otherwise, he was always listening to Kenny Chesney and Toby Keith on the Blazer's six-disc CD changer. Me? I preferred Hootie & the Blowfish and, as my "golden-oldie" choice, the Doobie Brothers (another one of Daddy's cassette tapes). And I really liked Bill Withers, especially "Lovely Day," because he'd been a sailor like Grandpa. For her part, Aunt Elaine was always playing a Mary Chapin Carpenter or Sheryl Crow or Norah Jones tape in the car, and they were OK, too.

Anyway, the tune Alan and Bo were listening to turned out to be "Skyland" Scotty and Lulu Belle Wiseman performing "The Legend of the Brown Mountain Light." It was the original version whose lyrics I had read in the library book. Bo was explaining again how popular the Wisemans' national radio show was back in the 1950s.

I walked to the Blazer, since its engine was still running and neither Alan nor Bo had made any effort to get out. "Going somewhere?" I teased Alan, as I approached the driver's side.

He threw up his hand. "Hi, cuz. Yeah, I'm just dropping off Boo-Boo here so I can go get Lacey. She's down at her house." He looked past me toward the Ranger Station. "You seen Sonny? He still working on Mom's car?"

"I don't know," I replied. "I guess so. He isn't in the lodge. I was just getting ready to check when you drove up." Now that Alan had reminded me, I wasn't sure I wanted to see what Sonny had done to the Beetle. It would break my heart to see those decals and racing stripes on it. *Herbie the Love Bug*, indeed.

"Well, say 'hey' for me," Alan said, as Bo retrieved his disc and got out of the Blazer. "I talked to Sonny this afternoon, and he knows the plan. We're gonna use CBs to talk back and forth, since our cell phones are pretty much useless out here. I'm gonna take the CB out of Lacey's truck and put it in here. And Sonny's gonna get Miss Faye to come back here and watch the lodge while we're all out. She can man the base station in the office and talk to us on the CBs and then talk to Mom and Sonny over in Blowing Rock by phone. Lacey's granddad has an old police scanner that picks up all the CB channels, so he'll probably be listening in, too. But if we *were* to get in trouble or something, I don't know how he'd call for help. They don't have a phone."

"Why don't you get him to blow his bugle, and you could blow *your* horn, your car horn, to answer him?" I quipped, remembering, though, that I wasn't supposed to reveal Oren and Miss Faye's secret little communication system. "You could toot once for 'yes,' two times for 'no' and three times for 'get your bony old butt on your horse and come help us!' And then Oren—I mean, Mr. Green, Mr. Buck—could blow 'Reveille' or 'Charge' or something on his bugle as he rides up the road to save you, so you know he's coming." I thought I was being funny.

Alan didn't get my little joke. "What are you talking about?" he asked. "Where'd you get *that* idea—about Buck blowing a bugle? Or riding a horse, for that matter?" By this time, Bo had joined me by the driver's-side window. "Little Boo-Boo here is the only bugler *I* know," Alan added with a grin, nodding toward Bo. "And that old horse Buck plows with isn't a horse, anyway; it's a mule. It's colored like an appaloosa, like that spooky-looking horse Clint Eastwood rides in some of his movies, but it's a mule all right. And that jackass—the mule, not Buck—it's as stubborn and crazy as the old man himself, not to mention it's blind in one eye, too. Why Buck doesn't just shoot the old thing and put it out of its misery, I'll never know, but Lacey says he still goes coon hunting on it sometimes, you know, at night, 'cause it knows all the trails down in there. Who told you all that stuff, anyway? Miss Faye?"

"Well...," I began, not wanting to betray Miss Faye's trust.

"Well, nothing," Alan said. "She means well, but you can't believe everything she says. Sometimes she exaggerates things a bit or is just mistaken. Sonny's been worried about her for a good while. That's another reason Sonny keeps an eye on Buck, 'cause wouldn't *that* be a pair—old Buck and Miss Faye? Could you see Buck as Sonny's step-dad?" He grinned and threw up his hand again, then backed the Blazer out of the space and wheeled around the lodge toward the highway, leaving my friend and me standing there.

"So how you been doing?" Bo asked.

I was so happy just to see Bo, but I didn't really know how to say so, or if I should. "I'm OK, I guess," I said, "but I didn't think this day would ever end."

He smiled. "It hasn't—yet," he said. "Come on. Let's find that guy and see what car I'm gonna be driving. You think he'd let me drive the 'Vette?" We started walking toward the Ranger Station, where we figured Sonny was still working. "You know," Bo added, "Miles had a Ferrari. Man, I bet he looked *bad* in it, too." We stopped to knock on the door to Sonny's workshop.

"I'd let you drive a Ferrarri if I had one," came Sonny's voice from behind the door. "Come on in, you guys. I'm about done in here."

Sonny was seated in an old straight-back chair next to Aunt Elaine's Beetle, which he had completely covered in a translucent plastic dropcloth and blue polyeurothane tarp so we couldn't see any of the work that he had done on it. The odor of fresh paint still hung in the air. "But we aren't quite ready for the unveiling just yet," he said, noticing I was looking at the car. "I figure it'll be ready for a test drive in, oh, about two weeks or so. But, Lionel, I really *will* loan you my Ferrari—when I get it. Of course, the car I want has to be a red 308 like the one Tom Selleck drove in *Magnum P.I.* You guys ever watch that show?"

"You can call me 'Bo,' Mr. Rose," my friend said. "Everybody does. 'Lionel' was my dad's name."

"Sure, Bo. And you can call me 'Sonny.' I was named for my daddy, too, and it used to bug the crap out of me when teachers called me 'George' or 'George Wayne' on the first day of school. And then, of course, the mean kids would call me 'Georgie Porgie Puddin' and Pie' for the rest of the term.

"I got in so many fights over that—and got quite a few paddlings, too. And then I'd get another one when I got home. That's the way my daddy was—and Mama, too. It didn't matter if I had an explanation or not, 'cause there wasn't any explaining to it, far as Daddy and Mama were concerned. When it came to paddlings and whippings, everything was pretty much cut and dried. There wasn't any such thing as a 'timeout' back then, either. No, sirree, when Rev. George W. Rose, Sr., got home from the church and heard that Master George W. Rose, Jr., had got a paddling at school, it was time-*in*, old buddy, time-*in*, and Daddy used his leather belt, too."

Bo and I both nodded, as we had heard similar stories from older folks before, just like how they walked miles to school barefoot and coatless through six-foot snow drifts all winter. "How much have you done to the Beetle so far?" I asked, still curious about the little sky-blue VW's transformation into *Herbie*.

Sonny made no move to uncover the car. "I finally got it repainted to suit me," he said, "and now I'm working on the interior. You know, the seats were in bad shape, it being so old and all. I would've been done by now, but I had another little project to take care of the past couple nights. Come on, I'll show it to you—my other project, I mean."

He led us from the workshop into the Ranger Station's showroom space, where all of his finished vehicles sat on display before the floor-to-ceiling windows that allowed guests to look in from the outside. All of his pop-culture vehicles were there, except for the lime-green *Mod Squad* Challenger, which Aunt Elaine was still driving, and the bright-orange *General Lee* Charger from *The Dukes of Hazzard*. In the *General Lee*'s spot was another Charger, this one, though, with a jet-black paint job. It was surrounded by four portable heat lamps on six-foot-tall stands.

"Here she is," Sonny said. "This is your ride tonight, Bo. You think you can handle her?"

Bo's eyes almost bugged out. "Woh!" he yelled. "This is one of the rides in that cop movie with the jammin' car chase! You know, Val?!" No, I *didn't* know, but I was glad that the car pleased Bo, since its earlier incarnation definitely would have been a problem.

"Well," Sonny said, "actually, it's a year off—a '69 instead of the '68 in the movie—but the body style's close enough, for government work. And I still need to reinstall a black vinyl top." He opened the driver's door. "You gotta be careful, 'cause the paint job hasn't really cured yet." He paused. "Look, I'm not gonna try to trick you, guys. This was the *General Lee*. But when Alan said you'd need a good car and a good CB, this was the one I thought of. I mean, I could give you a little walkie-talkie CB radio, but it wouldn't have near the range this one does. And you can't do anything to hurt *this* car. It's built like a dang tank. Matter of fact, it's original color *was* black, 'cause I think the old boy I bought it from ran moonshine in it. But that's another story, and I don't really want to go into that right now."

"Hey, it even has an eight-track!" Bo yelped, having already warmed up to the idea of driving the Charger. "How does it handle?"

"Oh, it handles like a dream," Sonny replied. "Just be careful on the curves when you're coming back up the mountain from the overlook, especially that first big curve after the straightaway where the road goes back to two lanes, as you're coming back this way. That's a bad spot, especially at night and you in a black car. I have to watch out there myself in my Mustang." He nodded toward his black convertible.

"You know you got the wrong Mustang, man," Bo stated flatly. "You need you a '68 Fastback GT in highland green—if you want a *really* fast machine, man."

"I know, I know," Sonny said. "I'll get that one *after* the 308, if I have any money left over. Oh, by the way, I topped off the gas tank before I pulled the car into the shop, so you don't need to worry about driving near any gas pumps or gas stations or gas cans or anything that might go *boom*, if you know what I mean."

"Dig, man," Bo laughed. "I dig."

Turning the key already in the ignition, Bo carefully backed the Charger into the open floorspace between the two lines of vehicles and pulled forward through the garage door that Sonny had opened at the end of the building. Bo stopped in the driveway for me to join him in the car, as I followed Sonny outside and waited as he closed the garage door and locked it. "Thanks, Sonny," I said. "Thanks for painting the car. We'll take care of it."

"Oh, sure, no problem" he replied. "But there *is* one small favor you can do me, just to be on the safe side."

"What's that?" I asked. I figured he was going to tell me to encourage Bo not to drive too fast or not to take any unnecessary chances in the car, or, maybe, he was going to speak for Aunt Elaine and diplomatically tell me not to try out the reclining seats or the back seat while we were parked at the Brown Mountain Overlook—

something he *didn't* have to say to either Bo or me, because we were just friends and had spent time alone many times in the past without anything happening.

"Well, it's kinda like this," Sonny said. "I was so busy with the paint job and all, and with the Beetle, that I kinda forgot one little detail." He leaned over to whisper in my ear, "*Whatever happens, don't let him blow the horn. It still plays 'Dixie.'*"

"Gotcha," I promised, with a grin. "But don't worry. It'll be OK. Thanks, Sonny."

I jumped into the passenger's seat next to Bo and buckled the old-fashioned lap belt. As we tooled through the parking lot and around the building to the highway along the same route that Alan earlier had taken, Bo looked over at me and asked, "What was that all about?" Since he didn't sound mad, just curious, I told him about the horn and about Sonny's warning. Bo just laughed. "It may come in handy, you never know," he chuckled. "If a county mountie sees me driving this thing tonight, I may need to play 'Dixie' just so he'll stop and salute and give me time to open up the four-barrel."

"Huh?" I asked. "The four-barrel?" This was a Bo I'd never met before.

"Just hang on, baby," Bo said, taking a right onto the highway, then shifting down into second gear and tromping the throttle to make the tires squeal. "Since you're riding shotgun, you gotta let me know if you see a dark-green Mustang in the rearview mirror. Watch my back, OK?"

"Huh? You mean Sonny's car? It's *black*. And he isn't gonna follow us."

"Bullcrap," Bo fairly shouted above the engine's roar. "Now let's get the heck outta here. Hey, how 'bout pushing that Doobies tape into the deck. Man, I wish I had my Gov't Mule or Derek Trucks!"

"Huh?"

"Just turn it up," he said.

I think the first tune that played was "Rockin' Down the Highway," but I was so busy holding on for dear life as we rocked down the highway for real that it could have been "Jesus Is Just Alright" for all I knew right then. If we reached that overlook in one piece, Jesus would be more than just all right with me, and I thanked my lucky stars that Sheryl Crow's "Steve McQueen" was too new to be on eight-track tape.

TWENTY

I don't really know where to start, to tell you what happened with Bo that night at the Brown Mountain Overlook. Nothing bad, necessarily. Just kind of weird. I don't know exactly how to describe it, because I don't know exactly what I saw. And I was the only one who saw it. Not Bo—he didn't see it, even though he was sitting right there beside me. Not Alan or Lacey parked at Wiseman's View. Or Aunt Elaine and Sonny at that restaurant in Blowing Rock. Just me. I was the only one to see what I saw, whatever it was. It could have been a lot of things, but it wasn't exactly like anything I had ever seen before, at least not until that night.

There we were in the black Charger, parked at the roadside overlook, which was a flat graveled lot about sixty yards long and thirty yards wide, with an opening in the steel guardrail along the highway for entry and exit at each end of the parking area. There were no signs or picnic tables or charcoal grills or waste receptacles or anything, really, to indicate that this was a popular gathering place for anyone hoping to spot the Brown Mountain Light—well, nothing official, anyway. On the other side of the guardrail that ran along the far side and kept vehicles from rolling off the embankment were scattered piles of trash left behind by previous visitors, mostly grocery bags containing torn cardboard twelve-pack boxes of emptied and crushed cans and stained once-white fast-food bags with wadded wrappers and the half-eaten odds and ends of burgers and fries.

We were parked almost perpendicular to the far guardrail so we could view the valleys and ridges that spread before us in lighter and darker shades of blue to the distant horizon. Grandfather Mountain was farthest from us to the north at about eleven o'clock, then Brown Mountain itself, the closest crest to us, at about two o'clock. According to a cellphone-sized Magellan SporTrak GPS unit that Bo pulled from a black nylon holster on his belt, sunset would occur at 7:48 that evening. "It's a new moon tonight," Bo added, "so it'll be dark enough to see *anything* that lights up over there on Brown Mountain." My friend pointed out the windshield toward the mountain's long low ridge running to the east beyond our line of sight.

"Don't people ride motorcycles and four-wheelers and stuff over there?" I asked, remembering something I had read—maybe in one of the brochures on the counter at the Jonas Ridge Library—about Brown Mountain being a favorite place for all-terrain vehicles like motorbikes and Jeeps.

"Yeah," Bo replied. "The official name is the Brown Mountain Off-Highway Vehicle Area. The map I looked at back at the college library shows miles and miles of bike trails and jeep roads all over the mountain, and, far as I could tell, it's open twenty-four seven. They even allow camping over there. But if we can't tell the difference between four-wheeler headlights and a Brown Mountain Light, we're in bad shape, you know?"

"I guess," I said. "You say it's a new moon tonight? That means you can't see the moon, doesn't it?" I'd have had enough trouble sitting in the dark car on a regular moonlit night, but this situation—no moonlight—was something I definitely wasn't prepared for.

"Yeah," Bo said, "that's why Alan picked tonight—'cause it's a Friday night, yeah, but mainly 'cause it'll be darker than usual. That's when you can see the Light best, they say."

"Who's *they*?"

Bo grinned. "You know. *Them.* The *they* that knows everything. Dang, Val, you sound like my mama or somebody." He toyed with the GPS unit, pressing different buttons and looking out the windshield at various landmarks in the vista before us. "Alan said for me to get a fix on this location, so he can put all three points in his computer and roughly triangulate anything we all see—you know, be able to kinda pinpoint where the light's coming from."

"That his gadget?" I asked, referring to the GPS unit.

"Yeah. He said it comes in handy when he's mountain biking down in Lost Cove or Harper Creek." Bo punched a couple of buttons and held the unit so I could see the tiny monochromatic display. "This is cool. See? It'll mark your trail as you go along, so you can *never* get lost. This is a ride he took on—let's see—on the fifteenth of April. Income tax day. Ain't that his birthday, too?"

"Yeah," I replied. "Uncle Lance must've sent him this thing for a birthday present, and he was trying it out. Uncle Lance is *always* giving him expensive stuff—like the Blazer and his mountain bike and skis and stuff. He tries to *buy* Alan's love—and make Aunt Elaine look bad."

"Alan's not that stupid," Bo said. "He knows what's going on. We were talking about it just the other night in the library."

That Bo and Alan had gotten together to talk about anything was a surprise to me. "What night?" I asked.

"The other night," he said. "Was it Monday? Yeah, I guess it was. You know, the night you called and wanted to talk, and I couldn't say a whole lot. That was why. I was sitting in the library, whispering to Alan, and a librarian kept shushing us. And then the cell phone went off. I didn't want to keep causing trouble and get kicked out of there. You know, if Mom gets a bad report on me, she might make me go back home early, and then I wouldn't get to go see Doc in a couple weeks."

"Why? You sick?"

"No." He gave me a funny look. "Earth to Val. Earth to Val. Doc Watson? Guitar player? Music festival? You said you'd go? Any of this ring a bell?"

"I know, I know. I was just trying to be funny."

"Well, try a little harder," he said, slowly shaking his head. "Now, it's not this coming week. It's next week—the weekend *after* the Fourth of July weekend. The Fourth's on a Friday this year, right?"

I shrugged. "Yeah, I guess so." Just thinking about the Fourth of July kind of made me sad, as it used to be one of my favorite holidays back home—back on the coast, that is, and back before I started being afraid of the dark. Every year Grandpa would get ahold of some skyrockets and Roman candles and stuff like that somehow, and as soon as it would get dark, we'd all go down to the dock—my mama and daddy and even Grandma, believe it or not, and Aunt Elaine and Uncle Lance and Alan, when they were there visiting—and we'd have the most fun shooting all that stuff off. We'd shoot it out over the waterway toward a little dredge spoil called Monk Island, where nobody went after dark.

And if it was a clear night, we could sit there after we'd shot everything and watch the fireworks display up the coast at Southport, where the state's official Fourth of July Celebration was, or we'd watch all the different fireworks displays down toward Myrtle Beach in all those little towns down that way. I especially liked those huge jellyfish-looking fireworks whose golden tendrils would gracefully arch outwards away from the body of the initial explosion and then burst into little whistling stingers that would dart in all directions. They were my favorites.

But that was back before getting caught out in the dark made me so panicky that about all I could do was curl up in a little ball with my eyes shut tight and with crazy little fireworks going off in my brain. And I would stay that way until the sun decided to rise, finally. Sometimes, when I'm really tired or when things are just getting to me, I still feel that way—like I just can't spend another night alone in the dark, waiting for the sunrise and for someone to come save me from myself. I know it's all in my head, but that doesn't make it seem any less real.

As Bo and I sat there at the overlook that night, other vehicles came and went. Even then, the highway was a fairly busy thoroughfare, as it connected Morganton—a good-sized town with factories, a mental hospital, an academy for deaf children, a treatment center for retarded and severely-handicapped individuals, two prisons and a community college—with the mountain communities of Jonas Ridge, Pineola, Newland and Linville, not to mention all of the ski resorts in the High Country. According to Sonny, many of the regular mountain folks drove down to Morganton to work every day, even in the winter when the long and winding road could be treacherous with ice and snow. Many of the vehicles that passed the overlook that evening, especially those around dusk, undoubtedly were some of those workers on their way home; however, many of the passing autos, after dark, anyway, were, like Bo and me, curiosity seekers who would pull off and park for varying lengths of time and then lose patience and drive off after not seeing anything resembling a Brown Mountain Light.

Bo remarked that some of the people must not have even known where to look, because he could see them staring off into the distance, in a direction away from Brown Mountain toward other knolls or ridges that he identified as Chestnut, Little Chestnut, Woodcock Knob and Adams mountains. Some of the people who stopped at the overlook stayed in their cars and trucks; others got out and walked around. Some folks were quiet, as if they were in a church or library, or maybe they just didn't want anyone else to hear their theories about the Brown Mountain Light. Others talked and got kind of loud, even rude and obnoxious, as if they had been drinking or were *still* drinking, from the looks of the trash we had seen lying about before dark. The only good thing about having other people around was that they were always shining their headlights on us or opening their car doors and lighting up the overlook. And, for my benefit, Bo let me hold the penlight he had brought along so I could turn it on whenever I started feeling anxious, which was every few minutes.

It was around 9:30 when I saw it—that thing I saw, whatever it was. Bo was talking about something—I can't remember what—when I saw a faint blue light, maybe about the size of a child's balloon, appear in the sky above the crest of Brown Mountain. It was so faint, though, and I was feeling so ill at ease, anyway, that I wasn't sure I was really seeing something. It could have been one of those spots I would sometimes get in my eyes—a "floater" was what Grandma called them, because she had trouble with them, too. Or maybe it was that shadowy reflection a person sees after closing her eyes to a bright light. I didn't know *what* it was—or *if* it was really anything. But by the time I decided to call Bo's attention to it—to that faint blue light that looked like a child's balloon—it had disappeared. "Did you see that?" I asked.

"See what? Where?"

I pointed toward the dark sky above Brown Mountain's faint ridgeline. "A little blue light," I replied. "Over there. At first I thought it was a star, but then it started moving down, and then it changed directions, so I thought it was a plane. But then it just went *poof*. It disappeared."

"Really? You're not kidding me?" Bo strained to look in the direction I was pointing. "A *blue* light? And it just disappeared?"

"You didn't see it, too?" Now I *was* starting to get scared, flashlight in hand or not.

"No," he said, "and I was kinda looking over that way, too. Dang. Lemme call Alan and see if they saw it." He grabbed the CB microphone and depressed the button on the side. "Breaker, breaker, one-eight. Breaker, breaker, one-eight. This is Bullitt Bo. You read me, uh, Steve McQueen? Come in, Steve McQueen." I didn't know why he picked those names.

We waited a few seconds and heard only the crackle of static on the CB before Bo tried again to hail Alan and Lacey at Wiseman's View, which was several miles behind and above us from our position there at the Brown Mountain Overlook. This time he used more familiar handles. "Boo-Boo calling Yogi Bear. Boo-Boo calling Yogi Bear. Yogi, you read me, man?" Still, we heard nothing but static on the speaker over the next thirty seconds or so.

But then, just before Bo tried one last time, a familiar voice broke the crackly silence—not Alan's strong youthful voice, but Miss Faye's weak elderly one. "Boo-Boo," Miss Faye called, "this is—pardon me—this is the Ranger Station, dear. I hear you loudly and clearly. Please go ahead, and I shall relay your message to, uh, Yogi the Bear. Do you hear me?"

Bo and I looked at each other, somewhat surprised that she had caught on to the CB handles so quickly. "Does she always talk that way?" Bo asked. "So, uh, proper?"

"No," I said. "She must think people are listening in, and maybe they are. Don't they use CBs around the campground? But you better answer her before she hangs up. Maybe she can hear us and hear Alan, but we just can't hear each other on these things, what with all the rock formations between us."

"Yeah, you're right," Bo agreed, then opened the mic again. "Ranger Station, this is Boo-Boo. Please ask Yogi if they saw anything a few minutes ago. Ten-four?"

"Excuse me?" Miss Faye asked. "For what? And whom, may I ask, is Yogi?"

"Ask Yogi—Alan—if they just saw a light," Bo said. "OK?"

"Very well," Miss Faye responded, then hailed Alan on the same channel. "Yogi the Bear, please. Do you hear me? Please say 'hello,' if you do." Alan must have answered her, because we heard more static on the CB speaker, and then Miss Faye's voice again. "Boo-Boo is asking if you saw a light just now." There was more static. Then Miss Faye asked us, "Boo-Boo, where did you see this light?"

The exchange went back and forth like that for several minutes, with us trying not to reveal too much information, knowing full well that other CBers could be listening to our three-way conversation. Miss Faye even called Sonny and Elaine in Blowing Rock on the telephone, to see if they had spotted anything. No such luck.

I was somewhat scared and even annoyed to learn that I alone had seen the Light and that the others seemed to doubt my reliability simply because they had noticed nothing out of the ordinary. Like a nibble on a fishing line, my dubious sighting served to keep all of us looking out over Brown Mountain for another hour or so; however, we got no more bites and eventually gave up for the evening. Sonny and Elaine left their post first, partly because the restaurant closed, and they didn't want to sit in the parking lot by themselves.

Alan and Lacey were *incommunicado* for much of that ensuing hour, for reasons Bo and I could only speculate upon at the time. We wondered if they were, in fact, seeing lights that looked like skyrockets in flight and were simply not commenting publicly on them. We did find out later, though, that Alan and Lacey had to leave the Blazer in the Wiseman's View parking area and walk about a quarter of a mile to the site's rock-walled observation areas perched above the Linville Gorge. Being away from their vehicle and the radio that Alan had installed that afternoon, they were forced to use a less powerful handheld model whose batteries ran down fairly quickly. At least Alan had remembered to pack the walkie-talkie. Though he had never been a Scout, he always seemed to be prepared.

I wouldn't have been able to think that far ahead or to anticipate that situation. Back then, back when I was still struggling with all my fears and with all my uncertainties about the future, I never felt prepared for anything—not for the curves in the road that everyone encounters, not for the roadblocks we often have to find some way around to get back on track, not even for the ride itself.

But later that night, as Bo drove back toward the lodge like he was going to a fire, slinging me from side to side as we flew around curves, I *did* know one thing for darn sure. I knew for certain that if I made it out of that black car alive that night without going up in a ball of flames at the bottom of some cliff, I would never ever get into that car again, with Bo or anyone else. But you know what they say about saying "never."

TWENTY-ONE

Saturday used to be my favorite day of the week, back when I lived on the coast with my grandparents and had to go to school Monday through Friday. It wasn't that I liked Saturdays just because I was off from school; I liked the sixth day of the week because that was when I could go shrimping with Grandpa on *The Lady of Shallotte*, while Grandma ran the shrimp stand near our house off Village Point Road. I manned the tiny tin-roofed stand on Sundays so Grandpa and Grandma could go to the little church they had attended ever since they got married there way back when.

For me, Sundays were OK, too, even though I had to work the stand in Grandma's place. Business didn't really pick up until noon Sunday when most of the churches let out. I kind of liked meeting tourists from different places and talking to them about where they lived and how they could fix the shrimp they were buying.

Every so often I had to deal with a real *touron* (a cross between a tourist and a moron), but they were the exception to the rule, as far as our shrimp-stand clientele went. Most of the folks who stopped there were nice to me. And many of our customers were locals who dropped by on a regular basis and would stand and talk about everything under the sun. That, actually, was how I first met Billy Joe Pearlman, long before I went to work for him at his golf course, as he was one of my regular Sunday morning customers.

In all the years I knew Billy Joe, he never went to church—well, not until he didn't have any choice in the matter. He always said he couldn't "praise God A'mighty around all o' them dad-blamed hypnocrites that lie and cheat and steal six blessed days a week and then go sit in a dang pew on Sunday and act like that makes everything

OK." He was well aware that Grandpa, his best friend, went to church every Sunday, but Billy Joe also knew that Grandpa went mainly because Grandma made him go, a situation perfectly understandable to Billy Joe.

Letting me run the stand on Sundays in season was the concession Grandma had made to get Grandpa into one of those church pews, even though he wasn't a "hypnocrite" by any means, and Billy Joe knew that, too. Later on, after my old boss had built the par-three course and driving range, he didn't go to church simply because Sunday was a big golfing day, even at the B.J., and he didn't seem to worry so much anymore about hypocritical church-goers, especially since some of them played his course through the week. Naturally, all that was after Grandpa had passed away and Billy Joe had given up on taking Grandpa's place with Grandma, if that, in fact, was what he had been up to.

Saturdays with Aunt Elaine, on the other hand, were no fun whatsoever during that summer of mine in the mountains, and Sundays weren't much better. After working all week at the newspaper, often sixty hours or more with meetings almost every evening, Elaine had only Thursday mornings and weekends free to clean house and run household errands. On Thursday mornings, as I've already said, she and Sonny played tennis with Duffy and Miss Kitty in Linville. So that left Saturdays and Sundays to do all our housework.

Until I moved in with them, Elaine had been able to get Alan to help out around the house, at least on Saturday mornings before he took off on some wilderness outing that might last until Sunday night, especially after he got his mountain bike. But once I was around to help his mother, Alan didn't even hang around on Saturday mornings. As I was usually lying awake anyway, I would hear him rise well before dawn, load his gear into the Blazer and roar off toward the Blue Ridge Parkway and some great biking and camping adventure. Sometimes I wondered if he wasn't really just spending the weekend with Lacey, whether they were camping out or not, but I never asked him about it. I could tell that the two of them were really serious about each other, and I didn't want him to think I was jealous of Lacey or disapproved of him spending so much time with her, even though he *was* ignoring his mom and me.

So Elaine and I worked around the house that first full Saturday I spent in the mountains. We vacuumed, mopped, swept, dusted, scrubbed. We emptied wastebaskets and trash cans, we washed and dried all the dishes that had been piling up all week in the kitchen sink—

or, rather, that Alan had been dirtying all week and had not bothered to wash—and, as soon as the dew-laden grass dried outside, I mowed the lawn. Taking a break on the porch with a cool glass of water, I looked out across the meadows and the Parkway lying between our house and the castle-like building in the distant trees, and I daydreamed of King Arthur and his Knights of the Round Table—which, for some reason, made me think of a Camelot-themed miniature golf course I had played once at the beach. Then I pictured Arthur, in full armor, playing golf in the meadow below me. Well, Arthur *was* from the British Isles, wasn't he? From the home of The Open Championship? Yes, I know. An idle mind is the devil's...what? Plaything? Playground? Play whatever.

In the afternoon, we went grocery shopping at a supermarket Elaine called the "old Winn-Dixie," as opposed to the new one across town, I guess. She explained that even though this older store wasn't as big and modern as other supermarkets, she continued to shop there because Grandma used to buy groceries once a week at the old "Dixie Home" store at the beach when Elaine was a girl. The oldest supermarket I could remember back home was the Piggly Wiggly, but I did recall hearing Grandma fuss about certain store brands of products that she wasn't able to buy anymore after the old Dixie Home closed. Aunt Elaine noted that shopping at the old Winn-Dixie helped her feel closer to Grandma, as if the two of them were pushing their grocery carts down those tiled aisles together still.

"I definitely was a daddy's girl," Elaine added, "but Mama and I were close, too. She tried her best to keep me from being a tomboy by making me go grocery shopping with her and doing things like that, but I just loved my daddy too much not to want to be around him as much of the time as I could and even be like him, for that matter. I probably would have been a shrimper, too, if I hadn't gone off to college and gotten into the newspaper business—and met Lance." She had been smiling until she mentioned my ex-uncle.

Late in the afternoon, after we had returned home and put up the groceries, Elaine called Alan's cell phone to see if he would be back in time for supper. When she got the automated message saying that the "customer" she was trying to reach was either out of the coverage area or away from his phone, Elaine hung up and dialed the lodge. Sonny answered and told Elaine that Alan wasn't there.

"Is Lacey working today?" Elaine asked her friend, then listened to his response. "Well, when is she coming in then?... Not until tomorrow morning? What time?... OK.... OK.... Uh-huh.... No, she won't mind.... Huh-uh.... OK.... Really? Yes, she's sitting right here at the table across from me. Really?"

When I became the topic of conversation, Elaine's eyebrows rose, and she glanced over at me, maybe to see if I could hear Sonny's side of the call through the earpiece. From where I sat, I couldn't make out what he was saying, but she kind of turned her head, anyway, to block any escaping sounds. "Well, that's so sweet.... I'll tell her.... OK.... Cross my heart.... OK, and hope to die. Honestly, Sonny.... OK, we'll see you in the morning.... Right. At the lodge.... OK, bye-bye."

She looked at me again as she returned the handset to its cradle. "Sonny wants us to go to church with him tomorrow morning," she said. "He's singing at that little church near Edgemont—Greenlee Chapel—and Miss Faye suggested he invite us, too. She's going along, and she doesn't want to sit by herself while Sonny's singing. You don't mind going with us, do you?"

"No," I replied. "So he hasn't seen Alan?"

Elaine shook her head. "No. And Lacey didn't work today, so I just imagine that's where he is—down there around Harper's Creek. I bet we'll get a call in the next hour or so, and he'll say he's camping out tonight. You wait and see. Now, if you take the call and I can't come to the phone, you be sure to tell him we're going to meet Sonny and Miss Faye at the lodge tomorrow morning at 8:30 and then we're riding down the mountain with them for church—the eleven o'clock service. Alan won't want to come along, but he *will* want to meet us back at Miss Faye's house for Sunday dinner *after* church. Sonny said it'll be a little late, though, probably around one or 1:30, 'cause it takes a while to drive back up the mountain on that old road with Miss Faye in the car. She doesn't like to be jostled around. Can you remember all that?"

"Yeah, I guess," I said, "but what did he make you promise—you know, when you crossed your heart and hoped to die?"

"Huh?" She gave me a funny look as she rose from the table. "I don't know what you mean." Her eyebrows were in the stratosphere again.

"Oh yeah, you do," I countered good-naturedly, sensing that Sonny and Elaine's pact somehow involved me, since she suddenly seemed to be in a big hurry to leave the room. "Is it where we're going to play golf Tuesday? Sonny said maybe he could fix it so we could play Linville. Is that it?"

Elaine smiled. "I promised I wouldn't tell," she said coyly, then quickly added, "I mean, I promised not to tell what it was we were talking about." Before I could question her further, she walked off toward the living room and kept going on out the door to the front deck, where she started straightening the deck furniture and fussing with potted plants. Whatever their secret was, she wasn't going to let me in on it.

That night, after I figured that classes and concerts and other activities had wrapped up at music camp, I called Bo's cell phone to see how he was faring since our outing the previous night at the Brown Mountain Overlook. He answered on the second ring and didn't hesitate to let me know that things hadn't gone well for him that day. Without repeating the entire conversation (because he was being moody again), Bo informed me that, thanks to our outing, he had been restricted to campus and that he would be lucky to get to leave even for the Fourth of July holiday. He had forgotten to sign in that night upon his return to his dormitory and, therefore, had missed curfew.

"Mom said it serves me right," he moaned. "She said I don't need to go anywhere off campus if I can't be responsible. At least she didn't pull me outta camp."

"Will you be able to leave for the Fourth?" I asked.

"She said she'd let me know," he replied. "That means I better watch myself, or I won't be watching anything but the Boston Pops' fireworks concert on PBS while you guys are out having fun."

Before hanging up, Bo promised he would call me as soon as he got word one way or the other from his mother. Alan had said something to me and Bo about maybe all of us going camping on the night of the Fourth, since it fell on a Friday and neither Bo nor Alan would have to worry about classes the next day. I wondered, though, if Sonny and Miss Faye would expect me to do anything for them on Saturday after taking Friday off to celebrate the holiday. Maybe not. Maybe they would give me a break for a change and let me enjoy a long weekend with my best friend and my favorite cousin and his girlfriend. Maybe they—and Aunt Elaine, too, for that matter—would let me start making some decisions for myself, even if what I decided wasn't what they would have had me do.

Alan *did* call later in the evening, and I was the one who talked to him, as his mother was soaking in the bathtub at the time. He didn't have much to say, just that he wouldn't be home that night, because he was "camping," as Elaine had predicted. He apparently wanted to get off the phone before his mom got out of the tub. Chuckling at my cousin's predictability, I asked where he was calling from, but all he would say was, "Lost Cove."

I assumed he was calling from his cell phone, since Lacey and Buck didn't have a regular telephone in their cabin. But I wondered where Alan could have been calling from in Lost Cove, since his tiny phone had had trouble connecting with a service provider on our earlier trips into the isolated area. I guessed that he and Lacey were on a high ridge, where his phone could hit a cell tower somewhere. When I relayed Alan's message to Elaine before going to bed, she just smiled sadly and shook her head, as if she knew it was inevitable that she would lose her son to another woman.

For the first time in my life, I read myself to sleep that Saturday night. Maybe it was because I was so tuckered out from having worked around the house most of the day with Aunt Elaine, or maybe it was because I had finally gotten interested in reading something more stimulating than *The Rules of Golf* in my spare time. I actually came within a single chapter of finishing *The Rub of the Green*, the golf novel I had taken from Sonny's bookshelf and had carried home with me earlier in the week.

It was the first work of fiction I had ever truly enjoyed reading, the first book of "make-believe" I had ever made myself believe in, the first story whose characters and situations I could see as reflections of real life. I was absolutely in love with Ted, the young golf pro and convict who was telling me his stories from the pages of this book I had borrowed. And I really disliked Trayn and Janice, that stupid girl the two of them were fighting over through most of the novel. I despised her, in particular, because of the way she was always manipulating them both. I hated girls like that and was determined not to be that way myself, a girl who was always trying to trick guys into doing things for her. I wanted to do things for myself.

That night I could have finished the book before I fell asleep, but I stopped reading when I came to the end of the thirty-fifth chapter. I just lay there a while, thinking about the decisions facing Ted and me both. He and I were a lot alike, even though I had never been behind bars and never wanted to be. Catching myself dozing after several minutes of musing, I turned the night light beside my bed on, snapped the lamp on the nightstand off and went to sleep as quickly as I could, because I did not want my relationship with Ted to end. I had already lost one golf pro too soon, also under violent circumstances, and I wasn't ready to lose another one just yet.

TWENTY-TWO

Greenlee Chapel was a lot like my old church back home in Brunswick County. The little white-frame church was already filled with people that Sunday morning when Sonny, Miss Faye, Elaine and I (wearing a borrowed blouse, pair of slacks and pumps, thank you very much) entered the sanctuary from the main door at the rear and looked for spaces in one of the pews down front. Sunday School had just let out, said the church's old preacher, a gray-headed man who identified himself as Rev. Hiram Vernon. Greeting us at the door, he explained that since it was Homecoming Sunday, seating would be tight, and we all might have to sit in the choir loft behind the pulpit.

"The choir ain't singing today," the elderly minister told us in a deep drawl, "since Brother Sonny here will be blessin' us with his special music and Reverend Bobby Lee there will be bringin' us God's Word this mornin'." He motioned toward a dark-suited younger man, handsome in a plain-featured and clean-cut way, though balding slightly and carrying just enough extra weight to give him the fatted look of privilege. The young evangelist already was seated on the platform in a throne-like chair to the right of and slightly behind the pulpit.

Sonny and Miss Faye seemed to recognize Reverend Bobby Lee and nodded their understanding to the old preacher. Elaine, on the other hand, made the mistake of asking if Bobby Lee was the man's full name and how long we might expect his sermon to last.

"Why, mercy me, you don't know of Reverend Robert Lee, Sr.?" the minister replied, with a look of disbelief. "He's Bobby's daddy, and he's just about one of the most Christian men in this whole God-fearin' nation. Don't you'uns turn to Channel 63 of a evenin' when his show comes on? Ain't you never seen it? It comes on ever' night but Sunday." He chose not to respond to Elaine's question about the service's length.

"I hope you'uns will stay with us for dinner on the grounds after the worship service," the preacher added, smiling at Miss Faye. "It would certainly be a pleasure and a blessin' to break bread with you good Christian brothers and sisters from the mountaintop. It has been quite a good many years now, ain't it, Mizzeriss Rose, since I run that revival meetin' for Preacher Rose up there at Jonas Ridge? How many years has it been?"

"So many years I've lost count, Hiram," Miss Faye said. "We do appreciate the invitation to stay for dinner after preaching, but I've been up since daybreak fixing my chicken 'n' dumplings and cube steak with mushroom gravy and buttermilk biscuits and two different kinds of homemade pies—fresh apple *and* fresh huckleberry pie—for these young'uns' Sunday dinner, and it's all up at my house on the mountain. If I'd thought about it, we could've packed it up and brought it down with us, but we weren't thinking. We thank you just the same, though." Miss Faye smiled politely, then turned away before the old man could invite himself home to dinner with us.

After we were seated in the choir loft, she whispered to Elaine that old Preacher Vernon, a long-time widower like Oren Green, had called on her a time or two over the years since her husband's death, the first time even before Hiram's own wife had been dead a full year. "I didn't think that was one bit proper, especially for somebody who calls himself a preacher," Miss Faye whispered, loudly enough that Reverend Bobby Lee overheard and turned his head to see who was sitting behind him.

The young evangelist nodded pleasantly at Miss Faye, then turned back to the Bible passage upon which he had been meditating while awaiting the start of the homecoming service. A moment later I saw him bow his head, as if in prayer. I wondered what he was praying for.

When the service finally got underway and Sonny's time to sing rolled around at last, he was accompanied by pre-recorded music from the portable sound system he always took to little churches. Sporting a similar Western outfit to the one he had worn the previous Sunday to the Singing on the Mountain, Sonny introduced himself—and us, to my embarrassment—then explained that he would not be singing any of his own original gospel tunes—namely the Rebel flag song that was usually such a hit—because he had learned the error of his ways and had "seen the light."

After that introduction, he broke into Hank Williams' "I Saw the Light," then "The Pale Horse and His Rider" and finished with "The Preacher and the Bear," for comic relief, I guess. By the end of that last song, Sonny had the congregation rolling in the aisles. He might have looked a bit foolish in his singing-cowboy getup, but he knew how to work a room.

Before Sonny had time to rejoin us in the choir loft, Reverend Bobby Lee was behind the pulpit, delivering the Word of God—or, at least, that was what he kept telling us he was doing, even though it looked more to me like screaming and shouting and pounding on his black leather-bound Bible. After about thirty minutes of that, I decided he had sat so quietly prior to the service simply to conserve his energy, like Duffy the other day on the tennis court during the changeover.

Reverend Bobby Lee, the Lord's annointed servant, yelled "hallelujah" time and again. He laughed out loud at his own jokes. He cried over the little lost lambs who were going to hell because they wouldn't listen to God's Word. He jumped up and down until he was drenched in sweat. He held up his hands to heaven and asked God to give us a sign of His glory. I'd never seen or heard anyone like him before. He even scared me two or three times.

The first couple of times were when the young evangelist unexpectedly shrieked in what Sonny later explained was "the unknown tongue," a spiel that sounded to me like gibberish but drew an enthusiastic response from many of the adults in the congregation. Then, toward the end of the sermon, Reverend Bobby Lee said something I understood perfectly and will never ever forget because of the shame it made me feel.

After an abridged retelling of the Old Testament story of Gideon and his three hundred chosen men who, with Jehovah's help, defeated the more powerful Midianites, Bobby Lee noted that even the great warrior Gideon had required a sign from God—also called "Jehovah" and "Yahweh," he digressed—before Gideon could bring himself to do God's will. On two successive nights, Gideon laid out a woolen fleece and told God first to make one side wet and then to keep the wool dry despite the morning dew, as proof God would help Gideon and his soldiers win the upcoming battle. And, according to Reverend Bobby Lee, God did as He was told. Gideon got his proof and went on to slaughter his enemies, thanks to God—Jehovah, I mean. Or Yahweh. Or Whatever.

What shocked me, though, wasn't that the Lord God Almighty had more than one name or that the old Jews were afraid to utter any of God's names and just referred to Him with the unutterable tetragram of YHWH, according to Reverend Bobby Lee. What scared me was that this so-called Man of God, who seemed to have no qualms whatsoever about calling the Lord any and all of His names, seemed to be talking directly to me as he finished his sermon. He even turned around once and looked me square in the eye.

"What if old Gideon had asked the Lord to prove Himself a *third* time?" Bobby Lee asked us. "What if old Gideon had said, 'I don't believe you yet, Jehovah God; you need to show me your power *one…more…time.*' What if old Gideon had said to that angel of the Lord, 'Mr. Angel, you go tell Yahweh—now listen to me—go tell Yahweh I need more proof. Tell Him I'm going to put out the fleece *one…more…time*, and *this* time I want Him to do such-and-such—I don't know, dye the wool blue, maybe—because I *still* don't believe in Him.'"

This was when Reverend Bobby Lee turned around and looked at me. "Young lady," he said sternly, even pointing at me for emphasis, "what do *you* think our Heavenly Father would say to someone for whom even a second chance isn't enough—now listen to me—for someone who asks for—no, for someone who *demands*—demands a third chance to get it right?" He fell silent, as if he actually expected me to answer him in front of the whole church. Or maybe he was just taking a second to catch his breath.

If I hadn't been so startled and frightened and embarrassed all at the same time, I might have given him a sarcastic Billy Joe kind of reply like, "Gee, I don't know, Bobby Lee—maybe, 'Another mulligan? Sure, why not?'" To me, anyway, God wouldn't be the type to worry about do-overs, especially with some young guy who was still learning the game. I mean, if Jehovah or YHWH or Whatever was a golfer, He'd be the most patient teaching pro you'd ever met, whether he was dealing with a scratch golfer or a regular duffer like me, even though I always *tried* to play by the rules.

Sometimes—like the week before when Sonny and I played Willow Creek—I couldn't help breaking a rule or two, no matter how much I studied my rulebook and how badly I wanted to do things right. Sometimes I just couldn't help it, like I couldn't help being afraid of flying or being afraid of the dark or being afraid of whatever. Now, I didn't actually say that or even think it until much later, but my mouth *did* fall open that morning as if I were *trying* to say something back to Reverend Bobby Lee. What it might have been, though, I don't know.

Before I could make any utterance whatsoever, the young preacher turned back to face the congregation again and answered for me. "*I'll* tell you what He'd say. He'd say, 'Depart from me, ye cursed, into everlasting *darkness*, prepared for the devil and his angels!' That's what He'd say to someone who *refuses* to believe, to someone who sees the evidence of God's greatness right in front of him and *still…does…not…believe*. The time is now, dear friends. The time is now. Don't put Him off any longer. Be like Gideon and accept the Lord's calling. Accept Him now, dear friends. Accept Him now, before it's too late."

Reverend Bobby Lee again turned toward us as he moved around the pulpit to step down from the platform, but this time he ignored me and whispered at Sonny to reprise the "Pale Horse" song as the invitational hymn. Without either explanation or apology, though, Sonny stood and sang the standard "Just As I Am" instead, *a cappella*. And he didn't waste any time packing his gear once Reverend Bobby Lee decided we'd had enough preaching and that it was time to eat. Leaving the sanctuary, Sonny did stop to whisper something into the evangelist's ear as they shook hands at the door. Reverend Bobby Lee didn't look pleased.

"What was that about back there?" Aunt Elaine asked Sonny, once we were in the Bronco and headed back up the mountain.

He acted as if he didn't know what she was talking about. "All what?"

"What did you say to the preacher?" she clarified. "He didn't seem to like it."

Sonny smiled. "I asked what version of the Bible he uses that says hell is everlasting *darkness*? My King James Bible says it's everlasting *fire*. Matthew 25:41."

Miss Faye jumped into the conversation. "Well, why didn't you sing the song he asked you to, Sonny? That was Reverend Bobby Lee. He's on television."

"I don't know," Sonny replied. "It just kinda hit me the wrong way, I guess. I don't like being told to do *anything*. I like to be *asked*, especially when I'm doing it outta the goodness of my heart. You know?"

"Oh, you were just being stubborn, Sonny," Miss Faye said, "just like Oren. You two stubborn little boys are always cutting off your noses to spite your faces."

"Huh?" Sonny said. "Where'd *that* come from, Mama? Why are you all of a sudden worrying about old Buck Green? Is there something you haven't told us about you two?" He waited to let that sink in, then added with a grin, "He ain't working on being my step-daddy, is he?"

"George Wayne Rose, Jr.!" Miss Faye shrieked, almost as loudly as Bobby Lee had screamed in his sermon that morning. "I never!" She muttered several other things, but they must have been in the unknown tongue, because I couldn't understand much of it.

"I'm just kidding you, Mama. I'm just kidding." Sonny laughed and looked up into the rear-view mirror, winking at Aunt Elaine and me in the back seat. We knew better than to get involved in that particular discussion, even though Elaine had started it. "No, seriously, Mama, why are you still upset with me? You know I'm just trying to look out for Buck."

"You embarrassed him," she explained, "just like Valerie was embarrassed when the preacher talked to her this morning in front of the whole church. Weren't you just absolutely mortified, honey?" She turned and looked at me.

"I guess so," I said. "I didn't know what to say." I could feel my face starting to flush again.

Miss Faye nodded. "See there. And that's exactly what you did to Oren, Sonny, by cutting his hair and making him shave off his beard. You took away his dignity, cut off his manhood, just like Samson."

"I guess that makes me Delilah," Sonny quipped. "Mama, that old man was scaring my campers off. I mean, half of them already think we're nothing but a bunch of crazy old hillbillies like the ones in *Deliverance*, and then they see Buck with his wild hair and beard and all, and they're convinced that's the way we are."

"Even so," Miss Faye said, "the Bible says respect your elders, and Oren Green has the right to wear his hair any way he pleases and wear a beard, too, if that's what he wants. My daddy wore a beard his whole life, 'cept for once when I was a little girl. He shaved it off, and I cried when I saw him the first time, 'cause I didn't recognize him and thought he was a stranger come to get me."

We rode in silence for several minutes as we continued up Mortimer Road (or was it Pineola Road?) toward Jonas Ridge. From having been there the previous weekend with Alan, I recognized the Darkside Cliffs and two Lost Cove Cliffs trailheads when we passed them, as well as the intersection with the road to Harper Creek and Kawana, near where Lacey and Buck lived.

"I just don't understand it, Mama," Sonny finally continued. "I mean, I think so much of Lacey—almost like she was my own daughter—and I know she's having it rough taking care of her granddaddy and all. But he *is* acting crazy, and he *does* scare people, and he—"

"He doesn't scare *me*," Miss Faye interrupted. "You all just don't know him. I've known Oren Green ever since we were young'uns, and I know he wouldn't harm a fly—that wasn't asking to be harmed."

"See there," Sonny said. "You admit he's dangerous. You've heard all the stories about him shooting at folks and getting in fights and doing all sorts of meanness. And that was back when he was supposed to still have his right mind. I figured he could handle keeping up the grounds at the lodge and maybe around your house and he wouldn't get into trouble doing that. But I think his mind has deteriorated so much lately that he can't be around people without acting crazy."

"He doesn't act crazy around *me*," Miss Faye countered. "And to tell you the truth, Sonny, I'd rather pass the time with Oren Green than with somebody like that old Hiram Vernon back there. Crazy or not."

"Why's that?" Sonny asked.

"Because," Miss Faye said, "Oren doesn't put on airs like a lot of folks. He doesn't try to be somebody he's not. Maybe he *is* getting on up there—like me—and maybe he *is* getting a little bit forgetful—like me—and maybe he's getting kinda ill about getting old and being treated like an idiot. Like me. Maybe he's just afraid of getting old and being pushed off in the corner where he'll be out of the way so everybody can forget about him. Maybe he doesn't want to be pushed aside. It doesn't mean he's senile."

Sonny glanced over at his mother. "You think we're pushing *you* aside?"

"Well, sometimes I do," she replied. "I don't think you believe what I say sometimes. I think you take everything I say with a grain of salt, like you think I'm lying or I'm crazy. And I'm *not* crazy, Sonny." Suddenly, she broke down and started to weep. "I'm not."

"Mama, I know you're not." Sonny reached across the front seat to touch his mother's shoulder. "I love you, Mama. And I'm sorry I'm not as patient as I oughta be sometimes. It's just that Buck's been acting so wild lately, I don't want him to hurt you, whether he means to or not. Nothing he does makes sense anymore—like riding off on my mower the other day. Val and Alan said they saw him down back there at the chapel. Who knows where else he's been lately?" (I kept quiet about having seen Buck on the mower in Linville.)

"He had to cut the grass," Miss Faye said. She seemed oddly calm again, as if she had already forgotten her earlier upset.

"Cut whose grass?" Sonny asked.

"Oren's been working at the C.C. camp down at Mortimer and cutting the grass there ever since he was a boy," she explained. "Sometimes he cuts other people's grass, too, if they talk nice to him. He said he cut the grass at the chapel, even though Hiram didn't even ask him to. That's 'cause Oren's a good hard-working man, Sonny. And good-hearted, too. He'd give you the shirt off his back if you needed it."

Now Sonny *was* confused. "Wait a second. In the first place, there isn't a Civilian Conservation Corps camp there anymore and hasn't been for sixty years. That's a Forest Service recreation area down there in Mortimer now. Matter of fact, it's a campground that I'm competing with for business, for Pete's sake. And you mean to say Buck rode my mower all the way down there to cut the campground's grass, and then back toward Edgemont and mowed that churchyard back there for nothing? Just to do old Preacher Vernon a favor? Great! He's riding all over creation mowing people's grass for nothing. On *my* mower!"

"No, not for *nothing*," Miss Faye said. "That's where a lot of his people are buried, back there at Greenlee Chapel, and he was doing it for *them*, it being homecoming and all. And not for Hiram. Oren doesn't care much at all for Hiram Vernon. Me neither. And he needed your riding mower just *this* time. Most times, he rides Niblick wherever he's going and uses his scythe to cut the grass the old-fashioned way, but he said it broke a couple weeks ago when he was cutting the grass there at the cemetery at Kawana. You know, Decoration Day is next Sunday. It's always the Sunday after July Fourth."

Elaine felt it was safe to rejoin the conversation. "Decoration Day? What's that, Miss Faye?"

Miss Faye turned to answer her. "Well, it's kinda like a church homecoming, honey, 'cept it's for family cemeteries that aren't connected with churches, like the little cemetery there at Kawana. It's really a big family reunion, and everybody comes from all over after they get out of church, and they have a big Sunday dinner together, like a dinner-on-the-grounds, and then they all clean and decorate the graves of their loved ones. It's a special day, 'specially for the older folks that don't get out and about much anymore. Decoration Day, they get to see everybody, all the young'uns that're shooting up like beansprouts and all the babies that've been born the past year. And they get to pay their respects to their loved ones that've gone on before them. That's important, too—that we don't forget what the old folks did for us."

Silence once again fell over us as Sonny guided the white Bronco around ruts and protruding stones in the winding roadway up the steep mountain. Occasionally, the road passed an open spot in the trees where I could see out over Lost Cove and catch a fleeting glimpse of the cliffs—specifically, the Little Lost Cove Cliffs, based on what Alan had shown me during our previous excursions on Mortimer Road. For some reason, I couldn't stop seeking out those picturesque gray granite cliffs set in their blue-green background of trees and sky, as if they were important to me for some reason I did not yet know.

While I had no reason to believe I would ever visit the cliffs, I also knew Alan was planning our camping trip for that coming Friday night, and I feared he just might pick a dark isolated spot like Lost Cove. It was, after all, one of his favorite places to mountain bike, and it was relatively close to Lacey and Buck's cabin.

Within the next hour, after we arrived at Miss Faye's house for Sunday dinner (little of which Sonny and Elaine could eat on their diet, by the way), my fear was realized, at least as far as Alan's plans were concerned. His bright yellow Blazer was parked in the driveway when we pulled up. Alan himself was fast asleep in a rocking chair on the front porch and didn't awaken until I snuck up behind him and rocked him forward, as if I were trying to dump him onto the plank floor.

"Hey, hey, hey!" Alan yelped, scrambling to right himself in the chair. "Come on, cuz! You trying to break my neck or something?"

Rounding the corner of the house on the stepping-stone path, Elaine answered for me. "You'd better have a good excuse for not coming home last night, young man, or I'm going to skin you alive."

"Oh, Mom," he replied. "What do you want me to say?" Blushing a bit from being questioned by his mother in front of us, he rose and stepped aside as Miss Faye, being helped onto the porch by Sonny, reached out to grasp the wooden rocker for support as she passed on her way to unlock the front door. Alan steadied the chair for the elderly lady. "Hi, Miss Faye," he greeted. "You doing OK this morning?"

"Not as well as *you* must be doing, young man," she said. "And how was Miss Lacey this morning?" She fumbled in her purse for her keys and took a bit more time than normal to find the right key and then the keyhole before opening the door for us. Sonny stepped inside first and held the door open.

"She's doing fine, Miss Faye," Alan answered. "I left her about an hour ago at the lodge, and I said I'd bring her and her granddad dinner, if you don't mind. By the way, Buck—I mean Mr. Green—asked for, let's see now, an extra-big helping of chicken 'n' dumplings, some extra mushroom gravy for his biscuit, and a slice of both kinds of pie. At least I *think* that was what he was growling at me. He was mad 'cause he was in the doghouse with Lacey and she made him stay in the lodge all morning. She wouldn't let him out of her sight."

"How did she manage that?" Sonny asked, suddenly interested in the conversation, as Miss Faye headed for the kitchen and the rest of us took seats in her living room.

Alan shrugged. "Aw, you know. He listens to Lacey, even if he doesn't like doing what she says. I guess he knows he'd be in a real fix if he made her mad and she took off like everybody else did." Then he added, with a laugh, "From what Lacey's said, the worst thing would be he'd have to eat his own cooking."

"Or Mama's," Sonny interjected.

"What was that, Sonny?" called Miss Faye from the kitchen.

"Nothin', Mama," Sonny called back, then turned to Alan again. "So how did Buck know to ask for chicken 'n' dumplings and mushroom gravy and *two* different kinds of pie? How'd he know what all we're having—or, I should say, what *you* guys are having, since Elaine and I can only eat the chicken but not the dumplings? I mean, I didn't even know what she'd fixed until just a while ago when Mama mentioned it at church, and I figured she was just telling the preacher that to get out of staying for homecoming dinner there."

"I guess Miss Faye told Buck yesterday," Alan ventured. "Lacey said he came up here to see her last evening. We walked over to the Harper Creek Falls and had just got back to the cabin when he took off on that crazy-looking old mule of his. It was almost dark, and he had a kerosene lantern in one hand and a big picnic basket over the other arm. I asked him what was in the basket, and he just said, 'Nothin' yet, Mr. Nosy,' and rode on off on the North Harper Creek Falls Trail, where we'd just come from.

"We got in the Blazer and went after him by Mortimer Road, but we never could catch up with him. We figured he took a side trail somewhere before cutting back to the road, just to throw us off—maybe up that loop trail that runs up past the Little Lost Cove Cliffs. We even hiked up there and looked for him, but we didn't see him. That's where I called you from, Mom—from that high spot on the cliffs where you can see 360 degrees. Matter of fact, that's probably where we'll camp Friday night, since the cell phone'll get out from there."

"Alan Delacruz!" Elaine scolded. "You hiked up there in the dark? Don't you *ever* do that again—taking a chance like that! You and Lacey could've slipped and fallen up there and really hurt yourselves—or worse—and it would've taken forever to get help to you! Don't *ever* do that again!"

"Oh, Mom, calm down. We both had good flashlights, and, besides, I've hiked and biked on that trail so much I could've done it blindfolded. Lacey, too. She said Buck used to take her there all the time when she was little, back after her folks went away, and they'd camp in the old apple orchard that's about halfway up the ridge. She thinks he was working a still somewhere around there, though, 'cause she'd hear him leave on his mule soon as he thought she was asleep, and he wouldn't come back until right before dawn.

"She'd try to find out where he'd been, and he'd just say he was out coon hunting, but she knew he wasn't 'cause he never took his coon dogs with him and he never brought back any coons. And if he disappeared during the daytime, he'd just say he was out huckleberry hunting or mushroom hunting or digging 'sang or something like that, so she never knew for sure what he was up to. Last night he came home around midnight and went straight back to his room without saying much of anything. Lacey talked to him this morning and found out where he'd been, that he'd come to see Miss Faye."

Sonny looked to see if his mother was eavesdropping from the kitchen. "Is he still moonshining? You know, Mama *has* been acting kinda strange lately, and that would probably explain it—I mean, if she's taking a little nip now and then. Maybe that's why he came up here last night—to deliver some, uh, 'recipe'—isn't that what those old ladies on *The Waltons* called it?" He winked.

Alan shook his head. "No, I don't think he's still moonshining. But he *did* bring Miss Faye something—whatever was in that picnic basket—'cause he didn't have it with him when he got back home. What he *did* have, though, was a great big Gala apple that Miss Faye gave him. He was eating it when he walked in the door."

"How in the world would you know it was a Gala?" Elaine asked.

"Lacey said it's the only kind he eats anymore, ever since he got into Sonny's stash at the lodge," Alan laughed. "She said he won't eat the little apples from his own trees or even the ones from that orchard near the cliffs, 'cause they're always so wormy. He mainly uses them for hard cider and applejack brandy. Those apples at Lost Cove aren't even ripe now, anyway."

Sonny thought for a second, then turned toward the kitchen door and called, "Mama? You hear me?"

"Yes, Sonny," she replied, wiping her hands on her apron as she came to the kitchen door. "Dinner's ready, children. I hope you don't mind sitting at the kitchen table. It's where Preacher Rose and I always take our meals when the weather's coolish. And I do hope the apple pie suits you. All I had were those apples you gave me to keep for you, Sonny, and I think they're just too sweet to make a good pie. I like Granny Smiths the best for a good-tasting pie."

Seeming not to notice his mother's reference to his late father, Sonny walked across the kitchen to the counter that ran along the wall and contained Miss Faye's double sink beneath an open kitchen window. On the counter next to the sink sat a picnic basket still half full of mushrooms and huckleberries. "Where'd all this come from, Mama?" Sonny asked, as if he didn't already know.

Miss Faye gave him an innocent little-girl look. "Well, of course *I* picked them, honey," she said, obviously fibbing to cover up Buck's visit the night before. "You don't have to worry about the mushrooms, dear. They're black trumpets—chanterelles. I looked them up at the library, and they don't look anything at all like the poisonous ones you always hear about people accidentally eating. You don't have to worry."

I could tell from the way Sonny just kind of looked at her for a second, he was trying to decide whether or not to confront her with what he knew about Buck's drop-in visit. He decided not to mention it.

"I won't, Mama," he said, then motioned for her to join us at the table. "Now, come on and let's eat. I'm half starved to death."

After dinner, Miss Faye silently emptied the picnic basket of its leftover mushrooms and huckleberries, then refilled it with Tupperware containers of food for Lacey and Buck. Alan left for the lodge with the filled basket, while Sonny and Elaine went to the front porch to sit and talk in private. I stood at the sink with Miss Faye and dried her pots and dishes as she washed and handed them to me. Despite the mountain chill in the air that she had mentioned earlier, Miss Faye left open the kitchen window above the sink and seemed to lean toward it from time to time, as if she were listening for something outside. About ten minutes after Alan drove away, I heard in the distance, in the direction of the lodge, what Miss Faye must have been listening for. It was the staccato call of a bugle saying "thank you" for dinner, I was sure.

TWENTY-THREE

The next few days leading up to the July Fourth holiday were nothing to write home about, really—if I'd had a home to write to, that is. I had hoped they would be fun. But Aunt Elaine and Sonny and Miss Faye had other ideas, and their plans for me were definitely at odds with my own. In the first place, Elaine was busy with the newspaper, getting ready to put out its big Fourth of July edition that many Linville area tourists would pick up. Sonny and Miss Faye were determined to prod me through their three-week summer-school crash course.

On Monday, I tried my best to read their plays—*The Amen Corner* for Sonny and *Twelfth Night* for Miss Faye. I kind of liked *The Amen Corner*, because it reminded me of the homecoming service we had attended the day before—except all of the folks in James Baldwin's play were black and everything happened in Harlem. *Twelfth Night* was quite another story—or play, rather. Try as I might, I couldn't make heads or tails of all that Shakespearean gooblety-gook, not until Tuesday morning when I complained about it to Sonny, and he found me a copy of Leon Garfield's *Shakespeare Stories*. It had *Twelfth Night* written in regular English that even I could understand. The story was OK but nothing spectacular, I thought.

My main question was, why did old Shakespeare name it *Twelfth Night*? What did *that* have to do with anything? Sonny said I'd just have to ask his mother. As a title, *The Amen Corner* made perfect sense to me, and I also liked it because that's what the toughest part of the Masters golf tournament course at Augusta National was called, even back when Billy Joe Patton—the *real* golfer, not my old friend who pretended to be a pro—almost won the Masters as an amateur. It was pretty easy to make connections with Sonny's assignments, not so easy yet with Miss Faye's.

I wasn't in the best of moods Tuesday morning with Sonny, because I learned that the secret he was keeping with Aunt Elaine didn't involve taking me to play the Linville golf course. Instead, after he listened to me gripe about having to read that old play for his mother, he made me sit there in his office at the college and wait for him to go to the college library to get their copy of *Shakespeare Stories*. When he got back, he handed me the book and told me I had to read Garfield's version of *Twelfth Night* before we could go play golf. It was the first story in the book and was only about twenty pages long, so I was able to skim it and take notes in a couple of hours.

But when I was finally done, Sonny said we only had time to play nine holes that morning, since it was already past ten o'clock. As we left the building and walked toward the parking lot where his red-and-white Corvette waited with its top down, Sonny nodded toward the full set of clubs I carried over my shoulder in my black Knight bag. "You're probably gonna have to hold them up front," he said, "'cause I doubt there's room for two sets in the trunk. I brought my big bag, too, and it's a real monster. You've seen it."

I nodded and smiled. "So we're riding today, even though we're only playing nine?" I asked, figuring Sonny wouldn't have brought his big bag and full set of clubs if he intended to walk the course or play Willow Creek again.

"Yeah," he replied. "You don't wanna walk *this* course, not even nine."

"Which course? Linville?" My heart had already started to sink, because I knew Linville had a fairly level design.

"Course not," Sonny said. "We're playing Hawksnest today, up there at Seven Devils." He nodded back over his shoulder toward the mountain looming behind us. "The front nine has some great views of Grandfather. You'll enjoy the course." I'm sure he could tell I was disappointed despite his assurances.

"So what about *next* week?" I asked. "You think we could play Linville next week?"

Before he answered my question, he helped me into the Corvette and lowered my bag to me after I buckled up. "I don't know," he said, as he turned the ignition key and revved the engine. "What other books are you reading for Mama this week?"

I thought for a second. "This book about the 'crack of dawn' or something and a Mark Twain book I never heard of before—not *Huckleberry Finn* or *Tom Sawyer*. I think it's *Punkinhead Williams*, or something like that."

"*Pudd'nhead Wilson*," Sonny corrected, as he wheeled the sportscar from its parking place and accelerated slowly through the lot toward the college's main drive. "What else you reading for *me*?"

"I don't know," I admitted. "You said I didn't have to read your books in any certain order, like Miss Faye did. What do you *want* me to read."

This time it was Sonny's turn to ponder his answer. He gunned the engine as we stopped at the intersection of the college's entrance drive and the two-lane road up the mountain to Seven Devils. "OK, how's this?" he said finally. "I think you're ready for *The Soul of Golf*, and, let's see, Maya Angelou's *Singin' and Swingin' and Gettin' Merry Like Christmas*. You'll enjoy the Hallberg book, 'cause it talks about him playing golf up here—well, at Linville Ridge, anyway—and on the coast, not around where you lived but down around Charleston—Kiawah Island, I think it is. You'll like Miss Maya's book, too."

"I really like Mr. Hallberg's other book—*Rub of the Green*," I offered. "I just have one chapter left." I wondered if telling Sonny that fact would impress him—how I had almost finished an entire novel that neither he nor his mother had assigned.

He nodded. "Really? You can set a book down with only one chapter left to read? Wow. That's something I can't do. Once I get that far, I've gotta finish it to see how it all comes out, you know?"

"I know how it's gonna end," I said. "That's why I don't want to finish it just yet."

Sonny was quiet for a second, then observed, "Well, if you know how *that* book ends without reading it, you oughta write one yourself—a novel, I mean. But I like the way that book ends. It's hopeful, you know?" He glanced over at me when I didn't reply. "So have you figured out what the author's doing with the two plotlines?" Sonny asked. "You see how he's intertwining the two stories to give you a sense of the past and the present coming together at the end of the novel? Neat, huh?"

I shook my head. "I didn't know he was doing *anything* except telling a story. Can't you just read a book and enjoy reading it, instead of picking it apart and trying to figure out all that stuff?"

"What stuff?"

"Like that—like what you just said—'the past and the present coming together,' or whatever it was—all that crap that teachers are always talking about." I could feel my head shaking again, though not by any choice of my own. My hands were trembling, too. As soon as I realized what was happening—that another panic attack was coming on—I knew I had to get out of the car immediately or else I would die.

"What's wrong?" Sonny asked, suddenly concerned. We rounded the next curve and pulled off at a gated driveway, but Sonny wouldn't let me get out of the car. "No, stay in your seat. You're safe here. Running from it won't help. You could get hit by a car coming down the mountain. We'll just sit here and be quiet until it passes."

And that's what we did. As hard as it was for me to do, we just sat there in Sonny's Corvette, and I rode out my panic attack, the first one I'd suffered since arriving in the mountains. I had come close to having one several times in the previous week to ten days; however, I had overcome my anxious feelings by "going to my happy place," as one of my counselors had taught me to do (or was that in *Happy Gilmore*?). Until I had the attack with Sonny, my happy place had been the most beautiful golf course on earth, even before I ever moved to the mountains and saw any part of it for the first time. It was my happy place even when I was having panic attacks on the coast, as I could see in my mind's eye the neat tee boxes, inviting fairways and immaculate greens without even knowing that this place I was visualizing actually existed. I think it became my happy place because it was the exact opposite of what I was trying hard to both forget and remember at the same time. Linville Golf Club—or, at least, the image of it in my fear-stricken brain—was everything that the B.J. back home was not.

What had happened to me during that last visit to thank Billy Joe for the Wilson sand wedge, his going-away present, was what I wanted to erase from my memories. At the same time, Billy Joe and, by extension, Grandma and Grandpa and Mama and Daddy—all the loved ones I had ever lost—were what I never wanted to forget. The problem was that in my mind, memories of them all were inextricably tangled together, as were the different sights and sounds that sometimes unexpectedly reminded me of them and pushed me ever so much closer to the edge of anxiety.

The attack in Sonny's car had been coming on since my arrival in the mountains. I didn't know if it was a good sign or not that it had taken that long to get to me. My counselor had identified it as a particular phobia; another analyst had said it was post-traumatic stress syndrome; still another doctor had just called it "growing pains." Whatever it was, though, terrified me, moreso than my fear of flying and my fear of the dark rolled together ever did. My counselor theorized that all three of my phobias were related, that they actually were just one great fear I could call *agoraphobia*, if I needed a name for what was making my life so miserable, if I needed a concept by which to measure my pain.

I tried to explain all that to Sonny, and I think he understood what I was saying—or, at least, he acted as if he understood the jumbled mess that had been my life to that point. When I finally calmed down enough to get back on the road, we drove on up the mountain to the golf course. As Sonny had promised, the course's front side was both enjoyable and picturesque, with spectacular views of Grandfather and Grandmother Mountains just across the Watauga River Valley in Avery County and of Mount Mitchell, the highest peak in the Eastern United States, to the southwest in neighboring Mitchell County.

I certainly didn't play well that morning, as I was still shaky from the earlier attack, but I really didn't care about my score and didn't even bother keeping it. Neither did Sonny, as far as I could tell. He just wanted to make sure we had a good time. Later, as Sonny was driving me to Jonas Ridge for my afternoon with Miss Faye, he promised that my next outing would be at my happy place. "I'll get you on that old Linville course," he pledged, "if it's the last thing I do."

Sure enough, that afternoon while I was staying with Miss Faye at the Jonas Ridge Library, Sonny phoned to say we had a three-thirty tee time at Linville Golf Club for Wednesday, the following day. He said he had called both Duffy and Kitty, and had talked them into playing a round of golf at Linville and into letting us join them as their guests. Our foursome's starting time was one of the last of the day, Sonny explained, mainly because Duffy couldn't take off work on such short notice and had to stay at his restaurant until after Wednesday's early closing time at two o'clock. Sonny added he had already gotten Aunt Elaine's OK for me to play so late the next day, since she probably would have to wait at the office for us to finish the course.

After giving me the good news, Sonny also talked to Miss Faye and got her permission for me to miss my studies with her on Wednesday afternoon, as long as I agreed to make them up on Friday morning instead of taking the whole day off for the Fourth. Right then, I would have agreed to almost anything in order to play Linville, my happy place, my idea of heaven on earth. I might even have agreed to go coon hunting with Buck on his crazy-looking one-eyed mule—or mushroom hunting or huckleberry hunting or even digging 'sang, whatever *that* was (Sonny told me later that *ginseng* is a medicinal root worth a lot of money to mountaineers, and that its Oriental name comes from its forked shape, like a little man).

OK, so everything was all set up. I was going to play Linville. Here's what I expected: After a morning of quiet reflection on *The Soul of Golf* (I wouldn't need any prodding to skim *that* book), Sonny and I would grab a quick bite of lunch in Linville (he'd pick up the tab since it was kind of like a date), probably at Duffy's place, to give the old Duffer a little extra business just to show our appreciation for his invitation; then Sonny and I would tool on over to the clubhouse in his, let's see, his black Mustang, yeah, his new car, not one of those old ones, not even the Corvette, as cool as it was; then we'd check in and change our shoes, in the clubhouse, of course, not in the parking lot; then we would saunter across the road to the practice range and hit a couple buckets of balls, before sauntering back to the practice green and chipping area near the first tee. We would greet Duffy and Kitty cordially, then agree on friendly wagers for the round (probably a modest Nassau), and then we'd be off on a four-hour tour of paradise, like the *Gilligan's Island* castaways on the *S.S. Minnow* (no, ours was better because theirs was just a "three-hour tour").

That's what I imagined, anyway, and was what I predicted that night when I called Bo to share my joyous news. Though he was happy for me, my best friend was more interested in getting me to find out times and places of the camping trip that he, Alan, Lacey and I were supposed to be going on that Friday night. Bo said he was still waiting for permission from his mother to leave campus on the holiday. She would come around after making him sweat for a few days, he ventured, and he wanted to be prepared for the outing.

Since I was totally in the dark about the camping trip, I was supposed to tell Alan to look Bo up on campus on Wednesday or at least no later than Thursday morning, so that the two of them could work out all the details of this big Brown Mountain Light hunting expedition we were going on. Bo needed to make absolutely sure he packed the right equipment and gathered all the right information—map coordinates and such—for a search of that magnitude, he said. He also wanted to know if Sonny would be loaning us the black Charger again. I didn't know the answers to any other questions Bo was asking, but I *did* know the answer to *that* one: I wasn't going to ride in that car again, at least not with Bo, and I told him so. As it turned out, that was just one of the many words I had to eat—and sooner than I thought.

Early Wednesday morning, after one of the best nights of sleep I'd had in ages (my lighthouse night light burned brighter than usual, it seemed), I arose to the news from Aunt Elaine that my golf outing was in jeopardy, not because of anything anybody could help, but due to an unfair act of God, a cheap shot from the Almighty, the threat of thunderstorms and locally-heavy rains, an unnatural phenomenon otherwise known as "the remnants of Tropical Storm Bill," according to the National Weather Service radio Elaine kept in the kitchen.

That afternoon, when Sonny and I arrived at the clubhouse under threatening skies (yes, in the black Charger, but with only the Allman Brothers' live acoustic version of "Midnight Rider" blaring, thankfully), we learned that there would be no more golf that day due to severe weather warnings in effect at that time. Sonny called Duffy and Miss Kitty to head them off, then dropped me and my clubs at the *Ledger* office, and headed on home himself.

I figured, though, that I wasn't going to let a little rain and maybe a thunderbolt or two keep me from a quick visit to my happy place, even if I wasn't going to get to play the course. I decided to grab my Wilson golf umbrella and maybe an iron from my bag and go for a little walk on the wild side, so to speak, before Aunt Elaine finished up at the newspaper and was ready to leave. Since I didn't have a one-iron to hold over my head in case of a lightning strike (because, according to the old golf joke, even God can't hit a one-iron), I pulled my Hogan six-iron and hoped to find some stray balls to hit, if not on the course itself, then maybe near the practice range along Roseborough Road.

With at least three hours to kill, I walked all the way down the main street through the village to the westernmost hole from the clubhouse, the 565-yard, par-five, number four hole. It was the longest hole on the championship course, with its green between one of Lake Kawana's small coves at the left rear and street along the right across a thin row of hemlocks and an eight-foot-high, chain-link fence.

When I reached the fence, which, by the way, was topped by three strands of barbed wire, I saw that entry onto the course there was impractical if not impossible, unless I chose to swim across Lake Kawana to reach the green. That, too, was hardly an option—that particular day, anyway—as someone had beaten me to the lake, someone I did not want to run into, for a number of reasons. It was someone who seemed to be having a perfectly fine time fishing in the rain, without being bothered by a girl who wanted to spend a couple of hours visiting her happy place.

That someone was Buck Green, who might have been a perfect gentlemen with Miss Faye, his sweetheart, but didn't seem to be warming up to me one bit, despite my budding relationships with both his old girlfriend and his granddaughter. At least his crazy-looking mule wasn't posted close to him; old Niblick wasn't anywhere in sight, in fact. And I didn't see Sonny's lawn mower, either.

Backing away from the fence, I figured I would be able to sneak away undetected, but as I started to turn away, Buck looked up from the red-and-white bob floating near the end of his line and spotted me. When I heard him yell something and saw him throw down his pole on the bank and start in my direction, I knew I'd better haul my butt out of there and quick, before someone else had to come haul *all* of me out of the lake. Buck wasn't going to catch me, not if I could help it.

And he didn't. As I ran all the way back up the road into the village proper, I looked back over my shoulder every few seconds to see if Buck was following me, but neither he nor his mule appeared on the avenue. If he was pursuing me, then he was crossing the course itself, either on foot or hoof, and I doubted that even Buck was crazy enough to try something like that in broad daylight—not unless he had highjacked Sonny's mower again and was posing as a groundskeeper. That idea *did* occur to me; however, I didn't worry too much about it, because I hadn't heard any mower engines start up since fleeing the lakeside.

Thirty minutes later, still carrying my umbrella and six-iron, and still smarting from the close calls I'd had with both heaven (almost getting to play the Ross course) and hell (almost getting caught trespassing by someone as scary to me as the devil himself), I wandered up Roseborough Road past the clubhouse, whose parking lot was now empty except for a white Caddy, a red Mercedes and a black Beemer.

Though I was still on the lookout for Buck and his mule, I did manage to find a single lost range ball in the deep rough on the shoulder of the road about 180 yards from the practice tees. I didn't dare pick it up, knowing the rulebook dictates that a ball must be played as it lies, so I couldn't read the ball's brand or number, as nothing but white showed. For all I knew, it could have been the very same ball (the Top-Flite Infinity 0 with the *pi* mark) that I had "holed" with Sonny's Hagen putter on the "green" at the cemetery and had later dropped near the river and then struck with the Wilson sand wedge that was like the one Billy Joe had given me as a going-away present.

Dropping my umbrella into the weeds and settling into my stance alongside the ball, I took the club away on my backswing, then brought the iron's silver blade down and through the ball, biting into the moist earth and slicing a grassy divot the length and width of an outstretched hand. As I carried the club through to its finish and twisted to face forward, the white sphere rose through the raindrops on a line toward the tees that would have made Billy Joe proud. Ordinarily, I was lucky to hit my six-iron 130 yards, which was about average for a lady golfer. This six, however, landed 150, at least, and ran another twenty-five or thirty before caroming off a four-foot-tall river-rock flower planter behind the tee boxes.

I was still admiring my shot when lightning flashed over Pixie Mountain and thunder cracked a split second later. Just then, the heavens opened and buckets of water fell from the sky, first in big drops, then in stormy sheets. As I unclenched from the thunderbolt's shock and fought to keep my eyes open in the rain, I saw standing at the back of the teeing ground—to my utter disbelief—the one and only Buck Green (but still no sign of his mule).

Buck stooped to look at my ball, straightened up again and lifted his green cap into the air despite the downpour, as if to celebrate my outstanding shot. When I didn't wave back, he returned the cap to his head, turned on his heel and walked down the stairs to the small parking area below the practice tees. Where he went from there and how he went away, I had no idea, because I wasn't about to follow him to find out. For all I knew, he could have simply disappeared into the fog rising all around us.

TWENTY-FOUR

The Fourth of July. Independence Day. Or as my old pro Billy Joe always put it, Happy Birthday, U.S. of A.! Billy Joe thoroughly enjoyed celebrating the Fourth, from the parades to the barbecues to the fireworks filling the holiday with smiles and laughter and good clean fun (except where Billy Joe's messy BBQ sauce was concerned—nothing clean about that).

That, in fact, was my old boss's big thing—cooking a pig and inviting all his friends and club members to drop by the course at their leisure in the afternoon between the Shallotte parade in the morning and the Southport fireworks in the evening. Billy Joe always drove his black pirate cart in the parade and tossed golf tees instead of candy to kiddies along the route. The morning of the event, he always went to Wal-Mart and bought a couple of economy-sized bags of regular store-brand natural-finish tees to throw, as he claimed that the absence of colored paint and a printed course name made his tiny wooden offerings more "biodegraphical," just in case they weren't picked up off the street.

There was nothing that *wasn't* biodegradable about the pig Billy Joe and I spent all night and the better part of a morning cooking for his July Fourth barbecue. In fact, when I worked for Billy Joe, I never got to go to the parade, because he always left me to watch the pig cooker at the course. It was one of those big black gas-powered grills made from a huge steel drum and mounted on wheels so it could be hitched behind a truck and pulled to the party. He was always afraid that some "yea-hoo" with a trailer hitch would drive off with our pig, if we were gone even for an hour. Also, I would be there to run the course itself, though Billy Joe usually didn't worry about people playing without putting their fees in the "Pirate's Chest" honor box on the clubhouse door whenever he had to leave the course unattended any other time.

Then, in the late afternoon, Billy Joe and I would drive down to Grandpa's dock near our house and watch the big fireworks display up at Southport, just like we used to do when Grandpa was alive. Later, we might do some floundering so Grandma would have something to fuss about when we asked her the next day to clean and fry up the fish we'd caught. Of course, that was before I developed my fear of darkness—and before Grandma made it perfectly clear she didn't want Billy Joe hanging around our house all the time.

My first Independence Day in the mountains promised to be quite different from all my previous July Fourths on the coast. Since I owed Miss Faye a half day of summer school, Aunt Elaine and I rose early, as usual, that Friday morning and drove to Boone, where we picked up Bo at music camp. He had phoned the night before to tell us his mother had finally given in and granted him permission to leave campus. "She still isn't happy with me," my friend noted. "She said if I mess up again, we won't get to go to DocFest next weekend—or *I* won't, anyway."

"Or go to the Highland Games," Elaine added. "It starts Thursday evening and runs through Sunday, so I'll be busy with it pretty much all weekend. When *is* Doc's festival exactly? It's in Boone, right?"

"No, ma'am, not really," Bo replied, as he leaned forward from the back seat of the Challenger. "It's Friday and Saturday at the Doc & Merle Watson Folk Art Museum at a place called Cove Creek. Do you know where that is?"

Elaine nodded. "When do you and Val want to go?" She glanced over at me to see how I was taking Bo's plans.

"Well, ma'am, I was thinking we'd go Saturday since that's the big day," Bo said, "and that's the only day I can ride the bus. If you or Alan or somebody can get Val to Boone Saturday morning and pick her up again that night, we'll be all set."

"We can probably work *something* out," Elaine agreed, looking at me again. "That OK with you, Val?"

"Sure," I said, "but don't you need me to help you at the Highland Games? I could take pictures or something, I guess, if you need me to."

Elaine smiled. "Yes, I probably *will* need your help, especially Thursday afternoon. That's when they run the Bear—*late* in the afternoon, actually. That's a footrace from Linville all the way to the top of Grandfather."

"Yeah, Alan told us about it the other day," Bo interjected. "On their way up the mountain, don't they run around the track there where we were the other Sunday for that gospel singing?"

"Well, they kind of cut across the track down the back stretch," Elaine explained, "and then they get back on the road and head on up the mountain all the way to the Swinging Bridge. The two winners—the fastest guy and girl—they finish before dark, and they're driven back down to the opening ceremony—a torchlight ceremony. That's held right after sundown there at MacRae Meadows."

"Torchlight ceremony?" I asked, with a frown. "After dark?"

"Yes, it's a beautiful ceremony," she said. "They get a representative from each clan—each family—and they divide them into four groups and put a group at each corner of the field there inside the track. Then, when it's dark enough, they carry the torches from the four corners—you know, to represent the four directions on the compass—and they place their torches in a holder that's set up in the middle of the field. It's really touching—you know, all of the families coming together for this big reunion and all."

Still leaning forward so he could hear us better, Bo must have sensed what was bothering me. "What you gonna need Val to do, Miss Elaine?" he asked. "I don't think I can leave camp that night, or I'd help her."

Instead of answering Bo directly, Elaine reached over and patted my knee. "Maybe I can get you to wait for the runners up at the Swinging Bridge, Val, and get their pictures when they cross the finish line," she said, then added with a laugh, "Sonny still says *he's* going to enter the race, even if he has to *walk* up the mountain. But we'll figure out some way to get you up there and back by dark. Who knows—maybe you'll have your own driver's license by then. You *have* been studying for the test, haven't you? Isn't Sonny handling that?"

"Well, yeah," I replied, "but I haven't practiced driving yet, not unless you count driving the golf cart the other day. Maybe *that's* why Sonny made me drive. I just thought he was being lazy."

Elaine smiled wistfully. "Remember when Daddy let you drive the Beetle down at the Point? You had to sit on his lap, and you still could just barely see over the steering wheel."

"That was your dad's car, Miss Elaine?" Bo asked. "I thought it was always yours."

"Well, it was my daddy's car first," she explained. "He loved that little car to death. He'd had it for years—I think he bought it brand new—but he gave it to me right after Lance and I split up, because I needed a car for work. I'd gotten a job at the paper down there. Daddy found himself another old car somewhere—it was always breaking down—and he drove the old Chevy until he…." She paused a moment. "And Mama—she never did drive. We wanted her to get her license after, after Daddy…. But she wouldn't." She didn't complete the sentences, but I was all too familiar with the word she was leaving out.

"There's something I need to tell you, Val, before we get to Miss Faye's," Elaine said, after regaining her composure. "Sonny told me yesterday he's done with the Beetle, and he wants to drive it in both parades today. The little Linville parade is this morning, and Newland's is this afternoon. He always drives one of his cars in both of those parades."

I shook my head as I pictured *my* Beetle as *Herbie the Love Bug*. "Did he really put those silly decals on her?"

"I guess so," Elaine replied. "He said he was done and she looks great. He'll be waiting for us at his mother's house, and then I'll ride with him back to Linville. So, Bo, you can drive this car down to the lodge after lunch—Miss Faye said she'd feed you—and then it'll be there tonight when Sonny and I get back from watching the fireworks displays. We're going to park at the overlook on Grandfather Mountain where you can see all the fireworks in towns off the mountain—Lenoir and Morganton and Hickory, if the weather's clear. Sonny said one year he watched *six* fireworks displays at the same time. It'll be fun."

Bo and I exchanged a mischievous look. "You and Sonny are going *parking*?" I gulped, trying not to laugh. "Does Alan know about this?"

This time Elaine slapped my knee playfully. "It's not like that," she scolded. "And, yes, Alan knows all about it. In fact, it was his idea, because he wants us to watch the Brown Mountain area, too. If we're up there at that overlook on the Parkway, Alan said we can even talk to you guys down in Lost Cove, either by phone or on the CB, if you don't have cell phone service down there. That's why Sonny's going to drive that old Charger, the one that *was* the *General Lee*, 'cause it has a CB in it. OK?"

"Whatever you say, Aunt Elaine," I said, then added with a giggle, "but will I have to call him *Uncle* Sonny?" She popped me again, a little harder this time, and changed the subject to me and my plans for the future. Within a matter of seconds, *I* was the one who wasn't in the mood to be forthcoming with any more personal information than was absolutely necessary, especially if it meant breaking the news to my aunt that I was still seriously considering a career in golf course maintenance and turf management.

She didn't seem to mind that I had suddenly clammed up. In turn, Bo took my cue and leaned back to listen to the MP3 player on his belt. With his earbuds in, I couldn't hear what he was listening to, but I could guess from his soft humming he was listening to Miles Davis. It must have been one of Miles' more sedate tunes, because my glances back at my friend caught him with his eyes closed and his face at perfect peace.

Later, after Elaine dropped us off at Miss Faye's house and then left with Sonny, I was actually relieved to have Bo around, because he made our discussion of my third English assignment that week easier and considerably more fun than usual. We spent the first three hours that morning in strict silence in separate rooms—me in the living room, Bo in the kitchen with Miss Faye—so I could try to finish reading as much of *Pudd'nhead Wilson* as possible. Then, about an hour before lunch, I joined them in the kitchen, and we discussed what I had covered, even though I hadn't finished the novel, which, I was surprised to learn, Bo *had* read in full the previous year at school and had even liked.

A few minutes into what I expected would be a tedious thirty-minute discussion (for every question I could answer, Miss Faye could think of three more that I couldn't), I started stumbling, as usual, over Miss Faye's literary hurdles about plots and subplots and protagonists and antagonists and conflicts and themes and devices and such. But this time Bo was there to pick me up and help me limp to the finish line.

"Mrs. Rose?" Bo began. "May I ask a question?"

With a look of mild surprise, Miss Faye replied, "Certainly, Linus."

"It's *Lionel*," I stated, drawing a frown from the elderly teacher, who didn't appreciate being contradicted by her student, "but he goes by Bo. That's why Alan was calling him Boo-Boo the other night on the CB. Remember?"

I don't think she *did* remember what I was referring to, but she didn't seem to let it bother her too much. "Well then, Lionel, you can call me Miss Faye. And what might your question be? About Mr. Twain's novel?" She didn't know yet that Bo had already read the book himself.

He nodded. "Yes, ma'am. I was just wondering what you think about the racial-stereotype issues in the novel—and the question of gender that's raised when Twain makes one of the characters a cross-dresser."

"Excuse me?" she said, looking and sounding as if Bo must have been referring to a different book from the one she had assigned me to read. She took up the small paperback edition I had earlier laid on the table, and she squinted down her nose at the small print on the back cover without commenting further.

"That's the same edition I read last year, Miss Faye," Bo noted, "and I really, really like Langston Hughes' introduction. I just like Langston Hughes, period. I found a first edition of *The Weary Blues* in the library the other day, and Mom said she'll download the whole Mingus album for me—Charles Mingus, he and another guy wrote some music, some jazz, to go with Langston Hughes' poems from *The Weary Blues*. Langston even reads the poems on the album. Anyway, he says this novel is a lot more serious about racial issues than *Huckleberry Finn* is, and, you know, I agree with him. And he quotes Mark Twain's saying about color, how it's 'only skin deep.' Do you agree with that, Miss Faye, that color is only skin deep?"

I think Miss Faye was still trying to figure out Bo's earlier "cross-dresser" reference, but she managed to reply, "Well, yes, I most certainly do, Lionel. Color is skin deep just like beauty is skin deep. I especially like another quotation…." She thumbed through the book, found her place, then continued, "Here it is—'Training is everything. The peach was once a bitter almond; cauliflower is nothing but cabbage with a college education.' And then the other quotation on the same page is, 'Remark of Dr. Baldwin's, concerning upstarts: We don't care to eat toadstools that think they are truffles.' Don't you agree, Valerie?" I got the distinct feeling she was passing the hot potato to me so I could help her take the heat from Bo.

"That's always been *my* position on that subject," I said, trying to stall for time.

But Miss Faye wouldn't let me. "Which of Mr. Twain's quotations spoke to *you*, Valerie?" she asked, apparently not wanting to give Bo a chance to horn in with more questions of his own.

I took the book back from her and turned through it slowly, looking at the quotations at the start of each chapter. "This one," I said presently. "It says, 'Let us endeavor so to live that when we come to die even the undertaker will be sorry.' I like that."

"Yeah, that's a famous quote," Bo observed. "Did you read the one about courage? It's farther back in the book. Here, I'll find it for you, Val." I handed him the slim blue volume, and he flipped from chapter to chapter as if he were so familiar with the book that he could find the epigrams after reading only the first couple of words. "Here it is, here it is. 'Courage is resistance to fear, mastery of fear—not absence of fear,' and it goes on and on, but that's the best part. That really is true, *isn't* it?" He wasn't looking at Miss Faye; he was looking straight at me, and he was waiting for an answer. "Isn't that true, Val? Just like in *The Wizard of Oz*, huh?"

"I guess so," I said, then looked at my teacher. "So, what *do* you think of the cross-dresser in the story, Miss Faye?" She chose not to comment, because—all of a sudden—it was time for lunch, after which we were to be on our way.

TWENTY-FIVE

When Bo and I arrived at the lodge office around one o'clock that afternoon, we learned from Lacey that Alan had left without us. It wasn't that we were late; in fact, we were earlier than I had thought we would be. Lacey explained that she and Alan had spent the morning gathering and packing all of the gear we would need for the outing and had loaded everything into the Blazer before he took off. The supplies for Bo and me—our sleeping pads and bags, backpacks, flashlights, first-aid and emergency kits, water bottles, freeze-dried foods, a propane-fueled backpacker stove, cooking and eating utensils, toiletry items and a second two-person dome tent—had come from the stockpile of camping supplies Sonny either loaned or sold to his guests.

"Sonny said I gotta wait until he gets back here from the parade before we can go camping," Lacey continued, "so Alan went ahead and packed everything up and hauled it on down there to save us time. He said he'd pack our stuff up to the cliffs and hide it real good so nobody'd mess with it 'til we got there, and then he was gonna drive his truck on over toward Brown Mountain and go bike riding up in there until about dark. He said he wanted to check on a couple things he read about."

"You mean we can't set up camp until after dark?" I asked. "How are we going to find our stuff?"

"Alan said he'd leave us a note with directions," she replied. "There's this little pile of rocks in the apple orchard going up the mountain, and he said he'd hide the note or map or whatever there."

"Cool!" Bo exclaimed. "A treasure map! That'll be a blast!"

I wasn't as enthused as my friend about the prospect of searching in the dark for our equipment and provisions. "But what if we can't follow his directions?" I asked. "Isn't there some other way we can find out where he put the stuff?"

Lacey nodded. "Yeah, he's got his cell phone with him, but Sonny said we should take a couple radios with us, too, just to be on the safe side. Alan always carries one, and he has it with him now. We can take the two Sonny keeps here."

"CBs?" asked Bo, apparently thinking about the communications problems we had on our Brown Mountain Light stakeout the previous weekend.

"Well, yeah, he *does* still have my CB in his truck," Lacey replied, "and he said he'd hide the walkie-talkie CB with our stuff. The radios Sonny meant we should take are these little two-way radios he loans to folks who wanna go hiking." She pointed toward the counter across the office area, where the lodge's telecommunications equipment sat, including a telephone, fax and answering machine combo and a tabletop police scanner, as well as two black breadbox-sized radios—a Cobra base station for the forty citizen-band channels and a Motorola base that could scan the public two-way frequencies, Lacey said.

Also, a pair of small blue Motorola Talkabout walkie-talkies sat in their recharger, waiting to be carried afield. "Just remember channel eighteen," she added. "Alan said we'd use eighteen on both radios." She clipped one radio to her belt and handed the other one to Bo, who already was toting his own cell phone and MP3 player.

I learned to really like Lacey that afternoon, and I came to understand why Alan was so crazy about her. Yes, she was pretty in a dark-haired, girl-next-door sort of way. And, yes, she was a dependable, hard-working young lady striving to improve the bad hand she had been dealt in life. But those qualities really weren't what made her so attractive, either to Alan *or* to Bo and me. It was that there seemed to be absolutely nothing phony or pretentious about the girl. Even though her family background was as unfortunate as my own—though for quite different reasons—she was one of the most plain-spoken and down-to-earth girls I had ever met. Sure, she acted shy at first, as Alan had warned us she would. But once she warmed up to us, she didn't hesitate to talk about herself and her family.

Sitting together in the lodge office as we waited to go camping, we talked about all sorts of things—our favorite music, favorite movies, favorite foods. Lacey said she loved Willie Nelson and *The Wizard of Oz* and hot cornbread with sweet butter and ice-cold buttermilk. She even revealed that Buck's favorite singer was Willie Nelson, too; that Buck had never seen a movie in his life and rarely watched TV; and that his favorite food was anything his late wife had ever cooked for him, he claimed. Lacey's favorite books were Langston Hughes' *The Dream Keeper*, Robert Frost's *You Come, Too* and Carl Sandburg's *Wind Song*, all of which she had been studying in one of her summer-school courses at the technical college.

We also talked about what we wanted for ourselves in the future, and Lacey admitted that she and Alan had already been discussing marriage, though she said they weren't even ready to get engaged yet, not until they both finished school. "We ain't gonna make the same mistake my mama and daddy did," Lacey said. "They were high school sweethearts and couldn't wait to get married. So both of them quit school soon as they turned sixteen, and they run off and got married down in Gaffney—that's where everybody went to elope. Granddaddy got Daddy a job in Linville, and everything was OK for a while, but then my big brother Bubba come along right off the bat and then me the next year, and that's when all the problems really started for my folks."

"*You* weren't the problem," I stated. "Some people just don't belong together—like Aunt Elaine and my, uh, my—"

"Sonny?" Lacey offered, trying to finish my sentence.

I laughed. "No, I was going to say 'my Uncle Lance.' Why? Are Elaine and Sonny a real couple? Do you think they're really dating?"

"Yeah, I think they are," she replied. "Alan thinks so, too, and he's OK with it. He says he don't want Elaine to be all by herself after we get married and he moves out of the house. And, you know, Sonny's a really good guy. Some people thought he was a dirty old man for hiring me to work here by myself with him, but do you know he's never so much as *looked* funny at me all this time, not even back before he started spending so much time with Elaine? Granddaddy's been mad at Sonny lately—for a lot of reasons—but it don't have nothing to do with the way Sonny treats me. He's always treated me really good. He's been like family to me—more than my own family's been."

Listening quietly until then, Bo picked up on something I had missed. "Did your grandfather work at the resort in Linville?" he asked Lacey. "And your dad, too?"

"They worked all over the village and did a little bit of everything," she said. "Mostly they did yardwork, same as Granddaddy does now for Sonny. Ain't that what you're interested in doing, Val? Alan told me something about you being good at mowing grass. That right?"

I blushed. "Well, sort of," I said, not yet ready to outline my dream in detail, either for her or for Bo. "Lacey, what do *you* want to do for a living?"

"Teacher, like Sonny and Miss Faye," she said, "but not high school or college. I want to teach elementary school. That's when young'uns still *like* going to school and want to learn a thing or two, when school's still fun."

"What would you teach?" Bo asked her.

She smiled. "A little bit of everything, just like my granddaddy," she replied. "But I especially like stories and poems and things like that. Language arts. You know what? My granddaddy is good at that kinda stuff, too. You wouldn't think so, would you? I think he's probably why I like it so much, 'cause when I was a little girl and I'd be upset about something and crying and all, he'd sit me down and tell me some crazy story or sing me a funny song—anything to get me to laugh or even just smile a little.

"I know what people say about him," she continued, "and most of it ain't true. Back when Granny was still living, he was a good granddaddy. The past few years, things ain't been going too good for him, not since Granny died. He don't act the way he used to when I was little. Sometimes he even scares *me*, the way he gets sometimes."

"You know, I was asking if he worked at the resort," Bo noted, getting back to the topic that had piqued his interest. "The other day I was in the Appalachian Room at the library, and I found some books about the history of Linville and the old inn, and it had a bunch of pictures of people who worked there."

Then, turning to me, he added, "And, Val, here's something you'll be interested in. It said the Eseeola had one of the first golf courses in North Carolina, back in the 1890s, I think it was. I don't remember the exact year, but it was a year or two *before* that famous course in Pinehurst was built—you know, the one you talk about all the time."

He was right; I *was* interested in that bit of information, especially since I had been under the impression that the Linville course—my idea of heaven on earth, though I was still in golf purgatory—hadn't existed in any form until it was designed by Donald Ross and constructed by Julian Morton in the 1920s, a good twenty to thirty years after the oldest of the Pinehurst courses was built. "Why were you looking *that* up?" I asked.

"Well," Bo began, "I started out looking up stuff on local musicians, like on Doc and Scotty Wiseman and the Hartley man who started that singing we went to. By the way, he even wrote a little book himself. And everything kept pointing me to the Brown Mountain Lights, which was OK, since I was going to do some research on that, anyway. The other thing I was looking for was—you remember,

Val?—you wanted me to see if I could find out more about that Morton lady with the rock monument at the stadium there at MacRae Meadows—Agnes Morton, wasn't that her?"

Lacey brightened at Bo's mention of the woman's name. "Agnes Morton?" Lacey said. "I think I've heard Granddaddy talk about her before. I think he called her 'Aggie,' though. Yeah, Aggie Morton. I'll have to ask him about her. I wish we had a phone down home, and I'd call him. I just can't remember the story."

"Well, anyway," Bo continued, "things I was reading about music kept pointing me at the Brown Mountain Lights, and they kept pointing me back to Linville and the Eseeola Lodge—like, where the best places were to see the Lights from Linville and what they looked like and stuff. One little book I found said Beacon Heights was the best place to see the Brown Mountain Lights. That's a place on the Parkway between Grandfather and Grandmother Mountain. And I'll tell you what. I found some *strange* stories about the Lights, especially one by the guy who said—"

Just then, an elderly couple entered the store to shop for supplies, and Bo cut short his recitation of what he had learned about the Lights. "I'll tell you later," he said. "Tonight, after we get camp set up. Maybe we'll see them." I was wondering if he had become a true believer, until he added, "—or not."

We finally got the green light to leave around five o'clock, not long after Sonny, Elaine and Miss Faye arrived at the lodge in *Herbie the Love Bug*. Miss Faye was there to man the office that evening while Sonny and Elaine were "out gallivanting around" on the Blue Ridge Parkway, the elderly lady said. Without even setting foot inside the lodge, the couple pulled the VW into an empty bay in the museum, then left in the black-painted former *General Lee*, not bothering to change clothes or pick up any food or other supplies for themselves.

"I don't know why they're in such a big hurry," Miss Faye said, as she walked through the lodge's back door into the store. "You'd think they were a couple teen-agers, the way they're acting."

Just then, the CB base station crackled to life. "Breaker, breaker one-eight," said a metallic voice on the speaker. "Breaker one-eight. Do you read me, Barkhouse? Barkhouse, do you read me? This is, uh, this is, uh.... Oh, you know who it is. Over."

Lacey took the handset microphone and depressed its key. "Go on, Sonny. We read you loud and clear."

"OK," Sonny said. "Just making sure this thing's wor—" Static interrupted the transmission momentarily, but then he continued, "—ave your phone numbers. We'll give you a call at n—" There was more static.

"Come back?" Lacey said. "Sonny, come back with that?"

"—ive you a call at nine o'clock," he finished. "Ya'll be careful. Have fun. Over and out."

"Ten-four, Sonny," Lacey replied. "Talk to you at nine o'clock. Over and out." Before she could return the mic to its hanger, the office telephone rang. "Barkhouse Lodge," she answered, then listened for several seconds. "OK, thanks, Sonny.... Well, I sure didn't think of that.... Yeah.... I sure am glad you and Elaine thought of us. Thanks.... OK, bye-bye." After hanging up, she explained that Sonny had said we should take his white Bronco into Lost Cove, instead of squeezing the three of us into the cab of her LUV truck.

"That's my Sonny," Miss Faye beamed. "He's always thinking of others. He's such as good boy. And he and Elaine make *such* a sweet couple." Whether to one or all the statements about her son, the three of us nodded in agreement.

TWENTY-SIX

By the time Lacey, Bo and I arrived at the Little Lost Cove Cliffs trailhead on Mortimer Road, we three had become fast friends. Though I was still apprehensive about camping that night in the wilderness, I felt better about it, because I now trusted all three of my companions and I knew they would help me any way they could if I ran into trouble. I just wished Alan hadn't decided to go mountain biking all afternoon and evening. He probably knew Lost Cove better than Lacey did, as he had spent much of his free time riding and hiking the trails crisscrossing the area. Lacey was more familiar with the adjoining Harper Creek basin, since she had been raised there.

Before we left the Bronco to look for the equipment and supplies Alan had hidden for us, Lacey pointed out the North Harper

Creek Falls Trail, which shared the same pulloff as the Little Lost Cove Cliffs Trail. "Down that path there is one way you can get to my house from here," she said, unfolding on the steering wheel a trail map of the entire Wilson Creek section of the national forest. "Let me show you exactly where we are—just to be on the safe side."

Bo leaned forward again to look over Lacey's shoulder. "Did Alan take the SporTrak with him?" Bo asked, referring to the GPS unit we had used in the car at the Brown Mountain Overlook the previous weekend.

"Yeah," Lacey replied. "That's the main reason he wanted to go riding up there at Brown Mountain before dark. He said he wanted to get a fix on a place he read about at the library—a place called Wildcat Holler. He said he couldn't find that name on any of his maps."

"Wildcat Hollow—I read that, too!" Bo exclaimed. "That's what I was gonna tell you guys before. One book I found was by a man who said the Lights are space aliens from Venus and that the best place to see them up close is from where Wildcat Branch starts as a spring in Wildcat Hollow. I remember reading all that and thinking we'd need to check it out, but I didn't have any idea Alan was gonna go looking for it. There's supposed to be a cavern there where the aliens keep their spaceship and everything."

"I don't believe that," I scoffed. "Space aliens?"

"Well, what about *The X-Files* theory?" Bo said. "That's pretty wild, too—a huge fungus or lichen or whatever growing right under the surface of the ground and covering the whole mountain and sucking people into it. There's a cavern in that story, too."

I just shook my head. "A big mushroom that eats people? Oh, come on."

"I like the old stories better—you know, the ones in the song," Lacey noted. "I think it makes more sense that the Lights are ghosts, if they're anything."

"You believe in ghosts?" I asked.

"Sure," she replied. "Don't you?"

I looked back at Bo. "*You* don't believe the Lights are ghosts, do you?"

"*I* don't believe in the Lights *at all*," he laughed, then added, "but, yeah, I kinda *do* believe in ghosts—or *spirits*, anyway. If there isn't such a thing as spirits, then there isn't such a thing as heaven—or hell either, as far as that goes. The Bible talks about spirits and angels and witches and *all* that stuff, so if you believe the Bible, you gotta believe in the supernatural—well, not believe *in* it, but believe it exists."

Lacey nodded. "Yeah, what about the Holy Ghost? That's in the Bible. Maybe the Brown Mountain Lights are the Holy Ghost. Or is it the Holy *Spirit*?"

"Same thing," Bo said. "The Holy Ghost is one part of the Trinity—God the Father, Jesus Christ the Son, and the Holy Ghost, the spirit that ties everything together—kinda like a computer network. Oooh, I've never thought of it that way before. I guess that'd make God the server and Jesus the work station. Hmmm, I wonder if He'd be Macintosh or PC." With a look of mock seriousness, Bo thought for a second, then added, "Nah, definitely a Mac—you know, fully integrated, more intuitive, user friendly, doesn't crash nearly as often." He chuckled at himself, as he was just getting started. "Or maybe *we're* the work stations—some of us are Macs and some of us are PC's, and some of us are just Palm Pilots and Playstations. Yeah, that's it. And the different operating systems are all the different religions of the world. So, let's see, that'd make the Holy Spirit the Internet, and Jesus your connection to it—the hardware, like your modem or router or whatever."

"So then what would God be in this little metaphor of yours?" I asked.

Bo smiled again. "Why, Microsoft, of course—creator of the source code."

I didn't ask, what if a person doesn't believe in all that technology crap? Instead, I gave Bo a gentle shove back into his seat and turned to Lacey so she could finish showing us the map. She pointed out the old forest roads and trails that Alan probably was biking around the foot of Brown Mountain as we spoke, and she outlined the circuitous route he undoubtedly would drive back to Mortimer and then through Edgemont to reach where we were parked on Mortimer Road near the lower trailhead to the Little Lost Cove Cliffs. We had passed the upper trailhead about a mile or so back up the road. The tip of her index finger tapped a light spot on the map to show us Kawana's location as an island within the national forest and another point where her grandfather's cabin sat. Finally, she traced the dotted lines representing the tangled web of trails connecting her home with Lost Cove.

"If you need water or if you want to see the two big waterfalls down there, you go down this way," Lacey said, pointing to the North Harper Creek Falls Trail on the map, then to the actual trailhead out the window. "That's it right there. It's one-point-three miles to the T-intersection at North Harper Creek Trail. You take a right, and that takes you to North Harper Creek Falls and then on to Harper Creek Road. You take a left, and you're at Chestnut Cove Falls, and that leads to Harper Creek Trail, then to Kawana, then to our place. There are some springs off both those trails. That's where you can get water, not from the creek."

"Why not?" Bo asked. "Giardia?"

"You mean, bad water?" Lacey said. "Yeah, you don't drink creek water unless you want to spend the next couple weeks in the bathroom. But it's OK if you get water from a spring—you know, right where it comes out of the ground. That's what Granddaddy says he always used—good clean spring water. Either way, though, I know Alan has a filter and some tablets to treat it, or we could just boil it good. That kills the bad stuff in it."

Still holding open the map, she pointed out another trail, a short spur off Mortimer Road. "Over here is the Darkside Cliffs Trail—remember where we stopped and hiked a couple weeks ago, coming back from the airport? And this trail on the other side of the road is called the Shortcut Trail, 'cause it's a shortcut from the Harper Creek Trail up to the road right there near the Darkside trail. Granddaddy takes that trail sometimes when he's on Niblick. It's the quickest way up to the road from our house."

Bo nodded. "Darkside? Wasn't that where you had trouble getting a call out on Alan's phone? That reminds me—I wonder if *my* phone can get out of here." He leaned to one side to unclip his cell phone, then checked to see if it registered service. "Nope, not a single bar," he said, referring to the signal-strength meter on the phone's LCD screen.

"That's OK," Lacey said. "Up where we're gonna be tonight—up at the cliffs—you oughta be able to make a call. Alan did say, though, we should set up camp near the lower cliffs, 'cause we don't wanna be at the highest point if a thunderstorm comes up in the middle of the night. But at those other cliffs—the high ones—you can see the whole area in a complete circle, it's so much higher than everywhere else. You can even see Brown Mountain real good from there and Morganton and Lenoir off in the distance. Alan said that's where we'll go to look for the Lights and watch all the fireworks—from up there at the highest point. He just doesn't want to take a chance and *camp* there."

In the two weeks I had lived in the mountains, thundershowers had been an almost daily occurrence, whether brief enough to be just a nuisance or long enough to completely alter the day, as had been the case a couple of days before, when I had come so close to my dream of playing that old Linville course. Locals were constantly complaining about how wet the previous spring had been and how wet the summer was shaping up to be; however, they invariably added that being wet was preferable to being as dry as the drought-stricken region had been in recent years. But on that particular day—on the Fourth of July—we were hoping the brief shower that had passed through the area while we were still at the lodge was the only shower we would see.

As the trail to the Little Lost Cove Cliffs was muddy from all the rain of late and from being shaded by a canopy of hardwoods, Bo and I tried to keep the moist red clay from caking the bottoms of our running shoes by walking in the grassy, less-worn strips on the edges of the path (Lacey was the only one wearing actual hiking boots). Eventually, the steep trail—which had begun as more of a rocky jeep road than a hiking path—began to level out, widen and become almost overgrown with course grass that also was wet from the recent rains. As we walked single-file up the mountain—Lacey leading, me next, Bo bringing up the rear—Lacey warned us to watch where we stepped. "You don't want to step on a snake hiding in the grass," she said, "and don't drag your feet in the weeds, either. That's how you pick up ticks, if you ain't careful."

"Tics?" Bo said, with a sly smile. "You mean, like twitching and stuff?"

Lacey laughed. "No, ticks—like ticks on a dog. Ain't you ever seen a tick where you're from?"

"I was just teasing you," he replied. "How much farther do we have to go?" I had noticed that Bo and I both were breathing fairly hard and had been from the time we ascended the first particularly steep section of the trail.

Lacey, on the other hand, seemed fit and as fresh as one of the wild daisies springing up in the path before us. "Not far. We're almost to the orchard. See, right here are some old apple trees. I guess they came up on their own. Granddaddy calls them *volunteers*." She pointed to two gnarled trees to the left just off the trail, then nodded ahead. "The big orchard is around the next bend up there. That's where the rock marker is, where Alan said he'd leave us a note."

The marker turned out to be a stack of brown stones sitting near a lone apple tree on the side of the orchard that opened to a view of the eastern mountains and foothills. The rockpile was not quite three feet tall and maybe about eighteen inches in diameter. It apparently was meant to mark the trail and not a property line, because it stood in the old orchard at the approximate midpoint between where we had emerged from the forest on the lower side and where we would reenter the dense foliage on the upper side. Without the cairn to point the way, our route through the orchard's tall grass back into the trees would not have been immediately evident, as the trailhead to the final upper leg of our hike was hidden by laurel branches and spruce boughs.

Lacey lifted one side of the marker's capstone and extracted what had to be Alan's note—a single sheet of college-ruled notebook paper that had been folded to a quarter its original size, then rolled up so it could be inserted down between the rocks supporting the larger flatter top one. After unfurling and unfolding the paper, Lacey carefully smoothed the wrinkles against her denim-clad thigh, then looked over the note before filling us in on Alan's directions.

"I'm gonna skin him alive," she said presently, still studying the paper. "This sounds more like one of Granddaddy's riddles than directions how to find our stuff. Listen to this—'One step at a time... climb the stairway to heaven that lies past the gate...bear to the right, then you can keep going straight...pass between two angels guarding your path...(watch out for them, though, because they're full of wrath)...turn right when you see their dark horns on the ground...keep going straight and don't you dare turn around...walk to the deer park on this side of the knoll...bear to the left where he sleeps in his hole.'

"That's what it says—I swear," she added. "Do you guys understand what he's saying? I sure don't, and we only got a couple hours to find our stuff and get camp set up before dark. You know, I wish he'd wrote it in plain English. I guess he didn't want somebody else to find our things right off if they found this note before we did."

"Yeah," I agreed. "It's like all the stuff Miss Faye's been making me read to get my English credit. It's in couplets, except for the first line. What was it—'Walk up the stairs one step at a time'?" I leaned toward Lacey to look at Alan's riddle.

"No," Bo interjected. "He means we should *take* 'one step at a time' following his directions. So...," he continued, taking the paper from Lacey, "we *should* find a 'stairway to heaven' on the other side of some kind of gate nearby." All three of us looked around. "There!" Bo almost shouted. "There's the gate." He already was heading toward the partially obscured trailhead on the upper side of the orchard.

The "gate" was a natural archway of fallen limbs about ten feet up the trail. Just beyond the arch, the path rose steeply in rocky rutted steps all the way to the top of the hill, where Bo, paper still in hand, waited for us to catch up. "Here's where the trail turns right and runs straight along the ridge, it looks like," he noted. "Are we headed toward the cliffs, Lacey?"

"Yeah," she replied. "There are two—no, three—side trails going up to the cliffs. The first two go to the lower cliffs, where we're gonna camp, and the third trail goes to that high place I was telling you about."

Bo snapped his fingers. "Two trails to where we're camping?" he said. "I bet the lines about the 'two angels' and turning right at the 'dark horns' have to do with which trail we're supposed to take."

"Duh, ya think?" I said. "Gee, I wonder how long it took Alan to come up with all that crazy stuff. It would've taken me all summer to write that."

Lacey took the lead as we followed the path toward the spur trails to the cliffs. "He's good at writing," she said, "just like his mama,

I guess. And he's *always* reading some book when he's waiting on me to get off work. The other day he was reading something about the Garden of Eden—*Dragons of Eden* was the name of it, I think."

"Yeah, that's Alan's hero, isn't it? Carl Sagan?" Bo asked. "I read that book at school last year for extra credit. It's a pretty good book, but I like *The Power of Myth* better. That's Joseph Campbell, Val. Ever heard of him? It was a TV series, too—on PBS, if you ever watch that channel." He laughed.

As we walked along, Lacey paused to indicate the first side trail on our right. "I ain't seen any angels yet or anything even close," she said. "Have you?" She moved on, with us still following closely behind.

"And then there's this book called *She*," Bo continued, ignoring Lacey's question about angels. "The author's Robert Johnson—no, not the blues singer. I checked that book out because I thought it'd help me understand women better. He wrote another book called *He*, too—about guys. You ever read it, Val? Might help you get yourself a man." He snickered again.

"Dad-gummit, Bo," I fussed. "Have you read *every* book in the darn library?" I was becoming a bit annoyed at my best friend, for whom learning seemed to come so easily. Sometimes I wondered if he knew too much for his own good—or for *my* good, anyway.

Bo just laughed at me as we continued along the path, with Lacey again out front, then Bo, then me. "Oh, Val, you just got out of the habit of reading books," he said. "Back when we first got to be good friends, *you* were the one always checking out library books. Remember? You were reading a book about King Arthur and the Knights of the Round Table when we met. Why'd you quit liking to read?"

"I don't know," I said, studying the ground as I followed him. Bo was right; I *did* read books for pleasure back before my experiences in high school turned me against reading. I could blame my English teachers; however, they were only assigning what they had to, what those people in Raleigh who came up with the rules for teachers to follow made them make us read. "Nothing was making any sense," I added presently, "especially after Grandpa died. Everybody kept telling me to read *this* and read *that*, but none of it made any sense. None of it. And I wanted something that—" I stopped dead in my tracks.

"What?" Bo asked, turning to see what was wrong. "Wait up, Lacey."

"There," I said, pointing to a patch of ground under an oak about ten feet to the left of the trail. "See it?"

"See what?" Bo replied.

"The angel—a destroying angel. Lacey, you see it?"

Lacey stepped off the path and knelt beside a relatively large white mushroom that was as beautiful as any fungi I had ever seen in the wild. It had an almost flat three-inch-wide top on a slender six-inch-tall stalk, with a pure white veil just under the cap. She brushed away the loose organic material around the mushroom's base. "Yep," she said. "You're good, Val. This sure *is* a destroyin' angel. How'd you know?"

I shrugged. "I saw it in a book at the library the other day. Somebody marked the page it was on, and I remember how pretty it looked."

"It *is* pretty," Lacey agreed, "but it's deadly. And what's so bad is, before it opens up all the way, it looks like one of the mushrooms you can eat. Granddaddy taught me that about them, 'cause he loves to pick mushrooms to eat."

"I know," I said, recalling the mushrooms Buck had picked for our Sunday dinner at Miss Faye's house.

Bo, who had wandered on down the path, yelped, "Here's another one! I don't see any more of them, and this one's on the other side of the trail from the one you guys are looking at."

"So?" I asked. "What difference does *that* make, one on each side?"

"Think a second, Val—Alan's riddle," he said, holding up the paper again. "It says we're supposed to 'pass between two angels guarding your path,' and then it says 'watch out for them, though, because they're full of wrath.' See, he's talking about these poison mushrooms, one standing on each side of the trail like they're guarding it."

"So where are their dark horns?" Lacey said, scanning the ground around us. "When we see their 'horns,' that's when we're supposed to leave the trail."

"You think he's talking about deer antlers, maybe?" Bo offered. "Or maybe a bull's horns?"

I shook my head. "No, he's still talking about mushrooms. That's why he said *their* horns—to connect them with these destroying angels. There must be some horn-shaped mushrooms where we're supposed to turn."

"Chanterelles!" Lacey announced. "That's what he means, 'cause they're shaped like horns. They're Granddaddy's *favorite* mushroom."

"Yeah," I added. "Miss Faye fixed some horn-shaped mushrooms for us last Sunday. She said *she* picked them, but everybody knew she was fibbing and that Buck—I mean, your granddaddy—had picked them for her. But she called them something else, not just chanterelles. I can't remember what—"

"Black trumpets!" Lacey said. "Look for little dark horn-shaped mushrooms. That's it—*dark horns*. They grow in patches under beech trees and oaks." She looked ahead on the ridge. "And there's a great big beech tree right up there—up there at the second trail to the cliffs! That's it!"

She took off and within seconds located a patch of the tiny dark-brown horn-shaped fungi growing right beside the trail at the second side path. From there, we had no trouble finding the four backpacks full of equipment and supplies that Alan had stashed in a cave-like hollow (the "bear's hole") under a Volkswagen-sized granite boulder about ten feet off the spur trail. Alan had marked the spot to enter the underbrush with an empty Deer Park water bottle stuck upside-down on a stick in the ground. He had indicated the right boulder—which may or may not have ever sheltered a real bear—by placing within easy sight an empty cellophane Harmony Gummy Bear wrapper under a fist-sized piece of white flint. Lacey identified the candy as the organically-sweetened brand Sonny now sold at the lodge and that Alan had bought with the bottle of Deer Park water before leaving that afternoon.

It was close to dark when we had finished setting up both tents—one near the cliffs, the other one about twenty yards away, off in the trees for privacy—and had gathered a pile of downed branches and limbs of all sizes to use in the existing rock-lined fire ring at our campsite, located in a thin grove of pines about twenty yards from the craggy granite cliffs. It was the most beautiful and awe-inspiring place I had ever camped, not counting overnight fishing trips on *The Lady of Shallotte* with Grandpa and those unbelievable sunrises over the ocean.

Our camp had everything—solitude within easy walking distance of our vehicle, shelter in the trees, and a great view of Lost Cove and the highest mountains rimming it (Blowing Rock, Grandfather, Grandmother and Jonas Ridge, from right to left). Lacey even dug a trench in an out-of-the-way spot and rigged up a couple of long sturdy pole-like limbs between two trees so we could use the restroom in the night without worrying about where we went or what we stepped in. Neither Bo nor I would have thought to dig a latrine, not until we needed to use it. Lacey, though, even thought to break off two branches on the two trees and leave nubs on which to hang our flashlights and biodegradable toilet paper. She obviously had camped in the wilderness before.

"Can we go ahead and start a fire before Alan gets here?" I asked, as we sat on the boulders near the cliffs in the gathering dusk.

To be honest, I didn't want to turn on my flashlight (one of those little black Mini-Maglites with two AA cells) so soon and risk running down my batteries. I was sure Alan had packed everything we needed for the outing; however, I hadn't been able to find extra batteries in my own backpack. He must have kept the extra batteries with him, just in case he needed them on the trail. Besides, we had already pulled all four backpacks up into a tree for safekeeping until Alan arrived and we could fix dinner, because we didn't want our packed food to attract any wild animals while we were on the cliffs.

"No fire," Lacey replied. "It wouldn't be safe to start one just yet, honey. Alan, when he gets here, might want to go up to the high cliffs to watch the fireworks. We couldn't leave it going, 'cause if the wind came up it might get out, and that'd be terrible."

"Well, we could put it out before we left," I offered weakly.

She shook her head. "No. That'd just be wasting our water. And you don't want to have to hike all the way down to the creek for more, do you? That's a long haul." Like I said, Lacey thought of everything, as she had done this before.

My friend Bo laughed. "We aren't gonna get Val to hike *nowhere* in the dark," he said. "She's afraid of the dark. Isn't that right, Val?"

Lacey answered for me. "I remember her saying that," Lacey said, referring to our ride together from the Hickory airport. "There ain't nothing wrong with being afraid of the dark. A lot of people are afraid of the dark. I use to be."

"Really?" I said.

She nodded. "Yeah, back when my folks was first gone. It didn't bother my big brother any. But I couldn't stay by myself with the light off at night."

"Why not?" Bo asked.

Lacey shrugged. "I don't know. I guess I thought some old boogerman was gonna get me or something." Nodding toward me, she added, "It was like Val here told you and Alan in the truck. Stuff like that don't make sense, but it's as real as can be to the person feeling it. Ain't that right, Val?"

"Yeah," I said.

Bo reached out and gave my arm a gentle squeeze. "I'm just teasing you, girl," he assured me. "Matter of fact, I got some tunes here to help you out tonight, just like on the flight from Wilmington." He patted a front pocket of his cargo shorts. "I been getting into Coltrane—John Coltrane. He's from Hamlet—you know, that little town on the other side of Charlotte. He's unbelievable. He played with Miles on *Kind of Blue* and on *Round About Midnight*. I'll let you hear him later, if you want to. The album's called *A Love Supreme*, and he even wrote a poem for it—not song lyrics, a real poem."

"How'd you find out about him?" I asked. "Miles?"

"Well, yeah," he replied, "but he's connected with Mingus, too—you know, the composer on *Weary Blues*?"

"Langston Hughes' 'Weary Blues'?" Lacey asked. "That's one of my very favorite poems in *The Dream Keeper*. He has a whole big section about the blues in that book."

At her mention of Langston Hughes, I remembered the poetry anthology Sonny had made me study the week before. "Yeah, I really like 'Weary Blues,' too," I said. "Lacey, you mentioned Robert Frost back at the lodge. Which poem of *his* do you like best?" I wondered if, by any chance at all, she might agree with me and name "The Bearer of Evil Tidings" instead of "The Road Not Taken."

She smiled as if she could read my mind. "My granddaddy's favorite poem is 'The Road Not Taken,' because it was in a book they give him in the service—back during World War II—and he used to always recite it to me, 'specially after Mama and Daddy went away. But *my* favorite poem by Robert Frost is one called 'The Night Light,' about a lady who couldn't sleep unless she had a night light burning beside her bed. I found it in an old book Miss Faye left at the lodge once."

"What?" I asked pointedly, wondering if Alan had told her about the night light by *my* bed and if she was simply teasing me about my fear of the dark, as Bo had earlier. "Are you kidding? That's *really* your favorite Robert Frost poem?"

She seemed surprised. "Kidding? You asked me my favorite poem of his. That's it, 'The Night Light.' Why would I kid you about that? It ain't one of his *big* poems, but I like it, anyway. It's about his wife dying, I think, and it's kinda like that little prayer young'uns say—you know, 'Now I lay me down to sleep, I pray the Lord my soul to keep.' My mama taught me and Bubba to say that not long before Mama and Daddy, uh, before they went away. And then afterwards, we'd say it every night after we got in bed, and it'd make me feel better 'til I could get to sleep." She paused to study my face in the growing darkness. "That's why I like that poem, 'cause it reminds me of back when I was still hoping Mama and Daddy would come back, instead of us having to go stay with Granddaddy and Granny. But they didn't come back." She smiled sadly.

"Where are they?" I asked. "I mean, are they still in prison? Do you ever go visit them?"

"Prison?" she said, surprised again. "Who told you they was in prison?"

I didn't want to say, *Your boyfriend, that's who*, because I didn't want to cause any trouble between Lacey and Alan, but Bo beat me to it. "That's what Alan said," Bo blurted. "He said your folks were sent off because of drugs. Your brother, too."

"He did?" Lacey asked. At first she looked confused, but a moment later she nodded her understanding. "No, they aren't in prison. They *were* in trouble a lot, like Alan said, and they *did* serve some jail time—both of them. Well, all three of them did, counting Bubba." She hesitated, as if she wasn't sure she should finish correcting Alan's version of her life story.

"And all three of them *are* gone now, Val, for good. They're all three dead. Bubba *was* in prison, and he got stabbed in a fight a year or so ago. Mama and Daddy—they was always fighting with each other, like I told you before, and Daddy got the idea one Wednesday night that Mama had been fooling around on him with somebody from up on the mountain—from Jonas Ridge. He thought it was somebody she'd met at church. She'd started going, to try to turn things around for her, but she never could get Daddy to go, too, 'cause he was just too stubborn—like Granddaddy. But Mama, she was in the church choir and everything. And so was the man Daddy thought she'd been messing around with—in the choir, I mean. She was late getting home from choir practice that night, and Daddy'd been drinking ever since he got home from work. Bubba and me was already in bed, but we heard the whole thing."

I wasn't sure I wanted to hear the rest of her story, as I could guess how it would end. Darkness was falling quickly, and I wanted Alan to get to camp so we could go watch the fireworks or start a campfire or just go to bed—whatever we were going to end up doing. Without mentioning it, I had been worried all afternoon and evening about the sleeping arrangements that night—whether Alan and Lacey would want to sleep together, leaving me and Bo to share the other tent. But right then I didn't care who I slept with, as long as they promised to hold me close and protect me—Bo, Lacey or even Alan, it didn't matter. And it wasn't my fear of the dark that was foremost in my mind right then.

"Do you know who the guy was?" Bo asked.

"It wasn't nobody," Lacey replied. "Mama kept saying over and over she wasn't doing nothing, and she never lied, but

Daddy wouldn't believe her. He thought she was doing something, 'cause some man had told Daddy he saw Mama talking to somebody outside the church building after prayer meeting the Wednesday night before—that's when they had choir practice, right after prayer meeting on Wednesday nights.

"He was all bent out of shape, too, 'cause she'd got some coins out of his bureau drawer to put in the offering plate at church, and one was this old coin Grandaddy'd found over on the Winding Stairs and give to Daddy when he was little—you know, where that Civil War battle was fought. She just thought it was a regular dime, and she said she was sorry and would try to get it back, but he didn't care.

"Well, before me and Bubba really knew what was happening, Daddy was yelling he was gonna kill that other man and that he was gonna make Mama pay for cheating on him, and Mama was screaming for him to stop hitting her or she'd leave and never come back, and then everything got real quiet." Lacey looked directly at me, as if she wouldn't end her story without my permission.

I closed my eyes and nodded for her to go on. "We couldn't hear Mama anymore, but Daddy was kinda crying to himself, saying he was sorry, he was sorry. He did that for a minute or two—or maybe longer, I don't know. I was so little, it's hard to know exactly how long it was, but it seemed like forever. Anyway, when we heard the gun go off, we thought Daddy had shot Mama, or maybe the other way around. But it was Daddy. He shot hisself. They was both dead."

No one said anything for several seconds. I was too mortified to utter even the simplest sound. Finally, Bo asked, "Was it you or your brother who found them?"

"No, Granddaddy did," she replied. "He and Granny lived right next door in their old shack—that was back before it burned down—and they heard the gunshot. Me and Bubba was too scared to come out of our room. Well, I was, anyway. Bubba went out to the living room and saw Mama and Daddy both, after Granddaddy'd went for help. There wasn't any helping either one of them, though. They was both dead. And that pretty much took care of Bubba, too. From then on, he hated everybody and everything. If he hadn't got killed in prison, he'd have eventually killed hisself somehow. He was looking for a way out, and he finally found it."

She was quiet for a second, then added, "I wish Alan would get here. I'm getting worried."

Bo squeezed my arm again, to see if I was OK. But I couldn't look at him—or at Lacey. I couldn't even open my eyes.

TWENTY-SEVEN

As I hid in the tent, curled up in back (not in a corner because there wasn't one in the dome tent), I heard Bo explain my reaction to Lacey, despite their hushed tones. I caught every word, though they weren't aware I was listening. He told her I had not only heard a person I loved die, as she had her parents; I had been so close at the last that I had heard that unmistakable death rattle in the man's throat and had seen him draw his last breath. Afraid to move, I had stayed there on the floor next to the dead man all night long, waiting for someone to find us, to tell me I was safe, that the killer really wasn't coming back as he'd said he would.

"He's still loose?" she whispered.

"Well, they caught the guy the next morning—they caught *three* guys—but they haven't been charged with the murder yet. They're still in jail on other charges—break-ins, mainly. They didn't have enough evidence to charge them with the old man's murder, 'cause they had a good alibi—they were breaking into another house that night about the time the man died.

"Besides," Bo continued, "the autopsy said the old man killed himself, like you said your dad did. It was his own gun, the one he kept in the cash box, and *his* fingerprints were the only ones on it, and he had powder burns on his right hand and all. Val couldn't get anybody to believe that wasn't the way it happened, that he didn't shoot himself. They all thought she was crazy, 'cause of the shape she was in when they found her. Hasn't Alan told you all this?"

"No. Well, he *did* tell me Val was all upset 'cause her old boss man died the week before she moved here from the beach, but he didn't tell me all *that*. Good Lord. You mean, he got shot right in front of her?"

"Well, no, she didn't *see* it. It was a robbery before she got there—or maybe even when she was there earlier in the day. Or at least that's what Val thinks happened. She saw a strange vehicle parked there that morning, but she didn't go in the building. It was probably happening right then or had just happened, and the robbers were still inside. If she'd gone in, they probably would've killed her, too—if it really was a robbery."

"But she found her boss later?"

"Yeah. She went back that evening to thank him for a going-away present he gave her and to tell him goodbye, and the door was open a little, like somebody left in a hurry and forgot to shut it all the way, and she found him on the floor in front of the counter. She tried to call for help, but the phone wouldn't work; the battery was dead from being off the hook all day. She was getting ready to go for help when she looked outside and saw the same vehicle turning off the road, coming back, so she hid on the floor *behind* the counter."

"Was it the three guys? The robbers?"

"I don't know if it was all three or just the one guy. Only one came in the building. He must've gone back to make sure the old guy was dead."

"He wasn't dead?"

"No, not when she first got there. He was just barely hanging on. She could see his face on the floor through this little open space under the counter, and he even opened his eyes and looked at her once—whether he could really see her or not, they don't know."

"Did he say anything?"

"Yeah, he said something—not much, though. Mom told me after Elaine told her. Elaine even got it second-hand, from her preacher—well, not *her* preacher, it was the old preacher at the little church where Mr. and Mrs. Galloway used to go. He's the only person Val's talked to about it. Far as I know, she still won't talk to anybody else, not even the cops. Or to me. It's really messing her up bad."

"You mean, that's what made her so afraid of the dark?"

"Well, that would do it, don't you think? But there's more to it than that."

"What else?"

"Well…I don't know if I should."

"What is it?"

"Well, right before the man died, he looked at her under the counter and told her to 'keep smiling.'"

"Keep smiling? She was smiling?"

"No, not according to what the preacher told Elaine. Val told him—the preacher—she told him she was *crying* the whole time and trying not to make any noise so the robber wouldn't find her—she had her fist stuck in her mouth to keep quiet—but the last thing the old man said was for her to 'keep smiling.' It didn't make any sense. The robber thought he was talking to him, and he said something back, but he just pulled up a chair and waited for the man to die, and then he cleaned up the gun and fixed it and put it in the guy's hand and shot it again, to make it look like a suicide."

"Keep smiling?"

"Yeah, they figured he could've been seeing things, if he was really seeing anything at all, maybe even the face of the guy who shot him, you know, smiling at him while they robbed him. It's weird."

"What did the robber say?"

"Well, when he heard the old man say, 'Keep smiling,' he cussed him—you know, the *big* one—and said something like, 'GD you, I ain't gonna leave 'til you die, so die, GD-it.' And he sat there for another hour or so and didn't leave until the man died. He even turned on the TV, and watched a couple shows. And then when he was finally leaving, he laughed and said, 'Don't go nowhere, 'cause I'll be back,' like he was the Terminator or somebody. She figured he meant he was coming back to carry some of the stuff off, like golf clubs and things. That's why she was scared to leave. But the thing that messed her up so bad was the 'GD' part."

"He said 'GD'?"

"Well, no, he said the real thing—or that's what Mom told me. I just don't like saying that word. It's about the worst thing you can say, whether you mean it or not—worse than the N-word. You know?"

"Yeah," Lacey agreed. "That was one thing my daddy kept saying over and over to my mama before he—before she died. Granddaddy used to say it all the time, too, but when me and Bubba went to live with him and Granny, he stopped talking like that so much—except when he got *really* mad. He went back to it for a while after Granny died, but he stopped again when he started working for Sonny—and for Miss Faye. Now when he's really mad, he says 'gall-durn,' like that old man on TV, that old McCoy man. But Granddaddy's still a pretty r—"

"Come in, Yogi the Bear. Come in, Yogi the Bear. This is the, uh, the Ranger Station at the Barkhouse Lodge. Do you hear me, Mr. Bear? Is your little blue radio on?... Come in, Mr. Bear. Are you listening to me?... Please, come in."

"Mrs. Rose?"

"Yes, I'm listening."

"Mrs. Rose, this is Lionel—Boo-Boo."

"Yes, Boo-Boo. May I please speak to Yogi the Bear?"

"He isn't here yet. We're still waiting on him. Have you talked to him?"

"Well, no, I have not. He called his mother on the telephone about an hour or so ago. Yes, it was about an hour ago; I think she

said it was about 7:30. Or maybe it was 7:45. Anyway, he said he was having difficulty contacting you on the telephone, and he wanted her to try to reach you. Did she call you?"

"No, ma'am. She did not—did *not*—call us. Let me check my phone...No, we do *not* have cell phone service at our present location. Do you read me? We do *not* have cell phone service where we are right now."

"Yes, Boo-Boo. I read you."

"Is there a message—from Alan, I mean, from Yogi? Or from, uh, Yogi's mom?"

"Yes, Boo-Boo. She told me to call you now—at 8:45—if I did not hear back from her by now."

"Uh, OK, what's the message, ma'am?"

"Well, Yogi the Bear said to tell you that he was leaving right then to meet you. He also said to tell you that he might not be able to get there where you are until after the agreed-upon time to talk to his mother and my son on the citizen-band radios. Nine o'clock? Wasn't that the agreed-upon time?"

"Yes, ma'am, it was. It's almost nine o'clock now. What time did Alan think he'd get here? Did he say?"

"No, he did not. No, he did not."

"Ma'am, where's Alan's mom right now? Where's Elaine—and your son? Where's Sonny?"

"Well, they were on their way to Grandfather Mountain—the Wilson Creek Valley Overlook, they said. They made me write that down. They're going to watch all the fireworks from up there and talk to you children on the citizens-band radio."

Lacey took the radio from Bo. "Miss Faye? Miss Faye? This is Lacey. Do you read me?"

"Yes, sweetie, I do."

"Alan should be here by now. I think I need to go and look for him."

"Yes, honey, that is probably a good idea, just to be on the safe side."

"Miss Faye, please write this down. OK? Can you do that for me?"

"I certainly can. What shall I write down? I have my pencil and paper ready."

"The three of us is gonna split up while I go and look for Alan. We're at the lower Little Lost Cove Cliffs right now. Write that down—Little...Lost...Cove...Cliffs. But one of us'll go up to the high cliffs so we can maybe call out on the telephone and talk on a radio, too. It'll probably be Bo. Val isn't feeling real good—nothing serious—but she'll probably stay here at the camp. But she'll have a little walkie-talkie radio, too, the one we're talking on right now. I'll give her this one we're using now. And she'll stay here, OK?—just in case Alan gets here while we're gone. Bo will have the other one—the other little blue radio—and I'll have the little CB radio. Did you get all that? Did you write all that down."

"Yes. Little...Lost...Cove...Cliffs. Go ahead."

"Miss Faye? Did you hear me say I'm gonna go and look for Alan? I'm gonna take the Bronco, so you can talk to me on the CB—the citizens-band radio. OK? It'll take me about thirty minutes to get to the truck, and then I'll call you on the citizens-band radio. I'm taking the CB walkie-talkie. Make sure the citizens-band radio is turned on. OK?"

"That's fine, sweetie. I'll be right here. Maybe you'll meet him on your way to the truck."

"I hope so. OK, Miss Faye. Over and out."

"Bye-bye, honey. I'll be waiting for your call. Bye-bye now."

"You think she understood what you told her—that you're going to call on the CB?"

"I sure hope so. I really *am* worried about Alan. He should've been here by now, if he left Brown Mountain over an hour ago."

"So you want us to go up to the higher cliffs?"

"No, just you, Bo.... Val? Do you hear me, Val?... Val, if you hear me, I need to go look for Alan. I'm gonna go back to the Bronco and drive down Mortimer Road, just in case he broke down or something. OK? Val?"

"You go on. I'll talk to her. She'll be OK."

"OK. So you'll have your cell phone and a walkie-talkie—I mean, a two-way—and I'll have the CB. If you need to get ahold of me, you can call Miss Faye and try to get her to relay the message to me. Sonny'll probably call on the CB before I get to the truck, so I'll tell him what's going on. OK?"

"OK. Be careful.... Wait a second. How do I get to the upper cliffs?"

"Sorry. Here's the map. Alan marked the little trail. You'll see it. But you just go back down to the main trail—you know, where we saw the mushrooms, the black trumpets, not the poison ones —and go right, up the hill. There's only one side trail to the right. That's the one. Kind of bear to the left, and you'll come out at the very tip-top of this ridge. It's where you can see all the way around in a circle. That oughta be the best place for your phone and radio. OK?"

"OK. See ya, Lacey."

"OK, I'll see ya later. Tell Val not to worry. Everything'll be all right."

TWENTY-EIGHT

As the crunch and thump of Lacey's footsteps down the trail grew fainter, I heard Bo walk around the tent to the mesh window in the rear where I lay. "Val?" he said, leaning down to the opening. "Val, you all right?"

"I guess," I replied.

"Did you hear?"

"Yeah. You going to those other cliffs now?"

"I have to. Will you be OK?"

"I guess so. Can I stay here?"

"Yeah," he said, "but let me give you the walkie-talkie." He walked back around the tent, unzipped the door and ducked inside. "Here's the flashlight out of your pack, and here's the radio. It's set on the right channel—eighteen—and it's still charged pretty good. I'll call you soon as I get to the other cliffs. You just, uh, sit tight. OK?"

"OK." Scrambling into a sitting position and crossing my legs Indian-style, I took the flashlight and twisted it on, illuminating the tent interior. The white light made me feel better immediately, as if I were home in my own bed, looking at my lighthouse night light plugged into the wall socket.

Bo placed the radio in my other hand. "If you need me—or if Alan shows up—call me, and I'll come right back. OK?" I nodded. "Oh, one other thing," he said, unclipping the MP3 player from his belt and taking the earbuds from his pocket. "If you start having another attack, stick these in your ears and close your eyes and just listen to what I loaded for you, 'til it passes."

"What is it?"

"Coltrane," he replied. "You might not like it at first, 'cause it's kind of different. But it'll take your mind off whatever else you're thinking about. OK? Here. Put it in your pocket so you have it close by, if you need it. OK?" As he handed me the cigarette lighter-sized player, he leaned down and brushed my cheek with his lips. "You'll be all right," my friend murmured in my ear. "I'll just be right up there, if you need me. If you do, just call."

I nodded as he turned and left the tent. After pausing to zip the tent door shut and repeat his goodbye, he hurried off at a quicker pace than I thought him capable of in the dark. Through the front tent flap, I watched Bo's light bounce into the dark woods and disappear below the ridge seconds later as he followed the path down to the main trail. It was then that I realized I was alone. All alone. In the dark.

Depressing the radio's talk button, I said, "Bo?"

"Yeah?"

I wanted to ask him—to *beg* him—to return to the tent and stay with me. To hold me. But I knew Lacey needed Bo to follow her instructions and position himself at the ridge's crest so he could relay information, if necessary, between her and Sonny, or maybe even between her and Alan. Even though I feared I was about to suffer another panic attack, I didn't want to make Bo do something that might hurt Alan—or, rather, *not* do something to help him.

"Val? You OK?"

"Yeah, I'm OK. Just testing the radio. It's working. Over and out."

"OK. I'll call you from the top of the hill. Over and out."

I wished Lacey had let us build a fire before she left. A roaring fire would have made me feel better than my flashlight did. A fire also would have warded off the night chill that was quickly enveloping me, partly from the dampness lingering from that afternoon's shower and partly from the mountains' naturally moist night air there in the dark forest. I guess I could have gone outside and taken down my backpack from its tree and checked it for one of those foil-like space blankets that backpackers carry, or I could have unpacked my sleeping bag and curled up in it. But then I would have had to leave the safety of the tent, my shelter from the elements, my sanctuary from the outside world, my hiding place.

"Val?"

"Bo?"

"Yeah, it's me. I'm there. And it's unbelievable! You should see this!"

"See what?"

"The view! You can see everything! Fireworks are going off everywhere!"

"Are you sure they're fireworks?"

"Well, I guess *they're fireworks. I mean, I guess some of them* could *even be the Brown Mountain Lights. And I just saw three orange*

streaks of light, like skyrockets or flares or something, on a ridge over in that general direction. You know, I think that is *Brown Mountain, Val! I think it is! Give me a second to check the map."*

"It could be Alan, Bo. Maybe he has a flare gun or something."

The radio was silent for a couple of minutes before Bo's reply. *"No, it wouldn't be Alan, I wouldn't think, 'cause he carries a red strobe light—one of those little survival lights. He just bought it the other day. I saw it. He showed it to me when we were sitting in his.... Hang on, Val. My phone's ringing. Sit tight."*

Since I really had no choice *but* to sit tight, I waited as patiently as I possibly could. Finally, after what seemed like a quarter hour but might have been only maybe three minutes, Bo came back on the radio and filled me in on what he had learned right then from Miss Faye, who had just talked to Lacey on Mortimer Road. Lacey, he said, had spoken to Sonny and Elaine, who had then been parked at the overlook on Grandfather Mountain.

The flares Bo had seen toward Brown Mountain *could* have been Alan after all, Bo said, because, according to Lacey, Alan had borrowed her grandfather's flare gun, a World War II-era German flare gun that Buck had taken off a dead Nazi's body. I learned later that with Lacey's help Alan had "borrowed" the gun without Buck's permission, and that my cousin had intended to use it both to celebrate the July Fourth holiday *and* to play a little joke on Bo and me that night—to let us think we had seen the Brown Mountain Light while he was off getting water or using the latrine.

Also, Bo said my quick-thinking aunt had gotten Miss Faye to call OnStar to get them to locate Alan's Blazer, and that they had pinpointed his vehicle's location in the parking lot of the Wilson Creek Welcome Center on Mortimer Road near Brown Mountain. With their theory being that the Blazer must have broken down, Lacey as well as Sonny and Elaine were all headed in that direction as we spoke—Lacey in the white Bronco, through Edgemont and then Mortimer on Mortimer Road; Sonny and Elaine in the black Charger, to Jonas Ridge by the Blue Ridge Parkway, down the mountain on the main highway, then to the welcome center by Brown Mountain Beach Road.

Bo added that Elaine had already called the Caldwell County Sheriff's Department—the law enforcement agency with jurisdiction in the Wilson Creek area—and that they, too, were sending a deputy to check the Blazer. The lawman, however, was stuck in traffic at a fireworks display on the other side of Lenoir, which was at least thirty minutes away even when the roads were clear.

"I told Mrs. Rose to tell them I saw those flares over toward Brown Mountain, so they're thinking maybe Alan is *in some kind of*

trouble—if that's him and not just kids shooting off fireworks. You know, three flares is a distress signal."

Yes, I knew that and had thought about that possibility minutes earlier when Bo had first mentioned seeing three skyrockets or flares toward Brown Mountain. It was one of the first things Grandpa had taught me back when I started sailing—that firing three flares one after another or blowing three short blasts on an air horn or blowing a whistle three times or even flashing a mirror in the sun three times was calling for help and that I should never, ever do any of those things unless I really needed help—I should never "cry wolf."

Something else had occurred to me—the possibility that the Blazer hadn't broken down but that Alan had tried to ride his mountain bike all the way from Brown Mountain to our campsite there at the Little Lost Cove Cliffs for the fun and adventure of it. And that he had run into some kind of trouble along the way. He was like that—a dare-devil, a risk-taker. After all, hadn't his last communication been from Brown Mountain—or was that merely what we had assumed?—and hadn't he said he was leaving for Lost Cove right then?

"Bo, could those flares have gone up *between* us and Brown Mountain? Were they *on* Brown Mountain or somewhere in between?"

"I don't know. It's hard to tell. That's why nobody's ever figured out what the Brown Mountain Lights are—because of all the rising heat waves and cool air currents and light refraction and all that kind of stuff in this basin around Wilson Creek. What I saw could've been an optical illusion of some kind—light deflected from the fireworks display near Lenoir. Or it could've been some kids shooting skyrockets at one of those campgrounds near Brown Mountain—or on past Brown Mountain, I don't know."

I started to reply, but Bo immediately came back on to tell me his phone was ringing again and that he would talk to me after he answered it. However, the seconds I waited became minutes, which began to drag by like time spent in Saturday detention at school. Several times, I considered calling Bo on the radio, but I didn't want to interrupt something more important than my uneasiness at being alone in the dark with only a dimming flashlight and a weakening radio to ease my fears. Time after time, I came within a hair of pressing the talk button, but I decided that—

"Hey!" growled a strange, deep voice outside the tent. "Git out chere you two!"

I squeezed the radio and screamed Bo's name, but I didn't release the button to hear his response, as if that would have mattered right then.

"Git out chere, you durn thief!" the intruder shouted. "Where's my gall-durn gun?! Git out chere right now!"

As I shrieked again into the radio, I heard the man struggling to unzip the tent door. "Gall-durnit! If you'ns don't open this door, I'm a-gonna cut it open!" he growled, still fumbling with the zippered flaps.

Within seconds, I heard the tent fabric rip, then felt a strong claw-like hand grab my arm and pull me into the night. The radio flew from my grasp and hit the ground with a crack. The tiny flashlight spun across the plasticized floor like a wild game of spin-the-bottle and ended up pointing back toward the freshly-slit opening in the tent. That was when I opened my eyes.

Knife blade glinting below one fist, the bear-like man shook me three times with his other hand before suddenly stopping and relaxing his grip but not letting me go. "You ain't that boy," the man rasped. "You're that gall-durn girl who won't let me alone."

It was Buck Green. "Whut're *you* doin' here?" he asked, only a bit less threateningly than before. "Where's my grandbaby and that boy? He's got somethin' that's mine, and I want it back—before midnight."

I could hear Bo yelling my name from the upper cliffs, but I was afraid to call back to him, with Buck still clutching my arm and brandishing his knife. "We don't know where Alan is," I insisted. "Everybody's looking for him right now."

"Whar's Lacey Mae?" he said. "She with him? Agin?"

"I don't know where she is right *now*," I replied, not realizing exactly what he was asking. "She *might* be with him by now."

Judging from his response, that wasn't what Buck wanted to hear, because he started pulling me by the arm down the path toward the main trail below. "M'on, little girl," he grunted, holstering the folding knife after closing it against his thigh. "You gonna hep me find 'em, you being that boy's next o' kin and all."

"Next of kin? What're you gonna do?" I tried to struggle free, but he was too strong for me, even at his age. Trying to twist out of Buck's grasp, I screamed for Bo to come help me, even though I knew my friend couldn't subdue the old bear by himself.

"Now quit yer squealin' like a little pig," Buck ordered, shaking me again. "You keep it up, and you'll spook Niblick." Sure enough, waiting there in the trees stood Buck's mule, far enough away from our camp that I hadn't heard their arrival as I was talking to Bo on the radio.

Before I knew what was happening, Buck stepped up into the stirrup and swung his body into the saddle, then hauled me up behind him. "Hode onto me, little girl," he said. "And quit howlin' like a banshee. Nib ain't like one o' them dang gub'ment mules that wuz use to all that screamin' and yellin' and such back durin' the war. You doan wanna git yer neck broke or nuthin'."

He was right about that; I didn't want my neck broken. I also didn't want to go trail riding on a dark summer night, especially with my arms wrapped around a knife-wielding homicidal-albeit-elderly maniac on a one-eyed appaloosa mule, but I had no choice. I heard a clank of metal and the hiss of a match being struck. The odors of sulphur and then kerosene tickled my nostrils, and I knew Buck had lit his lantern so we could be on our way. "Whut's goin' on?" he asked me. "Is my grandbaby awright? And that boy?"

"Alan's missing," I said. "He was riding his bike over near Brown Mountain, and he just disappeared. Lacey's gone looking for him." I heard Bo yell again. "And my friend back there is relaying messages to Lacey through Miss Faye, to help find Alan. My Aunt Elaine and Sonny and even a sheriff's deputy are looking for him."

"Humph," Buck snorted. "Bet I know where that boy is." In the soft yellow lantern light, Buck didn't look nearly as scary as he had minutes earlier in the darkness. "You better holler to that boy up yonder and tell him you're awright so he don't tell the sheriff I hauled you off or somethin'."

"Why do I have to go with you?" I asked, my voice trembling. "Can't I stay here?"

He shook his head. "No, ma'am," he said. "I need you with me if that boy's where I think he is. They's no two ways about it; you're comin' with me. You'll be awright. I won't let no boogers git ya." I think he tried to smile at me, but the shadows were dancing around his rough face under the bill of the green John Deere cap he was always wearing. "Go ahead and holler. I'll hold Niblick still."

Obediently, I yelled to Bo and told him I was OK and that Buck and I were going to look for Alan. "Tell Miss Faye I'm with Buck," I shouted, "I mean, with Oren. Oren Green."

Before Bo could answer, Buck dug his heels into Niblick, and we were off. At that point, there was nothing I could do but hold on for dear life, as the old man had instructed. As had been the case on the airplane flight from home two weeks earlier, closing my eyes so tightly that they hurt helped me control to some small extent the waves of panic that washed over me as our mount slid and jolted and scuffled down the rocky path. I would have reached into my pocket for Bo's MP3 player, to plug my ears (as well as my eyes) and listen to Coltrane, my friend's new hero, but that would have been impossible with both my arms around Buck's lean middle. I pressed the side of my face against his back and caught a whiff of sweaty flesh through the green work shirt he always wore.

In the distance behind us, Bo's shouts were fading fast, so I knew he would never be able to help me, not unless Buck decided to stop that stupid mule and turn me loose. But old Niblick hit the main trail, took a hard left and kept hauling it toward Mortimer Road. I peeked first when Buck yelled, "Duck," as we descended the hill before reaching the apple orchard, and I caught a glimpse of the gate of fallen branches just as we rode through it, our heads bowed to keep from being knocked off the mule. I glanced around again a few seconds later when we passed the pile of rocks where Alan had left us the treasure map.

Through the clearing in the trees there at the marker, I opened my eyes wide and looked off the mountain into the night. There I saw three pulses of reddish light blink near a dark not-too-distant ridgeline. "There!" I shouted. "Did you see them?!" I couldn't tell if the old fellow had heard me or not, or if he had heard but hadn't understood I was referring to what must have been Alan's red strobe light.

Buck must have seen the pulse of light himself and had evidently pinpointed its location, because when we reached Mortimer Road, Niblick took off down the graveled route toward Mortimer as if the devil himself were nipping at the old mule's hooves. We kept up that breakneck pace for several minutes, until Buck suddenly reined the mule to a skidding stop.

"Git down," Buck ordered. When I didn't turn him loose right away, he used his hand not holding the lantern to pry my arms from around his torso, one at a time. It was an impossible task, however, because as soon as he would pull one arm loose and reach for the other one, I would wrap him up again with the arm that he had just released. "Dad blast-it, little girl," he growled. "Whut are you, a octi-puss or somethin'? You gotta git down and look at that bi-cycle over thar by that sign. I seen it thar before, but I didn't know if it was that boy's or not."

I stopped struggling and looked to where Buck was directing the feeble lantern light. Leaning against one of the wooden Darkside Cliffs Trail signposts was a mountain bike that looked something like Alan's. With help from Buck, I slid off Niblick's back and carried the lantern to the sign, to inspect the bike—a red Iron Horse Maverick Sport.

"It's Alan's all right," I shouted back. "He must've walked over to the cliffs to use his phone. That's the only place he could get any signal when we were here before." I yelled Alan's name twice, but there was no response, other than the echo of my own voice off the ridges forming Lost Cove.

Buck dismounted and walked Niblick past the sign into the dark trees, stopping once he was out of sight of the road and wrapping the mule's reins loosely around a sapling along the trail. "Roll that contraption over here so it don't get stole," he said, referring to Alan's bike. "We gotta go see whut that boy's got hissself into. He coulda fell and got hisself hurt."

I remembered what Miss Faye had told me about one of Buck's sons falling off Harper Creek Falls near Kawana and breaking every bone in his body but not dying. Though I didn't mention it, I wondered if Buck was thinking the same thing right then. "Can't we ride the mule?" I asked, wondering, too, why Alan hadn't ridden his bike the quarter-mile to the cliffs.

"Nah," Buck replied. "Ain't no place to tie him, and I ain't gonna take a chance on him runnin' the three of us off that cliff. That rock's as slick as goose grease, what with all the rain we had of late. You ain't careful, you cain't stop, the way that little path runs downhill to the rocks, and you could go slidin' right off into nowhere, 'specially a dark night like tonight."

Buck held out his hand, and at first I thought he was reaching out to escort me up the ridge, then down the other side to the Darkside Cliffs. "Gimme the lantern," he said. "I kin hode it cuz I'm gonna be out front. You carry this." He unlooped a green webbed-cotton strap from Niblick's saddlehorn and handed to me an aluminum military-issue canteen covered in green canvas.

I noticed that Buck's battered bugle—the one Miss Faye had told me about—also was hanging by its cord from the saddle. After hesitating a second, he unhooked the bugle and handed it, too, to me. "M'on. But doan follow me too close or you'll get slapped by branches and briars." I tried to protest, but he had already started up the trail, and I didn't want to be left behind in the dark, even though I would have had the mule to keep me company.

As Alan himself had told Bo and me only two weeks earlier on our first day in the mountains, the Darkside Cliffs Trail probably *was* the easiest hike in the Wilson Creek Area, even in the dark. The problem I was having, however, had nothing to do with the difficulty of the walking itself; I was struggling with the possibilities of what Buck and I might find once we reached the cliffs, where Alan had gone before us.

Buck noticed a bootprint here and there in the moist earth as we hiked almost to the top of the ridge, then took the well-trodden path to the left when the trail forked. As we made the turn, Buck announced, "Up on the ridge up thar's whar I use to do my bidness in these parts." He swung the lantern toward the higher ground to point where he meant.

"Do your business?" I said, remembering that both my grandpa and Billy Joe had used that particular term for going to the restroom. I wondered why Buck was pointing that out to me right then.

"No, my *bidness*," he repeated. "'Shine. Moonshine—that good ole mountain dew."

"Oh," I said, finally understanding him.

"They's a big rock up thar—'bout six foot high and five or six foot wide and flat on one side. I use to hide my still behind it, so nobody'd see a far an' think I wuz one of the Lights or somethin'," the old moonshiner noted, as we continued down the left fork. "I wuz up thar just the other day fer Miss Faye. Anyways, up on the ridge, at the very tip-top, is another path that runs straight down to the cliff. It's a purty steep'en, though, a lot steeper'n this way. You think he woulda gone thataway?" He stopped to wait for my answer.

"I don't know," I replied. "Maybe—since that's higher ground than the cliffs. If he was trying to use his phone, he *might've* gone up there. I don't know."

"Me and you better split up then," Buck said. "Go back and take the path up the hill to the big rock. Make sure he ain't up there, then sit and wait on me. I'll come up that other path from the cliff and git you if he ain't down there neither. Just holler if you do find 'im."

I didn't like the way "find 'im" sounded or the way Buck wouldn't say Alan's name, as if the old man expected to find just my cousin's body instead of his whole live being. "If I find 'im, I'll holler, and you can come down and hep me with 'im," Buck added. "We ain't gonna be all that fur apart—me down at the cliff and you up on the ridge. It ain't *that* fur apart."

"But we only have one light," I said, pointing to the lantern he held.

He nodded, then stooped down to pick up a long club-like stick, which lay next to the trail as if someone had discarded their walking staff after it broke in two. Removing his work shirt and an old-fashioned "wife-beater" under it, Buck tightly wrapped and tied the stained white undershirt around one end of the stick, then doused it with kerosene from the lantern reservoir. With a chrome-plated cigarette lighter wider than the MP3 player in my pocket, Buck snapped the roller with his thumb to light the torch, then flipped the Zippo shut with a distinctive *chunk*.

"Here," he said, handing me the blazing torch. "You don't have as fur to go, case it goes out. Holler if you find 'im." He picked up the lantern, turned and continued down the trail.

I wanted to refuse to climb the ridge alone and instead follow the old man to the cliffs. But, for the second time that night, I felt as if my actions—or, rather, my inaction—might affect Alan's chances of being saved, since it was looking more and more as if he might be hurt. Or worse.

So, still carrying the canteen and bugle over my left shoulder, I held the torch as high as I could in my right hand to light the path ahead. As I had never carried a real torch before, I had no idea how long it would stay lit. That bothered me so much—the idea that I might be left in complete darkness—that I considered listening to Bo's

MP3 player as I ascended the trail to look for Alan. But, once again, I couldn't easily do that—put in the earbuds and turn on the music—unless I laid down the torch for at least a minute, and then I would have risked extinguishing it. Also, it occurred to me that I needed to keep my ears as well as my eyes open, in case Buck *did* find Alan and called for my help.

Minutes later, after I found the big rock and my torch did, in fact, go out, I thought again about curling up and listening to Bo's music next to the monolith where Buck's still had once stood. But, finally, I realized that the love inside me for my cousin was more powerful than the fear I felt for my own well-being. No mere song—no matter how moving its words and music might have been—could have swayed my devotion for Alan, who along with his mother were my only blood kin left. Who said blood was thicker than water? Besides, Buck had said that if he didn't find Alan at the cliffs, he would hike up the third trail and lead me back down to the road. As long as I didn't hear Buck "holler," I'd be OK.

But holler he did. His echoing voice was closer than I had expected. *"Hey! I found 'im. I found 'im. Come down here and hep me! Hurry!"* And he kept yelling until I answered that I was on my way.

I admit I was scared to death. But it wasn't the same kind of fear that had been paralyzing me over the past three weeks since I had hugged the floor in the B.J.'s clubhouse with certain death sitting in Billy Joe's chair watching TV and waiting for my friend, my teacher, my old pro to die—or should I say, while *we* waited and even wished, to my shame, that he would go ahead and die, so the killer would leave me alone.

Until that moment near the Darkside Cliffs in Lost Cove, I had not admitted to anyone, not even to the preacher back home—or to myself, for that matter—that I had actually welcomed another human being's death in order to save my own life. The guilt for which I sought forgiveness was one thing. My desire, my prayer, my hope for deliverance was something else. It was all I needed right then.

A light shone on my face. "Val! I finally caught you!" said Bo, running up the trail from Mortimer Road. "Where are they?" Bo added breathlessly, referring to both Buck and Alan. He shined his flashlight around the big rock, as if they might have been hiding behind it. "I heard him yell. And I saw Alan's bike. Where are they?"

Just then, Buck shouted again from below. *"Go git hep! Girl, go git hep! He's bleeding! We don't have time to carry him out! We gotta git hep here, quick!"*

Seeing that his cell phone had a strong signal where we stood on the crest of the hill, Bo dialed 9-1-1. As he waited for the connection, we both noticed at the same time the headlights of three vehicles slowly traveling Mortimer Road below us through the trees. Until then, I hadn't realized just how close I had been to the roadway.

The headlights disappeared one set at a time, then reappeared as the caravan rounded the nearest bend. It was then we saw that the lead vehicle was a squad car like the *Bluesmobile*, its blue light-bar on top reflecting the high beams from the two vehicles following in the slow-moving procession. We could count the six fixed beams of light illuminating the road ahead of the autos below us and a much stronger sweeping seventh ray probing the roadsides around the cruiser in front.

"Hey!" I screamed. "Stop! Up here! Stop!" But the vehicles continued creeping past us on the road below. Ignoring his cell phone for the moment, Bo yelled with me, but the line of cars did not stop.

We needed to get their attention, but our voices weren't strong enough, singularly or together. In a few seconds, they would be out of earshot around the next curve, and our last best chance for Alan's rescue would be lost. And unless the searchers got out of their cars, they wouldn't see Niblick or Alan's bike where we had taken them away from the road, out of sight up the trail in the trees. We had to get their attention right then. We had to make a noise, any kind of noise, that was loud enough for them to hear, even if the noise they heard made no sense whatsoever. All we needed was a sound that was strong and loud. And for someone to hear it.

For a reason I will never be able to explain, I looked down at my feet, where Bo's flashlight beam lit the ground around us. There, like on the ridge near the Little Lost Cove Cliffs trails, grew a thick cluster of chanterelles—black trumpets—evidently part of the same batch Buck had picked for Miss Faye days earlier. Seeing just one little horn-shaped mushroom would have been all I needed to realize that my prayer had already been answered and that help was only seconds away.

I couldn't see the expression on Bo's face as I pushed Buck's battered old bugle toward him, but I was sure my friend understood and was ready to perform. "What should I blow?!" he asked.

"Blow *anything*!" I screamed. And he did, as if his own life depended on it.

TWENTY-NINE

We got Alan to the hospital just in time. The worst injuries he had suffered in the fall were a broken right arm, a broken collarbone and a nasty head wound. That was the bleeding Buck had controlled with direct pressure, clamping his John Deere cap over his folded handkerchief on the point where Alan's blood seeped from the crown of his head.

The blow to the head in the fall kept Alan knocked out until we got him loaded into the squad car for the ride to Lenoir. Lacey got into the back seat with him and took over holding pressure on the head wound as the deputy roared away as if he were on a mission, which, of course, he *was* until he pulled up in front of the hospital emergency room.

Sonny and Elaine followed in the Charger, but not before Buck reached in the driver's-side window and snatched Sonny's ball cap off his head, to replace the bloodied headwear covering Alan's wound. Sonny was surprised but didn't seem to mind too much since he had other worries right then.

Bo and I loaded Alan's mountain bike into the Bronco, then looked around for Buck before Bo drove us back to the Little Lost Cove Cliffs trailhead so we could hike back to the lower cliffs and pack up our gear. We didn't get a chance to talk much to Buck. He mounted Niblick, cracked open his canteen and took a long swig to wet his whistle, then blew a rousing retreat on the bugle before spurring his mount toward the Shortcut Trail across the road.

We didn't see him again until a couple of hours later, around midnight, when we turned into the driveway at the Barkhouse Lodge and saw Buck—excuse me, Oren—and Miss Faye rocking together on the front porch, with the mule nibbling grass—and flower blossoms—

in the front yard. All of us stayed up that night until we got the call from Elaine saying Alan would be all right but that he would have to stay in the hospital for at least the next several days.

As the four of us sat together on the porch, the conversation somehow shifted from the evening's events to my plans for the next school year. Miss Faye pointed out that if I were to complete my high school studies with her and Sonny in the days ahead, as they had planned, I might have time to enroll at a good college for the fall semester and the next four to six years. "Who knows," Miss Faye added. "Once you get started, you may just keep a-going until you get your Ph.D."

"Yeah," Bo quipped. "Ph.D.—Piled Higher and Deeper." Even Buck laughed, though I don't think he knew or cared what the initials actually stood for. He just kind of smiled vacantly down into his lap, where he held the cap he had stolen earlier in the evening from Sonny. It was one of those green "1892" caps I had seen in the Linville pro shop. I wondered when and why Sonny had bought it.

"Naw," I said to Miss Faye, as agreeably as I could manage. "I'm going to finish reading all those books you and Sonny assigned me. And I'm going to get my diploma—and my driver's license, too. But, Miss Faye, I don't think I'm going to go to school this fall. Not up here, anyway. Probably not anywhere."

Miss Faye took my announcement with more grace than I thought possible. "What will you do with yourself, Valerie?" she asked. "Do you know?"

It was the question everyone had been asking me all my life—the question I'd been asking myself, if not all my life, then at least since my grandmother had died the previous spring and had left me orphaned for the second time.

"Yes, I do," I said, looking at Bo in the rocker next to me. "I'm going home—back to Village Point. That's where I belong."

"What'll you do?" Bo asked. "You know, Mom would be glad to have you stay with her. It's *your* house, and she wouldn't care. But what'll you do—for a living, I mean?"

I smiled wearily. "Well, for starters, I'm going to go back down there and make sure they put those guys away that murdered Billy Joe. That's one thing I can do for him."

"Murder?" Miss Faye said. "Good gracious." Buck reached over and patted her hand on the arm of her rocker.

"The other thing I'm going to do," I continued, "is see if I can do something with Billy Joe's golf course. I don't know who'll get it. I don't even know if Billy Joe *had* a will. But maybe whoever ends up with it will keep it a golf course, and maybe they'll need somebody to fix it up for them—make it a *real* golf course, not just a driving range with holes." I looked at Bo again, then at Miss Faye and Buck, to see how they were taking my announcement.

Miss Faye, in particular, had a somewhat quizzical look. "Well, now, I certainly don't want to be talking out of school," she said, "but I *think* I've heard my Sonny talking about buying a driving range somewhere, I can't remember where. I thought it had something to do with his automobiles—you know, a *driving* range. But if it's a golf course, Valerie, maybe you could stay here and work for him? He's just so busy with everything else he does."

I had no idea what she was talking about. "Well, anyway, *that's* what I'm going to do," I continued. "That's what I *need* to do—build my own golf course instead of trying so hard to play somebody else's. And, you know, I don't care if I *ever* get to play that old Linville course."

Buck perked up. "Hey, you wanna play ole Linville?" he asked, playfully snapping the green cap at me to get my attention. "That why you was out thar on the old course t'other day?"

I nodded, assuming he was talking about the time I had tried to sneak onto the Ross course but had changed my mind upon seeing him fishing in Lake Kawana. "Yes, sir," I replied. "I've been wanting to play that course since the first time I saw it. It's the most beautiful golf course I've ever seen."

"It *is* a perty place," Buck agreed, "and always was, even back when my daddy and me worked around there. Sometimes when he wasn't cutting the grass or trimmin' the shrubs—or fishin' in the ponds—he got to caddy them folks around like he was a big Ike hissef. My ole daddy knowed every bump and hole and laurel thicket on that old course like the back of his hand."

I smiled again. "Well, I don't guess *I'll* get to know it like that," I said. "But maybe I'll get to know my own course like the back of *my* hand, if I'm lucky."

"You sound jist like Aggie," Buck laughed, slapping his knee.

"Aggie?" I asked.

"Yeah," Buck replied. "Aggie Morton. I heard she got tired of waitin' to play Linville, too, so she went and built her own durn golf course. That's what *that* little gal went and done. That's how the Grandfather golf course come about."

"Agnes MacRae Morton?" Bo interjected. "The lady who started the Highland Games?"

"No, dear," Miss Faye answered. "Mrs. Agnes MacRae Morton was Miss Aggie Morton's mother."

Buck rocked back and forth in his chair, as if these thoughts of the past excited him. "That Aggie was somethin' else," he said. "She was the best lady golfer in the whole durn state—she shore was—and a durn sight better 'n a lot of men, too."

"And she built the Grandfather course?" I asked Buck.

"Yer darn tootin', she did," he said. "I was still workin' around Linville when she done it. I remember it like it was yesterday." He rocked quietly for a few seconds longer, as if he were picturing in his mind ghosts from his past. "I cain't get into Grandfather," he added presently, "but I *can* get you back on ole Linville, if that's what you really want, any time you want—just like the other day." He nodded at me. "Well, what d'ya say, gal?"

Though I doubted Buck could actually get me a tee time at Linville, I politely answered, "Sure, that would be great, Mr. Green," and changed the subject as quickly as I could. Any ordinary individual who thought he could tee off at Linville any old time he pleased—much less an old moonshiner with Alzheimer's—wasn't in touch with reality.

I returned Bo's MP3 player to him and inquired about the music he had meant for me to hear. He told me again that the music was Coltrane's *A Love Supreme*, an album he had been reading a book about. "It's amazing, isn't it?" my friend said. "And you've got to read the poem he wrote for the liner notes, too. Coltrane called it his 'gift to God.' It's supposed to be one of the most important albums ever made. What'd you think?"

When I said I hadn't had a chance to listen to the music yet, Bo told me to keep the player until we got together the next Saturday at the music festival. "I can go with you guys to Grandfather Mountain on Sunday," he said, "you know, to the Highland Games, if you're going the last day. But after that mess I got into last week, Mom says I have to stay on campus weeknights, so I can't go with you to the opening stuff Thursday night."

He added he was looking forward to the Celtic music at the Games, even if he had no Scots blood in him. "Coltrane was into folk music, too," Bo noted. "That's the best kind of music, the kind you don't have to think about, the kind that comes right from your soul, like a tuning fork going off—"

Stopping short, Bo looked at me and winked. I was glad he didn't finish that quotation from *Tin Cup*, one of my favorite golf movies, because I didn't know how Miss Faye would have reacted to hearing "like a tuning fork going off in your loins" as she and Buck sat together on her front porch. Besides, that particular quotation described the "well-struck golf shot," not necessarily folk music or anything else, I didn't think.

"It's like what I heard Doc say once about playing a solo," Bo added. "He said if he misses a note and just lets it go like that, it's called a mistake. But if he takes that bad note and does something with it—like, if he starts a fancy little run with it or something—well, then it's called *improvisation*, and that makes all the difference in the world.

That's the way life is, too, don't you think—learning how to make the best out of bad situations?"

"That's exactly right, Lionel," Miss Faye said, with a curt nod. "When people give you persimmons, make persimmon pudding."

Buck scrunched up his already wrinkled brow. "I thought you were suppost to make lemonade," he offered, with a mischievous grin.

"Oren Green, you're hopeless!" Miss Faye cackled. "Now, you stop making fun of me!" She leaned toward him and patted his old shoulder ever so lightly, as if she were scolding a schoolboy.

"I'll tell ya whut persimmon's good fer," Buck stated, liking the attention he was getting. "It makes the best play clubs. And brassies, too. They wudn't as light as these big high-priced clubs nowadays, but they got the job done, they shore did. Good enough, anyway. And they shore was a lot pertier than these big ugly clubs now. When I retired, I got it in my head that I's gonna take up golf like I's a rich feller or somebody, and I found me one 'o them big ugly play clubs that somebody'd fergot. Turned out I didn't need it, 'cause I didn't never git time to play none. Too busy with other thangs, ya know? 'Sides, if I was gonna pass my time playin' golf, I'd use a reg'lar play club off the tee, like they had back when I was a boy."

This time, I was the one who perked up. "Are you talking about a driver?" I asked Buck. While I knew old golf clubs had specific names instead of numbers—like brassie, spoon, mashie and niblick (yes, like Buck's mule)—I didn't know that the club used to drive the ball off the tee was called anything but that—a driver.

He nodded. "That's what they's called now," he replied, "but back when my daddy was caddying at ole Linville, they was called 'play clubs,' the driver was. Back in them days, all the clubs had a name, just like all the holes did, too. Nowadays, it's nothin' but numbers. Numbers ever'where. Numbers ain't got no soul."

"The holes had names?" I asked. "You mean, like Amen Corner at Augusta?"

Buck frowned. "Yeah, kinda like that," the old man said, eyeing me oddly, apparently surprised that a girl might know something about the greatest golf course ever built by the greatest golfer of all time. "I hate that durn hole. It cost me a perty penny when Billy Joe Patton went in the creek there." Buck studied for a second. "Yeah, at ole Linville, all the holes had names. They was 'Tanglewood Terrace' and 'Lenoir Park' and 'Hemlock Hedge,' and my favorite one was 'Arthur's Seat.' Ever' hole had a name—all fourteen of 'em."

"*Fourteen* holes?" I said. "Linville has *eighteen* holes. Donald Ross designed it with eighteen holes, didn't he?" As if she had just remembered something, Miss Faye quietly excused herself and hurried into the lodge.

"Not *old* Linville," Buck corrected. "Not the old *Tanglewood* course. It only had fourteen holes, really, and you had to play four of 'em twicest to git in a full round. Up 'til the '30s, they was *two* golf courses at Linville—the old Tanglewood course and the new Ross course. Most folks jist called the Tanglewood course 'Old Linville' and left it at that. Ever'body knowed whut they meant."

"Where *was* the old course?" I asked.

He grinned. "I figured you already knowed that," he said. "You was playin' it the other day."

"When you were fishing in the lake?" I said.

"Fishin'?" He looked confused for a second, then seemed to figure out what I meant. "Nah, not *there*. 'Member when you hit that ball up in the woods and almost hit me in the noggin? Whether you knowed it or not, you'd been walkin' Lenoir Park—and playin' Tanglewood Terrace, if you was hittin' to the green. It use to be up at the graveyard. I tend it ever' chance I git, 'cause that's where my wife's folks is buried."

He paused to study my look of befuddlement. "And then when you hit that shot at me in the rain the other day, that was Hemlock Hedge. It use to be the very first hole, and it even run down the hill the same direction you was hittin'."

I didn't know what to say—finding out I had unknowingly played if not heaven on earth, then at least the Garden of Eden. All I could do was try to remember how those spots looked now and visualize one of the oldest golf courses in North Carolina being there, maybe even older than Pinehurst No. 2 or Cape Fear Country Club and, for that matter, older than Bobby Jones's revered Augusta National.

Just then, Miss Faye returned carrying three books from the lobby sitting area, all three bearing old photographs of Linville's early years. One small volume (Shepherd M. Dugger's *The Balsam Groves of the Grandfather Mountain*, published in 1934) showed at least twenty men and women playing or watching the action on one green at "the golf course at Linville, N.C." I recognized the skyline in the photograph as the same view behind the *Ledger* office. In her second book (William S. Powell's *North Carolina: The WPA Guide to the Old North State*, published in 1939), Miss Faye showed me separate sections on North Carolina golf and Linville. The listing for the mountain resort stated that Linville boasted *two* golf courses with thirty-six holes.

Miss Faye's third offering was a colorful coffee-table book published for Linville's centennial in 1992 (Howard E. Covington, Jr.'s

Linville: A Mountain Home for 100 Years). A whole chapter of the book was dedicated to Linville's golfing history and featured several old photographs of the very "holes" I had unwittingly played—Lenoir Park, Tanglewood Terrace and Hemlock Hedge, which was the first hole on the resort's original nine-hole course in 1895 before five new holes were added around the turn of the century. There were even photos of Aggie Morton playing at Linville.

The picture that truly intrigued me, though, was one of "Arthur's Seat," with its sand tee overlooking Linville proper and its fairway running westward halfway across the Linville valley toward Pixie Mountain. "Where exactly is that one, Mr. Green?" I asked. "Have I played that hole yet? I was up there the other day, wasn't I?"

"Arthur's Seat?" he said, pausing again to remember his favorite old teeing ground in the picture I pointed to. "I don't think you was at Arthur's Seat. It ain't there no more, not where it use to be. Them days is gone." I think a tear came to his eye, though the shadows on his face from the porchlight made it hard to know for sure.

Oren Green didn't say anything for a few seconds, and at first I thought his mind had wandered from golf. But then he looked me straight in the eye and asked me point blank, "You wanna play Arthur's Seat? If you really wanna play that old hole, I'll do my best to hep ya play it—or the next best thang. You jist say the word, and we'll tee 'er up. I might even git out that ole high-priced play club I got and finally hit a ball with it. Or maybe I'll jist let *you* use it, and I'll be yer caddy." He chuckled. "Ya know—I hear a good caddy makes a perty penny these days. So when you're ready to go play, you make sure you bring yer money with ya."

"When can we go?" I asked, ready to put on my spikes and head out right then.

Oren smiled and started to reply but was interrupted by Miss Faye. "Young lady, you have *other* things to do," she said. "If I'm not mistaken, you have some books yet to read and a driver's examination to take and a cousin in the hospital who's going to need some cheering up. I don't think you and Mr. Green here will have time to tramp all over creation hitting little golf balls, not until you get *all* your assignments done."

I kept quiet, even when Bo nudged me with his elbow. "I guess you'll do your homework *now*, won't you?" he said.

Oren took off his cap and ran a gnarled hand over his closely-cropped hair. "That's OK, little Aggie," he told me. "We'll go out when the time's right, don't you worry."

I wondered if he didn't know my real name or if something about me reminded him of this great female golfer from the past. I hoped it was the latter, as the more I learned about this great woman, the more I wanted to be like her. Like my other two female heroes, she was a winner. Not a loser like me.

After all, no one gets to be a true champion by playing it safe, no matter how many strokes it takes to reach the green and how many hazards are encountered along the way. Someone once told me that, not in those exact words but close enough. I knew the time had come, finally, to think for myself.

THIRTY

As I had never before even ridden up a long and winding road quite like the one to the top of Grandfather Mountain, driving Aunt Elaine's newly-restored VW Beetle to the visitors center parking lot near the Mile-High Swinging Bridge was almost more than I could handle late that Thursday afternoon. Sonny had said it was my "final exam," to put my freshly-minted driver's license to good use while Elaine, Miss Faye, Lacey and Alan, just out of the hospital, attended the Highland Games' opening torchlight ceremony.

My assignment was to drive to the top of the mountain and wait there for Sonny to cross the finish line of the Bear, the footrace from Linville to the Swinging Bridge. I was to wait however long it took, even if he didn't get there until after dark. I didn't have to take any finish-line pictures for the paper, though. Elaine said she would photograph the race winners together when they returned to MacRae Meadows for their victory laps.

Elaine had passed up her weekly tennis outing with Sonny that morning, to take me to get my license at the Division of Motor

Vehicles office. Despite the expected case of nerves but nothing more serious, I had passed all the tests—the written test, the road test, the eye exam—with flying colors, according to the license examiner.

Did I say the VW was Aunt Elaine's? I should have said I drove *my* Beetle up the mountain that day, because Elaine and Sonny had been in cahoots all along over him fixing up the car for me. In order to keep it a surprise, he had pretended to convert it into *Herbie the Love Bug*, using magnetic decals that could be removed easily.

Elaine had told me the car was mine as we left the DMV office together. "It was my idea," she said, "but I couldn't have done it without Sonny." She explained that besides letting her keep the Challenger, Sonny had borne the entire expense of restoring the VW and that he was even loaning us enough money to get me on the road back to Village Point and to help me out until I got resettled. "He's even looking into buying Mr. Pearlman's golf course," she added, "as long as you'll run it for us."

"Us?" I asked.

My aunt just smiled and nodded. "It won't be right away," she said. "We're not in any hurry. That's why we haven't made it public, really. But I'm glad he asked me, and I'm glad I wasn't afraid to say yes. It's nice to trust someone again." She said Sonny popped the question as they were parked at the Wilson Creek Valley Overlook the night Alan was injured. She had given Sonny her answer long before they knew Alan was missing, she said.

Any other time, I might have teased her by asking if the two of them had seen any fireworks that night, but I didn't want to trivialize her announcement and suggest her knight in shining armor might have acted in a less than chivalrous manner. Besides, I doubt they even saw the three flares we all thought were Alan's signals for help.

When I asked him about that at the hospital, Alan denied firing any flares at all or setting off his emergency strobe light. He said he had left both the flare gun and light in his backpack with the rest of our camping gear at the Little Lost Cove Cliffs. He swore he had absolutely no idea what those reddish flares were that both Bo and I saw that night over toward Brown Mountain. My cousin, sticking to his role as a skeptical young scientist in training, refused to admit that those flares might have been the mysterious Light that so many people wait their whole lives to see but never do. I didn't argue with Alan the day I visited him at the hospital, because he was still hurting and because I knew what I had seen the night before on the mountain.

And, yes, I read the rest of those books to finish my summer school studies. For Sonny, I read the Giovanni, the Kerouac and the Hallberg (or was it the Walker Percy golf story that I was supposed to read for him?), and I read the Frost and Sandburg and Chase for Miss Faye. I even broke down and read the last chapter of *The Rub of the*

Green and noticed the irony in its reference to Frost's "The Road Not Taken," the poem that, whether I knew it then or not, I had been trying so hard to avoid that summer.

But what everything I had read had to do with golf, the blues and the Brown Mountain Light—and how those three things came together—I still had no answer, as I waited there atop Grandfather Mountain for Sonny to finish running the Bear (or crawling on all fours, if need be). Maybe some clues, but no real answer. Not just yet.

As I sat there in my car in the golden late-afternoon sunlight on the mountain, I reached into my pocket and felt for Bo's MP3 player. Yes, I still had it. I pressed in the earbuds and turned the player on, to hear this "divine gift" my best friend had wanted to share with me. Bo had been right—it *was* different, unlike any music I had ever heard before, unlike even the more unusual selections on the playlist Bo had put together for our flight to the mountains three weeks earlier.

At the close of the third movement in the four-part suite, I got out of the Beetle and walked across the parking lot to the rock stairway leading to the Mile-High Swinging Bridge. Though determined stragglers were still crossing the finish line as I climbed the rock stairs, the race had long been over and both winners had already been driven back down the mountain to MacRae Meadows to receive their medals before the torchlight ceremony. It was getting dark fast, and Sonny still hadn't shown up. Maybe if I walked over to the bridge, I thought, I could look down the mountain before it got too dark and spot Sonny coming up the road.

I had no intention of crossing the bridge itself, which had the reputation of frightening even big strong men—like Oren Green, who, to my utter surprise, was seated on the low rock wall that ran along the walkway to the gray-steel structure. As usual, he was wearing his old green work clothes, as well as his newly-acquired green "1892" cap.

"Mr. Green!" I said, removing the earbuds and stuffing them in my pocket without turning off the player. "What're *you* doing up here?"

He grinned. "I's wonderin' how long it was gonna take you to come up here and look at this scary ole thing," he said, nodding toward the bridge. "I been comin' up here ever' so often almos' my whole adult life, and—you know whut?—I *still* ain't got up the nerve to walk 'cross it, not the first time. Nossir. I know thousands o' folks has crossed it safe and sound—I know they has. But that ain't fer me, and I'm the first to admit it."

"Are you afraid of falling?" I asked.

"Nope," he said. "I'm afraid of hittin' the ground—of *dyin'*. Ain't you?"

I shook my head. "No," I said. "I'm afraid of *living*." He seemed to have nothing to say in return. He just kind of shrugged.

"Well, then why are you up here?" I asked finally, trying not to look past the bridge and into the gathering darkness off the mountain, where either torches or fireflies or car headlights or, for all I knew, maybe even Brown Mountain Lights were popping up all over the hills and valleys below.

"Here's why," Oren said, jerking his thumb back over his shoulder at a flat expanse of granite just across the rock wall. "You still wanna play Arthur's Seat? This ain't it, but I watched one o' the best golfers in the whole country hit balls off this very spot years ago. And he's good as royalty in my book." He took a yellowed newspaper clipping from his shirt pocket and handed it to me.

Unfolding the paper, I saw that it was a photograph of a man sitting next to what looked like a plot of grass boxed in by dark railroad ties. On the side nearest the camera, the platform bore a small wooden sign identifying the turf box as "Billy Joe's Tee." The simple carved sign also read: "Billy Joe Patton used this tee for a golf driving exhibition in September 1954. At his request it remains at Grandfather Mountain so other golfers may enjoy driving 'almost a mile' into the Linville River Valley below."

In both the picture and real life, I could see that the "teeing ground" before me pointed off Grandfather toward a distant lake, still visible despite the setting sun. "Is that Linville down there?" I asked. "Lake Kawana?"

Oren stood to see where I was looking. "Nah," he replied. "Linville's over the other way, down beyond the meadow. What that is you see down yonder is Grandfather—the course Aggie Morton built. Linville's on one side of this ole mountain's slopes, and Grandfather's on the other."

He stooped down and lifted a golf club he had stowed behind the rock wall where he had been sitting. "Here you go," the old man said, handing me the "high-priced play club" that he had acquired years earlier. I saw that it was a Yonex Super A.D.X. Zero driver. I knew from working with Billy Joe—*my* Billy Joe—that this club was one of the first graphite drivers to replace the old-fashioned persimmon woods. Printing on the toe of the club said the face had a nine-degree loft and that it had an "inner pressure molded graphite head for ultimate distance." It also had a metallic-gold graphite shaft and a black rubber Lamkin Cross Line grip. The club was as light as any three of my own clubs put together.

As I stepped over the rock wall, I noticed that Mr. Green had already teed up my ball. It was the Top-Flite Infinity 0 with the *pi* symbol, apparently the same one Sonny and I had found at the cemetery and that I had almost hit Oren with a couple of days later. Kneeling next to the ball to tighten my shoe laces, I saw that the white orb sat on what appeared to be a hand-carved wooden tee wedged into a tiny crevice in the granite. "What happened to the tee?" I asked. "Billy Joe's Tee, I mean."

"It got moved a while back, I think 'cause folks was shankin' golf balls into the parkin' lot," he replied. "But even the best hits a bad shot now and then. Even Billy Joe, and he *was* the best—always grinnin' and crackin' jokes and having a good time, even when he took a chance and hit his ball in the creek that time at Augusta tryin' to win the durn Masters. Ole Billy Joe, he just laughed and said somethin' like, 'This ain't no funeral, ever'body keep smilin'.' It was in all the papers."

Oren smiled again at the memory. "I don't care who else played them courses down yonder—Bobby Jones, Tommy Armour, I don't care who it was. Billy Joe was the best man ever to walk Linville fer my money, and Aggie was the best little gal. Simple as that." He moved away to give me room to swing. "Speakin' of money," he added. "Ya got my pay fer carrying yer clubs today? I tode ya the other night I ain't cheap."

I smiled, remembering that the three-cent piece Sonny had given me to use as my lucky ball marker was in my pocket along with Bo's MP3 player. "Yeah," I said, "I have your pay, Mr. Green. It's an old coin Sonny gave me—an old Civil War coin. He said it's only worth about ten dollars, though. You can have that, I guess. It's all I have." I figured it was all a joke, anyway.

But Oren's brow furrowed for a second as he studied my face. "A three-center?" he asked. "Silver?"

"Yeah," I said, wondering if I had offered him too little, even in jest. "Is that OK?"

The old man said nothing for a moment. Then, as if he had come to terms with whatever had bothered him, his face softened, and he nodded toward the ball. "I was just foolin' with ya, gal," Oren said. "Ya don't owe me nothin'. I'll caddy ya fer free. Now, come on and take yer cut, 'cause the time's right, right now. In a minute or two, it's gonna be dark as pitch up here, and I ain't got my lantern with me like the other night."

I stepped behind the ball and tried to visualize the trajectory of my tee shot against a less-than-spectacular but passable sunset behind clouds tinged in pink. After three tentative practice swings, I moved around the ball and took my stance to the left, planting my feet on the granite as firmly as my running shoes would allow. As I waggled the Yonex driver before starting my backswing, I noticed in the corner of my right eye that Mr. Green, standing directly behind the tee box, had taken off his cap and was slowly waving it back and forth in front of himself, as if he were *trying* to distract me.

"Hode on a second," he said, then stepped up next to me and looked off the mountain, where I could make out a cross of torchlight in the meadow below us. "Ya hear that?"

"What?" I asked, cocking an ear in the direction he was looking. "Bagpipes? What do they play when the clans get together down there—'The Campbells Are Coming'?" It was the only Scottish song title I knew.

"Nah," he said. "They play 'Amazin' Grace.' I *think* that's whut I'm hearin'. Ya hear it?" He stepped back over the rock wall and walked across the narrow ridge to an observation deck with two antique coin-operated telescopes that looked like oversized parking meters.

"M'on over here," he said, motioning for me to join him. But then he laughed and pointed at something else—or some*one*, as it turned out—on the trail directly beneath the Swinging Bridge. "They's a shortcut trail up here from down 'bout the Black Rock parkin' lot," he explained. "We shoulda knowed ole Sonny'd have to pick a new route to run. Ever'body else come up the road like they's supposed to."

Sure enough, just down the ridge from us and directly underneath the bridge, Sonny chugged up the path. Dripping with perspiration and stripped down to his running shorts and shoes, he wore a Sony Walkman clipped to his waistband and a headset clamped on his sweaty head. He bore no entry number on his shorts, as all the other racers did; I figured his sticker had been attached to his shirt and was still on it, wherever he had discarded the shirt and who-knew-what-else coming up the mountain.

"Hey!" I yelled. "Sonny! Up here!"

As if the plastic headset weighed pounds instead of ounces, Sonny lifted his head and managed a weak wave when his right arm rocked forward in his running motion. To describe Sonny as "running" was giving him too much credit. He wasn't exactly fast-walking, either. "Lumbering" would be a better word to describe his motion, especially as he mounted the rock stairs to join us, almost having to lift—with his arms, that is—one leg at a time from one step to the next. He didn't bother staggering all the way to the observation deck where we waited. He just collapsed on the rock wall next to "Billy Joe's Tee" and made us come to him.

"We're...gonna...have...to stop," Sonny gulped for air, "goin'...back down." He took off the headset and let it fall to the ground without bothering to turn off the Walkman. "Shirt...water bottle…fanny pack…Forrest…Forrest Gu-ump....” He gave up trying to explain and dropped his wet head into his hands.

“Ya better go ahead and hit, gal,” Mr. Green said. “Much longer and ya won’t be able to see the durn ball. ‘Course, it ain’t like ya gotta worry ‘bout gettin’ to the green or nuthin’.” He chuckled again. “This ain’t exactly like Arthur’s Seat, ‘cause them old holes had sand tees, and you’d build you up a little mound of wet sand to set yer ball down on—unless ya could talk my daddy or me into whittlin’ you a tee like that ‘un thar.” He nodded toward my Top-Flite Infinity 0 waiting for me on its homemade tee.

Having caught his breath well enough to finish what he had been trying to tell us a minute earlier—that he had dropped his shirt, bottle and pack at the so-called Forrest Gump Curve on the entrance road—Sonny figured out what I was preparing to do with Oren’s Yonex Zero driver, seeing me again addressing the teed ball. “With that club you gotta play it with a little bit of a fade,” instructed Sonny, always the teacher. “Just be careful not to shank it into the parking lot. You might hit *Herbie*.” He apparently didn’t know Elaine had already told me the Beetle was mine—and that *Herbie* wasn’t his real name.

“Oh, Sonny,” I said, backing off the ball a second time so I could go give him a hug. “Thank you for the car. Elaine told me. She told me this morning—and the other things, too.”

“Everything?” he asked. He seemed to blush, though it was hard to tell if the redness in his face was partly from bashfulness or all from running the Bear.

I nodded. “Yeah. Everything. I’m happy for you guys.” I hugged him again, and this time he hugged me back, as if I were already part of his family.

“Better hurry, gal,” Oren reminded. “They ain’t gonna let us stay up here much longer. The park closes at sundown.”

Taking my position again in the tee box and glancing up at the setting sun, I felt my eyes mist over a bit, not from the four winds sweeping up the mountain from the valleys below, nor from the crimson rays I had glimpsed on the horizon. I wiped my eyes, but all the feelings within me at that moment wouldn’t let me swing away. My joy and sorrow and relief had wound themselves into a big ball sitting on my heart, and I couldn’t swing just yet.

Mr. Green must have sensed I still wasn’t ready to hit, because he stepped up behind me on the tee. Holding the “1892” cap in his hands, Oren leaned down toward me, as if he were listening for something in the air that enveloped me. “You hear that?” he asked.

From the way he cocked his head toward the front pocket of my cargo shorts, I wondered at first if he were about to make a joke about a tuning fork going off in my loins, but then I remembered Bo hadn't finished that quotation the other night on the porch. And I doubted that Oren would have recalled it, anyway. Sonny might have remembered to tease me that way, if he hadn't been so bushed, but not Oren. As it was, Sonny just stared blankly at us, still trying to muster enough strength to walk back down the steps to the VW.

"Somethin' alive's in yer pocket," Mr. Green said, poking a long index finger at the front of my shorts. "I hear it buzzin' in thar, like a carpenter bee or somethin'. Ya hear it?" He looked genuinely concerned, as if I might actually be suffering an infestation of some type.

"Oh," I laughed, reaching into my pocket. "It's just this." I took out the earbuds from Bo's MP3 player and showed them to Oren, then to Sonny. "My friend Bo gave it to me to listen to while I was waiting. It's some music he likes."

"Miles Davis?" Sonny guessed, always interested in another person's musical tastes. "It's Miles, I bet, playing the blues. Am I right? Or is it Doc Watson?"

"No," I replied. "I don't remember the man's name, and I don't know what kind of music you'd call it. It's just—I don't know—*music*."

Oren straightened up and moved back again so I could address the ball for a fourth and hopefully final time. "It ain't *Willie*, is it?" he asked. "You cain't never tell *what* kinda music Willie's gonna sing from one day to the next. One day it's 'Summertime' or 'Sweet Georgie Brown' or somethin' like that, and next day it's 'Uncloudy Day' or some other church song."

Sonny got up and stood next to Oren, so they both could observe my swing from the same angle. "Yeah," Sonny agreed, "Willie's done all kinds of songs—country, rock 'n' roll, jazz, gospel, the blues. He does it all."

"That whut you was listenin' to comin' up the mountain?" Oren asked Sonny.

"Probably would've inspired me to run faster," Sonny replied. "No, I was listening to one of those audiobooks—*War and Peace*. Slow as I am, I listened to almost the whole thing. You ever read that book, Mr. Oren? *War and Peace*?" When Mr. Green asked if it was about married life, Sonny just smiled and didn't bother trying to explain his own little joke. Or maybe the joke was on him.

Sonny, my new teacher, reached up and laid his hand on my old caddy's shoulder, maybe for support, as they watched me waggle the club again behind the ball. "You know, Val, *Willie* plays golf," Sonny said. "He even owns a golf course down in Texas. Nine holes. Same number of holes as Mr. Pearlman's little par three, where you used to work." Then he added softly, "It's gonna be auctioned off, you know—Billy Joe's course, I mean."

Feeling my old pro's presence there on that tee, I closed my eyes again, though only for a second this time, and simply nodded that I understood, not only what Sonny had said just then, but what he and everyone else had been helping me to see and hear and feel. I couldn't have put it into words back then, but I knew what was in my heart.

It was that all things in life—yes, even random things like golf, the blues and the Brown Mountain Light—could have nothing or *everything* in common. It all depended on me and the choices I made.

Life is, like golf, a Quixotic quest for perfection and, like the blues, a heartbeat of hope from the depths of despair, and, like the mystery of the Brown Mountain Light, a never-ending search for elusive illumination, for the moonlight that reflects the sun, night and day, uncloudy sky or not.

Simply rising time after time to the challenges of this most ancient of games is what matters most. And *that's* what it's all about.

I looked down at the ball, the sun's waning rays making the Top-Flite's whiteness look almost optic-yellow. "If I hit it *now*," I said to Mr. Green, "you won't find it *this* time."

Oren chuckled. "But lookin' fer it shore will be fun," he said. Looking out over the sea of trees below, I knew for the first time exactly what he meant.

Putting the earbuds back in, I nodded once again, confidently this time, and waited to measure my swing with the music in my head (or maybe it was the beating of my heart). I drew back the light driver on one, two, three.... Then, on the downbeat of four, I swept the club forward and drove the ball high and far and straight into the purple haze of the horizon, where, in the arc of its fading flight, it looked something like stardust as it followed the sun.

* * * *

May the blessed sunlight shine on you and warm your heart till it glows, like a candle set in the window of a house, bidding the wanderer to come in out of the storm.

And may the blessing of the great rains be on you, and leave there many a shining pool where the blue of Heaven shines, and sometimes a star.

And may the blessing of the earth be on you—the great round earth. May you ever have a kindly greeting for those you pass as you are going along the roads. May the earth be soft under you when you rest upon it tired at the end of a day; and may it rest easy over you when, at the last, you lie out under it. May it rest so lightly over you that your soul may be off from under it quickly, and up, and off, and on its way to God.

—*from* The Celtic Blessing of Light

(Amen)

Selected Bibliography

For additional information on various subjects discussed in this work of fiction, consult the following sources:

Arora, David. *Mushrooms Demystified: A Comprehensive Guide to the Fleshy Fungi*. Berkeley: Ten Speed Press, 1979, 1986.

Boyette, John. "Playing on the Edge." *Masters 2004 Journal* <www.masters.org/en_US/about/patton.html>. Augusta National, Inc., 2004.

Brown, Bob. "Again, the Brown Mountain Lights." *The State* 1 May 1971.

"The Celtic Blessing of Light." Traditional.

Chase, Richard, ed. *American Folk Tales and Songs*. New York: Dover Publications, 1971.

Conarroe, Joel, ed. *Six American Poets*. New York: Random House, 1991.

De Hart, Allen. *North Carolina Hiking Trails*. Boston: Appalachian Mountain Club Books, 1988.

Dugger, Shepherd M. *The Balsam Groves of the Grandfather Mountain*. Banner Elk, N.C.: Puddingstone Press, 1974.

Hallberg, William. *The Rub of the Green*. New York: Ballentine Books, 1988.

Hartley, J.L. *The Mystery of the Brown Mountain Lights, combined with Singing on the Mountain [and] Walking for Health*. Linville: J.L. Hartley, 1962.

Holy Bible. King James Version.

Johnson, Earline F, ed. *A History of Jonas Ridge*. Banner Elk, N.C.: Puddingstone Press, 1974.

Lael, Ralph I. *The Brown Mountain Lights*. Ralph I. Lael, 1965.

Mansfield, George Rogers. *Origin of the Brown Mountain Light in North Carolina*. Washington: U.S. Geological Survey, 1971.

Morton, Hugh. *Hugh Morton's North Carolina*. Chapel Hill, N.C.: The University of North Carolina Press, 2003.

Percy, Walker. *Lost in the Cosmos: The Last Self-Help Book*. New York: Washington Square Press, 1983.

Powell, William S. *North Carolina: The WPA Guide to the Old North State*. Columbia, S.C.: University of South Carolina Press, 1988.

Prevost, Harris. "'Aggie' Morton Woodruff's Mountain of Achievements Mark Career." *Triad Golf Today Magazine* <www.triadgolf.com/Sep-Oct2001/majorplayers_aggie.htm>. Piedmont Golf Today, Inc., 2001.

The Rules of Golf. The United States Golf Association, 2002.

"Search Adds to Mystery of Brown Mountain Lights." *The Asheville Citizen* 13 Aug. 1962.

Twain, Mark. *Pudd'nhead Wilson (With an Introduction by Langston Hughes)*. New York: Bantam Books, 1981.

"W. C. Handy, Composer, Is Dead; Author of 'St. Louis Blues,' 84." *The New York Times* 29 March 1958.

Weston, Jessie L., ed. *Sir Gawain and the Green Knight*. New York: Dover Publications, 2003.

Wiseman, Scott G. *Wiseman's View: The Autobiography of Skyland Scotty Wiseman*. North Carolina Folklore Society, 2000.

Printed in the United States
25785LVS00003B/4-24